W9-BJZ-957

ATONEMENT OF BLOOD

Also by Peter Tremayne and featuring Sister Fidelma

ATONEMENT OF BLOOD

A Mystery of Ancient Ireland

PETER Tremayne

Minotaur Books
New York

ATONEMENT OF BLOOD. Copyright © 2013 by Peter Tremayne. All rights reserved. Printed in the United States of America. For information, address St. Martin's Press, 175 Fifth Avenue, New York, N.Y. 10010.

www.minotaurbooks.com

Library of Congress Cataloging-in-Publication Data

Tremayne, Peter.
    Atonement of blood : a mystery of ancient Ireland / Peter Tremayne. — First U.S. edition.
        p. cm.
    ISBN 978-1-250-04600-0 (hardcover)
    ISBN 978-1-4668-4624-1 (e-book)
    1. Fidelma, Sister (Fictitious character)—Fiction. 2. Nuns—Fiction. 3. Catholics—Fiction. 4. Women detectives—Ireland—Fiction. 5. Ireland—History—To 1172—Fiction. I. Title.
    PR6070.R366A86 2014
    823'.914—dc23

                                                                            2014007875

Minotaur books may be purchased for educational, business, or promotional use. For information on bulk purchases, please contact Macmillan Corporate and Premium Sales Department at 1-800-221-7945, extension 5442, or write specialmarkets@macmillan.com.

First published in Great Britain by Headline Publishing Group, an Hachette UK Company

First U.S. Edition: July 2014

10 9 8 7 6 5 4 3 2 1

For Tanya and Marianne in memory of the good guidance of
Cyrille (1899–1970) and Odeyne (1907–66)

Remember the days of our youth
And with fondness recall
Lemon teas in the garden
Those long summers of yore.

Anon

Quia anima carnis in sanguine est et ego dedi illum vobis ut super altare in eo expietis pro animabus vestris et sanguis pro animae piaculo sit.

For the life of the flesh is in the blood; and I have given it to you upon the altar to make an atonement for your souls, for it is the blood that maketh an atonement for the soul.

Leviticus 17:11
Vulgate Latin translation of Jerome 4th century

pRINCIpAL chARACTERS

Sister Fidelma of Cashel, a *dálaigh* or advocate of the law courts of
seventh-century Ireland
Brother Eadulf of Seaxmund's Ham in the Land of the South Folk, her
companion

At Cashel
Colgú, King of Muman and brother to Fidelma
Finguine, heir apparent to Colgú
Beccan, steward of the palace
Áedo, Chief Brehon of Muman
Aillín, Deputy Chief Brehon
Caol, Commander of the Nasc Niadh, bodyguards to the King
Gormán, a warrior of the Nasc Niadh
Enda, a warrior of the Nasc Niadh
Dar Luga, *airnbertach* or housekeeper of the palace
Brother Conchobhar, the apothecary
Muirgen, Fidelma's nurse
Nessán, her husband
Aibell, an escaped bondservant
Ordan of Rathordan, a merchant
Spelán, a shepherd
Rumann, inn-keeper

At Ara's Well
Aona, the tavern-keeper

Adag, his grandson

At the Abbey of Mungairit
Abbot Nannid
Brother Cuineáin, the steward
Brother Cú-Mara, of Árd Fearta
Brother Lugna, the abbey's horse-master
Brother Ledbán, *an elderly groom*
Maolán, a copyist

By the River An Mháigh
Temnén, a farmer and former warrior

At the Ford of Oaks
Conrí, warlord of the Uí Fidgente
Socht, a warrior
Adamrae (Gláed)
Brother Cronan
Sitae the inn-keeper

At Dún Eochair Mháigh
Cúana, steward of the fortress
Ciarnat, a servant

At the mill of Marban
Marban, a millwright

Near Rath Menma
Cadan, a farmer
Flannait, his wife
Suanach, an old woman

By the River Ealla
Fidaig of Sliabh Luachra, chief of the Luachair Deaghaidh
Artgal, his son

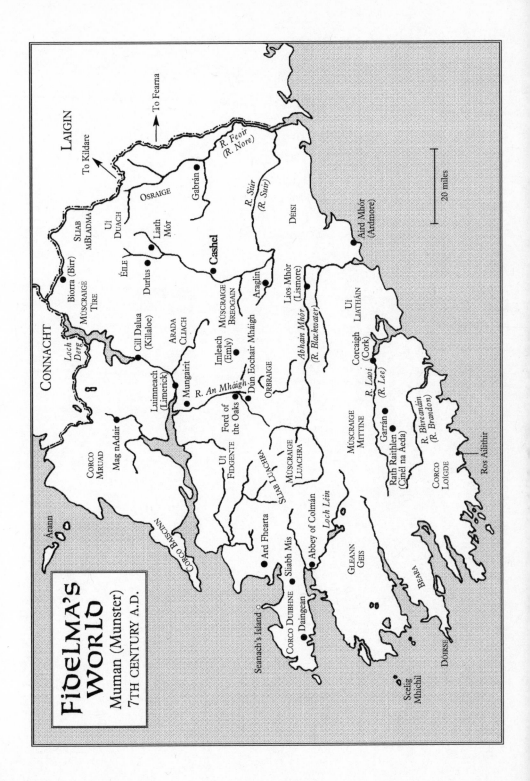

FIÐELMA'S WORLÐ
Muman (Munster)
7TH CENTURY A.D.

LAIGIN

To Kildare

To Fearna

CONNACHT

20 miles

Arann

CORCO
MRUAD

Mag nAdair

*Loch
Derg*

Biorra (Birr)
MÚSCRAIGE
TÍRE

SLIAB
MBLADMA

UÍ
DUACH

OSRAIGE

Gabrán

*R. Feoir
(R. Nore)*

*R. Siúr
(R. Suir)*

DÉISI

Aird Mhór
(Ardmore)

Liath
Mór

Durlus

ÉILE

Cashel

Cill Dalua
(Killaloe)

ARADA
CLIACH

Luimneach
(Limerick)

Mungairit

R. An Mháigh

Ford of
the Oaks

Imleach
(Emly)

MÚSCRAIGE
BREOGAIN

Araglin

Líos Mhór
(Lismore)

Dún Eochair Mháigh

ORBRAIGE

*Abhain Mhór
(R. Blackwater)*

UÍ
LIATHÁIN

UÍ
FIDGENTE

SLIAB LUACHRA

MÚSCRAIGE
LUACHRA

Corcaigh
(Cork)

*R. Laoi
(R. Lee)*

MÚSCRAIGE
MITTINE

Garrán

Rath Raithlen
(Cinél na Aeda)

*R. Bhreanáin
(R. Brandon)*

CORCO
LOÍGDE

Ros Ailithir

CORCO BAISCINN

Ard Fhearta

Sliabh Mis

Abbey of Colmán

Loch Léin

GLEANN
GEIS

BEARA

DOIRSE

Seanach's Island

CORCO DUIBHNE

Daingean

Scelig
Mhichíl

AUTbOR'S NOTE

The events in this story follow in chronological sequence those related in
The Seventh Trumpet. They are set during the month called *Cet Gaimrid*,
the start of winter, on the feast day of the Blessed Colmán mac Lénine
of Cluain Uamha (Cloyne, County Cork), which in modern calendars is
24 November.

CHAPTER ONE

E adulf was staring moodily out of the window at the darkening sky above the fortress of Cashel, the stronghold of Colgú, King of Muman. The Kingdom of Muman was the largest and most south-westerly of the Five Kingdoms of Éireann. The air was chill, and all day grey stormclouds had raced across the sky; low and intense, driven by strong and angry winds.

'It will snow before long,' he observed, turning to where his companion was seated before a mirror, putting the final touches to the position of a silver circlet which crowned her red-gold hair.

'Rain is more likely,' Fidelma replied, continuing to concentrate on her reflection. 'It is not quite cold enough for snow.'

'It's cold enough for me,' Eadulf muttered with a shiver as he left the window and crossed to where a wood fire was crackling in the hearth. 'At least, whatever arrives, it should come and go quickly, for the clouds are moving fast with this westerly wind.'

'It is the month of *Cet Gaimrid*, the start of winter,' Fidelma pointed out, rising from her seat. 'What do you expect but cold weather?' She turned again to regard herself critically in the mirror. 'Now, tell me truthfully, how do I look?' She moved her head from side to side in order for him to inspect her.

Eadulf smiled softly. 'Even more beautiful than the first time I saw you.'

Fidelma pulled a face at him in mock disapproval but she was not displeased with his response. Having finally left the religious, casting aside the robes of brown woollen homespun, she had now donned the clothes that revealed her as a Princess of the Eóghanacht. Eadulf knew that she only put on such fine clothes when there was an important occasion to be observed; this night was such an occasion.

There was a gentle tap on the door, and in response to Fidelma's invitation it opened to admit a middle-aged woman of ample proportions with greying, untidy hair. Judging from her weathered skin, she was more used to the open air than the enclosure of the palace. She was dressed in comfortable homespun. Clutching her hand was a young child, about three years of age, with a mop of bright red hair and features that resembled Fidelma's.

'I thought you would like to say good night to your little one before you go to the feast, lady,' the nurse, Muirgen, announced.

Fidelma immediately dropped into a crouch and held out her arms.

The boy ran forward to hug his mother. Then he pulled away from her with an anxious frown. '*Muimme* says you are going to a feast. Are you going away for a long time? When will you come back?'

Fidelma laughed easily and hugged her son again. 'We are only going down into the great hall, Alchú. You know where that is. We shall be back after our meal.'

Eadulf tried to conceal the emotion he felt. During the first three years of little Alchú's life it seemed that they had barely spent any time with the boy. They were always travelling on some errand, either on behalf of Fidelma's brother, the King, or on behalf of the clergy. Eadulf had seen what effect it had on the child, and he felt that it was time they settled into a more stable way of life. Their son was always nervous when there was any hint of them leaving. Eadulf's one abiding image of Alchú was of the boy, standing in the cobbled courtyard, clutching at his nurse's hand and trying not to give way to tears as he watched them ride out from Cashel.

'We are not going anywhere, Alchú,' he declared firmly, scooping the little lad in his arms and giving him a mock throw into the air.

The boy chuckled as he came down and clung to his father's shoulder, his blue-green eyes gleaming.

'Take me riding tomorrow, *athair*?' he asked.

'I'll take you, little hound,' said Fidelma, giving the literal meaning of his name.

'We'll both take you,' Eadulf promised, and set him down. Fidelma raised an eyebrow and smiled slightly, for she knew that Eadulf was not a natural horseman like she was and preferred to walk rather than ride. 'Now you run off to bed like a good boy. We'll look in on our way back from the feast and we'll expect you to be asleep.'

'Goodnight, *mathair*, goodnight, *athair*,' the boy said solemnly. Then he turned to his nurse with a skip. 'I am going riding tomorrow, *muimme*!' he shouted.

The elderly woman reached out a hand to take his. She acknowledged Fidelma and Eadulf with a quick nod before leading the boy from the room.

For a moment or two, Eadulf stared at the closed door. One thing he could never get used to in this adopted language of his was the fact that he and Fidelma were addressed by the formal *athair* and *mathair*, Mother and Father, while the intimate forms of *muimme* and *aite*, Mummy and Daddy, were reserved for foster-parents. He had heard the explanation many times but could never really understand it.

The clan society of the Five Kingdoms was also based on a fosterage system. When boys and girls reached the age of seven years old, they were sent away for their education in what was known as fosterage. It was practised by persons of all classes, but especially by nobles. Nobles fostered other nobles' children; kings fostered other kings' and nobles' children. There were two kinds of fosterage – for affection or for payment. Among the nobles it was usually for affection. In this manner, the closest of ties were developed between the ruling families and the relationship was regarded as a sacred bond, as if it was a blood tie. In such a deeply based kin-society it was a sure way of preventing conflict and warfare.

In many ways, Eadulf felt it was a laudable system. It was just that the closeness of the fosterage system seemed to have caused a change in language whereby the blood parents were addressed in formal terms while the foster-parents were addressed in intimate terms.

'What are you thinking about?' Fidelma's voice cut into his thoughts.

Eadulf turned and gave her a quick smile. 'I was wondering what the reason was for this special feast that your brother has called for this evening?'

'It is held in memory of a great poet and churchman of our people who died seventy years ago,' she replied. 'His name was Colmán mac Lénine.'

'And are his poems worthy of such a celebration?'

'Some would appear to think so,' she said. 'He was acclaimed as the royal poet of Muman. However, it is his services to the Faith that the abbots and bishops of Muman feel should be celebrated. He left the service of the King of Cashel and decided to travel through the kingdom preaching the New Faith. He finally established his own abbey at Cluain Uamha.'

'The meadow of the cave?' translated Eadulf. 'Isn't that an abbey to the south-west of here?'

'Your knowledge is very good.'

'So I suppose Abbot Ségdae of Imleach will be attending this feast?'

'No. The Feast of Colmán keeps him in Imleach. One of Colmán's achievements was to find the lost shrine of the Blessed Ailbe of Imleach, who brought the Faith to our kingdom. The ancients who buried Ailbe had kept his shrine a secret for fear it would be molested. The time came when no one left alive knew the secret. It was Colmán who solved the mystery and so he is blessed at Imleach and remembered there each year accordingly.'

Eadulf wondered aloud, 'So does tonight's feast commemorate the religieux or the poet?'

'This feast celebrates the whole man,' Fidelma replied.

The chamber was suddenly lit by a flash of white light, followed within a split second by a crash of thunder. The echo rumbled in the distance, then died away. There was a moment of silence, then a sound like pebbles being scattered on stone. They could see the urgent flurry of lumps of water-ice landing on the window-ledge. Eadulf peered out, through the hailstones, to the dim outline of the town below. A moment later, the hail gave way to heavy rain.

'You are right, Fidelma. Rain, it is. But let us hope that I am also right and this is no more than a passing rainstorm.'

A short while later, the couple made their way towards the great hall where the young warrior Gormán, of King Colgú's élite bodyguard, the Nasc Niadh, stood sentinel at the doors. He grinned as they approached, for he had shared many adventures with them.

'Are you not joining the feast tonight?' Eadulf greeted him as they came up.

The young man shook his head. 'Tonight I have drawn the short straw for guard duty here. No matter.' He opened the doors of the feasting hall to allow them to pass inside.

The great hall was a long, narrow room. Along each wall were the tables, leading to another placed broadside on at the head of the chamber and raised on a dais. This was where the King and his personal retinue would sit. On the walls behind the benches were hooks from which shields or pennants, depending on the rank of the guests, were hung. Seated at the tables were some of the lords of the territories of the kingdom, each attended by their shield-bearers. With them were their wives. No one sat opposite one another; only one side of the table was occupied, that being the side next to the wall. Fidelma did not need to examine their shields or pennants to recognise them all. She also knew that each guest had been seated by the steward of the household according to a known priority, thus avoiding any unseemly dispute.

On the dais, Fidelma's cousin Finguine, the young heir apparent to the kingdom, was already in his position to the right of the empty chair designated for the King. To the right of Finguine were the Chief Brehon, Áedo, and his deputy, Aillín. The commander of the King's bodyguard, Caol, the only man allowed to carry his sword into the feasting hall, stood behind the empty chair. To the left were others of the King's household and their ladies. Acknowledging greetings, Fidelma and Eadulf made their way to their appointed seats on the left. In all, it seemed that there were about forty people gathered for the feast.

In one corner, behind the top table, stood a *fear-stuic*, a trumpeter who, at some secret signal, raised this instrument to his lips and let forth three short blasts.

There was a movement of the curtain behind the King's chair and through this hidden entrance came the rotund figure of Beccan, King Colgú's newly appointed *rechtaire*, the steward of the palace, with his staff of office. He took his position at the side of Caol and thumped the end of his staff three times on the floor. The assembly rose to their feet. There was a moment of silence before Beccan cleared his throat and announced the presence of the King.

Colgú came pushing through the curtain behind his chair, seemingly embarrassed by the official attention. With his red hair and features, there was no mistaking him for other than brother to Fidelma. Beccan was banging his staff again and starting to intone in a loud voice: 'Give welcome to Colgú, son of Failbhe Flann son of Áedo Dubh . . .'

Colgú slumped in his chair and raised a hand as if to silence his steward.

'Thank you, Beccan,' he said gruffly. 'I am sure that all here will know my ancestry.'

Beccan blinked and a hurt look came over his features.

'But protocol dictates . . .' he began to protest.

'We are among friends tonight, Beccan,' smiled Colgú. 'We may dispense with the protocol. There are times to stand on ceremony and times when we can relax among those who know us well.' He motioned to one of the attendants who was waiting patiently with a pitcher of wine. The young man came forward dutifully and poured the liquid into the King's goblet. Then Colgú rose and raised his goblet to the assembly.

'My friends, it is I who bid you welcome this night. Health to the men and may the women live forever!'

It was an ancient toast and the assembly rose and responded in kind.

As the guests settled back, the side doors opened and a line of attendants came forward bringing in the freshly cooked dishes of roasted boar, venison and even mutton. Each dish was attended by the *dáilemain*, the carver, whose job it was to carve the meat for the guests, and the *deogh-bhaire* or cupbearer, whose task was to keep the guests supplied with drink. In addition, there were platters of goose eggs and of sausages, various cabbages spiced with wild garlic, and leeks and onions cooked in butter. And this was just the first course!

'I wonder who will get the hero's morsel this evening?' whispered Eadulf with a smile. He had come to know that at major feasts the person who had performed an outstanding act of bravery was symbolically rewarded with the *curath-mir*, which was a choice cut of the main meat dish.

'I expect Beccan will announce it shortly,' Fidelma whispered, '*if* he can overcome his dismay at my brother interrupting his attempt to bestow etiquette on these proceedings.'

There was a movement at the doors of the feasting hall and the young warrior, Gormán, entered and stood for a moment frowning uncertainly. Beccan, with a glance at Colgú, now busily engaged in conversation with Chief Brehon Áedo, went scurrying down the hall towards him. Fidelma watched as the two engaged in a swift and animated exchange. Then

Beccan hurried back to Colgú's side and bent to whisper in his ear. They seemed for a moment to be disagreeing about something and then Beccan appeared to shrug before he rose and signalled to Gormán. The warrior turned and left the hall.

'I wonder what that is all about,' muttered Fidelma to Eadulf, who had been hungrily sizing up the joint of venison, which was waiting to be carved. He turned absently, having missed the incident.

But the door was opening again and Gormán was ushering into the feasting hall a nondescript-looking man clad in religious robes. The religieux stood for a moment as if examining his surroundings, unsure of himself. The guests fell silent, their eyes resting on the unknown guest.

'Come forward, Brother Lennán, and join us,' Colgú called. 'I am told that you have journeyed from Mungairit with an important message for me? Come – you have had a tiring journey, so share our feast and we will speak of this matter as you refresh yourself.'

The newcomer glanced around, quickly examining the company from dark, sunken eyes set in a sallow face.

Apparently interpreting his hesitation as awe at being in the company of the nobles of the Eóghanacht, Brehon Áedo rose from his seat next to the King and, with a friendly smile, motioned for the man to take his place.

'Come and sit by me,' Colgú invited. 'I know Abbot Nannid of Mungairit well. How is the uncle of Prince Donennach? Does he continue in good health? Come, Brother, and you may tell me what message Abbot Nannid sends while we feast.'

The religieux gathered himself and his shoulders seemed to straighten – and then he strode towards the dais. As he did so, his right hand slipped into his robe as if to reach for a document. Instead of seating himself at the chair that Brehon Áedo offered, his stride brought him to the side of Colgú – and then the unthinkable happened. A knife appeared in his hand as if it had been conjured out of thin air and he lunged forward. 'Remember

Liamuin!' he cried in a tone that was almost a scream and struck Colgú full in the chest.

The King stared uncomprehendingly at the blood spreading over his tunic. Everyone seemed frozen in a moment of silent shock. Then, as the knife descended once more, Brehon Áedo, with a cry, threw himself in front of Colgú. The knife struck him in the side of the neck, sinking deeply and killing the Brehon.

The attacker was struggling to retrieve the knife from Áedo's inert body as if he intended to strike again. He was still yelling the same words: 'Remember Liamuin!' Then he glanced up and saw Caol, commander of the King's bodyguard, moving forward, his sword in hand, and renewed his frantic efforts to recover his knife. He had partially succeeded when Caol struck at him. The sword blow went straight to the man's heart and it was obvious that he was dead even before he reached the floor.

The cries of horror now rose in a deafening roar. Beccan was standing as if rooted to the spot, his face a deathly pale.

Eadulf was the first to reach Brehon Áedo but one look told him that the Chief Brehon was beyond help. He pulled the body off the slumped figure of Colgú and made a quick examination. The King was unconscious and blood still seeped from the wound in his chest. Eadulf was aware of Fidelma standing anxiously just behind him.

'He is still alive, but only just,' he said.

'With respect, I am best qualified to attend to the King.' It was the voice of old Brother Conchobhar, the physician and apothecary who had tended Colgú and Fidelma since they were children.

Eadulf immediately moved aside. The old man was right. There was no need to debate the issue.

'Will he live?' Fidelma demanded, her voice cracking with emotion.

'I can only do my best,' replied Brother Conchobhar tersely. 'The rest will be up to God.' He knelt at the King's side and began to remove Colgú's tunic and shirt, to examine the wound.

People were still milling about the feasting hall, their voices raised in disbelief, some trying to tell the story as they had seen it.

Now Finguine, the heir apparent, sprang up on a table and called for silence, clapping his hands to add emphasis.

'This noise is not helping,' he called, when the level of cacophony receded. 'You must all disperse and allow our physicians to take care of the King.'

Reluctantly, the guests began shuffling to the door of the feasting hall, which had been thrown open. Gormán stood to one side, sword in hand, awaiting orders.

Brother Conchobhar glanced up at Eadulf. 'We need to have him removed to his own bedchamber where we may treat his wound in more comfortable circumstances.'

Eadulf looked round to find Beccan, the steward. The man still seemed to be in a state of shock. 'Help me to carry Colgú to his bedchamber.'

Beccan stared at him as if he did not understand.

'I mean now!' Eadulf said harshly.

The steward blinked and then became aware of his responsibilities. He carefully helped to lift the inert body of the King while Brother Conchobhar moved forward, guiding the way from the feasting hall.

Realising that Fidelma was about to follow them, Eadulf told her: 'There is little you can do to help; better surely to find out who this assassin is and why he struck!'

Fidelma stared at him for a moment, as if she would disagree. Then, knowing he was right, she turned back into the hall to where Brehon Aillín stood looking down at the bodies of Brehon Áedo and the dead religieux. Then Finguine was at her side with a goblet of wine. He held it out to her without speaking. She took it and swallowed two mouthfuls, feeling its warmth in her body, helping her blood to flow once more after the trauma of the last few moments. Everyone seemed to be confused, not knowing what to do.

'I must take over until . . . until Colgú is recovered.' Finguine's voice was quiet. It was as if he were asking for her approval.

Brehon Aillín coughed nervously before she could respond.

'And as poor Brehon Áedo is dead, as his deputy I should therefore take charge of the legal matters.' It was true that Brehon Aillín was next in seniority among the Council of Brehons. 'But, of course, as the King's sister as well as a *dálaigh*, I would appreciate your assistance, lady,' he added courteously. 'Your experience in such matters is well known.'

'Very well, Brehon Aillín,' Fidelma replied after a moment or two. 'Any advice that you or my cousin Finguine need, is yours for the asking.'

Finguine looked relieved that a possible awkward moment had been avoided. He turned to Brehon Aillín. 'It was Gormán who admitted the assassin to the hall,' he said. 'I presume you will want to question him first?'

The place was almost empty now. Apart from Brehon Aillín and Fidelma, only Finguine and Caol now remained amidst the empty tables still laden with uneaten food. Gormán had remained at the door and, on Caol's summons, the young warrior advanced, his face pale and his manner nervous.

'Tell me what you know about this man, Gormán,' Brehon Aillín said, indicating the corpse of the assassin.

Gormán pursed his lips and gave a little shrug. 'There is little I can tell you. I was on duty outside the doors of the feasting hall, for it was my turn to act as sentinel. One of the guards from the main gates approached, accompanying this religieux.'

'Who was the guard?' asked Brehon Aillín.

'Luan, the one they nickname the "hound".'

'Caol, send someone to find Luan,' instructed Finguine before indicating that Gormán should continue.

'Luan told me that the religieux had approached the gates, saying that he was Brother Lennán from Mungairit and had come with an important message for the King. He did not look suspicious. He looked just like an ordinary religieux. He confirmed his purpose to me and said his message was very important, but for the ears of Colgú only. Therefore I told him to wait outside while I entered the feasting hall and told the steward about him. Beccan went directly to Colgú and explained about the visitor. Beccan then signalled for me to admit the man and I did so. The rest you all saw for yourselves, for I had returned outside to my station.' He sighed, turning his worried expression to Fidelma and adding sorrowfully, 'I could not have prevented what happened, lady.'

'No one is blaming you, Gormán,' Fidelma told him. 'We were all taken completely by surprise.'

'So far, that tells us nothing,' Brehon Aillín murmured. 'We had better examine Brother Lennán's corpse.'

At that moment the door opened and Caol returned with another warrior. The man was looking about apprehensively as he was guided towards the group.

'Is it true?' the newcomer asked in a whisper. 'Is the King badly wounded?'

'It is true,' confirmed Brehon Aillín, 'but God be praised that he still lives. However, Brehon Áedo is dead. Now, I presume that you are called Luan? We need you to tell us about this man who has proved to be his assassin.'

'I did not know,' the guard burst out, obviously distressed. 'I should have been suspicious . . . but he fooled me.'

Brehon Aillín smiled thinly. 'Just tell us what happened.'

The guard stood frowning, as if forming his recollection.

'I was on guard at the gates when the figure of a religieux came up the hill, walking easily and openly. He came to me and announced that he was Brother Lennán from the Abbey of the Blessed Nessán and that he had walked from Mungairit to bring an important message to King Colgú. I knew that the King would be celebrating the feast of

Colmán and told the man so. He replied that his message was important, that he needed to see the King at once and that he would take responsibility for disturbing him. I ordered my companions to maintain their vigil at the gates and instructed Brother Lennán to follow me to the feasting hall. There I spoke with the warrior, Gormán, and handed over my charge to him.'

Brehon Aillín was about to dismiss the man when Fidelma turned to the guard with a thoughtful expression.

'One moment, Luan. Why did you say that you *should* have been suspicious? What gave you such a thought?'

The guard looked unhappy, licking his dry lips for a moment.

'Lady, it is a long way to come on foot from Mungairit in the land of the Uí Fidgente, yet this man strolled up to the gates here as if he had barely walked from the centre of the town, let alone from Mungairit. There was no sign of his having been on the road for any time. His clothes were not creased or dusty, and he did not even carry a walking staff.'

'He could have travelled by horse or some other means, and also stopped along the way,' Brehon Aillín commented. 'That is what taverns and hostels are for.'

'He did say that he had walked,' Luan repeated. 'I suppose that he could have changed his clothes and footwear before arriving at our gates. That would make sense.'

'It is a good point,' Fidelma said. 'But not necessarily something to be suspicious about. You should not rebuke yourself, Luan. Even if you had voiced your concern, it would not have stopped the inevitability of what has taken place.'

'There is something more . . .' began Luan.

'Which is?' asked Brehon Aillín, sounding impatient.

'Just before the feast started there was a downpour of icy rain. It did not last very long but it was heavy. Feel my tunic. I was on guard and could not find shelter in time.'

He held out an arm and Fidelma reached forward and touched it. It was still damp.

Luan continued: 'The Brother arrived in dry clothes, within a short time of the heavy shower ending. So he could not have come far.'

'You point is well taken, Luan,' Fidelma said softly. 'But even so, there could have been a logical explanation. I repeat: do not blame yourself. You may return to your duties.'

As soon as Luan had left the feasting hall, Fidelma turned to where the body of the assassin was still sprawled on the floor where it had fallen. Nearby was the body of Brehon Áedo.

'I think we can have poor Áedo's body removed to the chapel while we see if the murderer's body can tell us something as to his identity,' she suggested.

Brehon Aillín relayed the order to Caol, who summoned two attendants and instructed them to remove the body of the slain Chief Brehon of Muman. Aillín stood with Fidelma as she stared down at the body of the assassin before her. Then she knelt at his feet and, without touching anything, gazed at the man's shoes. They were of the type called *cuarán*, shoes of leather with seven folds or layers to make the sole, which gave them the necessary thickness for hard wear. Unusually, the leather was stitched to cover a piece of wood to support the heel.

'One thing is certain,' she said. 'Luan is correct. This man has not walked far in these shoes. They are fairly new and the leather on the soles has hardly been marked. They are of good craftsmanship, too. In no circumstances are they the footwear of a poor religieux. Oh, and can you see those score-marks on the leather on the inside parts of the sandals? What might that mean?'

Brehon Aillín pursed his lips. 'That this fellow had some impediment in walking, one foot scraping the other?'

Fidelma shook her head. 'We saw no such impediment when he walked into the feasting hall. There is another explanation – that the score-marks were made by stirrups when the man was mounted.'

Brehon Aillín looked a little embarrassed at this obvious deduction. 'It is possible,' he conceded.

Fidelma continued her examination. 'The robes are ordinary religieux robes without adornment. They are of good quality wool and woven well, but nothing remarkable.'

'Except that the robes are dry,' muttered Brother Aillín, 'as Luan duly noted.'

'He wears a *criss*, a belt of cordage,' Fidelma continued, 'but nothing else. One might expect a purse to be attached, such as that worn by a religieux who is travelling. Now let us turn him over on his back and see what else we can find.'

They carefully turned the body onto its back.

Fidelma allowed Brother Aillín to make a quick search of the clothing but he moved back and sighed, 'There is nothing hidden other than what you see, but I will observe that his undershirt is unusual.'

Fidelma leaned forward, and even before she felt the texture she could recognise the material. '*Sróll*?' She did not hide her surprise.

'Satin, indeed. A shirt of satin, not of flax or wool which most religieux would wear,' confirmed the Brehon.

'The clothing must be examined carefully to see if there are any marks of embroidery which might identify its origin,' Fidelma told him. 'It is strange that this man carries neither purse nor anything else that one would expect on a journey. So let us see what we can tell by his appearance.'

She gazed down at the face of her brother's attacker. It was only now on close examination that she realised the dead man was only in his mid-twenties or so. His gaunt, sallow face had, at first glance, made him appear far older. The cheeks and upper lip were cleanshaven, but with that telltale bluish quality which indicated that he had to shave more frequently than most. The hair around his tonsure was thick and almost blue-black, as were his eyebrows. The eyes, vacantly staring upwards, were dark as well. Having observed their colour, Fidelma bent forward and closed them, trying to disguise her distaste for the task as the body had now begun to grow cold. Then she forced herself to touch the skin where the tonsure of St John had been shaved, after the manner of the Five Kingdoms rather than that of St Peter of Rome.

'You note how his pate is pale – a white circle of skin that is at odds with the sallow and weather-tanned skin of his face and arms? I think this tonsure was but recently cut.'

'You doubt that he was a religieux?' asked Brehon Aillín.

'You must admit, he has proved to be an unusual religieux,' replied Fidelma dryly. 'But we can make no such deduction as yet. We only remark that the tonsure is but recent. Now let us remove and examine his clothing and see what we can make of his body.'

'His body?' frowned Brehon Aillín.

'The man can change his clothing, the cut of his hair – even his features to some extent – but he cannot disguise his body.'

'Perhaps I should examine the body, lady,' muttered Brehon Aillín uncomfortably.

'I have seen and examined enough corpses in my time, Aillín, as you well know. I do not need anyone to spare my modesty.'

At that moment, Eadulf re-entered.

'The King still lives,' he announced, before anyone could ask the question. 'The wound went deep but it is clean and there appears to be no infection. The bleeding has been halted and Brother Conchobhar is in constant attention. However, the King is still unconscious and perhaps that is a good thing, for sleep will help to heal the wound.'

Fidelma compressed her lips for a moment. The only question in her mind that Eadulf had not answered was one that no one could answer at that time: would Colgú live? She took in some deep breaths before she indicated the corpse.

'You come at an opportune time, Eadulf, for we need your skills. We were just about to examine the body of the assassin.'

'What of his words before he struck? Has anyone recognised them?'

They stared at him blankly for a moment.

'Remember Liamuin!' Eadulf reminded them. 'Who is, or was, Liamuin? What does the name mean?'

'It is not a common name,' replied Fidelma, disconcerted that she had forgotten all about what the assassin had called out as he struck with his dagger.

'It is a female name,' replied Finguine. 'Doesn't it mean "the comely one"?'

'Liamuin is an unusual name but not an exclusive one,' Fidelma reiterated. 'Anyway, let us continue our examination of the assassin, for I think we were about to come to a conclusion that he was not necessarily a religieux.'

'There seems to be no identification on the man to show where he comes from,' Brehon Aillín said. 'He could be disguised as a religieux. Under his robe he wears a satin undershirt.'

Eadulf's mouth twitched slightly to hide a cynical expression. 'It is not exactly unknown for abbots, bishops and other wealthy prelates to clad themselves in such finery,' he said.

'But not a man purporting to be just a messenger and clad in simple robes as these,' objected Brehon Aillín.

'A point that is well taken,' confirmed Eadulf. 'Anything else?'

'He has good shoes, hardly worn, that do not reflect any lengthy walking. They have scuff-marks that might indicate he rode a horse,' replied Fidelma. 'He was certainly not caught in the rain shower which occurred not long before he arrived here.'

'And have you noticed the other curious thing?' enquired Eadulf.

Fidelma raised an eyebrow slightly, but said nothing.

'So far as I saw, when he attacked Colgú and now as he lays before us, there was no crucifix around his neck. Neither one that showed his poverty nor one that showed rank. It is odd that a member of the Faith would be without a cross.'

Fidelma smiled approvingly. 'A very good observation, Eadulf.'

Eadulf regarded the corpse for some time in silence before he realised that the others were waiting for him to make some further comment.

'His hands show that he is no manual labourer for the skin is soft and the palms exceptionally so, for that is an area where manual work leaves an impression. The fingernails are carefully cut and rounded and,' he took the right hand in his, pointing to the thumb and forefinger, 'there is a dark stain here on the side of the thumb as well as the forefinger. I would say that it is ink. His hair is cut and his face shaven. All in all, I would say he was a man used to keeping up a good appearance.'

'Anything else?' asked Fidelma.

'The main thing we must consider,' Eadulf insisted, 'is the name of the woman he shouted. Whoever she is, or was, it was meant to be recognised immediately by your brother. As this man struck him, he shouted: "Remember Liamuin!" Surely someone here should recognise that name and what it means?'

CHAPTER TWO

ॐ

Eadulf lay awake that night, aware of Fidelma tossing fitfully beside him but not daring to say anything in the hope that she would eventually sink into a much-needed slumber. He must have dozed off eventually – until something suddenly awoke him. He eased a hand across the mattress, finding the bed deserted and cold. It was dark, even though the stormclouds had disappeared, pushed away by the strong west winds. He blinked for a moment to adjust his eyes. The moon had only just reached its first quarter and was shedding little natural light.

A figure was standing at the window, gazing out into the night.

'Fidelma?'

The figure turned and said, 'Eadulf, sorry. I did not mean to disturb you.'

There was a tone in her voice that he had never heard before, and he swung out of the bed, hurried across to her and caught her cold hands in his.

'You've been crying.' He lifted one hand and gently wiped the wetness from her cheeks with his fingertips. She sniffed a little but made no reply.

'Your brother is a strong man. He is in the best of care with Brother Conchobhar.' Eadulf tried to sound reassuring.

Fidelma nodded slowly in the shadows. 'I have known Brother

Conchobhar since I was old enough to remember. There is no physician in the world that I would rather entrust with my brother's life.'

And then, to Eadulf's astonishment, she gave a heartrending sob. Fidelma was not one to let her emotions show. Only a few times had Eadulf been allowed to see behind the cryptic exterior that she had developed over the years; only now and then was he privy to flashes of her real feelings, her sensitivity, her vulnerability which she had learned, as a lawyer, to disguise with her cutting logic, a refusal to treat fools and prejudiced people with tolerance, her sharp speech and feisty attitudes. Eadulf was the only man who could see through her camouflage to the real person beneath, but even he was amazed to see her so emotionally reduced by the attempted assassination of her brother.

He knew that he could not comfort her by telling her that to cry was a normal release, nor that things would turn out all right in the end. He knew her too well to come out with such platitudes.

'I know you love your brother very much,' he said quietly, his hands squeezing her cold ones tenderly.

'He is all the close family I have left,' she wept. 'Our mother died giving birth to me and our father died soon after. My eldest brother, Forgartach, died when I was studying law. So Colgú and I are close.' She gave a shuddering sigh. 'We remained in touch with one another even when were studying and I went into the religious. We saw each other whenever we could.'

'And yet it seems that you have so many cousins. Finguine, your brother's heir apparent, for example.'

'But none of them are as close as Colgú and I, even though we are a kin-based society. Family is very dear to us and our genealogists are strict in recording our ancestry. Our genealogies go back to the beginning of time.'

Eadulf inclined his head in acknowledgement. 'I have heard your *forsundud* – your praise poems of your ancestry.'

'Neither king nor chieftain can be installed without the *forsundud* of his ancestry sung before the assembly,' agreed Fidelma and then, with some pride she dashed away the last of her tears and added: 'Colgú is the fifty-ninth generation from Éber Finn, the son of Milidh, and founder of this Southern Kingdom. It was the eight sons of Milidh, the warrior, whose birth name was Golamh, who landed with the Gaels on the shores of this island and established themselves here. That was in the time beyond time when they had to fight with the ancient gods and demons . . .' She paused and Eadulf was almost sure she was smiling in the gloom. 'Or so our legends tell us.' There was a pause and then she sighed: 'It will soon be dawn. No more sleeping. Light a candle, Eadulf, and fetch some wine.'

Eadulf felt satisfaction that he had distracted Fidelma from feeling sorry for herself. He could understand why she could not sleep, but he himself felt tired and would have liked to go back to bed. However, he picked up a candle and, knowing a lamp was always lit in the corridor, he went outside to ignite his candle from it. He had opened the door of their chamber when he heard a movement.

It was Enda, one of the young warriors of the King's guard. He was standing sentinel.

'Anything wrong, friend Eadulf?' Enda demanded.

Eadulf shook his head. 'We could not sleep, that is all.'

Fidelma appeared at the door, pulling a woollen shawl around her.

'What is it?' she asked. 'Is there news of Colgú?'

'No, lady,' replied Enda. 'Caol has placed me here to watch. I am sorry to disturb you.'

'You did not,' replied Eadulf, lighting the candle from the lamp. 'Good night.' He went back into their chamber with a nod towards the warrior and shut the door behind him.

'Caol is obviously worried that this assassin might not have been acting alone,' mused Fidelma, sinking back onto the bed while Eadulf placed the candle to give the best advantage of its dim, flickering light.

'He is cautious, and rightly so,' agreed Eadulf as he poured two goblets of wine and brought them to the bed. 'It is always best to be on guard until we know all the facts.'

'And we can't begin to gather the facts until it is lighter,' Fidelma sighed. 'Is that what you are thinking?'

'There is truth in that. The answer does seem to lie in discovering who Liamuin is or was, and why she should be remembered by Colgú at the hour in which this assassin intended his death. We were speaking of ancestry a moment ago. Is there anyone in your ancestry who bore that name?'

Fidelma drew her knees up to her chin and wrapped her arms around them.

'I do not think so.' Then she raised her head with a gasp. 'How foolish! Wasn't Liamuin the name of one of the five sisters of the Blessed Patrick? Wasn't she the mother of Sechnall? Sechnall the poet who wrote that famous song about Patrick?'

'*Audite, omnes amantes Deum* . . .' intoned Eadulf, remembering the opening of the song. '*Sancta merita viri in Christo beati Patrici Episcopi* . . . Listen, all you lovers of God, to the holy qualities of Bishop Patrick, a saintly man in Christ . . .'

His voice died away as a thought struck him. 'Do you think this attack might have had some religious connection? Is not the feast day of Blessed Sechnall the day after tomorrow?'

Fidelma pursed her lips, pausing for a second before shaking her head. 'These are traditions of the North and of the Middle Kingdom, Midhe. What quarrel would Colgú have had about the mother of the Blessed Sechnall of Midhe?'

'There is conflict enough between the Abbeys of Imleach and Ard Macha about Ard Macha's claims that its abbot should be chief among the bishops of the Five Kingdoms,' Eadulf pointed out.

Fidelma shrugged. 'That is purely an argument between the religious.

Anyway, apart from the mother of Sechnall, there must be other women bearing the name Liamuin, although I can't remember anyone else so called. But it is too early to say.'

'Let us be practical then,' Eadulf said. 'The cry was meant to mean something to your brother, so he must hold the answer to this mystery. Let us hope . . .' He paused in embarrassment before he hurried on. 'When he is better, the question must be put to him.'

Fidelma was quiet for a moment before agreeing. 'You are right and I shall put it to him as soon as I can. I was thinking,' she went on, then sighed. 'I believe the point Luan made is worth following when it is light.'

'You think the assassin stayed somewhere in the town while it was raining and then came up to the palace after the rain stopped?'

'Exactly so. If he rode to Cashel he must have found a place to stable his horse and change his clothes. If he was not a religieux then the clothes might offer a clue to his identity. But did he stay at an inn, or was he given shelter by a fellow conspirator?'

'Let us hope we can resolve the mystery.'

Eadulf glanced towards the window, where the sky was rapidly getting lighter, and blew out the candle. There were already the faint sounds of movement throughout the palace. Eadulf stretched and yawned. It was going to be a long day.

It was still early when Brother Conchobhar met Fidelma and Eadulf outside the doors that led into Colgú's private apartments. Two of Cashel's élite warriors stood on guard outside. They were Dego and Aidan, and both were well known to Fidelma and Eadulf. Their faces were set.

'What news?' asked Fidelma immediately as the apothecary came forward.

'He is conscious but in some pain. It has been a bad night but there is little fever, thank God.'

'Can he speak?'

The old man looked troubled. 'I'd rather he did not exert himself. The wound is deep and he needs stillness and tranquillity.'

'One question,' Fidelma pressed, after a moment. 'That's all I'll ask and then no more.'

Brother Conchobhar had known both Fidelma and her brother Colgú since they were babies. Even before they were born, he had served their father Failbhe Flann when the latter had ruled Muman. He had been with King Failbhe when he died. The elderly physician realised that Fidelma would not insist unless the question was absolutely necessary.

'One question,' he warned, standing aside.

'You go in,' Eadulf told her. 'We do not want to tire him with too many people crowding round.'

As Dego turned the handle to allow her entrance, Fidelma seemed to brace herself for a moment and then passed through the doors. Dego silently shut them behind her.

Eadulf turned to Brother Conchobhar. 'I suppose there is no one in this palace who knows Colgú as well as you do?'

The other man replied, 'I would agree, although no one is ever privy to all the thoughts, emotions and deeds of another.'

Eadulf accepted the caveat. He went on: 'You know that the assassin called "Remember Liamuin!" before he struck?'

Brother Conchobhar inclined his head.

'Would you have any idea of what that meant?'

'None at all. I have never heard of anyone called Liamuin. I presume that is the question that Fidelma will ask her brother? I regret I cannot help.'

'Then let us hope Colgú can supply an answer,' Eadulf said.

Fidelma moved across the large outer chamber where her brother usually received his advisers, members of the family and inner circle of friends.

A log fire was crackling in the hearth. She strode directly to the door of his bedchamber. A male attendant, seated outside, rose nervously to his feet but Fidelma motioned him to reseat himself. She opened the door and entered silently.

The bedchamber was in semi-gloom and Colgú lay on his back on the bed, his chest tightly bandaged. His face was pale. Sweat glistened on his forehead and cheeks, and his fiery red hair was plastered to his forehead. The King's lips were pale; his breath was uneven, coming in wheezy grasps.

As she approached the side of the bed, it seemed that Colgú became aware of her presence for his eyelids flickered and then opened. His grey-green eyes focused on her. The pain-wracked face tried to smile but it was more a grimace.

Fidelma held a finger to her lips.

'Hello, "little thorn",' she said softly, using her childhood nickname for her brother. His name actually meant anything sharp and pointed like a sword or a thorn, and when she had discovered this, she had bestowed 'little thorn' as a pet name on him. 'How are you feeling?'

He grimaced again. 'Like someone who has been stabbed,' he replied in a thick tone with an attempt at dry humour.

'The man who attacked you is dead.'

'I was told that Caol killed him.'

Fidelma nodded. 'But, sadly, not before the assassin killed Brehon Áedo.'

Colgú went to move but grunted in pain.

'Stay still!' Fidelma admonished. 'You must rest all you can.'

'Are you in charge of the investigation?' Colgú forced the words out.

'Have no fear,' Fidelma smiled cynically. 'Technically, it is Brehon Aillín who is in charge, but I am helping him.'

Colgú's lips compressed for a moment. 'Áedo was a good man,' he said hoarsely. 'He had hardly been a month or so as my Chief Brehon.'

Fidelma was aware of the passing of the time and did not want to tire the sick man. 'There is one question I must ask,' she said. 'Who is, or was, Liamuin?'

Her brother gazed up at her blankly. 'Liamuin? I don't understand.'

'When the assassin stabbed you, he was shouting, "Remember Liamuin!". It was obviously intended to mean something to you.'

Colgú closed his eyes and moved his head restlessly. 'I know of no one by that name.'

'No one at all? No one from the distant past – any relative, friend or acquaintance?'

'No one. Truly, sister – the name means nothing to me.'

Fidelma leaned over the figure on the bed and took one of his hands for a moment.

'Rest well, little thorn,' she told him. 'Do not worry about anything. Just concentrate on getting better.'

Colgú gasped, 'I'll do my best, sister.'

Outside Colgú's chambers, Fidelma greeted Eadulf with a disappointed shake of her head before he could ask the question.

'The name meant nothing to him,' she said.

'Then it becomes a mystery. Why would a man attempt to assassinate someone, knowing full well that he was likely to be killed in the process, while shouting a name in justification when it meant nothing to anyone?'

'The name meant something to the assassin,' Fidelma replied.

'Well, of course it would, but—'

'Perhaps it was meant for the assassin's own understanding and no one else's,' Fidelma interrupted. 'It was a justification to himself.'

'That is very deep.'

'There is nothing so deep as a disturbed mind.'

'Well, it does not help us discover who or why.' Eadulf glanced at the drifting clouds through a nearby window. 'We should make a search of the town for the assassin's horse, but . . .'

She heard the hesitation in his voice. 'But?' she prompted.

'We did promise little Alchú to take him riding.'

Fidelma sighed in annoyance. She had not forgotten but was hoping that Eadulf had.

'Can you explain the situation to Nessán while I go on ahead to the town to make enquiries at the inn?' she asked.

Eadulf shook his head. 'It is Alchú who will stand in need of the explanation, not Nessán,' he said firmly.

For a moment Fidelma looked as if she were about to argue and then she shrugged.

'Come on, then.'

'Lady! Eadulf! Wait!'

They turned at the urgent call. Gormán came hurrying along the corridor towards them.

'I've just come from my mother's house. She has some interesting information that might help identify the assassin.'

Fidelma stared at the young warrior in astonishment.

'Is Della well?' she asked immediately. Gormán's mother had become a friend to Fidelma. She had once been an outcast, a *bé-táide* or prostitute, whom Fidelma had successfully represented when she had been raped. Her defence demonstrated that the law allowed protection for prostitutes if they did not consent to the sexual act. Della had then given up her way of life but Fidelma had had to defend her again – this time from a charge of murder. It was then that Della had admitted she was the mother of the young warrior Gormán.

'My mother is in good health,' Gormán reassured her. 'It is about the speculation that the assassin might have left his horse in the town last night. I think you should both come with me.'

Fidelma glanced at Eadulf. She had no need to articulate the question.

Eadulf shrugged. '*Primum prima* – first things first. We will return to give young Alchú his riding lesson later, but first we must hear what Della has to say.'

Della's house was on the western side of the township that spread below the Rock of Cashel, on which the palace of the Kings of Muman arose, dominating the surrounding plains. Her home was set a little apart from the others with outbuildings and a paddock at the rear. The paddock led onto larger fields and an area of dense woodland, stretching to the south. As they approached, a large dog came bounding out of the house, barking noisily until Gormán called to it sharply. Then it gave one or two short barks and stood with its tail wagging. It was a fairly large animal, what many called a *leith-choin* or half-dog – a cross between a wolfhound and something else. Perhaps a terrier in this case.

Alerted by the dog, Della came to stand at her door. A small woman of forty years of age, her maturity had not dimmed the youthfulness of her features nor the golden abundance of her hair. She was clad in a close-fitting robe that flattered her figure, revealing that her hips had not broadened and her limbs were still shapely.

Della was clearly anxious as she greeted them. 'What is the news of your poor brother, the King?'

'Colgú lives, but is poorly. The next few days are crucial,' Fidelma replied. 'But is all well with you, Della?'

'I am well, lady, but mystified,' she said. 'Has my son explained?' She glanced at Gormán.

'Best if we hear it from your mouth,' returned Fidelma solemnly.

'Of course. Yet it is not so much what I can tell as what I can show you.'

She walked past them, beckoning them to follow, and turned around the back of the buildings towards the paddock. There, she pointed. A couple of horses were in the small field. One of them Fidelma recognised as Della's own workhorse; she had often seen it harnessed to a small *fén* or cart. The cart was a solid-wheel affair because spoke-wheels were expensive. Della was of a frugal disposition in spite of her son's position in the King's bodyguard.

It was the second animal that caught her attention. Taller and sturdier than the other horse, it was a well-muscled hunter that a warrior might ride, grey in colour but with white legs above the hocks.

'I presume that is not your horse?' Fidelma said.

Della made a face. 'Would that it were, lady. That animal would fetch a good price. Or my son might have a pride in riding it.'

Gormán shifted his weight impatiently. 'The truth is that my mother found it in our paddock this morning and in view of what has happened . . .'

Fidelma had already moved to the paddock gate; she swung up and over it with impressive agility, and went towards the animal. It stood docile enough, although its ears went back and its nostrils inflated as she approached. Eadulf had followed her to the gate, concern showing on his face. He was not a good horseman.

Catching his anxiety, Gormán said quietly, 'Do not concern yourself, friend Eadulf. That breed is usually quiet and intelligent, and the lady Fidelma is a good horsewoman. She will not disturb it.'

Fidelma came to the animal, reached forward without hesitation and petted its muzzle, allowing it to smell her hand while examining her with its large soulful eyes. She spoke softly to it. Eadulf was too far away to hear the words – if, indeed, they were words and not just the musical rise and fall of her voice. Then, still speaking, Fidelma began to move around the beast, patting its strong shoulders, but being careful not to go near its hindquarters, where many a nervous kick had injured the unwary. It stood patiently. When she turned and began to walk back to the paddock gate, the horse ambled after her.

'Do you have an apple, Della?' she called.

Della nodded and hurried back to her house where, on the porch, there was a small barrel. She withdrew an apple, went back to the gate and handed it to Fidelma. The horse gently took it from her outstretched palm.

'There is nothing to identify the beast,' Gormán commented. 'I could see no marks of ownership.'

'There is certainly nothing that I can see,' affirmed Fidelma.

'If that is the horse that the assassin arrived on, and he abandoned it here, then he must have found a dry place to store the saddle and his clothes and change them before making his way to the palace,' Eadulf suggested.

Della was shaking her head. 'We looked through the outbuildings and found nothing.'

'Did you hear anything last evening? No sound of restless horses? The paddock is near your house. No barking of your dog?'

'Nothing at all.'

'And you were here yesterday afternoon and evening?'

'I was. My son had left during the afternoon. He had guard duties at the palace last night for the feast in honour of the Blessed Colmán. He told me he would not return until very late last night.'

'As you know, that is correct,' Gormán said.

'And so what did you do last evening?' queried Fidelma.

'I ate my evening meal alone,' Della said. 'When I had finished, I made sure the lamps were lit, including the one over the door because it would be very dark when Gormán returned here. I spent some time darning and mending, then I grew tired and went to my bed.'

'You really heard nothing all this time?'

'Nothing.'

'Even when you went to bed?'

'I sleep soundly these days, lady,' Della smiled sadly. 'Ah, but I did stir when Gormán returned from the palace. I merely turned over when I recognised his step crossing to his bed. Then I must have slept until dawn. The dog was awake and I went to take oats to my horse – that was when I saw the other horse. I returned to the house and woke Gormán. When I told him about the horse, he became excited and related what had happened to your poor brother last night.'

Fidelma turned to Gormán. 'Did you come straight back here when you left the palace?'

'I stopped at Rumann's tavern on the square,' Gormán admitted sheepishly. 'But I had only one beaker of his ale before I returned here and went straight to my bed.'

'You don't lock your door?' Eadulf asked Della.

She laughed pleasantly. 'Locks and bolts are for nobles, brother. We poorer folk do not bother with such things, for who would want to intrude on us?'

Gormán was nodding agreement when Fidelma suddenly asked: 'The dog made no sound when you came in?'

'He must know my step by now, but . . .' Gormán broke off as if a thought had struck him.

'But?' echoed Fidelma.

'If truth be told, he usually barks and snarls until I call out to him and he recognises my voice.'

'And last night he did not?'

'He seemed to be sleeping soundly.'

'He does not appear to be a docile dog,' remarked Eadulf. 'I have seen these cross-breeds before. They are good for hunting.'

'How was your dog's behaviour last evening?' Fidelma asked Della thoughtfully.

Della shrugged. 'How do you mean?'

'Was he alert? Or did he become sleepy?'

'He was running about all afternoon. I think he tired himself out . . .' Her voice suddenly trailed off.

'You've thought of something?' prompted Fidelma.

'Yes, something curious. He came back just before I had begun to prepare my evening meal. He was carrying a bone. I presumed that he had helped himself to a bone given to one of my neighbour's dogs. He went quietly to his spot and lay down. I usually give him a slice of meat if I am eating it for the evening meal.'

'And last night, you were eating meat?' Eadulf asked.

'I was. I threw him a small chunk, but he didn't even touch it.'

'Where does he sleep?'

Della took them to the porch of her wooden cabin and pointed to where some sacking was spread in a dry spot. As they moved towards it, the dog trotted forward and picked up the remains of a piece of meat and, growling softly, began to chew it. However, it was a bone that lay on the sacking that Fidelma was after. She reached down and scooped it up. There were still strands of meat hanging from it. She sniffed at it cautiously before handing it to Eadulf.

Eadulf grimaced at the strong and disagreeable odour. '*Cáerthann curraig*,' the Irish name came immediately to his lips.

'What is that?' asked Della, puzzled.

'Valerian root,' he translated. 'Apothecaries use it to allay pain and promote sleep. It tranquillises the mind.'

'Except that this seems stronger than the usual valerian that I know,' commented Fidelma.

Della was looking horrified. 'Are you saying that someone tried to poison my dog?'

'Probably not,' Eadulf said. 'They just wanted to ensure that he was sleepy enough not to arouse any alarm, and then they could paddock the horse and change any clothing without being challenged.'

Fidelma was looking unconvinced. 'Why go to all that bother? Our assassin would have already arrived here with his horse and the dog would have had the chance to raise an alarm before the tranquilliser had been given to it.'

'I have no understanding of this, lady,' Gormán said.

'And I have no explanation to offer at the moment,' replied Fidelma. 'Let us see if we can find the bridle and saddle that belong to this horse and the clothes belonging to the assassin.'

'As I said, lady, we have made that search already and found nothing.'

'Perhaps he used some other shelter nearby,' offered Gormán, 'rather than our outbuildings.'

'Do you have any suggestions?' Eadulf asked.

Gormán pointed to the treeline at the far end of the field. 'There is a small woodsman's hut among those trees. The rider could have used that to change in and to store his clothes. I know of no other shelter nearby.'

'Then let us examine it.'

Gormán gave his mother a reassuring smile and indicated that she did not have to accompany them before turning and leading the way across the small field, passing the now indifferently grazing horses. A short distance beyond the back fencing of the paddock, the edge of the forest began to stretch south of the township, and beyond that was a large area of grassland, the Plain of Femen. It was an area abounding in ancient legends, so Eadulf had learned, and much associated with the stories of the ancient gods and heroes, goddesses and heroines of Fidelma's people. However, the forest was large enough to supply the townsfolk of Cashel with many kinds of wood. Eadulf knew that the ancient Irish laws were very specific about the illegal felling of trees, with fines according to each class of trees. He noticed that this area was composed of birch and elm, which were fairly common, but it also had several tall yew trees which were highly valued.

Gormán saw his wandering gaze and smiled.

'This wood used to abound in yew when I was a boy. It's why the old woodsman's hut is there. It's a difficult wood to work and they say it requires much skill, for it is used for so many things.'

'I have noticed it is prized for making beds and couches as well as decoration in the houses of nobles,' replied Eadulf.

'The ancient law has a special provision for protection of items that are made of yew,' Fidelma put in. 'The law lists fines for damage caused to such articles by visitors to places where they are displayed. So if you visit a person's home and damage furniture made of yew, then you are in trouble.'

Gormán led them down a short path through the trees. A few moments later, they came to a small clearing in which stood a hut hardly big enough for an average man to stand up in or to lie down in, full length. In fact, a man could stand in the centre and stretch his hands out to touch each wall. They could not easily discern what wood it was constructed of because it was almost obliterated by thickly growing ivy.

Eadulf was moving towards the door when a rustling sound from within caused him to halt, head to one side, not sure whether it was merely the wind among the ivy leaves.

A hand fell on his shoulder. Gormán, behind him, had raised a finger to his lips. So he had heard it too. The young warrior drew his sword and motioned Eadulf and Fidelma to stay back. He paused for a moment and then raised his right foot and kicked out, sending the door flying inwards. The crash of the shattering wood was accompanied by a frightened cry. Sword at the ready, Gormán moved quickly inside and a moment later dragged a small figure out, screaming and struggling, and threw it on the leaf-strewn floor of the glade before them.

Straddling the figure with his sword pointing downwards in readiness, Gormán commanded, 'Identify yourself, boy!'

The figure rolled over and scowled up at him.

Fidelma turned to Gormán in amusement. 'You have your sexes mixed, Gormán. This is clearly a girl.'

CHAPTER THREE

ᕫᕫ

Gormán stood staring down in astonishment at the young woman. Her tousled blue-black hair was cut short, not in the usual fashion, and it was quite dirty, scattered with dead leaves and wisps of straw. There were patches of dried mud on her face but, nonetheless, the features were quite attractive, symmetrical with a splash of freckles on the cheeks, dark flashing eyes and full lips that needed no berry-juice to enhance them. At the moment, those lips were drawn back in a snarl showing very white and even teeth. Her clothes were of poor quality, soiled and torn, and there were no shoes on her feet.

'What are you gawping at, you big bully!' she growled at the young warrior.

Gormán started at being addressed in such a fashion. Then he slowly replaced his sword in its sheath before reaching out a hand to assist the girl to rise.

She ignored him, rolling quickly over and scrambling to her feet. They could see now that she was no more than twenty.

'And who are you?' Fidelma asked mildly.

The girl turned on her with an unfriendly expression.

'What business is it of yours?' she replied pugnaciously.

'The lady is Fidelma of Cashel and a *dálaigh*,' Gormán said in a shocked tone. 'When an attorney of the courts of the Brehons asks, it is your duty to give your name.'

The girl raised her hands to her hips and stared truculently at him.

'My name is mine to keep.'

'Watch your manners, girl!' Gormán replied, anger in his voice. 'You are speaking to the King's sister.'

There was a slight narrowing of the girl's eyes, which was the only reaction to this information. She remained as belligerent as before.

'And that makes a difference as to whether I care to give my name or not?' she sneered.

'Not that I am a King's sister,' replied Fidelma. Her voice was dangerously cold and even. 'But that I am a member of the courts of the Brehons and that I am qualified to the level of . . . ah, but I doubt whether that would mean much to you. Sufficient to say that my office gives me the right to question you and places you under the obligation of answering.'

'You use long words,' sniffed the girl.

'It means that you are required to answer,' snapped Gormán, clearly outraged by the girl's behaviour. 'And you should do so with deference.'

'Words I have no use for,' the girl went on.

'Do you have a use for the word "punishment"?' asked Gormán, taking a menacing step forward.

The girl wheeled around towards him, almost in a crouch. In her hand there had appeared a small glinting dagger.

'Try to attack me, bully, and you are a dead man!'

Gormán took a step back, surprise clearly showing on his features.

Eadulf, who had been standing in silence during this time, leaped forward, grasped the girl's wrist and twisted it slightly, so that the knife dropped from her hand onto the forest floor, then kicked it out of her reach. She spun round, her eyes flashing and her teeth bared. For a moment or so it seemed she was about to launch herself on Eadulf, her hands clenching and unclenching like claws.

'The hellcat!' breathed Gormán, recovering his poise. He made to move towards the girl but Fidelma held up her hand to stay him.

'Why are you so frightened, girl?' she asked gently.

The young woman relaxed and straightened herself, but her jaw remained thrust forward combatively.

'Who says that I am frightened?' she demanded.

'You do,' replied Fidelma. 'Otherwise you would not be behaving in this manner.'

'Clever, aren't you?' was the insolent response.

'It does not require cleverness. However, I cannot sympathise with you about the troubles that afflict you unless you tell me what they are and allow me to do so.'

The girl still stood silently defiant. Fidelma sighed. Authority was of little use unless it was freely recognised.

'Gormán,' she said to the young warrior. 'Search the hut.' Then: 'Eadulf, pick up this woman's knife and return it to her.'

Eadulf made to protest then went to find the knife he had removed from the girl's grasp. He handed it to her hilt first, but warily. She snatched it from him without thanks and replaced it in the worn leather sheath that hung from the rope belt at her waist. She remained regarding Fidelma with suspicion.

There was a cry of triumph from within the hut. A moment later, Gormán emerged with a saddle-bag in one hand and a saddle and bridle in the other. He was grinning.

'A bag of clothes.' He held it up. 'It seems we were right. This is the place where the assassin changed.'

Eadulf, watching the girl, saw an expression of bewilderment spread across her face.

'Let's examine the clothing. It might tell us something,' Fidelma instructed. Then she paused and looked at the girl. 'Did you know these things were in there?'

Once more the pugnacious look returned.

'Why should I?' she countered.

'You were asked *if* you knew that they were there,' Gormán demanded. 'Not *why* you should know.'

The girl blinked at the intensity of his tone and replied sullenly, 'No, I did not know they were there.'

'How long have you been in the hut?' Fidelma asked.

'I came here just after dawn. I wanted to sleep.'

'You were not here last night?'

'I said as much, didn't I?'

'So you did. And if you came here just after dawn, where did you spend the night?'

'I was walking, most of it,' conceded the girl.

'Walking through the night? Alone?'

'Have you found anyone else with me?' she sneered.

'That does not prove you were walking alone during the night,' Gormán said irritably. 'Do you know who left this bag here?'

'I did not even know it was in the hut. How many times must I tell you?'

'Whether you knew or not, we have yet to discover. But you are in serious trouble.'

For the first time the girl looked uncertain. 'What do you mean?'

'There was an attempt on the life of the King last night. This is where the assassin sheltered. Now we find you here, and with his belongings,' replied Gormán.

Fidelma was watching the girl's expression closely. There was a subtle change, a hint of fear as the girl seemed to realise the seriousness of her position.

'That is nothing to do with me. I arrived here during the morning. There was no one here.' The words were truculent but some of her confidence had gone.

'And your name is . . . ?' Fidelma asked sternly.

The girl hesitated and gave in. 'If you must know, my name is Aibell.'

'And where are you from?'

'From the west.'

Fidelma smiled sceptically. 'That is a large area.'

'I came from An Mháigh, the River of the Plain.'

'And that is a long river,' murmured Eadulf.

The girl glanced at him in annoyance. 'I was born and raised by Dún Eochair Mháigh.'

Gormán's eyebrows rose a little. 'That is the fortress on the ridge of the Mháigh. It is the principal fortress of the princes of the Uí Fidgente.'

'So, what of it?'

It seemed to Fidelma, watching her closely, that this Aibell was in constant battle with the world around her.

'But the Uí Fidgente . . . Mungairit is not far,' the young warrior protested.

Fidelma's glance was expressive enough to silence him. She turned back to the girl.

'The attempted assassination of the King is a very grave matter, Aibell. It will go better with you if you tell us the complete truth.'

'It is the truth.'

'So you travelled through the night – all the way from the fortress of the Uí Fidgente?'

Aibell saw Fidelma's disbelieving look and bit her lip. 'Not exactly.'

'Then how . . . *exactly*?'

'I left my father's house there as soon as I reached the age of choice.'

'When I asked you where you are from, I did not mean where were you born, or even where were you raised, but from whence you travelled last night.' Fidelma spoke firmly.

'Last night I met a merchant who was travelling here. He offered me a seat on his wagon. I accepted it.'

'A merchant who was travelling at night?' Gormán snorted. 'That is unusual.'

'He said he wanted to be at his destination by dawn.' It was the first time Aibell had bothered to explain her short answers.

'And where did you meet this merchant?' Fidelma enquired.

'I had reached the banks of a great river just west of here and had resigned myself to trying to sleep near a ford there when I saw this wagon crossing.'

'Did you know the name of the ford?' demanded Gormán.

'I am a stranger here,' she replied. 'How would I know it?'

'Tell us about this merchant, then. Did you find out *his* name?'

'As a matter of fact, I did. It was a stupid name for a merchant – something about dignity and honour.'

Fidelma wrinkled her brow in perplexity but Gormán's eyes widened.

'Ordan, lady,' he said. 'Ordan often trades in the west. "Dignity" indeed is the meaning of his name.'

Aibell nodded confidently. 'That was his name. Ordan. A fat, ugly man as far as I could see in the light of his lantern.'

'He has that land just east of here, lady,' the young warrior reminded Fidelma.

'I know it. He calls it Rathordan.' Fidelma turned back to the girl. 'So you were picked up by Ordan the merchant?'

'He offered me a seat on his cart,' affirmed the girl. 'He would have offered me much more had I agreed to it. He was a pig of a man!'

'When was this? When did he pick you up?'

'About midnight.'

'And why did he put you off here, on the western edge of the town at dawn?'

'Because I made him do so.'

'Why did you not want to go into the centre of town?'

'Because I refused to share his bed, which was his intention. As soon as I saw the outskirts of the town, I demanded that he let me off his wagon. In fact, I had to jump from it.'

Gormán was thinking carefully. 'The road from the Ford of the Ass, which I presume must have been the ford Ordan crossed over the River Suir, runs by the far side of that field.' He pointed to the north side of his mother's paddock. 'There is no other ford nearby, only the road across the bridge further to the north.' He turned to the girl. 'Are you trying to tell us that you came across the paddock and into this wood and found this hut purely by chance? Or did someone guide you here?'

Aibell glowered at him. 'I did not say that I had found my way here by chance.'

'That is true,' said Fidelma slowly. 'Therefore we would be interested in knowing exactly how you came here.'

'Simple enough. I was told the hut was here.'

'By whom?'

'By a man going early to the fields.'

Fidelma tutted in exasperation. 'A man who just happened to be passing in the darkness of early morning? Do you expect us to believe this?'

'I do not expect anything. It is the truth.'

'Why are you here, Aibell?'

The girl laughed for the first time.

'Why should I not be here?' she countered.

'What are you doing in Cashel?' Fidelma insisted.

'Because this is where I have stopped to rest. Had I been left in peace, I would have been elsewhere when the sun reached its zenith.'

'Brother Lennán!' It was Eadulf who suddenly rapped out the name. 'What is he to you?'

The girl regarded him for a moment in silence before she said, 'I know no one of that name and am now tired of all these questions.'

'As we are tired of asking them and receiving no convincing responses.' Gormán was clearly irritable.

'I can only respond as I see fit. Whether you accept my replies is no concern of mine.'

'Oh, but it is,' Fidelma said tightly. 'I am afraid that you will have to come with us until we are satisfied that you are telling us the truth.'

'Under what authority?' challenged the girl, her truculent manner returning.

'Under my authority as a *dálaigh*, under the authority of the Chief Brehon of this kingdom, under the authority of—'

Aibell interrupted with a derisive snort. Fidelma wasted no more time on her. 'Eadulf, help me carry the things that Gormán found in the hut. Gormán, take charge of this woman. We have stood long enough in this wood. Let's go back to Della's place, so that we can examine what you have found in more comfortable circumstances.'

At once the girl started to protest but Gormán seized her right arm in a firm clasp.

'By order of the King's sister and a *dálaigh* of the courts, you are to accompany us until we are satisfied that you have given us a truthful account of yourself. There are two ways for you to accompany us – of your own free will or by force.'

She glared up at him. 'You wouldn't dare use force!' she said. But there was no conviction in her voice.

'Oh, but I would,' he replied grimly. 'And don't try to use your knife again, because this time you will get hurt.'

They stared at each other for a moment before the girl recognised the determination in his fierce gaze and then tried to feign indifference. She fell in step beside Gormán, who kept his hand on the hilt of his sheathed sword.

Eadulf and Fidelma picked up the saddle-bag and the horse's equipment and led the way back towards Della's cabin. Della had seen them advancing across the paddock and came to open the gate for them. She seemed surprised to see the young woman.

'We need to request your hospitality for a short while, Della,' explained Fidelma.

'Come in and be welcome, lady,' she replied.

'This is Aibell,' Fidelma added, as they entered.

Eadulf left the saddle and bridle on the porch outside. They all went into the large room where crackling logs produced a fierce heat. A cauldron of aromatic-smelling stew was simmering above the fire. The morning's autumnal sunlight shone through the southern-facing windows so that the room was bright in spite of the weakness of the pale yellow orb.

Della bade them be seated and asked if she could provide refreshment. Fidelma had spotted the girl's eyes lingering on the cauldron and saw the quick, nervous movement of her tongue over her dry lips.

'I should imagine that Aibell has not yet broken her fast. I am sure she would like something to drink and eat, if you can manage it.'

'Of course!' At once Della became almost a mothering figure, making sure the girl was comfortably seated at one end of the table and fetching a small mug of ale and a wooden platter containing some cold meat and cheese with a hunk of freshly baked bread. The girl hesitated at first, but as Della turned to enquire if anyone else wanted refreshment, she immediately began to tackle the food. Although Fidelma appeared to be ignoring her, out of the corner of her eye, she saw Aibell was consuming the food as if she had not eaten for many days. She hoped that none of her companions were watching the girl so as not to embarrass her.

'First we need to examine the contents of this saddle-bag,' Fidelma announced as a way of distracting them.

Eadulf opened it and took out the garments inside, placing them one by one on the table for everyone to see.

There was a *bratt*, a cloak of a striking blue colour that would stretch to the knees of an average-sized person. It was loosely shaped and had a fringe of beaver fur around the neck and down both edges in front. There was an over-garment, a coat without a collar, ending about the middle of the thighs, and a pair of *triubhas*, sometimes called *ochrath* – tight-fitting breeches made of thin, soft leather, which were drawn on over the feet. The *criss* or leather belt had a purse attached to it, containing some silver.

Eadulf examined the bag and the clothing to make sure there was nothing hidden inside. Having satisfied himself, he turned to Fidelma and said, 'There is nothing here that would give us a clue to the assassin's identity.'

'What of the clothes themselves?'

Eadulf lifted them each in turn. 'They are not the kind of clothing worn by a noble; that is for sure. But then neither are they the apparel of a poor man or a labourer.'

'That is true.' Fidelma was approving. 'However, these must be the clothes that our assassin changed out of when he put on religieux robes.'

'That would be supported by the fact that there are no shoes here – but our assassin was wearing the sort of footwear that could go with such clothing. There is no underwear here either, but our assassin was wearing a shirt of *sróll* or satin which is more likely to go with these clothes than those of a poor religieux.'

'You seem certain then that the clothes are those of the assassin?' Gormán asked.

'The clothes fit the pattern,' said Eadulf. 'He's not a noble or a warrior, nor one pursuing a physical trade or an artisan . . . They confirm what I said when I examined the corpse.'

'What about the tonsure?' demanded Gormán.

'As Fidelma observed, the assassin seemed to have shaved his tonsure recently,' Eadulf said. 'He disguised himself as a religieux deliberately. I stick to my opinion that he was a poet, a copyist or illustrator.'

What makes you think that?' Fidelma asked.

'Last night, we saw that the assassin's hands showed that he did not do physical work. The fingernails were well cared for. However, his right-hand thumb and forefinger were stained.'

'And that indicated?'

'They were stained by ink, which meant that he often had a quill in his right hand. Who works with a quill and ink if they are not scholars? He could have come from an ecclesiastical college or even from one of the secular schools, but I believe he was not a religieux.'

Gormán was staring at the clothing moodily as if he were trying to gather more evidence from them. Then he suddenly gave a soft exclamation and picked up the saddle-bag, turning the leather over to examine it more closely.

'It's just a plain leather saddle-bag, Gormán, my friend,' Eadulf commented. 'Good quality and well-stitched, but—'

He was interrupted by a grunt of satisfaction from the young warrior, who had turned over one of the flaps and pointed to something underneath.

'The leather has been marked – seared by a hot needle. See.' He held it out for inspection.

Fidelma took the bag from him and peered closely. 'A serpent entwined around a sword. Why, that is the mark of . . .'

'. . . the Uí Fidgente's princes,' Gormán finished with emphasis.

Fidelma turned to where Aibell was finishing her meal.

'When did you leave Dún Eochair Mháigh?'

'I told you, as soon as I reached the age of choice. Four years ago.'

'So you are now eighteen? And where have you been since then?'

Once again, the girl showed reluctance in answering, but seeing the frown gathering on Fidelma's brow, she changed her mind.

'I was a long time in the country of the Luachra.'

'What were you doing there?'

'I served in the household of Fidaig.'

Fidelma was surprised. 'Fidaig, the lord of the Luachra?'

'Yes. I worked in the kitchens of his household.'

'And why did you leave?'

'If you must know, I ran away,' the girl replied defiantly. 'I was sold to him as a bondservant and I ran away.'

Fidelma's brows rose in astonishment. 'You said you were born and raised at the capital of the Uí Fidgente. Who was your father?'

'He was a fisherman, an *iascaire*, on the River Mháigh.'

'Of what class was he?'

'He was a *saer-céile*, a free-tenant, who rented his cabin and stretch of the river from a prince of the Uí Fidgente.'

'So what do you mean when you say that you were sold to the Luachra? Why would a free man of the Uí Fidgente allow his daughter to be sold to a neighbouring tribe?'

'My father declared me to be a *daer-fudir* and sold me.'

Fidelma breathed out sharply. *Daer-fudirs* were the lowest members of society, mainly criminals who had refused to meet their fines and pay compensation, or captives taken in battle. In other words, they were slaves – often foreign – people who had fallen foul of the law and were unable to extricate themselves. However, the fate of these slaves was not hopeless, for the law favoured their emancipation – and with diligence and perseverance they could raise their status and even come to be a free person in the clan.

'How would you become a *daer-fudir*?'

'My father sold me, to pay his debts.'

'But that is illegal!' exclaimed Fidelma.

'My father was a beast.'

'And your father's name was . . . ?'

'Escmug.'

'A name well-suited for a fisherman,' muttered Gormán. The name meant 'eel'.

'He was a beast,' repeated the girl. She looked directly at Fidelma and said: 'At first I was not sorry to escape from my father. If you are as knowledgeable as you seem, then he was similar to Oengus Tuirbech in the stories told about him around the winter fireside.'

Eadulf noticed that this meant as much to Gormán as it did to himself, because the young warrior was also looking puzzled. However, Fidelma appeared shocked by what she had heard.

'Then you have led a sorrowful life, Aibell,' she said. 'Now I begin to understand your bitterness.'

'Never!' The word came out like the crack of a whip. 'No one will ever be able to understand me, to understand what I have had to endure. But I will do so no more. If you try to send me back, I shall resist.'

'You shall not be sent back. If you were at the age of choice when you were sold, then your father was contravening the law in selling you as much as Fidaig was in buying you. Both will answer to the law. I promise this.'

The girl sniffed; scepticism was clearly on her features.

'My father is dead and who is going to punish Fidaig? He is powerful and rules the mountains of Sliabh Luachra.'

It was Della who intervened. 'Young girl, I do not know your troubles but I will tell you this – when the lady Fidelma says that something will be done, then it will be done.' Her voice was vehement and, for a moment, seemed to impress Aibell. Then the girl turned away with a defensive movement of her shoulders.

Fidelma glanced at Gormán. 'Keep an eye on our young friend here,' she said quietly before turning to Eadulf. 'Eadulf, come with me to the paddock. I want your advice.'

Eadulf was about to comment when he saw her expression and so followed her without demur. They walked slowly down to the paddock gate.

'What is it?' he asked, when they stopped. They both leaned on the wooden bar of the gate watching the two horses that still stood grazing contentedly in the field.

'This is perplexing,' she sighed.

Eadulf grinned. 'It is not often that you admit to being perplexed about anything.'

Fidelma said, 'Well, I am now. When we found this girl, I thought we would be reaching a rapid conclusion in this matter.'

'I am not so sure that we have not,' replied Eadulf. 'We know the assassin came here on horseback. He arrived, put some narcotic on the meat for Della's dog so it wouldn't cause an alarm, and thus was able to place his horse in Della's paddock. Then he changed into the guise of a religieux from Mungairit, leaving his clothes in the woodman's shed, and came to the palace. His saddle-bag is branded with the symbol of the Uí Fidgente, not just any of that clan but the mark of the princely family itself. The Eóghanacht and Uí Fidgente have been blood enemies for generations . . . you know well enough that if there is any rebellion in the kingdom, the Uí Fidgente are usually behind it.'

'Not always,' objected Fidelma. 'Not since my brother defeated them at Cnoc Áine.'

Years before, Colgú had crushed a rebellion mounted by Eoghanán, the prince of the Uí Fidgente, on the slopes of Cnoc Áine. Eoghanán's warlike sons, Torcán and Lorcán, also met their death during the same conspiracy. And when the princedom of the Uí Fidgente passed to Donennach, son of Oengus, he had agreed a peace with Cashel; since when an unsettled calm had been maintained over the kingdom.

The cause of the friction was thus: the Uí Fidgente had long insisted that they should be in the line of the rightful rulers of the kingdom and not just the Eóghanacht, the descendants of Eóghan Mór. They claimed to be descended from Cormac Cass, the elder brother of Eóghan Mór, and sometimes called themselves the Dál gCais, descendants of Cass. But outside of their own lands, they found little support for the claim.

'True, your brother defeated the Uí Fidgente and that could be the reason behind this attack. The assassin could have come to enact vengeance on him for defeating them in battle. Their capital is Dún Eochair Mháigh where this girl says she came from. We find her sheltering in the very hut the assassin used. She is truculent and uncooperative. What more is needed to make the connection?'

Fidelma was looking unconvinced. 'These things make sense only superficially.'

'Superficially?'

'Your arguments are correct, Eadulf. But they need to be tied together by logic.'

'I thought the logic was clear.'

'Let us put ourselves in the place of this assassin. He has come to take revenge on my brother for some crime. We think it is something to do with a woman called Liamuin – a name that means nothing to Colgú, incidentally. The assassin appears to be a scholar rather than a warrior.'

'Agreed.'

'We presume that he arrives unseen on the outskirts of Cashel. Why does he come to this spot? Darkness must have fallen for it does so early at this time of year. Yet he is able to have a potent mixture at hand, ready to smear on a joint of meat to send Della's dog to sleep. How does he even know that Della has a dog? He then unsaddles his horse and leaves it in her paddock, even though the horse is bound to be noticed, come daylight. Then he is able to find his way to that hut in the forest, which even I did not know existed, and changes his clothes to assume the guise of a religieux. He waits until the rainstorm is over and enters the palace on the pretext that he has an urgent message from the Abbey of Mungairit; once inside, he makes his attempt on my brother's life.'

'When you put it that way, it does throw up several questions,' Eadulf said. 'They could be answered by the fact that perhaps he had been here before and thus was no stranger to this area. Could that be why he was able to feed the dog with the tainted meat without the animal causing an outcry?'

'But why go to all that bother? Why not just take his horse into the woods and leave it there?'

'Perhaps the man cared about his animal and didn't want any harm to befall it. There are wolves and boars that roam the woods around here,' Eadulf replied.

Fidelma shook her head. 'There are too many oddities that need answers.'

'I think it is more than mere coincidence that we found the girl in the same hut the assassin chose,' Eadulf said firmly.

'Yet she has told us enough to find proof how she came there. We will have to ride out to Ordan's place and question him, and we must make enquiries about the man she encountered who told her where the hut was. There will not be too many men on their way to the fields at that hour at this time of year.'

'Perhaps she thought that we would simply take her word for that?' Eadulf said.

'Perhaps, but I do not think she is so naïve – not if her experience of life is as she says. We will take her up to the palace and keep her in safe custody while this investigation is going on.'

'Do you really think that her story has merit? I mean, can you believe that her own father would sell her to this chieftain . . .'

'Fidaig of Sliabh Luachra? Such things, while against the law, are not unknown, I'm afraid. Sliabh Luachra is a strange, brooding place. It's the Mountains of Rushes – a marshy area among the mountains for it is not just one mountain. You may have seen the twin peaks from a distance on your journeys to the west. Those peaks mark the southern extremities of Luachra territory. They are called the Breasts of Danu, she who was the ancient mother goddess of our people before the new Faith came to us.'

Eadulf suppressed a slight shiver.

'I have seen them when I passed near those mountains tracking down Uaman, Lord of the Passes of Sliabh Mis, when he kidnapped little Alchú. I remember how a local inn-keeper told me that the ancient gods and goddesses still dwell among the marshes up there.'

'Indeed. I have passed through the territory only once and had to spend a night in a small glen called the Glen of Ravens, where it was said the ancient goddesses of death and battle dwelled. It is not a place to stay if one is of a nervous disposition.'

'We certainly seem to have avoided it in our travels,' observed Eadulf, 'and we have been to most other places in this kingdom. What of this chieftain, Fidaig?'

'I know of him as a profane and evil man. He once came to Cashel to pay his respects to the King at the time of our wedding feast. You probably don't remember him.'

'As I recall, there was a great deal happening at the time,' replied Eadulf dryly. 'Among other distractions there was the murder of Abbot Ultán. However, when Colgú defeated the Uí Fidgente at Cnoc Áine, I presume that Fidaig was their ally?'

'Curiously, he was not, although I heard that the Luachra had a small band that fought there, commanded by a son of Fidaig. Fidaig claimed that they had mustered without his consent and therefore he was not responsible.'

'To my mind, it seems that the girl is connected in this,' Eadulf repeated.

'But would she have been that forthcoming about being a bondservant in the household of the Luachra chieftain if there was such a conspiracy and she was part of it?'

'It is the only explanation I can see. But that reminds me – what did she mean when she said that her father was like Oenghus Tuirbech? You seemed to understand, but I do not think Gormán or Della did. I certainly did not.'

Fidelma's expression was serious. 'Oenghus Tuirbech was supposed to be an ancient King descended from the race of Eremon. He was called Oenghus the Shameful because he forced his own daughter to go to bed with him and begat a son called Fiachaidh Fear Mara. Oenghus had him put into a canoe and pushed out to sea because he could then claim that his son's blood was not on his hands.'

For a few moments Eadulf stood frowning at her and then he realised what she was saying.

'So she meant that her father . . . ?'

Fidelma sighed deeply, cutting him off and saying, 'Let us get back to the others. We will have to keep the girl at the palace while we go to see Ordan and check out her story. Perhaps we can also verify the matter of the man going to the fields who told her where the hut is.'

Eadulf suddenly looked nervous. 'We did promise little Alchú to take him riding.'

Fidelma was about to make an exasperated retort when she suddenly relaxed, saying, 'The rath of Ordan is not so far distant. Our son can ride with us when we go to see the merchant.'

'That's a good idea,' replied Eadulf with relief. 'I would not like him to be disappointed again.'

Fidelma glanced sharply at him: was there a hidden criticism in his tone? Then she decided to let the matter pass. Eadulf was touching a tender spot because the life the couple had led since little Alchú had been born was such that the boy had been well-nigh neglected by them. Had it not been for Muirgen, whom Fidelma had appointed as nurse to the boy and, indeed, foster-mother, she did not know how they would have managed.

Fidelma led the way back into Della's cabin. Gormán looked up in relief as they entered. The girl was sitting in brooding silence while Della was washing dishes. It turned out that she had tried to engage the girl in conversation a few times but without success.

'What now, lady?' asked the young warrior, rising from his seat.

'Now we shall return to the palace. I must learn if there is further word of my brother's condition and then we will continue our enquiries. Thank you, Della, for your hospitality. I will ask our *táisech scuir*, our master of the stables, to send one of his lads to remove the horse and the responsibility of feeding it from you.'

'Thank you, lady. Did you find the answer to what it was that you sought?'

As Fidelma shook her head, Eadulf added: 'We are as much in the dark about the identity of Liamuin as we were before.'

The reaction was unexpected.

'Liamuin?' The cry came from the girl. She had sprung from her seat, arms akimbo, body tense, and was staring at them with wide-eyed hatred. Her voice rose to the edge of hysteria. 'Then you knew? All along, you have known. How did you know? *How did you know?*'

chapter four

They stood astounded at the girl's outburst. Then Fidelma took charge. 'Tell us what you know of Liamuin,' she instructed.

Aibell was trembling uncontrollably so Della went to get a beaker of *corma* and motioned her to sit down again. She cast a reproving look at Fidelma before turning back to the girl. It was some time before Aibell was calm.

'There, my dear, take your own time and answer lady Fidelma's question,' Della said comfortingly. 'No harm is going to come to you.'

'Tell us what you know of Liamuin,' Fidelma said again.

'If you know the name of Liamuin, then you will know that she was my mother,' Aibell replied tightly.

Fidelma and Eadulf exchanged a surprised glance. Fidelma lowered herself onto a chair opposite the girl.

'Liamuin was the wife of Escmug, your father?'

The girl sniffed sourly. 'What do you know of my mother?' she grunted.

'Nothing unless you tell us,' Fidelma replied. 'Does she still live?'

For a moment Aibell hesitated before saying: 'I do not know.'

'That needs an explanation,' Fidelma commented, surprised by the girl's answer.

Aibell gave a sharp laugh. 'You mean, how do I not know whether she is alive or dead? The answer is simple. It was just after I reached the age of choice. I had been working in the fields and came home to find that my mother had vanished. Later, when my father returned from his fishing, she still had not returned. She never returned.'

'And from that day to this, you do not know what happened to her?'

'I think she could no longer stand the beatings my father gave her when he was drunk. I think she ran away.'

'And left you behind?' Fidelma's tone was slightly incredulous. 'She left you behind without protection and knowing the man he was?'

Aibell shrugged but made no reply.

'You say this was just after you reached the age of choice?'

'I remember the very day, for it was on the next day that we heard the news of the great defeat of Prince Eoganán at Cnoc Áine.'

'The victory of King Colgú over the Uí Fidgente uprising,' muttered Gormán in correction.

'Was any search made for your mother? What about her relatives?' asked Fidelma hurriedly, before the girl could respond to Gormán.

'My father was angry that she was gone. He went to bó-aire, the local magistrate, but nothing was done. I think my mother had a brother but no one was allowed to speak about him because my father hated him. I do not even know his name. There was also another relative who owned a mill some distance from us. One day, my father came home and told me to get my things together. He said that we were going to see my mother.'

'So what happened? You told us that you had not seen her again after she left.'

'My father lied. We travelled south for a while, towards the mountains of Sliabh Luachra. Then we met a band of people and my father handed me over to them. They gave him money . . . he sold me!'

The girl's voice had faltered.

'And you were forced to go with these people?' Fidelma asked in a gentle tone.

55

'They were Luachra. I remained a bondservant with them until a week or so ago, when I was able to seize the opportunity to escape.'

'Where were you heading?'

'Anywhere to the east, as far away as I could get. I now suspect that my father killed my mother on the day she disappeared and that his anger was merely a sham.'

'What makes you say that?' asked Eadulf.

'When I was packing my things, I went to get something I had left in one of the outhouses and found some bloodstained clothes. The significance of them did not strike me until the long years when I brooded over my mother's disappearance.'

'What motive would your father have to kill his own wife?' Eadulf asked.

'Motive enough. I have told you that my father was *colach*,' she spat the word. Eadulf had to search his acquired vocabulary before realising it meant an act of sexual corruption; a term for abuse. 'My mother had realised what he was doing to me. She tried to protect me when she was there, but he beat her. I think she finally ran away and abandoned me to him. Or, as I now believe, he had found her and killed her.'

'Tell me, Aibell, did your mother have any links with Cashel?'

The girl frowned. 'I do not understand what you mean.'

'Did she ever say anything to you about my brother, King Colgú?'

'Why should she? I have told you that we were a poor family. My mother's father went into an abbey when his wife died. My father was, as I have said, a fisherman. We had nothing to do with nobles.'

'But you dwelled not far from the fortress of the princes of the Uí Fidgente. Did your father take part in the uprising led by Prince Eoganán?'

'My father was too much of a coward to do that. No, he stayed safe on the river.'

Fidelma paused for a moment in thought. 'Answer me this, then, Aibell. Why would the man who attempted to assassinate my brother cry out, as the knife descended, "Remember Liamuin!"'

'I have no idea,' the girl said dully. 'Why do you suppose this Liamuin would be my mother?'

'It is not a common name,' Gormán interposed harshly. 'And it seems extraordinary for you to appear in Cashel on the same night as someone attempts to assassinate the King, shouting that name. Further, we find you in the very same hut where the assassin had left his clothes and saddle.'

'So far as I know, my mother ran away from my father four years ago and I was sold to the Luachra. I have nothing to do with Cashel.'

Fidelma let out a soft breath of resignation. 'You will have to come to the palace and view the body of the assassin. Perhaps you will be able to recognise him.'

Fidelma watched the girl's features carefully as Eadulf removed the covering sheet from the corpse. There was no sign of any recognition at all, and after Aibell had shaken her head to the unasked question, Fidelma accompanied her from the chapel.

'I am afraid you must stay as our guest until we find out a little more about your arrival in Cashel at this particular time,' Fidelma advised Aibell. To her surprise, the girl made no protest but was looking intently at the great buildings of the palace, obviously impressed. Fidelma led her across the courtyard in search of the matronly Dar Luga who served as the *airn-bertach* or housekeeper of the palace. Her role, of course, was different from that of the steward, Beccan, for she attended to the more domestic chores of the King's household, and saw to the comfort of the guests as well as the King's family.

Fidelma caught sight of Caol emerging from a side door and hailed him, saying, 'Have you seen Dar Luga?'

Caol swung round. 'She's in . . .' He stopped and regarded the young girl at her side with a puzzled look.

'This is a new guest,' Fidelma explained. 'Her name is Aibell. She will be staying with us for a while.'

It seemed that the commander of the guard had difficulty dragging his eyes away from the attractive, dark-haired girl.

'You were saying?' Fidelma went on.

'Oh yes – Dar Luga? You will find her beyond that door.' He pointed. As they moved away, Fidelma was aware of Caol staring after them.

She made sure that Dar Luga understood that Aibell was to be treated with courtesy as a guest, but was not allowed to leave the palace, unless such instruction was given by Fidelma. Leaving the girl in the care of the housekeeper, Fidelma then went to see old Brother Conchobhar the apothecary. Eadulf, meanwhile, had gone to prepare Alchú for his promised horse-ride. Gormán had been asked to ensure that their mounts were ready and had agreed to accompany them.

Brother Conchobhar greeted Fidelma with a smile, but told her: 'There is little change from when you saw him this morning, Fidelma.'

'When will we know that he is out of danger?' Her voice was anxious.

'With such a wound, we can never be certain. At least it was a single stab wound, but the knife went in deep. It would have been worse had not poor Brehon Áedo thrown himself across the body of the King, and had not Caol despatched the assassin before he could do further damage.'

'You will keep me informed?'

'Naturally.' As she made to go he added: 'I heard that you have brought back a prisoner to the palace.'

'You have eyes and ears everywhere,' she replied, turning back to the old apothecary with curiosity. 'I am only returned a short while ago. How did you hear this?'

Brother Conchobhar chuckled. 'I would be a poor servant, having served the Eóghanacht in this palace since the days of King Cathal son of Áedo Flainn, if I did not hear what happens in any part of the palace. Even a thought articulated in the stable will not escape my attention. Do you say that this girl is part of the assassin's conspiracy?'

'I have no idea, old friend,' Fidelma replied. 'I feel there is some connection that I cannot understand. All I know is that her mother's name was Liamuin . . .'

Brother Conchobhar's eyes widened. 'Now that *is* interesting.'

'But this Liamuin disappeared years ago. The girl claims she does not know what became of her, but suspects her father killed her. She was the wife of a river fisherman. How could that Liamuin have any connection with my brother?'

'That is even more interesting,' confirmed the old apothecary. 'You will have to delve further into this matter, that is for sure. Is the girl from a far distance?'

'She is of the Uí Fidgente,' Fidelma told him. 'Her father was a fisherman as I have said, on the River Mháigh just by the principal fortress of the prince of the Uí Fidgente.'

'Ah,' the old man's voice was soft. 'Then you must avoid springing to conclusions, however logical. Be careful that she is not condemned for the one fact of her mother's name.'

'Don't worry. Anyway, she is here in the palace as a guest. She is not confined within her chamber but I have asked Dar Luga to place a restriction on her freedom. She cannot leave the palace and is not to approach the King's chambers. As you say, there are aspects of her explanation as to why she came to Cashel that must be carefully checked.' Fidelma sighed. 'Don't forget to let me know if there is any change with my brother.'

As Eadulf had entered their chambers, he found Alchú sitting on a chair while Muirgen the nurse was pointing out various objects in the room and getting the child to name them. As soon as the boy spotted his father, he jumped up and ran towards him with outstretched arms. Eadulf scooped him up and twirled him round, which caused the child to gurgle happily.

'When are we going riding, Father?' the boy demanded, after his fit of giggling abated.

'Very shortly,' Eadulf assured him. 'As soon as your mother returns from seeing her brother.'

'King Am-Nar?' queried the little boy.

Eadulf chuckled. Alchú had managed to understand that Colgú was 'king' and that Colgú was his mother's brother, his uncle. The word for a maternal uncle was *amnair* and this was as close as he could come to naming his uncle.

'Is King Am-Nar very ill, Father?'

'He is not well, son,' Eadulf prevaricated.

'Will he die?' the boy asked.

Eadulf set him down and took a chair. 'All things have to die sometime.'

'The cat died last week,' the boy told him. 'Mother said it was old. Is King Am-Nar old?'

Muirgen cast a meaningful glance at Eadulf. It was obvious that she thought such subjects should be avoided with such a young child. Eadulf suppressed a sigh.

'I heard you showing your knowledge of objects when I came into the room, Alchú.'

The little boy pouted. 'Oh, that is all easy stuff. Table, chair, cupboard . . . I can do other things. Listen, Father, I am counting in the language!'

Eadulf smiled to himself. Alchú always called Eadulf's own language 'the language', *berla*, to differentiate it from Fidelma's Irish, which was the language of every day and with which he was surrounded.

'Go on then, son,' Eadulf encouraged.

'An, twegan, thrie, feower, fíf, six, seofon . . .' The boy paused. For an instant, Eadulf was going to make the mistake of helping him but, after a moment, he added, with a broad smile of triumph: *'Eachta, nigon, tiene.'*

'Well done.' Eadulf clapped his hands. 'You will soon be able to converse fluently.'

Muirgen sniffed in disapproval. 'I don't see the sense in stuffing the boy's head with that nonsense,' she said. 'What avail is this Saxon gibberish when you are trying to buy cattle in Cashel market?'

Eadulf said sadly, 'I swear, Muirgen, you must broaden your mind a little. To speak other languages is a great asset. Besides, it is the language of my people – the Angles.'

'It's all right for you, Brother Eadulf, but you no longer live in the land of the Angles. The boy lives here and it will not help him. Surely, there is no room for a child's mind to be filled with something that will stop him learning his own language properly. He'll be mixing things up next, not knowing what words to speak. Too much learning damages the mind.'

Eadulf chuckled. 'Do you suggest that my mind is damaged or, indeed, that the lady Fidelma's mind is damaged?'

Muirgen flushed. 'I have suggested no such thing at all,' she bridled.

'But the lady Fidelma speaks her own language; she also speaks Latin, Greek and also some Hebrew – the three languages of the Faith. She even speaks my own language, which gives her some knowledge of that of the Franks and, indeed, she has knowledge of the language of the Britons. According to your philosophy, she should be unable to absorb these languages for they would damage her understanding.'

'The lady Fidelma is a wise and an exceptional person,' replied Muirgen undeterred. 'But have not the priests warned us of the confusion of the Tower of Babel? They say it is God's will that we should all speak one language, but that it was the Devil who made us speak many tongues.'

'Now I heard a similar story,' corrected Eadulf. 'In that version it was God Himself who scattered the language of Babel to the four corners of the earth to create many languages.'

'That is not what the priest told me, Brother Eadulf. He said that after the dispersal of the language it was our great King Fenius Farsaid who sent scholars to the four corners of the earth and, with God's blessing, they gathered a knowledge of the seventy-two languages that had come from the dispersal and had then put together the best of each of them, trying to recover the one true language. And they did so and the language was called after Fenius' fosterling Gaedheal Glas, and that is why our language is called after Gaedheal for he brought the language to this country.'

'So what language did God mean us to speak, Muirgen?' Eadulf tried to sound solemn but he knew laughter was not far away.

Muirgen saw his expression and flounced off in annoyance. At once Eadulf felt contrite. He realised that he should have known better than to make sport of other people's beliefs and he called her back with an apology.

'I meant no disrespect to you, Muirgen. All I say is that, in place of a common language, the more languages we can absorb the more we can understand and communicate, especially with our neighbours. I believe it will be a sad day when languages are destroyed because we do not appreciate them. Why, just think what would be lost if, in the fullness of time, the very language of the Kings of Éireann is destroyed and its culture lost?'

Muirgen turned with a laugh. 'Now you are making fun, Brother Eadulf. Sooner will the mountains disappear than that will ever happen. But I will allow that Alchú, if his mother so wills it, may speak what languages he likes. That is because the lady Fidelma is a noble, the sister of a king and a descendant of kings,' the woman said, as if that was the explanation.

'And is not Alchú my son as well?' Eadulf found a note of hurt creeping into his voice. He felt guilty once more for snapping at the woman, for she was a simple soul and did not mean to rouse his insecurity. Under the law of the country he had been classed as a *cú glas*, literally a 'grey fox', which meant an exile from over the seas without any rights and no honour price. On his marriage to Fidelma, her family had acknowledged him and he was elevated to the status of *deorad Dé*, exile of God. He therefore was bestowed with half the honour price of Fidelma's rank, but without the rights or responsibility for rearing his own children. It was Fidelma who had the final say in such matters. But Muirgen would not, perhaps, have known this. She would not have questioned him on that account. Nevertheless, it was often difficult for Eadulf, as a foreigner in this land, to feel totally secure.

He was about to frame another apology when the door opened and Fidelma herself came in.

'Are you ready, both of you?' she asked brightly.

'Yes, yes, yes,' cried the child. 'Are we going riding? Are we?'

'Yes, we are,' answered Fidelma. She fussed over the boy, making sure he had the right clothes and cloak and then she and Eadulf led their son down to the courtyard.

Gormán was already there with the horses. There was a small piebald pony for Alchú, and Eadulf's roan-coloured cob, which he had actually come to enjoy riding, though still admitting that he was not a good rider. Fidelma preferred her short-necked, ancient breed from Gaul, which she called Aonbharr, the 'supreme one', after the horse ridden by the Ocean God, Mannanán Mac Lir. Gormán was accompanying them on his cob.

'Where are we off to?' asked the boy again. He sat on his pony with ease and without fear, much to Eadulf's quiet admiration.

'We are going eastward a little way, towards a place called the rath of Ordan,' Fidelma replied with a smile.

'What's a rath?'

'It can be many things. It can be goods, chattels, property that is given as surety in law . . .'

The boy looked blank and Fidelma realised that the lawyer in her was speaking. It was Gormán who explained.

'A rath is also the ramparts that surround a chieftain's residence; it can be his fortress.'

'Oh.' Alchú was excited. 'Are we going to see a fortress?'

'Except Rathordan is no fortress,' muttered Gormán. 'It is just a pretend chieftain's residence, for Ordan is certainly no chief.'

Alchú either didn't hear or had lost interest as he guided his little mount out of the courtyard between his parents on their horses. Gormán brought up the rear.

They had descended from the Rock to the road that led towards the eastern hills when they saw a man walking up in the direction of the palace. He was elderly and dressed in clothes that easily identified him as a shepherd. It was Muirgen's husband.

'Hello, Nessán,' called Fidelma.

Little Alchú smiled broadly and waved a tiny hand, 'Nees-awn, Nees-awn!' he chanted.

The shepherd touched his forehead nervously at the party. He always appeared uneasy in the presence of Fidelma and Eadulf even though his wife was nurse to young Alchú. He could never forget that when the boy had been kidnapped as a baby, he and his wife had been given the child to raise as a shepherd by the kidnapper, the evil Uaman, lord of the Passes. The motive of the kidnap was vengeance. Nessán and Muirgen were to have taken in and hidden the child without them knowing whose son he really was. Fidelma and Eadulf had tracked down their son and, instead of punishing the elderly couple for their unwitting role, they had invited Muirgen to be Alchú's nurse at Cashel while her husband had been employed to look after Colgú's sheep.

Nessán cleared his throat. 'There is great sorrow on me at the news of the attack on your brother, lady. Is there better news of his health?'

'He is doing as well as can be expected.'

'He is in my prayers, lady.'

'Thank you, Nessán. It is good that we should meet you on this road. Perhaps you can help us?'

'If I can, lady.'

'Were you abroad early this morning?'

'As you know, I attend your brother's sheep in the northern rough pasture, behind the Rock. But I was up late last night, lady. I am afraid I went to Rumann's tavern in the town and so it was after dawn that I left to tend the sheep today.'

'At An Screagán – I know the place.' Fidelma was disappointed because Della's homestead lay on the other side of the township. Then a further thought occurred. 'Do you know any of the other shepherds around the township? Those that pasture their flocks to the west of the town?'

'I dare say, lady. I meet with them on lambing days and when the time comes to shear the flocks. And when there is no work in common, we gather in Rumann's inn.'

'Do you know anyone who would be going to the fields to the west, just beyond Della's homestead, very early this morning? You see, I am trying to find a man, a shepherd, who was abroad before dawn and said he was going to tend his sheep. Would you know who that was?'

The shepherd replied almost at once.

'Well, that might be Spelán. Doesn't he have a flock along the road of rocks to the west of her place? I met him in the tavern only last night, and he was complaining about trouble with one of his ewes. That might have caused him to stir early this morning. He was truly concerned.'

'Spelán, I don't think I know him.' Fidelma glanced at Gormán, and the young warrior nodded quickly.

'I know the man,' he said, 'and if he is not up with his flocks, then he may well be found in Rumann's tavern. It is a favourite place of the shepherds here.'

With a wave of farewell towards Nessán, Fidelma indicated that they should ride on.

The rath of Ordan was certainly no rath, as Gormán had foretold. The attempt to construct ramparts was no more than a ditch which would scarcely keep livestock in. However, the gate to the homestead was more substantial. It consisted of two stone pillars through which one passed into a large yard before coming to the single-storey house of stone. On top of each pillar were geese carved with beak and wings extended as if threatening the visitors – an odd symbolism for a merchant, thought Eadulf. Indeed, the building beyond seemed full of the owner's aristocratic pretensions but did not quite measure up to the houses of nobles that Eadulf had seen throughout the country. To one side of the complex were a number of large sheds where the merchant presumably stored his goods, and outside these were two large wagons. To the other side were some buildings that showed that Ordan was self-sufficient in livestock, with pigs and some milch cows in a fenced area.

Three or four people were moving about, pursuing various tasks. One of them, having spotted their arrival, had run to the house, doubtless to inform his master of the arrival of guests.

A moment later, a man emerged through the door, crossing the porch to meet them as they halted in front of the building. He was balding, of stout proportions running to fat, his eyes almost buried in his moon face. His lips were thick, and even when closed presented an ugly shape, and his skin was pale, where it was not blotched with unhealthy pink on his fleshy cheeks. His clothes were certainly of fine quality but hung on his ill-shapen figure without disguising it. He was rubbing his pudgy hands together as he approached and bowing rapidly from his neck.

'Lady Fidelma! Brother Eadulf! I am honoured, extremely honoured that you have come to my humble house. You are most welcome.'

Little Alchú, seated on his pony now behind Eadulf, with Gormán at his side, spoke up clearly.

'Who is the ugly fat man, Mother?'

Fidelma's mouth tightened to hide the smile that twitched at the corner. Ordan wheezed as he forced what passed for a laugh.

'The little prince is not shy in stating his mind.'

'Would that all people were as forthright in their opinions,' muttered Eadulf piously.

'Come in, come in. My steward will attend to your horses.'

'We were just passing,' Fidelma replied firmly. 'So we will remain seated and not trespass on your hospitality. It was only a brief question.'

Ordan looked disappointed. He had already been mentally building the story of how the sister of the King had visited him and taken his refreshment.

'As you wish, lady. But my humble house is your house and you have but to ask.' As he spoke, he kept bowing and they found it distracting.

'Why is that man doing that?' Alchú piped up. 'He's very funny.'

Fidelma caught Gormán's eye. 'Take Alchú to show him the animals,' she instructed. 'Go with Gormán, Alchú, and when you come back you can tell me what animals you have seen.'

She and Eadulf waited until Gormán led the boy's pony towards the barns.

Ordan was waiting, his hands still clasped together in front of him.

'I am told that you have been away and only returned here last night,' Fidelma began.

Ordan nodded, but he suddenly seemed uneasy. His eyes narrowed, if such a thing could be possible in his plump features. 'And, indeed, on my return I heard the terrible news of the attempt on the life of your brother,' he said unctuously. 'May the devil take the soul of the assassin. I was told that Brehon Áedo, who was my very good friend, was slain but that the King, God be merciful, has survived. How is your brother, lady? Does he fare well?'

'He fares well enough.' Fidelma almost snapped the words to quieten the flow of honeyed tones of the merchant. 'It appears that you had a passenger on your wagon on your return.'

Ordan blinked rapidly. 'What has that girl been saying about me?' he asked nervously.

'Should she have been saying anything?' Fidelma asked innocently.

'Of course not. It's just . . .' The merchant seemed uncomfortable and then closed his mouth.

'I believe you arrived in Cashel in the hours before dawn?'

'I did so, and have barely slept since my arrival for I promised to meet a smithy from Magh Méine to do some trade with him. At first I thought it was he who was arriving when I was told you were here.'

'What I want to know is about your passenger,' cut in Fidelma, holding up her hand to stem his outpouring.

The pudgy-faced man scowled. 'Is she making a complaint about me? I swear I gave her a lift for charity's sake. She was full of bile, that one. She even threatened me with a knife. I was well rid of her when I made her get down on the edge of town. I cursed the goodness in me that prompted me to give her passage on my wagon.'

'I want to know where you found her,' Fidelma said.

The merchant raised his arms in a helpless gesture. 'Found her? More like she found me and thought I was a generous soul whom she could beguile . . .'

'Where did you meet her and when?' It was Eadulf who snapped the question.

Once more Ordan blinked. 'It was at the Ford of the Ass, on the River Suir, Brother.'

Fidelma nodded at the confirmation of their deduction. 'So that would have been around midnight or just afterwards?'

'It would, lady,' confirmed Ordan.

'Why were you so late abroad? Is it not dangerous for a merchant to travel alone at night?'

'I had to meet a fellow merchant from the honey fields.'

'Where had you been?'

'I had been with my very good friend, your cousin Congal, the Prince of Iar Muman, the Prince of the Eóganacht of Locha Léin.'

Fidelma stared for a moment at the merchant. 'And what would you be doing at the fortress of Congal?'

'I was buying badger and fox fur and trading honey from the honey fields and hence . . .'

Once more Fidelma cut in. 'It is several days' journey from the territory of Locha Léin to the River Suir. You would have passed through the territory of the Uí Fidgente or, indeed, the Luachra?'

'I would.'

'You did not find that dangerous?' asked Eadulf.

'I have no fear of either the Uí Fidgente or Luachra, Brother Eadulf. I know the country well. There is peace between our people now so I often trade among them.'

'And you did not meet this girl until you came to the River Suir?'

'That is as I said. The heaviness of my eyes was pressing me to stop but I would be a poor merchant if I did not reach here in time to conclude a good bargain with the smith from Magh Méine. So I had pressed on even though night was upon me.'

'So you came to the Ford of the Ass. What then?'

'I saw the girl sheltering by a tree and stopped.'

Eadulf smiled cynically. 'I thought you said that the girl stopped you?'

The merchant was unabashed, 'Ah, so it was, Brother. So it was. She asked me to take her as far as Cashel. Out of my generosity, I did so.'

'Did she tell you what she was doing, camping out by a tree at midnight?'

The fat merchant shrugged. 'I presumed that she was just an itinerant. One of those wanderers in search of work, who are not to be trusted.'

'Not to be trusted? Then why did you give her a lift?'

Ordan's smile was sly. 'Have I not been telling you that I am a generous man and hate to see poor creatures suffering without a warm bed of straw to lie down in for the night?'

'So you brought her all the way to Cashel and made her get off your wagon before you even entered the town, leaving her in the darkness of the night. Wasn't she a stranger to the area and without knowledge of the place, and therefore generosity would surely dictate that you might drop her at the door of a *bruden* or tavern?'

'She insisted that I let her down at the edge of the township. Frankly, I was glad to do so. She was of a volatile disposition, Brothel Eadulf. She could well have attacked and robbed me, for she had a knife and it was sharp.'

'How did you know that? Did anything occur which drew the knife to your attention?'

It seemed the red blotches on the face of the man deepened in intensity.

'Nothing occurred, and if she tells you different then she is a liar. I am a respectable merchant. I have friends in high places. The girl was merely an itinerant and I was pleased to be rid of her.'

'You never saw the girl before you met her at the Ford of the Ass?' Fidelma asked.

'I did not.'

'You never saw her in the country of the Luachra?'

The merchant started. 'The Luachra? Why do you mention them?'

'I would have thought that the quickest way from the Eóganacht Locha Léin was through the mountains of the Luachra,' she replied.

He hesitated a moment and then said: 'I have told you the truth, that I did not encounter her before I crossed the Suir.'

Fidelma suddenly smiled and said pleasantly, 'Then we shall delay you no longer, for I see a wagon approaching and that must be the smith you are expecting from Magh Méine.'

She turned her horse, with Eadulf following, while the merchant peered after them with an uneasy expression on his blotched face.

'I think he spoke the truth in its main essentials,' Eadulf commented, 'except . . .'

'Except it was probably a good thing that Aibell was carrying that knife with such a man as Ordan about,' finished Fidelma with a grim expression. She turned and waved to Alchú and Gormán to follow them.

'What now?' asked Eadulf. 'It looks as though the girl was telling the truth.'

'About her arrival in Cashel? I agree, but we should make every check. I do not believe in coincidences. The name Liamuin continues to have significance. And we cannot deny the fact that she was in the very place where the assassin changed into his disguise.'

'Coincidences sometimes happen,' offered Eadulf.

'It would be a fool who denies it,' she replied evenly. 'At the same time, assumption is never a good method of investigation.'

'Then we should try to find this shepherd mentioned by Nessán.'

'I think so. If he was the person who directed the girl to the hut, that would also confirm that part of her story. But there are other questions which remain.'

They found the shepherd, Spelán, in Rumann's tavern, which was situated on the main square of the township. When Rumann pointed him out after Fidelma and Eadulf asked the inn-keeper to identify him, the man rose respectfully from his bench in a corner by the smouldering turf fire. Fidelma motioned for him to reseat himself.

'I am told you have a ewe in bad health, Spelán?' she began, taking a settle beside him.

The shepherd was nervous. 'I did, lady.'

'Did?'

'She died this morning.'

'I am sorry to hear it. What was wrong with her?'

'The other day she began to have difficulties with breathing, shaking her head and sneezing. There was a discharge from her nose. When I went to see her this morning, she was dead. I fear it was the *cuilí biasta* – evil flies which sometimes choke the noses of sheep. She had probably picked them up grazing in the marsh areas.'

Fidelma made a sympathetic sound. It was not an uncommon occurrence among the sheep flocks.

'So you were abroad early this morning? Before first light?'

'That I was, lady.'

'I understand you keep your flock on the western side of the Road of Rocks?'

The man started to look worried. He nodded in confirmation.

'Did you meet with anyone on your way there this morning?'

'It was dark,' he began. 'I was up beyond Della's paddock when I saw that fat merchant, Ordan, on his wagon going along the road. I don't think he saw me, as the wagon had just passed me when I emerged into the road. But I did see someone else.'

'And who was that?'

'A young girl.'

'How did you know that, if it was dark?'

'Didn't I have a lantern?'

'So what happened?'

'She wanted a dry place to rest for she said she had been travelling all night. I told her there was a *bruden* in the town but she said that she wanted a barn or shed where she would not be disturbed. I thought it odd, as she did not appear to be one of those itinerants or beggars. I suggested Della's barns which were nearby, but she asked if Della had a dog and when I said, yes, she asked if there was anywhere else. Then I remembered the old woodsman's hut just a few yards into the forest here. I took her to the edge of the forest, for it skirts the Road of Rocks, and pointed the way. It was easy enough to find.'

'And she went off in the darkness, just like that?' Fidelma sounded incredulous.

Spelán chuckled. 'Bless you, no. I gave her my lantern. I know the road well, see, and knew it would be dawn before long. The lass had the greater need of the lantern to guide her along the path to the hut. I told her to leave it there and I would pick it up later today. Did I do wrong?'

Fidelma paused thoughtfully for a moment and then spoke.

'No, Spelán. And you parted company with her and went off to tend your ewe. Did you see the girl again?'

'I did not. You don't think that she took the lantern with her?' he asked anxiously.

'She did not,' smiled Fidelma. 'I think you will find it in the hut still.'

She rose and thanked him, before turning to Rumann and handing him a coin. 'You may give Spelán a drink on me to help him with his loss.'

She and Eadulf left the inn with the thanks of the shepherd echoing after them.

As they rejoined Gormán and Alchú outside and mounted their horses, Eadulf declared, 'Well, all we have learned is that the girl spoke the truth about how she came to the hut. So now do we let her go on her way?'

'Not at all,' Fidelma replied, much to his surprise. 'Our task has only just started. I told you that I do not believe in coincidences. Now we must find out more about Liamuin.'

chapter five

❧

D arkness had already fallen that early winter afternoon by the time
six solemn-faced people gathered in a circle of chairs in the small
council chamber of the King's palace. Finguine, the heir apparent to Colgú,
assumed the chair of office in the absence of the King. By his side sat
Brehon Aillín, acting Chief Brehon since the death of Brehon Áedo. Caol,
the commander of the élite warriors of the Golden Collar and bodyguards
to the King, sat next to him. On the other side of the circle sat Beccan,
the King's steward. The only person missing from the King's intimate
council was Abbot Ségdae of Imleach, as senior prelate of the kingdom.
A messenger had been despatched to advise him of the attack on the King.
Fidelma and Eadulf had been invited to join the council. The lamps had
been lit and the attendants had withdrawn.

The members of the council listened in silence to what Fidelma had to
report. As if by unspoken consent it was Brehon Aillín who was the first
to question her when she had finished.

'So you believe that this girl, Aibell, is who she claims to be?'

'It would seem so,' Fidelma replied. 'But we are faced with accepting
two improbable coincidences, and I say that we must take them both into
consideration. We found her in the hut where, a short time before she
arrived, the assassin changed his clothing, and near where he tethered his

horse. Then there is the fact that her mother, who disappeared four years ago after the Battle of Cnoc Áine, was called Liamuin.'

Brehon Aillín made a wry grimace. 'We should bear in mind what Cicero said: *vitam regit fortuna non sapienta* – it is chance, not wisdom, that governs human life. So chance – coincidence, call it what you will – does have a part to play and is often dismissed when it should be accepted.'

'I will grant you that, Aillín,' Fidelma replied softly. 'In this instance, however, we cannot rely on accepting chance to make a decision about the involvement of the girl. We need evidence.'

'The evidence you already have may be circumstantial but it is still evidence,' replied Brehon Aillín.

'Do we not have an old saying "better 'it is' than 'it may be so'," Brehon Aillín?' Fidelma asked.

'Of course, of course,' interrupted Finguine impatiently. 'Suspicion is no substitute for fact, but how do we set about establishing what the facts are?'

There was a silence and then Brehon Aillín spoke again.

'I am sure the young *dálaigh* has some suggestions.' He looked at Fidelma as he spoke, his words deliberately placing emphasis on her age and legal status. He had not forgotten that a few months before, Fidelma had presented herself to the Council of Brehons of Muman as a candidate to replace the Chief Brehon Baithen, who had died from old age and infirmity. The council, however, had chosen Brehon Áedo as Chief Brehon and, as his deputy, the conservative Brehon Aillín.

It was Beccan, the steward and controller of the King's household, who replied. 'Sister Fidelma . . .' He paused and smiled apologetically at her. 'The lady Fidelma as she chooses to be known now, although to most of us she will remain as Sister Fidelma . . . the lady Fidelma has served both the law and the Eóghanacht well. I think her views and suggestions are well worth our careful attention.'

Brehon Aillín flushed. 'I would not suggest otherwise, Beccan.'

'Nor would I have misinterpreted you would do so.' The steward bowed his head towards the Brehon as if to disguise his sarcasm. 'I merely emphasise that her view is of importance to us.'

Finguine turned to his cousin, anxious to avoid an argument. 'You have some suggestions as to how we should proceed, Fidelma?'

Fidelma acknowledged his intervention. 'We have some clues as to who the assassin was. Each piece of information must be followed and examined.'

'And these pieces of information are . . . ?' Brehon Aillín enquired, in a patronising manner.

'Firstly, the assassin introduced himself as Brother Lennán of Mungairit. Now, I suspect that his name was *not* Brother Lennán. Perhaps he did not even come from Mungairit. Nevertheless, this must be verified or excluded. Secondly, we were able to confirm that he had changed his clothes before arriving at the palace to attempt his assassination. He rode a good horse, but did not appear to be a warrior, and this evidence leads us to the conclusion that he was a scholar of some description. More importantly, his leather saddle-bag was scored with the sword and serpent symbol of the Uí Fidgente.'

They each nodded in silence as if concurring with the points she made.

'We found the assassin's horse left in Della's paddock and his clothes stored nearby in a woodman's hut. In that same hut we found the girl, Aibell. Now, according to Aibell, she had run away from the mistreatment of Fidaig of Luachra, and eventually found her way to the Suir where she was given a ride to Cashel. She arrived here just before dawn. A shepherd then suggested the hut to her as a place where she could spend a few hours in the dry and get some rest. Both the driver of the wagon who brought her here and the shepherd who suggested the hut give testimony to the truth of this statement.'

Fidelma paused for a moment. 'On that basis, we can accept the girl's statement. However, Aibell also says that she is originally from Dún Eochair Mháigh, the chief fortress of the princes of the Uí Fidgente. She says that her father was a simple fisherman on the River An Mháigh, a man called Escmug who, she claims, was a depraved person and sold her as a bond-servant to Fidaig of the Luachra even though she had reached the age of maturity.'

Brehon Aillín could not help interrupting with a sniff. 'That is unlikely. Even among the Uí Fidgente such a transaction is against the law.'

'Nevertheless, this is what is claimed. Now, given the fact that our assassin has a saddle-bag with the brand of the Prince of the Uí Fidgente and the girl originally comes from the chief fortress of those people, we have another strange coincidence that is worth pondering on. It may well be just another coincidence – but we must gather more facts.'

Finguine sat back with a frown. 'You have a proposal as to how those facts may be gathered? I presume you mean to question the girl further?'

Brehon Aillín said deprecatingly, 'If she has lied already, she will lie again.'

'That is not what I propose,' Fidelma said hurriedly. 'I am afraid there is only one way to gather the evidence that might or might not confirm these matters.'

It was Caol, speaking for the first time, who understood her intent.

'You propose to go to the country of the Uí Fidgente and see if you can obtain this information?'

Brehon Aillín pursed his thin lips in disapproval. 'The land of the Uí Fidgente is dangerous to one of your blood, especially after your brother defeated the rebellion of Eoganán at Cnoc Áine.'

'You may recall that Brother Eadulf and I spent some time among the Uí Fidgente when we went to the Abbey of Ard Fhearta,' Fidelma said.

'As I recall,' Brehon Aillín responded in a pedantic tone, 'you went there at the invitation and under the personal protection of Conrí the son of Conmáel, the warlord of the Uí Fidgente.'

'That is true,' Finguine agreed. 'But since then there has been much disturbance in that country.'

'Disturbance?' Fidelma's tone was dismissive. 'That was mainly due to the fanaticism of Étain of An Dún and nothing to do with the Uí Fidgente. Even though they are reluctant to accept the rule of Cashel, Prince Donennach has made a peace with us and has kept to it.'

Finguine seemed to be struggling with the proposition. 'Do you think that such a journey is the only way to resolve this matter?'

'The corpse will not reveal any more information,' Fidelma replied. 'And if Aibell is lying, then she is quite proficient in her lies. Her story of her arrival is supported by two independent witnesses. Yes, I think there is more to be discovered – and the means of doing so is not, sadly, in Cashel.'

Finguine suddenly turned to Eadulf, who had been sitting silently at Fidelma's side.

'You do not speak, friend Eadulf. What have you to say in this matter?'

Eadulf stirred himself. 'I do not speak out of respect to this assembly for it is not my right, being a stranger in this kingdom.'

'Nonsense!' Finguine almost snapped the word. 'You are no longer a *cú glass*, an exile from over the sea. When you married our cousin you were accepted as a *deorad Dé*, an exile of God, with an honour price in your own right. Colgú the King has always respected your advice. So do I, and now I ask for your opinion on this matter.'

Caol muttered something in support and even Beccan nodded assent.

'Very well.' Eadulf learned forward slightly in his seat. 'I think you will all agree that since my partnership with Fidelma, we have spent longer away from Cashel than in its vicinity. You may also know that it has been my preference to stay in one place long enough to see our son, Alchú, grow to the age for what you call *áilemain*, the act of education. Personally, I would prefer to be the boy's teacher myself, but this I know is not your way.'

Brehon Aillín seemed to suppress a snort. 'I fail to see how this is answering the question of the *tánaiste*, the heir apparent.'

'I preface my remarks in order that you will know that I am not responding lightly,' replied Eadulf, looking him straight in the eye.

'Continue,' Finguine ordered, casting a frown at the Brehon.

'I have said what I have said so that you will know that my preference would be for Fidelma and me to stay here to look after the wants of our son. However, in this case, the only logical path to discovering who is behind the attempted murder of Colgú and the death of the Chief Brehon, is to follow what little information has been given to us. That is the path Fidelma has outlined to you. If there is any other way we can proceed, then let me hear it now.'

There was a silence among the gathering. It was finally broken by Brehon Aillín. 'This opinion contains a rather arrogant presumption.'

Fidelma's head came up quickly. There was a dangerous look in her eyes.

'I was responding to a question,' Eadulf said quietly. 'I fail to see the arrogance in my response.'

'Perhaps "arrogance" is too strong a term,' Brehon Aillín replied with a thin smile. 'And yet the opinion you express is that only you and the lady Fidelma would be fit to take on the task of investigating this matter among the Uí Fidgente.'

Eadulf witnessed the stormclouds gather on Fidelma's features and put his hand on her arm.

Finguine also noticed, for he said immediately: 'You are quite right, Brehon Aillín. You do well to remind us that you are senior in this matter.'

Fidelma noticed there was a twinkle in her cousin's blue eyes as he brushed his Eóghanacht red hair away from his forehead.

'As the senior Brehon, Aillín himself might want to take on this task of riding into the country of the Uí Fidgente to discover what more can be found out,' explained Finguine.

The heir apparent's voice sounded innocent enough, but Fidelma was sure he was inwardly laughing at the crusty old judge, whose features had whitened considerably at the suggestion.

'It would be an honour to undertake this task,' Brehon Aillín stuttered a little. 'Of course, I could do so . . . But – but I am now acting Chief Brehon following the death of poor Brehon Áedo.' His voice grew stronger. 'It is therefore my duty to remain in Cashel as your adviser, Finguine, until the King returns to health. Perhaps a more junior *dálaigh* would be capable of gathering what additional evidence there is to be garnered?'

'Naturally,' agreed Finguine solemnly. 'And since Fidelma has investigated thus far, and with some notable success, I would suggest that she continues to fulfil this task.' He turned to Fidelma. 'And in accepting it, I suggest that our friend Eadulf be at your side as always.'

Fidelma bowed her head so that her amusement was not seen by Brehon Aillín.

'I will carry out the wishes of my cousin, the *tánaiste*,' she forced a sombre note in her voice. 'And I am sure that Eadulf, in spite of his stated reluctance,' she glanced meaningfully at the old judge, 'will be happy to accompany me.'

'But you cannot go into the country of the Uí Fidgente alone.' It was Caol who protested. The commander of the élite warriors of Cashel turned anxiously towards Finguine. 'They must be accompanied by a bodyguard of warriors.'

But Fidelma was already protesting. 'If we go into the country of the Uí Fidgente with a company of warriors, we will be asking for trouble. There is peace between Prince Donennach and Cashel. Armed warriors riding into his territory will be seen as a sign of aggression. Best go there as what we are – two people who travel in peace.'

'We cannot trust the Uí Fidgente,' Caol said obstinately. 'I have fought against them at Cnoc Áine, and I am responsible for your safety as a

Princess of the Eóghanacht. Remember that Abbot Nannid of Mungairit is the uncle of Prince Donennach. I cannot allow . . .'

Fidelma's eyes flashed suddenly. 'Cannot allow?' she demanded coldly.

Finguine once again raised his hand for silence. 'I am inclined to agree with Caol, Fidelma. It crosses my mind that this is an interesting time for this attack to have happened.'

'Why so?' Fidelma was impatient.

'Because Prince Donennach is due here before the next full moon. He is coming to negotiate a new treaty with Colgú to supersede the one concluded at the end of the Uí Fidgente uprising against us four years ago.'

Fidelma was surprised. 'I was not told this. I had heard that he was going to pay his respects to the High King at Tara, but not that he was returning through Cashel.'

'It was felt best not to make the negotiation too widely known.'

'Donennach is a wily politician,' muttered Caol. 'That is why I should go with you. You stand in need of protection.'

'Eadulf and I can protect ourselves . . .' began Fidelma.

Finguine intervened again: 'Your brother has come close to assassination. If there is a danger in the country of the Uí Fidgente then you must take what steps you may for your protection. On the other hand, Fidelma, I can appreciate your argument that it would be ill-advised for you to take an entire band of warriors as your escort. That would draw too much attention to yourselves and might well restrict your enquiries.'

'What middle path do you suggest?' Fidelma asked.

'I would suggest that one warrior of the Nasc Niadh, the Golden Collar, should accompany you.'

Fidelma thought about it and then shrugged. 'Very well. One warrior will not attract as much attention to us as a band of warriors.'

'Then it is agreed,' confirmed Finguine.

'I will make sure that you are both kept safe,' Caol promised them with a confident smile. 'It will be like old times.'

Finguine was shaking his head. 'I did not mean you, Caol. As commander of the warriors in Cashel your task must be to remain close by my side during this time of unrest. If news of the severity of the King's injuries becomes known among his enemies, then we may stand in need of your skills.'

Caol's expression fell in disappointment. 'But I know the Uí Fidgente,' he repeated. 'They are not to be trusted. I was one of the warriors who went with Uisnech, the lord of Áine, to pacify them after they were defeated at Cnoc Áine. And didn't they assassinate Uisnech before they agreed the peace with Cashel? You must remember that, Finguine. You are of the Eóghanacht Áine and were you not kinsman to Uisnech?'

Finguine would not be moved.

'My mind is made up, Caol. Your duty is here. Now, who would you recommend to accompany the lady Fidelma?'

Caol looked as if he would argue further, but seeing the determination in the *tánaiste*'s features, he shrugged. Before he could speak, however, Fidelma had answered her cousin. 'Let Gormán come with us. He has had a great deal of experience.'

'An excellent choice,' Finguine agreed, turning to Caol. 'Do you raise any objections?'

'He is a good man,' Caol admitted reluctantly.

Finguine turned back to Fidelma and asked: 'Do you know when you will leave?'

'Tomorrow, at first light.'

'How will you proceed?'

Fidelma glanced at Eadulf and then said confidently, 'First we will go directly to the Abbey of Mungairit. It may be that something is known there of Brother Lennán. The road is not too difficult beyond Ara's Well. Two days' riding should bring us safely to the abbey.'

'But if you have no success at Mungairit, what then?'

'Then we shall ride south-west. We'll follow the river, An Mháigh, to

Dún Eochair Mháigh and see what is known of this girl and her mother Liamuin. That's no more than a day's ride from Mungairit. A further day's ride would put us in Luachra territory if our enquiries force us there. From the territory of the Luachra we could be back in Cashel after two or three days at most. Of course, it all depends on how long we stay in each place pursuing our task, but the minimum we should be away is seven days.'

Finguine was calculating the time. 'I cannot say I feel comfortable about this, but if there is no other way . . .'

'This has to be done so that we can learn if there is more danger threatening,' Fidelma insisted.

Finguine nodded briefly before glancing around at the assembled company. 'Then it is agreed?'

They assented one by one, although Caol still looked disappointed that he would not be going with them.

Outside the small council chamber Fidelma turned to Eadulf and apologised.

'For what?' he asked.

'Once more we have to leave little Alchú behind.'

Eadulf smiled at her. 'In this case it seems necessary. Let us hope it will not be for long. The boy is bright and I feel he now needs our attention. He is beginning to have dexterity in counting and speaking. He is even picking up some of my language, in spite of Muirgen's disapproval.'

Fidelma laughed easily. 'Take no notice. It is what *we* think that is important. Indeed, this is the best time for the boy to learn languages. We should talk to Brother Conchobhar about it. He always says that the younger a child starts learning languages, the more naturally they can pick them up.'

'Well, I am certainly impressed by the way he counts and with his vocabulary. I nearly flushed in embarrassment when he commented on Ordan's appearance, but he was accurate. He puts words together to communicate, he knows the difference between time words – *yesterday* and *next week* – and he knows emotional words – *happiness* and *disappointment*.'

Fidelma said teasingly, 'I have to say that little Alchú is only showing that he is a normal child.'

'But he can relate the spoken numbers to objects,' protested Eadulf.

'As can any average child at his age.'

Eadulf realised that he was sounding like a proud and boastful father.

'Let's go and find Brother Conchobhar now,' Fidelma suggested. 'We'll make sure he keeps an eye on Alchú while we are away. Muirgen means well and the boy will be safe in her hands, but now he is learning so rapidly, she needs a little help. What was good for her when she was growing up at Gabhlán in the shadow of Sliabh Mis is not quite good enough for an Eóghanacht . . .' She was about to say 'an Eóghanacht prince' but hesitated in case Eadulf was offended. Eadulf pretended he did not notice the slip of the tongue.

They crossed the cobbled courtyard to the small apothecary shop where a dim light could be seen through the window. Fidelma tapped on the dark oak door before seizing the handle to open it. Immediately she and Eadulf were engulfed in the pungent aromas of herbs and dried flowers, combining in an almost overpowering smell that caused them to catch their breath. It took a few moments for them to grow used to it.

From the gloom of the interior Brother Conchobhar moved forward, a lamp in his hand.

'Ah,' he smiled as he recognised them. He put the lamp down on a workbench and proceeded to light a stronger lantern to illuminate the scene. 'There is still no change in the condition of your brother, Fidelma,' he said at once. 'I left him but a short time ago. I do not expect any further change one way or another until tomorrow. At least his heart is strong and the bleeding has stopped. It is not the first time the King has suffered grievous wounds.'

Fidelma drew her brows together. 'I do not recall him suffering a serious wound previously?'

'You were away at that time, lady – at the Abbey of the Three Wells, as I recall. It was during the Battle of Cnoc Áine when we defeated the Uí Fidgente.'

'I did not know.'

'He still bears a scar on his right side. One of the enemy struck his shield from his hand and managed to bite into the flesh with his sword. He was carried barely conscious from the field even moments before the Uí Fidgente admitted defeat. He recovered quickly, as I am sure he will recover from this wound.'

'Thank you, Conchobhar,' Fidelma said quietly. 'We will pray that you are right.'

'We came to speak with you on another matter.' Eadulf intervened to break the awkward silence.

'Another matter?'

'Fidelma and I have to leave Cashel,' explained Eadulf. 'We need to follow some information which may lead us to discover who the would-be assassin was and whether he was working alone or in some conspiracy.'

Brother Conchobhar's expression was one between resignation and disapproval.

'Then I presume that you will both be heading off into the country of the Uí Fidgente?'

'Gormán will come with us,' Fidelma said, and when the old man did not show any enthusiasm, she added: 'Have you seen some warning in the heavens?'

Brother Conchobhar was not only a gifted apothecary but he was a keen observer of the heavens and had a gift for making observations from the stars as to the best and worst of times. It was an art that had helped Fidelma several times in the past and the old man had once advised that it was a gift that Fidelma should develop herself.

Brother Conchobhar, however, simply shrugged. 'The wheel of the sun can tell many things. Some are clear, some are obscure. What I see presently is that it could be a time of ill-judgement.'

Eadulf smiled and said: 'I have never known a time when one could not make an ill-judged decision.'

'True for you, friend Eadulf. But the Red Mare consorts with the warrior and the Fair Mare drinks at the watergate of heaven. It is compounded by the star of knowledge being in the company of the bees while the star that defends is in the sign of the reaping hook.'

Eadulf looked blank as he tried to interpret the unfamiliar names and connect them to the stars.

'It means,' went on the old apothecary patiently, 'that there is much restlessness, impatience and hot temper at this time which could lead to quick judgements and wrong conclusions.'

'I've no understanding of these matters,' protested Eadulf.

'The Red Mare is what we sometimes call the sun; the Fair Mare is the moon. We call what you might know as Sagittarius, the warrior; the watergate of heaven is Aquarius and the star of knowledge is . . .'

'I know that is Mercury, and the Defender is what you call Mars,' interrupted Eadulf irritably. 'I know those names.'

'And it means one is in the sign of Scorpio and the other in that of Leo,' explained Fidelma.

Brother Conchobhar smiled in approval. 'Exactly so, my young friends. I do not say this will be the entire influence but, if you find that you are given to impulsive behaviour and decisions, then be warned. Avoid such tendencies.'

'That we will,' Fidelma solemnly assured him.

'Yet that is not what we came to see you about,' Eadulf added.

The apothecary's eyes widened. 'Then . . . what? Oh, about the girl Aibell? Have no fear. I shall keep an eye on her. I have already spoken to Dar Luga and together you may trust us to keep her safe and secure.'

'It is not even about her, this time,' Fidelma said. 'It's about Alchú.'

'He is a bright, intelligent boy,' Eadulf added.

'And that is natural in view of his parentage,' observed the old man with a smile.

'In seriousness, he is learning many things and his mind needs to be engaged so that he continues to learn,' pressed Eadulf. 'While we are away, we thought you might speak with him, teach him things, and especially watch his vocabulary and his knowledge. He is already counting in my own language.' Eadulf spoke the last sentence proudly.

Brother Conchobhar's smile broadened. 'Alas, I do not know much of your language, friend Eadulf. But you may rest assured that I can impart a little of Latin and Greek and much of my own mother tongue.'

'That would be of tremendous help,' Eadulf assured him. 'It is just that . . .'

'Just that you realise that the boy is of an age where he is absorbing information very quickly,' suggested Conchobhar. 'While Muirgen can teach many things, she is not exactly of a scholarly disposition. The time has come when his mind needs to be engaged with knowledge that she cannot impart.'

'Exactly so,' said Eadulf, feeling a little guilty over Muirgen's role for she had been essential to them in the early days, especially when Fidelma had been seized with a curious depression about the baby and her behaviour had begun to worry Eadulf.

'Do not worry, my friends. I understand. As a matter of fact, I have recently made a purchase from your old college, Eadulf, which I was going to tell you about before . . . before . . .' He raised a shoulder and let it drop.

'What sort of purchase?' asked Fidelma curiously.

'One that will help with the education of the young. It is a book that has been copied at Tuaim Drecain and much of it is attributed to Cenn Fáelad who was a chief professor at the school. I am told, however, that it was Longarad of Magh Thuathat who devised the entire book. It is a book called *Auraicept na nÉces – The Scholar's Primer*. It gives knowledge on grammar, rhyme, and the meaning of the old alphabet we called after Ogma, the old God of Literacy. It has the new alphabet and shows how children may remember the letters by calling each one after a known tree.'

'I don't understand,' frowned Eadulf.

'Easy enough. A is *ailm*, a pine tree; B is *beith*, a birch tree; and C is *coll*, a hazel tree and so on.'

'Ah, it is the way some of our scholars teach young children. A is for apple; B is for boy; and C is for cat.'

'It seems a good idea,' Fidelma conceded. 'So long as someone in the future does not think that there is more symbolism in the concept and start forming other ideas beyond seeing it as a simple way of children remembering their letters.'

Brother Conchobhar chuckled. 'I don't think we need have any fear of that.' He turned and picked up a leather-bound vellum book from a shelf and showed it to Eadulf. 'I shall leave it in the *tech screpta*, the library, for your return, friend Eadulf. Then you will see some of the matters that I shall pass on to your son.'

'Fair enough,' Eadulf nodded. 'I will rest easy now that you will look after him, for he is an intelligent lad and has the sharp mind of his mother.'

Fidelma playfully punched Eadulf on the arm for she was not displeased with the compliment.

'And now we must find Gormán and warn him of our journey tomorrow,' she said.

As Eadulf was about to pass out of the door after Fidelma, Brother Conchobhar suddenly tugged at his sleeve and pressed something round and metallic into his hand. The old man said softly: 'Fidelma has left the religious, I know. She believes that she no longer needs their help. The time may come when you might – especially where you are going. This is the silver seal of Ségdae of Imleach, whose authority is known throughout Muman. He gave it to me some time ago. Show it to any religious in the kingdom and they will respect its authority.' Then he raised his voice and wished Eadulf 'good luck' on his journey.

They left the apothecary, with Fidelma not seeming to have noticed the exchange, and made their way across the shadow-filled courtyard, lit by several brand torches. The shadows darted this way and that as warriors moved here and there, fulfilling their duties as sentinels. They found Gormán at the stables checking the tackle. He looked up as they entered and grinned. He was clearly in a good mood.

'Caol has already told me,' he greeted them. 'We shall journey together. I don't think Caol was too pleased that he has to stay behind tomorrow.'

'I suppose he feels responsible that he was not able to defend the King against the assassin's blow before the damage had been done,' Eadulf commented. 'Perhaps there is vengeance in his mind.'

'That's probably it,' agreed the young warrior. 'He would doubtless like to reinstate himself in your eyes.'

'He has no call to feel any guilt in that respect,' Fidelma replied. 'It happened so fast that none of us were able to move until it was too late. It was so unexpected.'

'Are you prepared for tomorrow?' asked Eadulf.

'The horses will be ready in the courtyard before dawn, friend Eadulf.'

'We will make our journey in slow and easy fashion,' Fidelma promised, knowing full well that Eadulf did not regard himself as the best of horsemen.

'I have ridden to Mungairit in a single day,' said Gormán solemnly, 'but that was on a warm summer's day and I rode from dawn to sunset with scarcely a pause. But do not fear; with these shorter, winter days, we have only half the time to be on the road, otherwise darkness and cold will overcome us. Nevertheless, we could stay overnight at a place called Ulla, among the rounded hillocks. There is a good tavern there, as I recall. We could reach it before dark tomorrow. Then by the next day we will be safely in Mungairit.'

'It is a good suggestion but we will let the day and conditions dictate our pace,' Fidelma said sensibly. 'There is no need to rush, for we are not in pursuit of anyone . . . yet we are travelling through the country of the Uí Fidgente so we must be vigilant.'

'That is understood, lady; yet it would be a bad thing when a warrior of the Golden Collar is fearful of travelling in any part of the Kingdom of Muman because of a rebellious clan who ought to have learned their lesson by now.'

'Even so, as the philosophers say – *in ominia paratus*. Be prepared for anything.'

'Then we shall be prepared, come what may, lady.'

chapter six

The early morning frost had vanished rapidly soon after they had set out from Cashel. They had taken the westward road with the sun rising behind them, spreading a mild warmth in a cloudless blue sky that was surprising for the time of year. Aware of the length of the journey they were embarking on, and understanding horses and the conditions well, Fidelma had decided they should keep their pace to a slow trot unless faced with an emergency. So it was mid-morning when they were following the track through the marshy approaches to the River Ara, surrounded by the fen sedge and wilting bulrushes, to the spot called Ara's Well. This was a settlement of a few isolated homesteads sprawled carelessly on both sides of the river.

Fidelma led the way across the shallow ford to where a large building stood near a smith's forge and other outbuildings. An elderly man was seated outside the door in the lukewarm sun, polishing leather. Hearing the sounds of the horses' hooves squelching along the muddy path from the river, he glanced up and then rose with a smile of greeting, tossing the piece of leather down on the bench behind him as he strode forward to meet them.

'Is it truly yourself, lady?' the old man beamed in disbelief.

'It is I, Aona, and Eadulf is with me.'

She slid from her horse, as did Eadulf and Gormán, with Gormán moving to take their reins while they went forward to greet the man called Aona.

The tavern-keeper, for such was Aona's profession, took Fidelma's hand shyly, and then extended his greeting to Eadulf.

'It is a while since you have passed this way, lady. But, praise be, time has been kind to us all.' He glanced at their companion. 'And is that not young Gormán who rides with you? How are things with my old companions of the Nasc Niadh?'

As a young man, Aona had commanded a full *catha* or battalion of the bodyguards of the Kings of Cashel, before his retirement to become a tavern-keeper at the Well of Ara.

'May good health attend you, Aona,' smiled Gormán. 'But there is sadness on me that, because of my youth, I cannot bring news of any of your former companions as a new generation now serves the King.'

Aona grimaced. 'Sometimes I forget my age. Those I served with during the days of King Failbhe Flann are all long retired from the service of Cashel or passed on to the Otherworld. But what am I thinking of? You must come inside and drink *corma* with me.' He turned and shouted: 'Adag! Adag!'

From the side of the building a youth came hurrying. He halted a moment at the sight of them and then his face broadened into an urchin grim. Adag had been about eleven years old, the last time they had seen him as a boy fishing on the riverbank. Now he was almost as tall as them.

'Lady! Brother Eadulf! It is good to see you both again.'

They returned the boy's enthusiastic welcome.

'Well, Adag, you must soon be nearing the age of choice,' remarked Eadulf, as the boy went to take their horses from the care of Gormán.

Aona chuckled. 'My grandson lacks another year or two before he can make his own decisions, according to the law. But I have no fear that he will make the wrong ones. He is a good boy and a good helper. Now, come in and tell me all the news from Cashel.'

It was some time later as they sat before the smouldering fire, sipping Aona's home-brewed *corma*, and talking over the news from Cashel, that the old man turned a worried face to Fidelma.

'If this is something to do with the Uí Fidgente, then I do fear the future, lady. Why are you and your companions intent on entering their territory? Was there not enough conflict the other month when that crazy woman, Étain of An Dún, escaped from the Glen of Lunatics and persuaded some of the Uí Fidgente to follow her?'

'Only a few of them were foolish enough to follow her,' corrected Eadulf. 'Prince Donennach actually sent warriors to help Cashel confront Étain and her ragtag of fighters.'

Aona made a dismissive gesture. 'Isn't there an old saying that there are four things not to be trusted: a bull's horn, a horse's hoof, a dog's snarl – and the friendship of the Uí Fidgente?'

'Do not concern yourself, Aona,' Fidelma replied solemnly. 'We shall take special care. Anyway, this afternoon we hope to reach Cnoc Ulla before dark and there is nothing to fear along the valley between here and there.'

'It is afterwards that I fear, lady. If this is some plot of the Uí Fidgente, then they will not be content until it is successful or until they are destroyed.'

'But we don't know that it is,' Fidelma said firmly. 'And that is the purpose of our journey into their territory – to find out what, if anything, is going on.'

'You are in a good position to hear news from merchants coming out of Uí Fidgente country,' Eadulf said now. 'If anything was stirring there, then surely the merchants would have some gossip to spread?'

Aona smiled in acknowledgement. 'True – merchants always have gossip to spread, Brother Eadulf. The problem is judging whether the gossip is true or false. I swear some of that lot are better than the bards at their storytelling.'

'But the resourceful listener, such as yourself, can surely detect a lie from the truth?' Eadulf said.

The tavern-keeper grinned modestly. 'That is true. Take Ordan for example . . .'

'Ordan?' Fidelma frowned. 'Ordan of Rathordan?'

'Himself, no less,' nodded Aona. 'He is a frequent traveller between here and the country of the Uí Fidgente and Luachra. When he came here the other afternoon—'

'When was this?' Fidelma interrupted.

'It was three days ago. He arrived about midday.'

'But that was the day of the assassination attempt,' Eadulf said. 'Midday? Don't you mean midnight?'

'I may be old but I still know the difference between midday and midnight,' chided Aona.

'Go on,' Fidelma said with a warning look at Eadulf. 'You were saying . . . ?'

Aona cleared his throat, took a sip of his *corma* and then continued: 'Well, he arrived at midday saying that he had come from Uí Fidgente country. He wanted a meal and he took his time about it. I had the impression . . .' He seemed to ponder.

'You had the impression?' prompted Fidelma.

'I might be wrong but I thought he was very preoccupied. You know what a vain man Ordan is, full of bombast and stories. That was why I mentioned him, because of his usual gossip and storytelling. Well, this day he was as quiet as a lamb. He was sitting over there.' Aona pointed to a dark corner by the window.

Fidelma glanced across. 'Not by your fire? These are cold days and often raining, when a fire's warmth is welcome.'

'Indeed, lady. Usually Ordan would make himself comfortable on a chair before the hearth and be talking non-stop. But that day he went and sat over there alone while I remained at the fire.'

'So?' Fidelma prompted again when he paused to take another swallow from his beaker.

'He had eaten his meal and was having a drink when another traveller came in. He was difficult to place for he wore a long cloak and was hooded. I know he arrived on horseback, because Adag went to tend to it. The traveller asked for *corma* and went to sit just there, between the fire and near where Ordan was sitting.'

'You saw nothing by which you could identify this man?'

Aona shook his head.

'Was his cloak of good material; and what of his boots?' asked Eadulf, meeting Fidelma's nod of approval.

'Ah, I see. His cloak was of heavy wool. It was a good weave, edged with beaver fur and doubtless expensive. He kept the hood covering his face. The cloak was tightly pinned with something . . . now, what was it? Ah, I have it. A polished bronze brooch. I can't remember the pattern, but I know it kept the cloak so tight around him that I could not see what manner of clothes he was wearing beneath. The boots I noticed were of treated leather and appeared well-made.'

'Are you suggesting that Ordan might have been waiting for this person?' Fidelma asked.

Aona shrugged. 'I can't swear it was so, lady.'

'Yet you felt it? Did they speak to one another?'

'No more than a curt acknowledgement as the man entered. The sort of greeting strangers give when they confront one another in a confined space.'

'But you're not convinced?' Fidelma said, picking up on the intonation of the tavern-keeper.

'Funny thing – the newcomer asked me to make sure that Adag was looking after his horse correctly. I assured him he would be well cared for, but he insisted that I go to check. On my way back, I thought I heard quiet voices, but no – when I re-entered, the stranger and Ordan were still sitting in the same places. Some time later, the stranger rose, made his farewell, collected his horse and left.'

'Do you recall what his horse looked like?' Eadulf asked suddenly.

The old inn-keeper looked surprised for a moment but then said: 'As a matter of fact, I do. It was grey in colour with white legs above the hocks. Even young Adag remarked on it, as it was the sort of hunter that a noble would ride.'

Eadulf smiled in satisfaction. 'So the stranger left. What did Ordan do?'

'That was what puzzled me. He stayed here, sipping at his ale until it began to grow dark and then he demanded another meal, it being so late. It was not until near midnight that he rose to pay his dues and said he would travel on to Cashel. I asked, was it wise to travel on during darkness? After all, I saw that his wagon was heavily laden with goods and it is not unknown for merchants to have been waylaid and robbed at the bridge over the River Suir on the road that leads to Cashel. There are some wild youths among the Múscraige Breogain who dwell in that area.'

'And what was his answer?' prompted Eadulf after the tavern-keeper hesitated.

'He did not seem worried. He said that he was under the protection of the King's warriors and that no one would dare molest him.'

'It is true that Ordan often carries a banner on his wagon.' Gormán spoke for the first time. 'It is a symbol of the Nasc Niadh which he uses to frighten any would-be robbers.' He added with a smile of pride: 'Often, it works – for the warriors of the Golden Collar have a reputation.'

'Indeed,' nodded Aona. 'That's what I mean. The fat merchant often boasts of his personal friendship with the King of Cashel and how well-protected by the Nasc Niadh he is. Of course, it is all arrogance. Tall tales.'

Fidelma wore a thoughtful expression. 'You say that he was heading with his wagon for the bridge across the River Suir?'

'That was the peculiar thing,' the innkeeper replied, scratching his head. 'He said that he would go by a safer route, away from the bridge. He had decided to go south and cross by the Ford of the Ass.'

'That is a longer route,' Gormán pointed out. 'And you say it was near midnight when he left?'

'How far south of the bridge is it to the Ford of the Ass?' asked Fidelma.

'It is quite a distance from the main track, lady. It would add extra time on one's journey and in a heavy wagon . . .' The warrior shrugged.

'But it would explain why Ordan was crossing the Ford of the Ass and picked up the girl, arriving in Cashel before dawn,' observed Eadulf.

There was a silence and then Fidelma heaved a sigh. 'You have told us a strange story, Aona. Can you give us nothing further about your unknown guest?'

The elderly tavern-keeper shook his head. 'Alas, lady, if there was more to tell then I would tell it. I have searched my mind. As I said, he had a hood over his head, although I caught sight of a sharp chin and the fact that he was badly in need of a shave. I had the impression of gauntness. That is all I can say.'

Eadulf chuckled and laid a hand on the elderly inn-keeper's arm.

'Well, friend Aona, for a man who says he did not notice much, you seem to have noticed a great deal.'

For a moment or two Fidelma sat in silence and then she rose and stretched. 'It is time to be off,' she said decisively. 'We need to reach Cnoc Ulla before the winter darkness is upon us and I don't want to exhaust our horses by needless speed.'

After Aona had gone off to the stables, shouting for his grandson to get the mounts ready, Fidelma turned to her companions. 'Well, we know that Ordan came here and that he met the assassin. We cannot be sure that they knew each other, but Aona suspects they exchanged words. But what were these words? Then the assassin left on his way to Cashel. Why did Ordan stay until midnight and then take the long way home? Did he stay because he knew what was going to take place at Cashel that evening? As Eadulf observed, at least Aibell's story of being picked up by Ordan at the Ford of the Ass is confirmed.'

'I think we should ride back to Cashel and have a word with that merchant,' suggested Gormán.

Fidelma thought for a moment and then shook her head. 'The merchant will keep until our return. We have other matters to pursue.'

As Eadulf knew, the road running directly to the west would bring them to the famous Abbey of Ailbe at Imleach, but they soon left this road and turned northwards, along a stream which fed the Ara. While riding at Fidelma's side, with Gormán a little way ahead, Eadulf re-opened the subject that had been worrying him.

'Have you considered that Ordan may have taken the detour towards the Ford of the Ass because the girl was also involved in the conspiracy?'

Fidelma smiled at him. 'At the moment, we are not even sure it is a conspiracy. And if Ordan and Aibell were fellow conspirators, they are poor ones to concoct a story that paints Ordan in such a bad light.'

Eadulf relapsed into silence and in this fashion they continued onwards for a while.

The day was turning colder as the sun started its descent towards the rim of the western hills. Dark clouds began to race across the sky. A bitter wind was gusting across the narrow valley through which they were travelling along the bank of the stream. Had they been on higher ground, unsheltered by the surrounding hills, the cold would have been sharp. They drew their cloaks more tightly around them.

'Let's hope the wind remains strong,' muttered Fidelma.

Eadulf glanced at her in surprise. 'Why would you wish that?'

'Because if the wind blows those clouds away, it will not rain. Those are heavy stormclouds and I would not like to be drenched before we find shelter.'

Eadulf saw the logic in the observation and glanced up at the clouds that were racing along, almost at hilltop-level.

'How far is it to this place where we intend to stay tonight?'

'Not far now, if we can keep up this pace,' replied Fidelma.

As she spoke, they both became aware that Gormán had halted and was peering in the direction of a small copse of trees that grew to one side of the track.

'What is it?' called Fidelma as they came up to him.

Gormán merely pointed. Among the trees, a black shadow seemed to be moving in the wind. As they stared at it, the horrible realisation dawned that it was a human body hanging from a branch of one of the trees. The young warrior had already unsheathed his sword and his gaze scoured the surrounding woods.

'Wait here,' he ordered, and nudged his horse across the short distance to the edge of the little wood, his keen eyes alert for any danger.

They waited while he entered the wood, halted and looked about. Then he turned and waved them forward.

The body was hanging by the neck: it was clear that he had not come to that position through his own means. Eadulf noticed that the skin of the arms and hands was mottled, the features deathly white.

'He has not hung here very long,' Eadulf ventured. 'No more than a day or two, perhaps less.'

The body was that of a young man. The face was cleanshaven. His hair was corn-coloured, long but dishevelled, with dirt and dead leaves mingled in it. The clothes, too, were torn and caked with dirt and dried blood. He wore a linen shirt covered by a short, tight-fitting jacket that had been ripped open so that the fixings had been torn away. He wore *triubhas*, trousers that fitted snug from hip to ankle with straps that passed underneath the feet to keep them in place. The man's feet were bleeding and there was no sign of any footwear. It was hard to discern the quality of the clothes. They had once been bright and possibly of good craftsmanship. There was no jewellery on the corpse.

As they stared up at the dead man, Gormán appeared a little impatient.

'Is it wise to tarry here, lady? After all, this is the border of the Uí Fidgente territory.'

Fidelma grimaced. 'I doubt whether the Uí Fidgente do anything without a purpose, so I do not think they would attack us for merely looking at this unfortunate. If they did not want travellers to observe this body then they, whoever they might be, would have cut it down, not left it hanging in this place.'

Gormán did not appear reassured. He kept his sword ready in his hand while his eyes darted here and there in case of unexpected dangers.

'I wonder who or what this young man was?'

Fidelma suddenly bent from her horse and reached out to take the left hand of the corpse, peering at the palm and fingers. She then stared awhile at the fingers of the right hand before letting it go with a sigh.

'And what does that tell you?' Eadulf asked with an expression of repugnance on his features.

'It tells me that the young man wore a ring on the third finger of his left hand which, over the years, has left a mark. His palms and fingers are soft, so he did not do manual work – but the nails are torn and there is blood under them, so he must have either used his hands to fight his captors or tried to dig himself out of some prison.'

'You think he was a noble?'

'There are other people in society who do not do manual work,' she replied.

'Well, this is a frustrating trip,' Eadulf complained. 'We have moved from one mystery to another and there is no information to take us forward to a resolution of either of them.'

A small smile flickered on Fidelma's lips. 'If life's mysteries were easy, Eadulf, then there would be little for me to do and I should doubtless pine away with boredom.'

They had reached the marshland country around Ulla with its small hill called Cnoc Ulla rising barely fifty metres above them but seemingly out of place on the flat plain. Below the hill was a collection of buildings, which was where Fidelma had proposed to spend the long winter night before moving on to Mungairit. It was twilight as they approached, that strange grey light that appears in the moments approaching sundown. And it was in this light that Gormán, once more riding a little way ahead, saw the condition of the buildings they were approaching. His hand again went to his sword-hilt.

'The buildings are in ruins,' he muttered as they came up alongside him. 'We must be careful.'

Fidelma examined them for a moment. 'Some time has passed since this was done. This probably occurred during the raids that Étain of An Dún and her followers made.'

Gormán relaxed a little. 'I had forgotten they were active in this area. You are right. They wreaked much devastation here.'

Being mainly wooden constructions, the fires had consumed almost all the habitations. There was little left but the three travellers were thankful that there were no signs of human remains. From the look of things, either the attackers, survivors or those who had come later had cleared up the human debris. Étain of An Dún, in her attempt to create war in the kingdom, had exacted a high price for her madness. But now she was dead and the kingdom was supposedly at peace.

'A pity,' Fidelma said, regarding the ruins.

'Where is the next settlement?' asked Eadulf. 'We can't stay here.'

'There is no other settlement close by that I know of,' replied Gormán. 'At least none that we can reach before darkness.'

'Then there is nothing for it but to find the least damaged of the buildings and make ourselves as comfortable as possible for the night,' decided Fidelma.

'At least we have firewood enough,' Eadulf observed with cynical humour.

At one end of what had been the settlement they found the remains of a substantial construction. It appeared to have been built mainly of stones, although the door and windows had been burned away.

'A chapel, I think,' Eadulf observed. 'I wonder where everyone went?'

'If any of them survived at all,' Fidelma commented dourly as she dismounted. 'Let's look inside and see if we can make it habitable for the night.'

A corner of the drystone-built chapel seemed surprisingly undamaged. The roof of wooden planking had fallen, but against a beam which kept it secure from the ground so that one could still stand up with head clearance in the area. Apart from dust, the flagstones were relatively clean, enough to provide a comfortable sleeping area.

'We can lay a fire here,' Fidelma pointed to an area before this sheltered section, 'and that should keep us warm.'

Eadulf set off to gather firewood, while Gormán saw to the horses in a small enclosed space behind the building. Perhaps it had once been the garden of the religious who had occupied the little chapel. The wooden fencing had only been damaged slightly and the warrior was able to rearrange the railings to make a secure paddock. The grasses had grown wild and were enough for the animals to graze upon.

Fidelma had asked Gormán to locate a spring or brook where they might find fresh water. No settlement was built without a supply of fresh water. Gormán, who had brought the goatskin water bags with him, set off to look amongst the burned ruins of the homesteads that had sprawled around the stone church. There was no immediate sign of a brook flowing through the centre of the settlement and so the young warrior realised it must run outside its blackened borders. Logic told him that if there was a spring it would rise on the hill behind. He began to move in that direction when a faint sound caught his ear. It came from the far side of the desolate remains of the buildings. Once more, he eased his sword in its scabbard and moved forward carefully and silently, making sure that he stayed close to the cover afforded by what remained of the buildings. As he grew nearer to the sounds, he recognised them as the high-pitched yelping and growling of puppies.

The end of the ruined village was marked by the very gushing burn he had been seeking. It came tumbling down the hillside of Cnoc Ulla, snaking its way onwards across the plain. In and across this small burn frolicked four clumsy grey puppies, snarling, biting and play-fighting with each other. Gormán smiled and was about to relax when his eyes caught sight of a majestic, immobile figure. Seated on a round rock by the burn was a magnificent slate-grey animal, the mother wolf watching her progeny at play through slanted green eyes, edged with red. There was white fur around her muzzle, her sharp yellowing fangs snapping now and then as one of the puppies came tumbling too close.

Gormán froze as he watched her, for he knew how dangerous it was to be close to a mother wolf protecting her young offspring at play. He knew of the ferocity and might of those sharp fangs, the power of those muscles in that heavy-set animal. He hardly dared breathe in case the intake of his breath came to the sharp ears of the wolf. His blood turned to ice as he saw the ears of the beast prick forward and the muzzle rise as her nostrils sniffed the air. A moment later came a sound high above on the hillside. The she-wolf rose and it seemed her mane stiffened and she bared her fangs. Now, clearly, above them, carried on the breeze, came a curious wailing sound. Gormán recognised it as the hunting call of the wolves. The beast turned and let out a series of short, sharp barks, before trotting off up the hillside. The four puppies ceased their play immediately and, in obedience to her call, went scampering after her.

It was some time before Gormán felt the tension in his body release. When he was sure that the vixen and her brood were gone he made his way slowly to the burn, following it up the hill a little before dipping his hand into the water to taste it to ensure it was clean and fresh. Keeping one eye on the slopes of the hill for any threatening movement, he filled his water bags. The sky was almost dark when he returned to the chapel where Eadulf had already lit a fire which provided both light and heat for the cold night that would soon be upon them. They could already feel a chilly breeze crossing the plains and whispering around the isolated hill under which they sheltered.

'Is all well, Gormán?' Fidelma asked as he entered the ruins of the chapel. She had been preparing a cold meal. 'You were a long time.'

'I came upon a she-wolf and her offspring at the far end of the village,' he told her. 'I felt it wise not to announce my presence. The animal was watching over her cubs. Anyway, they have gone up the hill now but it would be wise if we made sure the fire was well lit through the night. There is a pack nearby.'

'A wise precaution,' Fidelma agreed. 'Did you see anything that might give a clue about the destruction of the village?'

'So far as I can tell, the whole settlement seemed totally abandoned after its destruction,' Gormán replied. 'That is,' he added, 'if there was anyone left to abandon it. Either there were some survivors or others came along and tidied away any human remains. It seems that Étain's rebels from the Glen of Lunatics did a thorough job of destruction.'

'Well, at least we do not have to worry about them,' said Eadulf as he stacked more wood on the fire. He had brought in quite a store to last them through the night.

'Perhaps,' Gormán said shortly.

Fidelma's eyes narrowed in interest at his comment. 'You'd best explain.'

'I was thinking. The attempt to kill your brother, the King, must surely be an act of vengeance for the defeat of Étain's rebels and their allies in Osraige. It is unlikely to be connected with a defeat that happened four years ago. On the other hand, it is only a few weeks ago that our armies defeated Étain and stormed Cronán's fortress at Liath Mór.'

Fidelma regarded the young warrior thoughtfully. 'An interesting point. But it is only speculation and . . .'

'. . . without information, speculation is a waste of time,' piped up Eadulf.

Fidelma was about to express her annoyance but then shrugged. 'I have always said so,' she acknowledged.

'But sometimes such thoughts are a logical process,' protested Gormán.

'I will not deny it. However, if one acts on speculation only, therein lies a danger. Do not disregard speculation but do not act solely upon it.'

'Surely that is difficult? For example, if I have chosen a tender joint of meat for my supper and placed it on the table, then I am called away for a moment and on my return I find the meat on the floor and my hound standing over it, it is logical that the hound must be guilty of theft. However, I have not *seen* the hound take the meat from the table. So that is speculation.'

Eadulf chuckled. 'That is a good example of a legal argument. But as I understand your law, a witness is called *fiadu*, one who "sees". So what does not take place before the eyes of the witness is irrelevant.'

'Well done, Eadulf.' Fidelma smiled in approval. 'You have obviously read our text, the *Barrad Airechta*, on the law of evidence. It does say that a person can only give evidence as to what they have seen and heard – and that would imply that speculation must be eliminated.'

Eadulf smiled smugly. Over the years that he had been with Fidelma he had tried to learn as much of the laws of her country as he could, spending time among the law texts in the *tech screpta* or libraries.

Fidelma turned thoughtfully to Gormán. 'However, you have also made a good example, for the law texts admit that indirect evidence can be presented if there are grounds for suspicion. But because your hound is standing by the meat which is on the floor, that cannot be the only grounds for blaming the dog. Were the doors and windows closed in the room where the dog was found with the meat? Was the hound enclosed in the room when you left? Could some other animal have entered and could the hound have chased them off after they had taken the meat and left it on the floor? You see, your speculation must be extended to full capacity. When all other avenues are closed then a judge is allowed to decide if there is only one explanation and accept that as indirect evidence which otherwise would be inadmissible. And yet I would still be unhappy with that decision.'

The young warrior was frowning as he followed her reasoning. 'Unhappy?'

'There is still room for error unless there is proof. When speculation has convinced people to condemn another, the truth will remain the truth and it is the truth that must prevail.' Fidelma gave a sudden yawn. 'And now, we should eat and then get some rest. If we leave after first light, we will reach the Abbey of Mungairit just after midday.'

They sat before the fire and consumed bread, cheese, some cold meats and an apple, all washed down with cold spring water. As frugal as it was, the meal tasted good after their long journey. Eadulf banked the fire again.

'Do we need to keep a watch?' asked Gormán.

'It is not necessary,' Fidelma replied. 'Just so long as we do not let the fire go out. Although I doubt whether the wolves will bother us.'

Her sentence was curiously punctuated by the distant howling of the animals on the hillside. It started with a solitary cry from what could only be the leader of the pack; this, after a moment or two, was joined by others. The whole chorus was eerie, rising gradually to a crescendo, until the wolf-pack fell silent.

Eadulf shivered a little. A nearby sound caused him to start nervously before he realised it was only the mournful call of an owl, perched on the ruined wall above him. He found Fidelma trying to hide her amusement, pulled a face at her, and turned to find a comfortable spot for a bed.

It seemed that he had barely stretched out on his cloak in the corner of the ruined chapel than his eyes opened to the cold grey light of morning. He blinked and sat up. The fire was no longer blazing but a plume of smoke was rising where Gormán had placed some dew-dampened wood on it in an attempt to rekindle it. The young warrior was kneeling by the side of the fire, poking at it. Beside him, Fidelma was stirring. Eadulf rose to his feet, stretched and smothered a yawn.

He was about to make a remark to Gormán when the whinny of a horse outside stayed him. The young warrior came quickly to his feet, head to one side in a listening attitude. Fidelma also jumped up, exchanging a glance with Gormán. To most people, one horse sounds much like another. But to someone who has spent their life with horses, there is an ability to detect differences as another might observe the contrast in the sound of people's voices.

It was at that moment when a harsh voice called from outside of their makeshift compound.

'Come on out, strangers! And if you have weapons, discard them. I have bowmen here, and their arrows are strung and ready. If we see a sign of any weapon, you will have seen your last dawn.'

chapter seven

❧

'Put down your weapon, Gormán,' Fidelma ordered quietly as she saw the warrior clutch the hilt of his sword in automatic reaction. 'We have no reason to suppose whoever is outside is not speaking the truth.'

Gormán slowly drew his sword and placed it on the ground. Fidelma then went to the doorway and pulled aside the temporary barricade they had erected to protect themselves from stray animals during the night.

'We are coming out – unarmed,' she called.

'Come forth, then,' invited the grating voice.

She glanced over her shoulder at Eadulf and Gormán. 'Do nothing foolish until we see who summons us in this fashion.' Then she turned and took a step outside.

The man who had summoned them had not been lying. Five men sat on their horses forming a semi-circle before the ruined chapel. Those at either end of this semi-circle had bows strung with arrows aimed. Two others had their swords ready while only the central figure sat at his ease on his horse without a weapon in his hand.

Fidelma automatically noted that once this man might have been handsome. He was tall, muscular, with a shock of sandy-coloured curly hair and a beard to match. However, his face was disfigured by a scar that caused a white welt from his forehead diagonally across his left eye, nose and cheek. It was not clear whether the eye was blind but it was certainly a pale, opaque colour compared to the restless blue orb that was its companion. He stared at them almost with disinterest. There was no way of telling whether he was smiling or not, for the thick beard hid all his lower features.

'Well, now, what have we here?' he muttered as Fidelma, followed by Eadulf and Gormán, appeared through the doorway. 'A warrior.' The glance fell on Gormán's empty scabbard. 'You were wise to abandon your sword, warrior. Now raise your hands just in case you are tempted to seek the knife I see still in your belt. Quickly!'

Keeping a rein on his anger, Gormán did as he was bid.

The man nodded approvingly. 'Bowmen, keep a watch on that one. He wears a golden circlet around his neck. You know what that means? He is a warrior of the Nasc Niadh, the Golden Collar, who regard themselves as élite champions. They don't surrender easily and are full of tricks. If he even moves a finger to scratch his nose, loose your arrows.'

Fidelma took a step forward.

'If you recognise a warrior of the Nasc Niadh, the bodyguard of your King, you know that you trespass on dangerous ground, whoever you are. Name yourself!'

This time there was no doubting that the sandy-bearded warrior was laughing, as a deep throaty sound issued from where the beard hid his mouth. He then focused his gaze down on Fidelma.

'I have no wish to name myself,' he replied evenly. 'I am the captor and, in case you have missed it, you are the captives. Now, who are you that travel in the company of a foreign religious and a warrior of the Golden Collar?'

Fidelma thrust out her jaw pugnaciously. 'I am Fidelma of Cashel, sister to your King, Colgú.'

'Not my King, woman,' replied the man, as if amused. 'And if you are Fidelma of Cashel, why do you sport clothes of this fashion. It is well known that Colgú's sister went into religious service. Does not everyone talk of Sister Fidelma?'

Fidelma's eyes narrowed dangerously. 'So might they. But since you know so much, you may know that I have left the religious and pursue my rôle as *dálaigh*, an advocate at my brother's court.'

The sandy-haired leader grunted indifferently and glanced at Eadulf. 'So who is the foreigner?'

'I am able to speak for myself,' Eadulf snapped. 'I am Eadulf of Saxmund's Ham in the Land of the South Folk, among the Angles.'

'There is a sound of arrogance in your voice, Saxon,' sneered the man.

'I am an Angle,' replied Eadulf.

'Angle or Saxon – what matters? You are a foreigner.'

'And now you know who we are, I suggest you identify yourself,' Fidelma said again, to show she would not be intimidated.

The man turned his gaze on her for a moment and then said, 'I see no reason to do so.' He addressed one of his companions. 'These folk have no use for their horses. Turn them loose.'

With a grin at his leader, the man trotted off to the makeshift paddock where Gormán had left their horses. A few moments later came the sound of shouting and the thud of hooves on the soft ground. Then the man returned.

'In more arduous times,' the leader of the group addressed them languidly, 'we might have had need of your horses. But we can dispense with them.'

Once again he signalled to his two immediate companions who, leaving the others with their arrows still strung and threatening, dismounted swords in hand and moved towards the captives.

'This can either be done easily without the shedding of blood, or the harder way which will cause you much suffering,' the leader called.

'What is it that you want?' Fidelma demanded suspiciously.

'Only that which is valuable,' replied the man. 'We will take your belongings and leave.'

Fidelma's eyes widened in surprise. 'You are just thieves? Robbers?'

'Were you expecting that we were warriors with some lofty purpose in mind?' The sandy-haired man laughed in amusement. 'I regret that I have disappointed you. Alas, I am no more than a simple brigand who would relieve you of the burden of carrying such items as the golden torque that your friend of the Golden Collar wears around his neck.'

Even as he said this, his two men began to search Gormán at sword-point, removing his dagger that he wore at his belt, the gold circlet showing his rank, a ring from his finger and a few other trinkets. Then they moved on to Eadulf, taking the silver crucifix he wore and a few other items of value including the silver seal that Brother Conchobhar had given him.

Fidelma glared at the leader of the brigands. 'You may regret this day,' she said fiercely.

The man made a bored gesture with his hand. 'Indeed, I may. But "may" is a word of uncertainty. I may regret it and I may not. That is something only the future and soothsayers can tell.'

While the arrows unwaveringly covered them, the two men searched Fidelma with professional detachment, removing her jewellery and the smaller version of the golden circlet she wore at her neck. In her *marsupium* they also discovered a small wand of white rowan wood on which was fixed a figurine in gold. It was the image of an antlered stag, the emblem of Fidelma's authority when acting for her brother. They added this to their store of booty while Fidelma and her companions looked on powerlessly. When they had finished collecting the spoils, one of the men packed the loot into a bag and tied it to his saddle while the other went into the ruined chapel and apparently searched the belongings they had left there. He came out after a few moments, holding Gormán's sword which he handed to the leader. The sandy-haired man glanced at it, weighed it in his hand and muttered approval.

'A good blade, warrior,' he said. 'I expect it has been put to expert use. I could use a better blade than I have.'

Gormán gritted his teeth in impotence. The sword had been an especial favourite of his.

The leader of the brigands now glanced at his comrade but the man shook his head.

'That is all,' the man said. 'But the trinkets and gold torcs will pay well for this day's work.'

'That is true.' The leader turned to Fidelma. 'Think yourself lucky. I feel in a generous mood, so we'll leave you with your lives. Two days ago we encountered a young merchant who was not as accommodating as you. He objected to us in most aggressive terms. So we hanged him.'

He gestured to his companions, who swung up on their horses. The two silent bowmen remained with their arrows still aimed while this was done. Then the sandy-bearded man yelled: 'Ride!'

Before Fidelma and her companions could move, the band of five brigands had wheeled round and set off at a fast pace through the ruined village towards the western hills.

Gormán uttered a curse, hand to his empty scabbard. Then he was peering on the ground, apparently trying to retrieve his dagger.

Fidelma heaved a sigh, moved to a boulder and sat down.

'Well, what now?' Eadulf asked resignedly.

Gormán had recovered his dagger and rejoined them.

'They have driven off our horses,' he said, stating the obvious.

'In that they have made one mistake,' Fidelma replied confidently, suddenly rising to her feet again.

'I don't understand,' the young warrior replied.

'Had they been sensible, they would have driven the horses before them. Or, indeed, have taken them. Instead, they just turned them loose.'

Gormán and Eadulf looked puzzled as Fidelma strode back to the ruined chapel and, with some dexterity, managed to scramble to the top of one of the thick walls and stood eyes shaded against the rising sun. She caught sight of Aonbharr, her horse, some distance away, grazing unconcernedly.

She raised her voice and began a series of long, loud wordless calls. She saw the beast's head raise, the ears prick forward. Then the head shook up and down on its thick neck, the mane flowing in each direction. The horse gave an answering series of snorts and whinnies, pounding the earth with a front hoof, and then came trotting back towards the ruins.

Fidelma climbed down from her perch and went to stroke the muzzle of the animal as it came up to her.

'Obviously our thieves know little about the bonds that can develop between people and their mounts. Aonbharr is not one to be chased off like that.'

'That is well and good,' replied Eadulf. 'But I don't think our horses have the same affection for us.'

Fidelma gazed at him reprovingly. 'If you will look behind Aonbharr you'll see that he is not alone. Horses are herd animals. The other two beasts are following him back. All we have to do now is saddle them. But I think we should break our fast first and see what these brigands have left us.'

Indeed, there was little of value that had been left, although Fidelma always carried some gold pieces for emergencies and these the thieves had missed. However, the most important items missing were the symbols of office, the white rowan-wood wand and the golden torcs which showed her and Gormán to be of the Order of the Golden Collar. Jewels and rings could be replaced, but the symbols of rank and authority were more difficult to obtain.

'Perhaps we should turn back,' Gormán suggested uneasily. 'If we are to ride into Uí Fidgente country we will need to do so with some authority.'

Fidelma disagreed. 'We are less than a day's ride from the Abbey of Mungairit, and to turn back now would be an act of foolishness.'

'I have no sword, nor means to defend you,' protested Gormán.

'Surely a sword is easily replaced?'

'You do not understand, lady. That was a special sword.'

'A sword is only as good as the hand that wields it,' replied Fidelma firmly. Gormán knew when to give up the argument.

The remaining belongings were gathered. They ate sparingly, not having much appetite after the morning's encounter. Gormán went to refill the water bags before they mounted their horses and began to move off along the track that led to the north-west. For the main part, they journeyed in silence, a slow and thoughtful trek over the cold, undulating hills, fording numerous small streams and rivers. They passed close to the banks of a larger river, which Fidelma identified as An Mhaoilchearn.

Even Gormán, who seemed depressed over the theft of his emblem and sword, which Eadulf knew was considered a loss to his honour and status as a warrior of the bodyguard of the King of Cashel, roused himself from his torpor.

'You will never starve by those banks,' he assured Eadulf, who had asked about the river. 'It is a great spawning place of salmon and sea lamprey. Otters crowd its banks. It heads north to join the great River Sionnan. You know the story of its creation?'

Before Eadulf could answer, Fidelma intervened testily: 'There are several stories of its creation. There is even one that says that under the estuary lies a city of the Fomorii, the underwater people, which rises to the surface every seven years and all mortals who look upon it will die.'

Gormán shook his head slightly. 'I was thinking of the story of the daughter of Lodan, the son of the Sea God Lir. She was a wayward girl and one day went to the Well of Ségais, the forbidden Well of Knowledge. Because she did a forbidden thing, the well rose up and chased her across the land until she reached the sea, where she drowned. The waters of the well that chased her formed the path of the great river that is named after her.'

'That is one story,' agreed Fidelma. 'Yet another is that there was a great beast, a dragon named Oilliphéist. It was chased by the Blessed Patrick and the passage of the beast created the gorge which filled with water to become the river.'

Eadulf realised they were talking merely to ease the passing of time on their journey.

'Well, as stories go, I like the one about Sionnan,' he piped up. 'She seems like a real character to me – someone who is not afraid to look for forbidden knowledge in forbidden places.' His expression was bland.

Fidelma pulled a face at him. He had not seen her mischievous grin for a while and it comforted him to know she was still capable of humour.

'Tell me more about this Well of Knowledge,' he invited.

'That is your story, Gormán.' Fidelma glanced at the young warrior.

'The Well of Ségais? There are many stories about it. Two of them are associated with the formation of rivers. The well was said to be surrounded by nine hazel trees which bore the nuts of knowledge, and these fell into the well in which a salmon dwelled. Because he ate of the nuts, he became Fintan, the Salmon of Knowledge.'

Although they continued to keep the conversation light for a while, it was clear that the robbery had shaken Fidelma more than she would admit. The loss of the symbols of power and identity were the main concern. Even Eadulf knew how much such symbols mattered in the culture of Fidelma's people. Without them, Fidelma would find it hard to assert her authority over the rebellious Uí Fidgente.

It was well after midday that they came into an area of low-lying bog, covered in sedges and long grasses.

'It looks like a wilderness,' commented Eadulf.

'Well done, friend Eadulf!' Gormán told him. 'This area is called *Fasagh Luimneach*, the Wilderness of the Bare Place. That is why the abbey we seek is so named.'

Eadulf frowned. 'Mungairit? You'll have to explain that to me.'

'*Mun* comes from *moing*, the tall bog brass, while *gairit* is from *garidh*, a mound that rises above the low-lying boglands.'

It was not long before they came within sight of the great Abbey of the Blessed Nessán at Mungairit.

It seemed to Eadulf to be a grey and forbidding edifice. He counted six chapels nestling among the abbey buildings.

'It is larger than I thought it would be.'

'It is certainly a great seat of learning,' agreed Fidelma.

'When was it founded?'

'Nessán, its founder, died here well over a century ago. It is one of the biggest and most important abbeys among the Uí Fidgente, who claim to be the descendants of Cass.'

They followed the track, passing an ancient standing stone, to the walls of the abbey. The fields around were deserted but, in more temperate weather, it was obvious that the brethren used them to plant and then harvest the crops to sustain the inhabitants of the vast complex of buildings.

The gates stood open and they rode through into a large square. There were several religious moving here and there, apparently intent on various errands. A tall, burly member of the brethren, looking more like a warrior than a religieux, was striding towards them with a smile of welcome. He was a pleasant-looking man, with dark hair and sea-green eyes that were sharp and perceptive.

'You are most welcome, pilgrims. I am Brother Lugna, the abbey's *táisech scuir*, the master of the stables. How can I serve you?'

'Where may we find the *rechtaire*, the steward of this abbey?' enquired Gormán.

Brother Lugna turned and indicated one of the many buildings. 'You will find our steward, Brother Cuineáin, in there. Shall I take care of your horses while you consult him?'

'There is no need, Brother,' smiled Fidelma. 'Gormán here will look after them until we have spoken with the steward.'

'Well, if you need to have them stabled and foddered, you will find me in that building.' The man pointed. 'That's our stables. Just ask for me, Brother Lugna.'

'That is much appreciated, Brother Lugna.' Fidelma led the way forward and came to a halt in front of the building that the man had indicated. Dismounting and handing the reins to Gormán, Fidelma and Eadulf went to the main door of the building. A bell-rope hung by it. A distant chime came to their ears as Eadulf tugged on the rope. A moment passed before the door swung open and a grim-faced religieux stood before them. His expression was in contrast with that of the stable-master and he showed no sign of welcome.

'*Pax tecum*,' Fidelma greeted him solemnly. 'Are you the *rechtaire*, the steward of this abbey?'

The man's eyes flickered from side to side as he examined them each in turn. Then he turned back to Fidelma with a slightly hostile look.

'*Pax vobiscum*,' he replied. 'I am not the *rechtaire*. Who wishes to see him?'

'I am Fidelma of Cashel and my companion is Brother Eadulf; beyond, with our horses, is Gormán of the Nasc Niadh.'

The expression of hostility seemed to become more pronounced, as the religieux moved reluctantly aside.

'Enter in peace.' The words were uttered as an expressionless ritual.

They entered a dark antechamber and the religieux went to close the door on them, saying, 'If you will wait here, I will inform the *rechtaire* of your arrival.'

Without another word he turned and hurried away. The antechamber was bare of any furniture. There were no seats and not even a fire was burning in the hearth. The whole grey stone interior gave out an atmosphere of forbidding chilliness and dark. They could just make out a wooden cross hung on one of the walls but, apart from this, there were no other ornaments or tapestries to offer relief.

Eadulf shuffled nervously. 'Not exactly an effusive welcome,' he muttered.

'Did you expect there to be one?' Fidelma replied.

'Uí Fidgente territory or not, this is still a territory that is subject to the Kingdom of Muman, and you are sister to the King,' he pointed out.

'I do not have to remind you of the differences between the Uí Fidgente and the Eóghanacht,' she murmured. 'We are in their territory now and must accept that they do not love us.'

The door suddenly swung open as the grim-faced religieux returned, holding a lit oil lamp which spread some light in the gloom of the chamber. Behind him came a short but well-built man in dark robes, wearing the tonsure of the Blessed John. From around his bald pate, straggly grey curly hairs seemed to float in all directions. He was a fleshy-faced man with eyes of indiscernible colour, perhaps grey, perhaps light blue. They could not tell. He seemed to have a particular habit of rubbing his right wrist with his left hand.

'I am Brother Cuineáin, the steward of this abbey.' He looked at them expectantly.

'I am Fidelma of Cashel and this is Eadulf of Seaxmund's Ham, my husband. Waiting outside with our horses is Gormán of the Nasc Niadh.'

Brother Cuineáin inclined his head in brief acknowledgement. Then he raised his pale eyes to examine them closely.

'What do you seek here?' His voice was as lacking in warmth as that of the religieux who had opened the door to them.

'I wish to speak with Abbot Nannid,' replied Fidelma.

The steward regarded her without emotion.

'These are strange times, lady. Only a few months ago, this abbey was attacked by rebels commanded by Étain of An Dún. Now, I have heard of Fidelma and Eadulf – who has not? But it was of Sister Fidelma and Brother Eadulf that I have heard. While this Eadulf wears the tonsure of the Blessed Peter, you come in the robes of nobility, lady – you do not wear the robes of a religieuse. Perhaps you can let me have some proof that you are who you say you are?'

'Brother Cuineáin.' Fidelma was patient. 'You have made a reasonable request but one to which we cannot respond. On our journey here, at the Hill of Ulla, we were attacked by brigands and our symbols of authority, being valuable, were taken from us.'

The steward regarded them for a few moments and then sighed, rubbing the side of his nose with a pudgy forefinger.

'That presents me with an awkward situation. Without proof, I am not at liberty to accept that you are who you claim to be and therefore I can offer you neither admittance nor assistance. These times are fraught with unease and enemies can come in friendly guises. We must protect ourselves.'

Fidelma's eyes flashed. 'I am Fidelma, sister to Colgú, King of Cashel. I *demand* to see Abbot Nannid.'

'You can demand all you want, lady,' the steward said indifferently. 'However, until you can prove your identity I am only fulfilling my duty to the abbot of this place in refusing to admit you.'

'I come to him on a matter of law.'

The steward shook his head. 'That cannot be allowed. Abbot Nannid will not see strangers, moreover, strangers who have no proof that they are who they claim to be. I cannot admit you under the rules of this abbey, which are to safeguard it from any possible harm.'

Frustrated, Eadulf just restrained himself from taking a step forward. Brother Cuineáin's eyes narrowed quickly.

'Threats will do you little good, my friend. I suggest that, as the day darkens, you should all be on your way.'

'You do us an injustice, Brother Cuineáin,' Fidelma said softly.

'I can only obey the rule of this abbey.'

'Is it not said that rules are only for the obedience of fools but the guidance of wise men?' she snapped.

The steward pursed his lips in an ugly grimace. 'I would have to own, then, that I am either a fool or a wise man. The proof of which is difficult to discern at this time.'

'Then it seems we shall have to return when we are in possession of that proof,' Fidelma replied, suppressing her annoyance, 'and then we shall discuss the answer.'

Outside, Gormán was waiting patiently for them. Brother Cuineáin had followed them out into the courtyard to watch them depart. He glanced at Gormán and called with dry cynicism: 'I see that your companion, who you claim is Gormán of the Nasc Niadh, wears no Golden Collar and seems to possess no sword for his empty scabbard.'

Fidelma made no response.

'I knew something like this would happen,' muttered Gormán. 'We should have turned back and picked up other means of identity before coming into Uí Fidgente land.'

'The word "should" is as negative a word as "if", Gormán,' Fidelma said, her voice waspish. 'We have to deal with reality and not lament decisions that do not prove the right ones.'

'What now?' asked Eadulf.

'I can see no alternative but to find a place of safety for the oncoming night and then seek the help of my nearest cousin of the Eóghanacht Áine – and that's over a day's ride to the east.'

Fidelma was about to mount her horse when a shout came from the other side of the courtyard.

'Sister! Sister Fidelma!'

A young religieux was hurrying across the flagstones towards them, waving his hand in a manner undignified for one of his calling.

Fidelma turned to stare at the young man and then moved to meet him with a smile on her face; her hands were held out in greeting.

'Brother Cú-Mara!'

The young man came up slightly breathless and caught her hands. There was ill-concealed excitement on his youthful features.

'I thought I recognised you. What are *you* doing here?' He turned and clapped her companion on the back. 'And Brother Eadulf! I did not think to see you in this corner of the world.'

'It is good to see you again, Brother Cú-Mara,' Fidelma replied, smiling at the effusiveness of his greeting. 'And I might ask the same question of you? You are a long way from the Abbey of Ard Fhearta.'

The young man chuckled. 'I am, indeed, but on a visit to bring a copy of one of the books from our *tech screptra*, our library, to that of this abbey. I am due to return to my abbey tomorrow.'

Brother Cú-Mara was the steward of the Abbey of Ard Fhearta. He had once studied the art of calligraphy under Fidelma's own cousin, Abbot Laisran of Darú. It was while they were staying at Ard Fhearta that Fidelma and Eadulf had been able to resolve the evil threat of the person known as the 'Master of Souls'.

'It seems we might be in luck to have found you here before your return to the coast,' Eadulf said dryly.

Brother Cú-Mara looked puzzled. 'Why so, Brother Eadulf?'

Eadulf glanced over his shoulder to where Brother Cuineáin had been standing at the doorway, and was startled to find that the steward had moved forward and was now close behind him. He was staring at Brother Cú-Mara.

'Am I to understand that you know these people and can identify them?' he demanded in a heavy tone.

The steward of Ard Fhearta looked at Brother Cuineáin in astonishment.

'I do not know the warrior who accompanies them, but of course I know them! I thought everyone knew Sister Fidelma and her husband Brother Eadulf. If they did not know them in person, then their reputation is spread among the Five Kingdoms. I know them personally, for only a few years ago they spent time at our abbey and saved the kingdom from relapsing into war.'

The steward of Mungairit appeared flustered. A look of embarrassment began to spread across his features.

'Then it is up to me to offer my apologies.' He almost mumbled the words, addressing Fidelma. 'I have to say that in refusing you entry here

I was only acting by the rules and best intentions to protect our abbey from the many threats with which it is surrounded. I now offer you and your companions the hospitality of the abbey.'

'We will accept not only your apology but your offer,' replied Fidelma graciously, 'and with many thanks for we are exhausted since our experiences on the road here.'

Brother Cú-Mara was puzzled as he tried to follow the conversation.

Eadulf took pity on him. 'We were attacked on the road here by brigands. They stole what valuables we had, including all our means of identification, the symbols of office.'

'Ah!' the young man exclaimed. 'I begin to understand why the steward, if he did not know you, was reticent about your admittance to this abbey. You may recall the abbey was recently attacked by Étain of An Dún? But we must talk later for I have to meet the *leabhair coimedach*, the librarian, to conclude my business here. We will meet at the evening meal.' Then, with a wave of his hand, the young man was gone.

'He turned up at an opportune moment,' muttered Gormán.

Brother Cuineáin had signalled for his assistant and gave orders for their mounts to be taken to the stables. And, with their saddle-bags removed, he motioned them to follow him.

'I will ensure that the hospitality of the abbey is yours and beg your forgiveness, Sister.'

Fidelma coloured a little. 'I have left the religious,' she said. 'I am, as you may have heard, a *dálaigh*. I now serve the law on behalf of my brother, King Colgú of Cashel.'

'And the purpose of your seeking to speak with the Father Abbot, lady?' Only by the alteration of his means of addressing her did he indicate that he understood her change of status.

'An attempt was made on my brother's life; on the life of the King. The assassin identified himself as one of the brethren of this abbey, bearing an important message from Abbot Nannid. That is why we have come here.'

The steward halted in astonishment and swung round, staring at her. 'In that case I must take you to the abbot immediately,' he said. It was as if all the authority had suddenly left him. For a moment Fidelma was looking at a deflated and frightened man. He almost scurried along the long, gloomy corridors before them, barely taking time to light a lantern to guide them. Finally, with some breathlessness, he came to a halt before a dark oak door.

Here the steward paused, as if to gather himself, and then gave three loud raps on it. Then, with a muttered 'Wait here!' he opened it and disappeared beyond, appearing to forget that he had left them in the ill-lit corridor. It did not seem that long, however, before the door swung open again, shedding a little light on them, and Brother Cuineáin waved at them to enter.

The chamber of the abbot was well-lit by several lanterns. It was large, and the walls were covered in tapestries that gave warmth to the otherwise cold grey stonework. There was a yew writing table, elaborate and ornamental, which stood on a single support, balanced on three short legs near the base. On the top was an angle board on which the scribe could rest his book or vellum, or even *taibhli filidh*, tablets of poets that were usually beech or birch frames into which wax was poured. Notes could be made with a stylus and afterwards the wax was smoothed over again for reuse. To one side hung a number of book satchels. A few chairs and a large table on which two oil lamps stood completed the rest of the furniture.

A tall, thin man rose awkwardly from behind the table to greet them. It was difficult to see his features clearly, but his long robes and the ornate silver crucifix with its jewel insets proclaimed him to be abbot. He had a pale, gaunt face and wore the tonsure of the Blessed John, denoting him as a follower of the churches of the Five Kingdoms of Éireann rather than Rome.

In spite of the flickering shadows, Fidelma noticed, with some prejudice, that the man's eyebrows met across the brow; she had always been told that this was a sign of a bad temper. Although she knew it was folklore, she could not help but recall it. She also noted that his lips were thin and twisted in one corner. Fidelma mentally rebuked herself as the words of Juvenal came into her mind. *Fronti nulla fides*. No reliance can be placed on appearance. After all, her brother knew the Abbot of Mungairit and had a good opinion of him.

'I am Abbot Nannid,' the thin man said. 'My steward has informed me of the terrible news you bring from Cashel. How is the King, your brother?'

'He still lives,' Fidelma replied. 'Your steward will also have informed you that I am a *dálaigh*, as well as sister to the King?'

The man stared at her for a moment and then slowly nodded.

'This is my husband, Eadulf of Seaxmund's Ham. Our companion is Gormán of my brother's bodyguard,' she went on. 'You will excuse our appearance. On the journey here we were attacked by brigands, and our valuables and emblems of office were stolen from us.'

It was clear that the steward had already imparted this information, for the abbot made a sympathetic clicking sound with his tongue and waved them to chairs.

'Please be seated. Is my steward correct when he tells me that the assassin is supposed to be a member of our brethren? Who is this person?'

'I believe we should ask who this person *was*,' Fidelma said solemnly. 'The assassin was killed, you see – although not before he had seriously wounded my brother and murdered the Chief Brehon of Muman.'

'If the assassin is dead, how is it known that he came from this abbey?' the abbot asked defensively.

Eadulf was wondering whether the abbot was defensive because of guilt or whether he was considering the fact that as 'father' of his community, he would be responsible for the fines and compensation that were involved, should one of his community commit a criminal act. If Colgú died, that meant the value of forty-eight milch cows. As it was, the death of the Chief Brehon of Muman already meant a fine of forty-two milch cows. Eadulf mentally shook himself. He should not be thinking along such lines at this time.

'The man came into the feasting hall where my brother was seated, having gained access by introducing himself as a member of this abbey, further claiming that he brought a message from you. He said his name was Brother Lennán.'

'Brother Lennán!' The name came as an exclamation from Brother Cuineáin.

Fidelma turned quickly to him. 'It seems that his name is known, then?'

The abbot was sitting back with a curious expression on his thin features.

'His name is known,' he agreed quietly. 'Brother Cuineáin, will you go in search of Brother Ledbán and bring him here? Do not tell him the purpose.'

The steward nodded and immediately went off on his errand.

When he had gone, Abbot Nannid bent forward a little and said, 'Can you tell me the circumstances of this event? And could you describe this Brother Lennán to me?'

Fidelma told the story rapidly, in short sentences. She had just finished when there came a knock on the door and Brother Cuineáin re-entered and stood aside, holding the door to allow two figures to pass through.

One they recognised as Brother Lugna, the friendly stable-master, who had greeted them on their arrival. The other was an elderly man, walking unsteadily, hanging on his companion's arm and, with his other hand, using the aid of a heavy blackthorn stick. His back was bent, his skin like parchment, stretched tightly over his bones and across his sunken cheeks. Brother Lugna helped his companion shuffle to a halt before the abbot's table.

Brother Lugna turned to them with an apologetic smile. 'Brother Ledbán recently had a fall and that is why I help him. He was once an *echere*, a groom, in my stables.'

'This is Fidelma of Cashel,' the abbot said, raising his voice, for it appeared the old man was hard of hearing. 'She is a *dálaigh* and you must answer her questions.'

The old man turned colourless eyes upon her and waited expectantly. It was the abbot who finally asked the question.

'Tell her your name.'

'I am Brother Ledbán,' came the cracked, ancient voice. 'I came here to work as a groom. They used to call me Ledbán the Plaintive, but that was . . . that was . . .' He screwed up his eyes thoughtfully. 'That was many years ago.'

'And tell her of Brother Lennán,' went on the abbot.

'Lennán? Why, he was my son.'

'Your son?' Fidelma started in astonishment and was aware of Eadulf's gasp as he stood next to her.

The old man continued to stare at the abbot and went on, without glancing at Fidelma, 'He was my own son, as dear to me as life, bound in the bond of blood.'

'Did you know he was dead?' asked the abbot softly.

The old man's jaw rose pugnaciously. 'He was killed, as well you know.'

Fidelma stared amazed at the old man.

'How would you know that he was killed?' she demanded. 'Who told you?'

Now the old man seemed fully aware of her presence, turning to face her instead of addressing his answers to the abbot. 'He was my own son. How would I not know that he had been killed?' he replied, as if she had asked a question without logic.

'But . . .' began Fidelma.

Abbot Nannid interrupted, his voice loud and the words expressed slowly. 'Perhaps you should tell the *dálaigh* when it was that your son, Brother Lennán, was killed and where,' he instructed.

'Why, I am not sure how many years have passed now. Maybe four – but he was killed at the Battle of Cnoc Áine, when the Eóghanacht defeated the young warriors of the Uí Fidgente.'

CHAPTER EIGHT

∾

There was a silence before Fidelma turned to Brother Lugna. 'Perhaps Brother Ledbán had better sit down,' she said gently. 'Then he can tell us about his son, Brother Lennán.'

'Thank you, lady,' the stable-master said, and helped his elderly companion to a seat. When Brother Ledbán had settled himself, Fidelma suggested that the old man begin by telling them something of himself.

'Something of myself?' queried Brother Ledbán with a puzzled expression.

'I presume that you were not always a religieux?'

'Ah, no. I was a stableman for a chieftain who had a rath along the banks of the Mháigh, south of here. They were good days – happy days. My wife and I had no problems and raised our children under the shadow of Dún Eochair Mháigh.'

'So when did you leave there and join this abbey?'

'Oh, that was just after my wife died.'

'When was that?'

'My wife was a victim of the Yellow Plague. My son, Lennán, had already come to this abbey to study the physician's art, so I came here and joined him. I thought it would bring me closer to him. You see, there was nothing left for me at Dún Eochair Mháigh.'

Abbot Nannid was nodding in agreement. 'We were very happy to welcome Brother Ledbán into our community. We have a good stable. Brother Lugna has been our stable-master for many years, but he found Brother Ledbán an excellent asset. He was a good worker.'

'A good worker until I grew old and careless,' muttered the old man. 'I had too many accidents. Now I am just a burden.'

'Of course you are not,' boomed Brother Lugna, placing a large comforting hand on his shoulder. 'We all have accidents. I, myself, was bitten by a fretful horse.' He briefly showed a scar on his right wrist that had long since healed.

'So when did your son, Lennán, enter this abbey?' continued Fidelma.

'He was my eldest child. He came here a few years before his mother died from that fearful scourge which turned the skin yellow and from whose fever no one recovered.'

For many years the Yellow Plague had swept through the known world; prelates and princes succumbed to it – even two High Kings of the Five Kingdoms of Éireann fell to its ravages.

'Go on,' Fidelma urged.

'Well, after his mother died, my son concentrated his efforts on finding a cure for the pestilence that had devoured her.'

Abbot Nannid added: 'He was one of our most promising physicians. Then came the day when our Prince Eoganán sent the *crois tara* – the fiery cross, the summons to arms – throughout the clans and septs of the Uí Fidgente. As you know, he had declared that his line, the Dál gCais, were the rightful bloodline to be Kings of Muman. He raised an army to march on Cashel after your brother Colgú succeeded as King.'

Gormán stirred uneasily and glanced at Fidelma, who simply commented: 'Those were the facts and whether they were justified or not is another matter.'

'Just so,' agreed the abbot diplomatically.

'So what happened when the summons to arms reached here?' Fidelma asked, turning to the old man.

'My son left the abbey to accompany the Prince's army.'

'Understand, Brother Lennán went as a physician,' the abbot emphasised hastily. 'He did not go to kill but to tend to the wounded and injured during the conflict.'

'My poor son,' sighed the old man. 'When I heard that he had been cut down in the rage of that battle on Cnoc Áine, I could not believe it. He was merely tending the wounded. God's curse on him who struck that fatal blow. Survivors said that it was a man who wore the golden circlet around his neck. The Devil take them all.'

The abbot leaned forward and shook his head reprovingly.

'The pain of your loss is understandable, Brother Ledbán. But we must remember the teaching of Christ that we must forgive our enemies.' He glanced at Fidelma with an apologetic smile as if on behalf of the old man.

'We can appreciate your loss,' acknowledged Fidelma. 'Who identified your son's body?'

The old man seemed puzzled. 'I do not understand.'

'It seems someone has been making free with your son's name,' explained the abbot. 'I think that the lady Fidelma wishes to make sure that he is quite dead.'

'Did I not see the body of my own son when he was brought back here?' demanded the old man, his voice full of bitterness.

'Let me explain.' It was Brother Lugna who spoke. 'I knew poor Brother Lennán as well as any man. A report came to the abbey that he was one of the dead and so I rode to the Hill of Áine, found and brought the body back to this place for burial myself.'

'Does anyone here have any idea why someone would come to Cashel and announce himself to be Brother Lennán of this abbey?' asked Fidelma.

'I find it hard to believe that anyone could have done such a wicked thing,' replied Abbot Nannid, while the others shook their head.

'Not only did they do so, but they used the excuse that they bore a message from you, Father Abbot, in order to approach my brother,' Fidelma said, her emotions still very raw.

Brother Ledbán looked up at her and his old eyes were steady. 'Then all I can say is, they have sullied my son's name, for he gave his life for healing and not for killing.'

'Perhaps he had a friend who decided that he would avenge him?' suggested Eadulf.

Once more the abbot decided to respond on behalf of them all. 'Brother Saxon, may I remind you that Paul wrote to the Romans: *sed date locum irae scriptum est enim mihi vindictam ego retribuam dicit Dominus*. Is it not written "Vengeance is mine, I will repay," saith the Lord?'

'That is true, yet it is not a teaching that is universally obeyed, for even your own law provides reasons why, under certain conditions, vengeance killings may be excused,' replied Eadulf coolly. 'And I am not a Saxon but an Angle.'

Fidelma glanced at him in rebuke. She knew that Eadulf had discovered this ancient law when they were dealing with the mystery of the death of Brother Donnchadh at Lios Mór, but now was not the right time to debate such points with the abbot.

'Brother Eadulf makes a valid point,' she conceded. 'Would anyone spring to mind if we were seeking someone close to Brother Lennán whose emotions might well lead them to overlook the teachings of the Faith? Perhaps they might be thinking that they were acting under the ancient law?'

She was looking directly at the old man when she asked the question. There was no guile in his expression when he replied, 'There was no one other than myself who was as close to poor Lennán. Certainly, no one who would do this thing.'

'Very well,' sighed Fidelma. 'Oh, one more question. Perhaps it might mean something to you. When the person calling himself Brother Lennán struck the blows, he shouted a name. He shouted, "Remember Liamuin!" Does that—?'

She stopped abruptly, aware that the old man was completely still, staring at her with an expression that was almost akin to horror. Then a pale hue crossed his features. It spread noticeably, making his lips almost bloodless. His eyes rolled back and he slid unconscious from his chair to the floor.

Brother Lugna gave an exclamation of dismay and started forward, but Eadulf sprang up and was by the old man's side in a moment.

'He has fainted. Have you water?'

Brother Cuineáin went to lift a nearby pitcher of water to pour into a beaker but his hands were shaking and the water was spilling. Brother Lugna reached forward to take the beaker from him. The steward was apologetic.

'Sorry, it is an ague I suffer from which sometimes stops me picking up things unless I am careful.'

Eadulf ignored him and turned to the prone figure on the floor. They gathered round in a concerned circle while Eadulf tried to revive the man by coaxing the water between his lips. Brother Ledbán spluttered and coughed but he did not come back to full consciousness.

The abbot stood undecided for a moment. 'We'd best remove him to his chamber.'

'I can manage that, Father Abbot,' said Brother Lugna.

'Brother Cuineáin will help you carry him there.' Then Abbot Nannid added to his steward, 'You had best send for the physician to attend him.'

The steward and the stable-master picked up the inert man and carried him from the room.

After they had left, the abbot turned to Fidelma with a sad shake of his head. 'Poor Brother Ledbán is an old man. We have exerted too much pressure on him, conjuring painful memories. It is good that he has such a friend and patient helper in Brother Lugna.'

'He seems a kind person,' agreed Fidelma.

'Brother Lugna has been working at the stables of this abbey since he was seventeen years old, over twenty years. He is a generous and pious soul. He ran away from . . . from a good family to come here. Anyway, I hope Brother Ledbán will be better in the morning. A good night's rest is in order.'

'Perhaps in the morning he will be able to finish answering my question,' Fidelma said. 'We will leave matters until then.'

The abbot was quick to agree. 'It will soon be time for the evening service and meal. I will get someone to show you to the guest house.' He picked up a hand bell and shook it several times. In moments, there was a knock on the door and another religieux entered, waiting while the abbot issued instructions. 'A bell will be rung for the evening services which are held just before the meal. Either follow the sound of the bell or ask any of the brethren to take you to the refectory.'

The Abbey of Mungairit was obviously a rich one. In spite of the frugality of the entrance chamber where Brother Cuineáin had greeted them, once beyond that the wealth became obvious. The fact that it possessed its own large stables should have been an indication. When Nessán had founded the abbey, it was under the patronage of Lomman, son of Erc, Prince of the Uí Fidgente. When Nessán died it was endowed by Prince Manchin, son of Sedna, who claimed descent from Cormac Cas, who maintained that his people were senior to the Eóghanacht in their claim to the Kingdom of Muman. It was a claim that the Eóghanacht denied.

The abbey had grown in influence and learning and housed several schools of learning which brought it wealth and prestige. As they were conducted through the corridors and halls to their chambers, Fidelma and her companions could not ignore the riches that adorned the abbey walls. Great tapestries hung there, depicting all manner of religious scenes as well as scenes of hunts, horse races and battles . . . scenes from every aspect of life in the country. There were carved statues and gold and silver religious icons that the steward of a king's palace might envy.

Fidelma disappeared to the guests' bathing room for the traditional evening *dabach* or hot bath while Eadulf joined Gormán in a more Spartan strip wash with a section of the brethren of the abbey.

Later that day, after the evening meal, when they were back in their chamber in the guests' hostel, Fidelma sat down next to Eadulf. It was the first time they had been alone and could speak privately. 'Was Brother Ledbán truly unwell or did his fainting attack have something to do with my mentioning the name Liamuin?' she asked.

'He really did faint,' Eadulf told her. 'It could have been a co-incidence, or perhaps the old man recognised the name and reacted badly to it.'

Fidelma sighed wearily. 'Well, there is nothing else we can do but wait until the morning before we can ask him.'

'I did not see Brother Cú-Mara in the refectory for the evening meal,' Eadulf said.

'That is true. Perhaps his business with the librarian has kept him busy. It was good luck that he should have been here just at the very moment he was needed.'

'Coincidences still seem to occur frequently at the moment,' Eadulf remarked.

Fidelma looked at him curiously. 'Explain,' she invited.

'The fact that we found that girl, Aibell, whose mother just happens to bear the name shouted by the assassin. The fact that she just happened to be in the woodshed where the assassin changed his clothes. The fact that Brother Cú-Mara, all the way from the Abbey of Ard Fhearta, just happened to be in this courtyard and was able to identify us. There is the fact that Brother Ledbán happens to come from the same place as the girl and faints when the name Liamuin is spoken. And didn't Aibell mention that her mother's father had joined an abbey? It crossed my mind, could it be that old Ledbán was Liamuin's father?'

Fidelma chuckled softly. 'I swear that you are looking for coincidences in everything.'

Eadulf joked, 'Suspicion is something easily acquired when one lives with a *dálaigh* in this country.'

Fidelma pulled a face at him. Then, thinking of her brother, she had a moment of guilt that she could still be light-hearted.

'Anyway, the stable-master seems a pleasant man, giving such time to look after old Brother Ledbán,' she said, changing the subject. 'There is a particular friendship among people who look after horses.'

Eadulf knew that one of Fidelma's loves was horses and it seemed true that she had an empathy with people who worked with them.

'Anyway, we have many things to consider here,' she said.

'And best we consider them after a proper rest,' Eadulf advised, yawning. 'Last night, sleeping in ruins and then being robbed by brigands, before riding all the way to this place, was hardly conducive to our being able to reflect clearly on these matters.'

'You are right,' Fidelma sighed before turning and blowing out the candle by their bedside. She was asleep almost immediately.

In the morning, when Fidelma arose, Eadulf was already awake, washed and dressed. She washed her face and hands as was the custom, before joining Eadulf in making their way to the *praintech* or refectory. They were met at the door of the dining hall by Brother Cuineáin.

'Would you come with me?' he requested without preamble. It was clear that something was worrying the man.

Abbot Nannid enlightened them as soon as they entered his chamber.

'I am afraid Brother Ledbán passed to his eternal rest during the night,' he intoned solemnly.

'He was quite old,' added Brother Cuineáin as if anxious to give an explanation. 'Perhaps the remembrance of what happened to his son caused such distress that the strain was too much for him to bear.'

Fidelma received the news with feelings of suspicion and frustration.

'Does your physician concur with this cause of death?' she asked brusquely.

The abbot blinked briefly before he responded. 'Of course. Brother Ledbán was a frail and—'

'I would like Brother Eadulf here to examine the body,' cut in Fidelma.

The abbot drew in his breath in irritation. 'I see no reason—'

'The reason is that I am a *dálaigh* and the acting Chief Brehon will require it,' she said firmly. 'Brother Ledbán died in the middle of answering my questions.'

Abbot Nannid hesitated. 'If it is required by law, then that is the law. Though it seems strange that the word of our physician is not to be trusted.'

'I have not said that the word of your physician is not to be trusted. I am investigating the attempted assassination of the King. I have a responsibility to answer to the Chief Brehon that all was done as the law requires.'

The abbot glanced at his steward and gestured indifferently.

'Very well. Show Brother Eadulf to the chamber of our departed brother.'

Fidelma decided to follow Eadulf and Brother Cuineáin through several stone corridors and across a yard into a building close to the stables and paddocks of the abbey. They entered a small cell with room for a bed and little else.

The body of the old man lay stretched out on his bed. He had not yet been bathed nor had his body been wrapped in the *racholl* or shroud as the winding sheet was called, in preparation for the *aire* or watching which would last presumably until midnight – the traditional time of interment.

Brother Cuineáin stood back and allowed Eadulf to bend over the body. He waited by the door as Eadulf made his examination, which was not a long one.

'It certainly seems that he expired in the night, for the body is cold and stiffening.' He turned to the steward. 'When was the physician called to examine the body?'

The steward paused for thought and then said: 'At first light. I was about to attend early morning prayers when Brother Lugna came to find me and told me that old Brother Ledbán appeared to be dead. He had been worried when the old man passed out last evening and decided to check on him at dawn. The physician was then called and confirmed the death.'

'In what condition was the body?' asked Eadulf.

'I do not understand.'

'Did the body show signs of contraction, the experience of any agony which sometimes overtakes one in a seizure? Or did it lie peacefully as now?'

'Oh, he was almost exactly as he is now. I doubt if he knew he was departing life, for he left it while asleep and at peace.'

'Very well.' Fidelma saw that her husband had a resolute expression but something prevented her from asking further questions. 'There is nothing to keep us here.'

A sigh of relief seemed to come from Brother Cuineáin. 'Then I suggest we return to the abbot's chamber.'

To Fidelma's surprise, Eadulf replied, 'We have not broken our fast yet. May we therefore return to the refectory and take some sustenance? I think we shall be leaving the abbey soon as there is a long ride before us.'

Another look of relief crossed the steward's features and then he assumed a sombre expression and nodded.

'You are quite right, Brother Eadulf. I should have let you attend to the morning meal before I broke this news to you. I will go to the abbot and report that you are in concurrence with our physician and that you will shortly be leaving us.' He conducted them back to the refectory and left them at the door.

They found Gormán striding up and down, looking anxious. He seemed relieved to find them safe and sound.

'I wondered what had happened to you both,' he said. 'I heard there was a death last night but could find out no other details.'

'There was a death,' replied Fidelma grimly. 'Our main witness, old Brother Ledbán, has died.' She swung round to Eadulf with a frown. 'What was the meaning of your telling the steward that you agreed with his physician and that we would be leaving shortly? I had the distinct impression that you did not agree at all with his deduction.'

'Firstly, I really do think that we should all break our fast,' Eadulf smiled briefly. 'Secondly, there is nothing that I can prove about the old man. He did die in the night, but . . .'

'But?' snapped Fidelma, irritated.

'There is something I cannot explain. I noticed there was blood in the corner of his eyes, and blood in his nostrils that someone has tried to clean: you have to look carefully to see it. And there were specks of blood at the corners of his mouth. I have seen such conditions before.'

'And what do they signify?'

'Such signs are usually consistent with someone having such a powerful seizure that bleeding occurs from these orifices. If he did not have a seizure then he was smothered.'

'You mean that he was murdered?' gasped Gormán.

'The trouble is, I cannot make a definite pronouncement because he could have had a seizure,' replied Eadulf.

'Yet surely, had a seizure been the cause of death, the body would have shown clearer signs of it,' mused Fidelma. 'It would not have been in the state of repose the steward said it was in, when he and the physician examined it.'

Eadulf was in agreement. 'Exactly. That means, if we accept the murder theory, that someone in this abbey did not want him to speak further to us.'

'He collapsed as soon as you uttered that name – Liamuin,' Gormán caught on.

Eadulf glanced round. 'We'd best have our meal and not stand here for all to see like a group of conspirators.'

They entered the almost empty refectory and were given bread, boiled fish, apples and a jug of water. When they were seated in a corner, Fidelma said: 'But you told the steward that we agreed with the physician and would soon be continuing our journey. If this is murder, then the murderer is here and we must stay here to discover him.'

'I do not think that will avail us anything,' Eadulf argued. 'If old Ledbán was killed to prevent him talking to us about the identity of Liamuin, then only three people were in the room when the matter came up and it became obvious that he had reacted to the name.'

'You mean – Abbot Nannid, Brother Cuineáin and Brother Lugna?'

'And if they, one or all, are behind this, how long should we be left unmolested in this abbey? We are here on sufferance because Brother Cú-Mara vouched for our identity. But remember, we don't have any means of asserting our authority. It would be difficult for us to pursue enquiries among a community which is in the heart of the Uí Fidgente country and where folk are hostile. It would be easy for us to "disappear".'

Fidelma looked shocked. 'You cannot mean that the abbot would allow the law to be flouted and would fail to respect my position as an attorney of the courts of this country?'

It was Gormán who answered. 'I am afraid friend Eadulf is right, lady. If there is a conspiracy here, then the life of a king or a Chief Brehon would not be valued by these conspirators. That being so, what would the life of a mere *dálaigh* be worth – meaning no disrespect, lady.'

'Are you suggesting we abandon this investigation?' Fidelma's voice was hard.

'I am suggesting a strategic withdrawal,' Eadulf replied. 'Let whoever killed the old man enjoy a false sense of security while we pursue the investigation elsewhere. We may then be able to return here in a position of authority.'

'I think friend Eadulf makes an excellent point,' confirmed Gormán.

'Where do you propose that we pursue the investigation?' demanded Fidelma.

'Where we would have gone anyway, had nothing happened here.'

'I am not sure I follow . . .' Gormán began and then he sighed. 'Oh, you mean go south to the Dún Eochar Mháigh?'

'Exactly,' confirmed Eadulf. 'We have had several interesting strands and they all seem to lead to Dún Eochair Mháigh.'

'So we leave the abbey pretending that we have noticed nothing unusual? Very well. Shall I get our horses ready for the journey?' asked Gormán.

'We will have to officially bid farewell to the abbot,' Fidelma said.

Just then, a voice hailed them from across the refectory. It was Brother Cú-Mara.

'I was wondering whether you were still here, lady,' he said as he came up to their table and seated himself. He greeted Eadulf and Gormán with a nod. 'I became involved with the librarian last night and could not join you for the evening meal. How long are you here for?'

'We are departing now,' Fidelma told him. 'We were lucky that you were here to identify us yesterday.'

'I was pleased to be able to help,' the steward of Ard Fhearta said. 'You rendered our abbey great assistance when Eadulf and you were there. I have not forgotten, lady.'

Fidelma glanced at Brother Cú-Mara with interest. 'Have you known Brother Cuineáin for some time?'

'I think he joined the abbey back at the time when Prince Eoganán rose up against Cashel. Ah, no, it was shortly after that. I have been an inter-mediary between my abbot and Abbot Nannid several times. That is why I am here now. Our copyists have just completed a copy of *Aipgitir Chrábaid – The Alphabet of Piety*. It was made at the request of the librarian here and so I came to deliver it.'

'Well, it was fortunate that you were here. It seems Brother Cuineáin was fully intent on denying us entry because we could not prove who we were.'

'Some of the brethren here would say he was too conscientious,' replied Brother Cú-Mara. 'Do not get me wrong. He is good at administration but his devotion to the Faith has been questioned several times.'

Fidelma was surprised. 'Has it really? In what manner does he lack devotion to the Faith?'

'Oh, perhaps I should not spread gossip, but then gossip always spreads in a confined community like this.'

'He who goes about as a tale-bearer reveals secrets,' Eadulf added almost sanctimoniously.

Fidelma glanced at him in disapproval. 'I am sure the quoting of Scripture is appropriate in its place but in this instance I would be interested to know what it was the brethren complained of.'

'Well, they felt that it was unjust that Brother Cuineáin should be made steward before other, longer-serving candidates.'

'I am not sure I understand. The brethren usually elect the officers of the abbey from the most suitable candidates in accordance with the law.'

Brother Cú-Mara smiled briefly. 'In this case, it was Abbot Nannid who appointed him. His argument was that the death of Prince Eoganán at Cnoc Áine and the defeat of the Uí Fidgente warriors had thrown this land into turmoil. Stability was needed both across the land as well as in Mungairit. Therefore someone used to administration was needed as a temporary measure.'

'Someone used to administration? So Brother Cuineáin had been an administrator in the abbey before this?'

The steward of Ard Fhearta shook his head. 'My understanding was that he was newly arrived at the abbey.'

'But from where?'

'That, no one knows for certain. No one, of course, except the abbot himself. The end of the war here was a tough time for all of us. It changed the lives and attitudes of many. For example, Brother Lugna, the stable-master, was a more humorous man before the conflict. Now he seems just as pleasant but more reserved than before. He no longer tells jokes as he once did.'

'The abbot appointed his steward?' queried Fidelma. 'It is unusual, not only to appoint someone without the approval of the brethren of the abbey but to appoint someone who is not even from the abbey; someone whose background seems shrouded in mystery. Has anyone challenged Brother Cuineáin on his background?'

'Brother Cuineáin claims that he spent time on a mission to the Kingdom of Neustria in Gaul. Some years ago, a missionary named Fursa set up an abbey at a place called Latiniacum . . .' He halted, for Eadulf had made an involuntary movement. 'Does that mean anything to you, Brother Eadulf?'

'Nothing of significance in this matter,' replied Eadulf. 'But it was Fursa who came to my country, the Kingdom of the South Folk of the East Angles, and converted them to the Faith.'

'So Brother Cuineáin was in Neustria and then came back here?' Fidelma pressed. 'That must have caused some annoyance to those religieux who have spent years in this abbey.'

'It certainly did, according to the stories I have heard,' agreed Brother Cú-Mara. 'And I have also heard other stories about his origin.'

'Such as?'

'He came to Mungairit soon after the Battle of Cnoc Áine and the stories about being in Gaul are lies. They say that he commanded a company of warriors during that battle and that he was a favourite cousin of Prince Eoganán. The story is that he fled to this abbey after the defeat and was given shelter by Nannid, who is uncle to Prince Donennach.'

'I knew of Abbot Nannid's relationship to the Uí Fidgente princes.'

'I suppose it is logical that all the Uí Fidgente nobles are related,' muttered Eadulf. He was thinking back to the proposition he had put forward. If Ledbán had been killed to prevent him from being questioned further about the identity of Liamuin, then only three people knew – and one of them was Brother Cuineáin. At the moment, it seemed to him that Brother Cuineáin was the most likely candidate to be the murderer.

A prayer bell was chiming in the distance and Brother Cú-Mara stood up.

'I presume that you are taking the road south to Cashel?'

'No,' Fidelma said. 'We'll take the road west and join the river An Mháigh before turning south. We intend to visit Dún Eochair Mháigh before we return.'

'I heard about the attack on King Colgú,' the young steward said in a low voice. 'Do you really think there is another Uí Fidgente conspiracy against your brother?'

'We are here to find out.'

'I have heard no whispers in my travels across the territory. I know Prince Donennach has gone to pay tribute to the High King in Tara. Indeed, the wounds of the war are such that I do not think anyone would contemplate a renewal of it, especially in Mungairit.'

'Why do you say that – especially in Mungairit?' Eadulf picked up on the point.

'I was speaking to one of the scribes when I first arrived here. That was over a week or so ago. Maolán was his name. He told me that the abbot kept a small chamber containing a shrine to the memory of the Uí Fidgente defeat at Cnoc Áine. The room is filled with swords and shields, spears and battle helmets, even emblems of the warriors gathered from the battlefield. This was done so that the battle could be remembered.'

Fidelma was not impressed. 'A strange thing to do. What is it, a shrine to be worshipped?'

The young man shook his head. 'Shrine was not perhaps the best word, for I understand that the abbot has ordered the door to be kept locked; only he and the steward have the key to it. It was created, we are told, to remind the abbey of the evil consequences of war.'

'How does this Maolán know of this shrine if it is kept locked?'

'That I am not sure.'

'I would like a word with him.'

'He is no longer in the abbey. He left a day or so after I arrived. I think he said he was going east where his calligraphical talent was needed. I don't think he was expecting to return.'

'Well, let us hope that there is no conspiracy at all. Nevertheless, my brother lies close to death and the Chief Brehon of Muman is dead. Whether this is an isolated case of vengeance or part of something more widespread and serious, we must find an answer.'

'I trust you will.' Brother Cú-Mara's face suddenly brightened. 'But if you are leaving shortly and going towards An Mháigh, we will be taking the same road. Perhaps we can travel together as far as the ford, where I continue on towards Ard Fhearta?'

Fidelma agreed as she rose. 'It is always good to have companions on the road. And now Eadulf and I must make our farewells to Abbot Nannid. Gormán will go and ready our horses.'

Brother Cú-Mara also rose. 'Then I will accompany Gormán here to the stables for I have to collect my own beast.' He chuckled. 'Only an ass, I am afraid. Religious without rank do not have the privilege of riding on horses unless by special dispensation.'

Fidelma and Eadulf made their way to the abbot's chamber and found Abbot Nannid closeted with Brother Cuineáin. The abbot seemed nervous and preoccupied.

'We have come to say our farewells,' Fidelma announced.

Almost at once there was a change in the man's features.

'Are you leaving us already?' The regret in his voice was so obviously feigned that Eadulf felt embarrassed.

'I am afraid we must,' he said.

'So where do you go now?' asked Brother Cuineáin.

'Why, we shall head west with Brother Cú-Mara,' Fidelma replied, but she did not elaborate further.

Abbot Nannid seemed surprised. 'I thought you had not known that Brother Cú-Mara was visiting us until you arrived here?'

'Correct – but what a lucky chance that he was here. He probably told you that Eadulf and I spent some time at the Abbey of Ard Fhearta a few years ago.'

'He did. Indeed, a coincidence.'

'We offer you and the abbey our condolences over the demise of poor Brother Ledbán. He obviously led a long and active life so I suppose death came as no surprise.'

'Death is the one event that is inevitable in all our lives,' Abbot Nannid intoned. 'However, we are sorry to hear the news of the death of Chief Brehon Áedo as we are shocked at the attempt on the life of the King, your brother. They will both be remembered in our prayers, but especially, we will pray for the recovery of your brother.'

'Please accept our gratitude for your hospitality,' Fidelma said politely.

'May you find God on every road you travel,' replied the abbot.

Thus dismissed, they followed Brother Cuineáin out of the abbey buildings and into the courtyard. Gormán was already there with their horses and nearby, Brother Cú-Mara was standing with his patiently waiting ass.

The farewell from Brother Cuineáin was less effusive than from his abbot and, as they passed through the gates of the abbey and turned westward along the road, Eadulf was uncomfortably aware of the steward standing watching them intently until the trees and shrubs that grew alongside the road hid him from sight.

CHAPTER NINE

T he day was damp and chill, the clouds dark and lowering, as Fidelma
and her companions progressed westward through the flat, marsh-like
countryside. Now and then they passed isolated fortified homesteads but
there was little sign of human activity.

'What do you expect?' asked Brother Cú-Mara, when Eadulf commented
on the fact. 'This is the start of winter. The harvest has been gathered in
and stored, and there is little enough to do but bring the animals into the
barns, keep them foddered and stay warm until the light returns.'

The bleak landscape and the big grey skies reminded Eadulf of his
own country. In this area there was hardly anything that resembled a
real hill, let alone a mountain. It was very much like the fens of the
Kingdom of the East Angles, a series of fresh- and salt-water wetlands,
often flooded by the rise and fall of the sea-levels from the Sionnan
Estuary, a short distance to the north of them. It was an area criss-crossed
by streams and rivers and a few meres or shallow lakes with the
surrounding areas of peat.

It was Gormán who suddenly articulated Eadulf's thoughts. 'This is an
inhospitable country. The Uí Fidgente are welcome to it.'

Brother Cú-Mara sighed. 'Don't forget, warrior, that the Uí Fidgente
claim the same descent as the Eóghanacht. From the time of Fiachu

Fidgenid, three centuries ago, they have claimed to be descendants of Cormac Cass, the elder brother of Eógan Mór.'

'Our genealogists have disputed that claim,' intervened Fidelma firmly. 'That argument was laid to rest when they were defeated at Cnoc Áine by my brother.'

'The only thing Cnoc Áine laid to rest was Prince Eóganan's uprising against Cashel,' replied the young steward.

Fidelma was reminded that the steward was himself a member of the Uí Fidgente. 'Well, there is a peace between us now.' She did not want to get into an argument with Brother Cú-Mara as she respected the young steward.

He smiled. 'That is true, lady. And such arcane matters of who is right and who is wrong should be best left to the old, white-haired genealogists, rather than settled by the shedding of the blood of young men.'

They eventually came to a substantial river flowing from the south which turned sharply along their path to the west.

'Is this the Mháigh?' asked Eadulf, wondering why they were not following it to its source southwards.

'No, it is a river called Bearna Coill – the River from the Gap in the Woods – which is exactly where it emerges,' explained Brother Cú-Mara. 'It flows into the Mháigh further on – and that river is much broader than this one.'

He was right. Soon they heard the rushing sounds of the meeting of the two large rivers. One broke into the other, causing a clash of currents, white-crested and billowing, before the reinforced waters roared on hungrily to the north where they would join the even mightier Sionnan.

Brother Cú-Mara flung out his arm dramatically. 'There is An Mháigh, the River of the Plain.'

It was, indeed, as substantial a waterway as Eadulf had ever seen. On the banks were several buildings and one of them, judging by a couple of boats outside, bobbing up and down in the currents, was the home of a ferryman.

'That is where I cross the river to continue to Ard Fhearta,' confirmed Brother Cú-Mara. 'So this is where I must take my leave of you.'

They waited until the young steward had led his ass onto the sturdy ferryboat. The ferry was pulled across the river with a series of ropes by a team of two men and two asses on the far bank. With the turbulent current at that point, any boat propelled by oars would have simply been swept downriver. However, it did not take very long before Brother Cú-Mara was leading his ass onto the far bank. Once mounted, he turned and waved before disappearing westward along the track.

Fidelma and her companions turned back the way they had come, for they had passed a wooden bridge a short distance back which led across the waters of the Bearna Coill to bring them southwards, along the eastern bank of An Mháigh. They were conscious of the skies continuing to darken now, and far to the south came a faint rumble of thunder.

'A storm approaching,' muttered Gormán unnecessarily, looking at the clouds that were beginning to race across the skies in ever-tightening dark billows, as if pushing each other out of the way in some curious race to the north-east. 'I doubt if we'll make the Ford of the Oaks before it breaks. That's the next township along the river,' he added for Eadulf's benefit.

His doubts were quickly confirmed as large splatters of rain began to come down, increasing in size and rapidity.

Gormán, screwing his eyes against the sting of the almost horizontal rain, suddenly pointed.

'There is a cabin ahead. It looks like a farmstead. Let's seek shelter there.'

Heads down against the now wild, wailing wind, which seemed to be throwing the rain in torrents against them, the crack of thunder and sudden bright flashes of lightning spooking their horses, they pushed on towards the buildings.

'You seek shelter with friend Eadulf at the cabin, lady,' yelled Gormán.

'I'll take the horses to that stable over there.' He gestured to a dark outbuilding.

Fidelma and Eadulf slipped from their horses into the squelching mud while Gormán gathered the reins and fought his way through the sleeting rain towards the stable. Wiping the water from her face, Fidelma hammered on the door. She heard a muffled exclamation and then the door swung open.

A tall, well-built man stood framed against the light of a lantern. The darkness of the storm had made it necessary for, although it was only midday, the heavy clouds seemed to have plunged them into the night.

The man seemed to be a person of quick comprehension and decision. He simply stood back and motioned them inside, shutting the door behind them.

'Stay, Failinis!' he shouted.

They turned to see that a large hound had risen from its place by the hearth and was sniffing enquiringly towards them. It immediately returned to its place, yet its eyes remained on them, watchful and ready.

'Our companion has taken our horses to your stable for shelter,' gasped Fidelma, still wiping the wetness from her face. 'We hope that you have no objections.'

'I would not deprive anyone of shelter on such a day as this,' the man replied. 'There is plenty of room in the stable. Will he need help?'

'He will manage,' Fidelma assured him. 'And we thank you for your hospitality.'

The man seemed to examine them for a moment or two from eyes that sparkled like points of fire, reflecting the flicker of the lantern. He was of middle age with lean features and tanned skin. The remains of youth and handsome good looks were still etched in his features and yet there seemed a tension around his mouth which gave the impression of age and weariness. Although he was dressed as a farmer there was something about his carriage, the upright way he held himself, that did not quite match.

'My name is Temnén,' he announced, as if he realised that they were waiting for him to introduce himself first. He turned to Eadulf with raised brows.

'I am Eadulf of Seaxmund's Ham, in the Land of the South Folk.'

'A Saxon?'

'An Angle,' corrected Eadulf patiently.

The man's eyes suddenly narrowed as if trying to remember something. 'Brother Eadulf . . . ?'

He was interrupted by a knocking at the door. He turned and swung it open and Gormán staggered in, mud-stained and soaked.

'Thanks,' he muttered, thrusting the door shut behind him. He stood leaning against it, breathing heavily from his exertion running through the mud and storm to the cabin.

Temnén nodded briefly and went to a side table where there was a jug and clay beakers.

'A drink of *corma* to keep out the winter chill?' he asked, his gaze sweeping over them. They assented readily.

He began to pour. 'We were in the middle of introductions,' he said across his shoulder. 'If this is Brother Eadulf, then you, lady, are . . .'

'My name is Fidelma,' she replied. 'Our companion is Gormán.'

Temnén swung round rapidly, beakers in hand, examining each in turn before he handed Fidelma and Eadulf their drinks. He then poured one for Gormán and one for himself, raising his drink in a silent toast as they all took a swallow of the fiery liquid. He motioned for them to seat them-selves round a central hearth in which a smouldering peat fire was sending out its warmth.

'The heat will quickly dry your clothes, but I would suggest that you remove your cloaks to allow them to dry more quickly. You are all soaked through.'

They did so with gratitude.

'So,' resumed Fidelma, 'your name, you say, is Temnén? I take it you are a farmer?'

149

The man bowed his head in a solemn gesture. 'That is now my lot, lady. I farm this small piece of land with some cattle, some pigs, two horses and my hound as my companion.'

'You do not look like a farmer,' Eadulf commented.

'What is a farmer supposed to look like?' laughed their host good-naturedly.

Eadulf shrugged. 'I suppose I could only give the answer that I will know a farmer when I see him. You do not look like a man who has spent his life tilling the soil or herding cattle.'

Temnén regarded him for a moment and then said: 'So what are a Princess of Cashel and her husband doing in the land of the Uí Fidgente?'

Gormán frowned and glanced at Fidelma. Temnén noticed and addressed him.

'Have no fear, warrior – I presume that you are a warrior of Cashel – although it is a strange Cashel warrior who carries an empty sheath and lacks the insignia of the Golden Collar. Anyway, there can only be one Brother Eadulf in these parts and the stories of Sister Fidelma and Brother Eadulf are told and retold around many a hearth at night.'

Fidelma inclined her head. 'That is flattering to know. I must tell you, however, that I am no longer in the religious.'

'I have heard that you prefer your role in the Law to your role in the Faith,' replied the man. 'So, as I was saying, what brings you here? Apart from want of shelter from the storm, that is.'

'You seem very well informed for a farmer, Temnén,' Eadulf observed.

'I have made it a rule in life to be as well informed as I can be. Is it not an old saying that knowledge is power?'

'It depends on what power you seek, my friend,' replied Eadulf.

'The knowledge to provide for myself and protect my people.'

Fidelma peered quickly round the house and the man caught her doing so. He chuckled again.

'You look for signs of a wife and children, lady? Alas, you will not find them. My wife was killed several years ago, as was my son. He was but a baby and died from want of his mother's milk. They were bad days.'

There was no rancour in the man's voice. It was almost emotionless, as if the stated facts were somehow unconnected with him.

'Are you referring to the time of the Yellow Plague?' asked Fidelma.

'It was the time following our defeat at Cnoc Áine.' A bitter smile came to his lips. 'Ah, yes. Bad days, best forgotten by those who can forget.'

'A lot of people were killed in that useless conflict,' Fidelma pointed out sharply.

'Too many,' agreed Temnén, and now there was a trace of anger in his voice.

'So you were a warrior?' interposed Gormán.

'Not by choice.'

'But you fought at Cnoc Áine?'

'I remember wandering over that dark hillside among the dead and the dying,' the man confirmed. 'I was lucky. A blow to the head rendered me unconscious for a while, and when I came to, the battle was over. I can remember the human vultures crawling over the battlefield and taking things from the slain, even from those who were not yet dead. Swords, jewels, torcs, shields, anything they could lay their hands on, all taken away as if they were prizes of honour. And I admit, the scavenging was not all done by the victors. Sadly, I saw many of the Uí Fidgente taking what they could before fleeing from the field.'

'Many were slain on both sides at Cnoc Áine,' Fidelma said once again, but this time she spoke sadly.

'And many slain *after* the battle on Cnoc Áine,' grunted Temnén.

Fidelma was puzzled. 'After the battle? I am not sure what you mean.'

'Many, like my wife and child, were killed after we had disarmed and surrendered.'

'My brother would not countenance that,' Fidelma protested, shocked at the assertion.

'Who did your brother send to ensure our people were pacified?' the farmer asked, his voice sounding tired, as if teaching a well-known fact to someone who would not learn.

'It was Uisnech, Prince of the Eóganacht Áine,' supplied Gormán, adding sarcastically, 'and he was ambushed and killed by your so-called disarmed warriors.'

Temnén turned with a grim smile. 'And deservedly so. He made this land a desert with his raids and burnings until at last the people could stand it no more and he was caught on a lonely hillside and cut down.' He sighed deeply. 'His death did not bring back my wife and child.'

Fidelma was quiet. Somehow she knew that the man was not making up the story. She had met Uisnech only twice and knew instinctively that he was a man not to be trusted. 'I did not know of this,' she said after a while, 'and I am sure that my brother did not know either. He had given command to Uisnech of the Eóghanacht Áine after the battle. Uisnech was to deal with any who objected to the surrender. Later Donennach came to Cashel and agreed a treaty on behalf of the Uí Fidgente. We knew, of course, that Uisnech had been killed in an attack and that was just before the peace was agreed.'

Temnén nodded slowly. 'Bad days,' he said, as if agreeing with her. 'Yet they are hard to forget.' He drew back his shoulders with a cynical laugh. 'I will say one good thing of Uisnech, if it is true. That he caught and slew Lorcán the son of Prince Eoganán, who was both a vicious and cruel man, although he was a Prince of the Uí Fidgente.'

'I thought Torcán was Eoganán's son?' Eadulf asked, remembering back to when he had been held captive before the battle and had encountered Torcán.

'Eoganán had three sons. Torcán was the eldest,' Temnén explained. 'The other two were . . .' He used a word – *emonach* – that Eadulf had not come across before.

Fidelma quickly translated for him. 'Twins.'

'They were as alike in looks as if they were one,' agreed Temnén. 'But in character they could have been born of different parents. Lorcán was ruthless and without morals even to his own people. No one shed a tear when he was killed. At Cnoc Áine, Lorcán had a moment of glory when it was thought he had killed King Colgú. He went round waving the King's shield and claiming that he had killed him. That soon turned out to be a falsehood.'

'So Lorcán was killed?'

'But that was after Cnoc Áine. Uisnech caught and slew him but Uisnech slew a good many of our people.'

'Why did you fight at Cnoc Áine?' Eadulf asked softly.

'I was a *bó-aire*, a young noble, and when Eoganán's rider came with the fiery cross to summon all the clans to his side, I took my arms and my horse, bade my wife and child farewell and rode off. We were young and our love of country sped through our veins like intoxicating liquor. We became drunk on it.'

'And you did not question the morality of Eoganán's cause?' asked Eadulf.

Once more there was a smile on the face of the man, albeit a bitter one.

'How does a simple warrior assess morality? Morality is for kings and philosophers, not for warriors.' He turned to Gormán. 'Do you ever debate with your King or even your captain when you are given an order? When you are told to do something, do you sit down and ask whether the order is right and moral?'

Gormán pressed his lips together nervously and glanced at Fidelma as if seeking guidance. Temnén saw the look and slapped his thigh with a sudden, unexpected hoot of laughter.

'So, my friend, you prove my point. You are not even sure that my question should be answered without receiving an order from your superior. Of course, you don't question your order. You fulfil it and, sometimes, if you have a conscience, you struggle with justifying your actions to yourself in the long dark nights that lie ahead.'

There was a silence and then Fidelma asked softly: 'Is that what you have been doing, Temnén?'

He glanced at her, his face angry for a moment, and then his facial muscles seemed to relax again. 'You are a wise woman, Fidelma of Cashel,' he said.

'Tell me, Temnén, what was the name of your wife?'

'Órla,' he replied, his eyes misting for a moment. Then: 'You have not told me what brings you here,' he said brusquely.

'We are on our way to Dún Eochair Mháigh,' she replied.

'You will waste your time if you are going to see Prince Donennach. He is in Tara.'

'We know that,' Eadulf blurted out and then regretted it, for the man turned to him with an interested look.

'So you are not here to see our Prince. What is your purpose then?'

'You will hear soon enough, Temnén, and so it will do no harm to tell you now,' Fidelma replied. 'My brother lies near death if he has not already passed to the Otherworld. There was an attempt to assassinate him at Cashel. At the same time Áedo, the Chief Brehon of Muman, was struck down.'

Temnén's eyes widened. 'And you are looking for the assassin? How could he have escaped from the middle of your brother's fortress?'

'I did not say he had escaped. He was struck down himself.'

'Then why do you come here?'

'The name he gave was Brother Lennán of Mungairit.'

Temnén sat back in astonishment. 'Lennán the physician? But I was told he had died on the slopes of Cnoc Áine!'

'We found that out when we went to Mungairit and spoke to his father, an elderly man named Ledbán.'

'Old Ledbán? Does he still live? He used to run the stables of Codlata close by Dún Eochar Mháigh. Codlata was Prince Eoganán's steward. He disappeared after Cnoc Áine. But Ledbán retired to a monastery some years before that.' He paused. 'I still do not understand. If Lennán was killed at Cnoc Áine, how could he have been killed at Cashel? Ah.' A look of understanding settled on his features. 'You are here to find out who the man who called himself Lennán really was – and why he used that name.'

'So you knew Ledbán, you say? What did you know of him?'

Temnén rubbed his chin reflectively. 'Little enough, except that some years ago he was in service to Codlata, whose rath was at the Ford of Flagstones. Ledbán must be elderly now. Brother Lennán was his son. I simply knew him as a physician from Mungairit who came to tend the wounded during the battle. He was no warrior. He should not have been killed.'

'You know nothing else about Lennán or Ledbán?'

'If you spoke with Ledbán at Mungairit you must have learned all he could tell you.'

'Ledbán died the evening we arrived there,' replied Fidelma.

There was a moment of silence and then Temnén said reflectively: 'That was bad fortune.'

'Indeed it was,' returned Fidelma. 'Then there is little you can tell us about Lennán or his family?'

'Little enough, other than what I have already told you. But there may be some left at An tAth Leacach, the Ford of the Flagstones, who still remember old Ledbán. As I recall, the old man was well known for his work with horses.'

'When the storm clears, we shall continue on there.' Her sentence was punctuated by another clash of thunder.

Temnén glanced up to the ceiling, as if able to peer through it to the storm raging above.

'This will not pass for some time. I suggest that you join me in the *eter-shod*, the middle-meal?'

It was usual to have a light meal between the morning breaking of the fast and the evening meal. Temnén was no poor provider. He produced some cold joints of ham called *saille*, deriving from the word for salt and applied to any salted meat, for the joints were salted for preservation. These had been mixed with berries of rowan to enhance its flavour. There were also *indrechtan*, sausages made of a pig's intestine, stuffed with minced meat, *creamh* or garlic, *folt-chep* or leeks, and *inecon*, carrot that had been cooked, pickled and placed on the table. There was also a dish of barley cakes, the inevitable basket of apples and a jug of ale.

'You serve an excellent table, Temnén, especially for one who lives alone,' Fidelma observed.

The farmer shrugged. 'I make use of that which I am surrounded by.'

'You work this farm alone?'

'During the summer months I sometimes share the work and produce with my neighbours.'

'I did not see any fences marking the boundaries of your farm,' observed Eadulf.

'What need?' replied Temnén. 'So far as the land is free from forest and bog, it is clan land, and as I was a *bó-aire* there was little need for fences to mark out my portions of it.' He hesitated. 'But after Cnoc Áine some of us are beginning to mark our land even though it was once common property.'

'It is true that as tillage increases, the Council of the Brehons have introduced new regulations regarding the erection of fences between farmsteads,' Fidelma agreed. 'The laws now state how such fences are to be constructed, and if they are not constructed well then the owner is liable if animals are injured by them. For example, if a fence was so constructed that stakes were too sharply pointed and placed in a way to cause injury, that would bring the owner into difficulties.'

'Doubtless Cashel will send a Brehon to teach our backward lawyers the new laws,' Temnén said sarcastically.

'Only if they need instruction,' replied Fidelma without taking offence. She felt that she should make allowances for the bitterness of the *bó-aire*. 'But this law does not come from Cashel. You know that every three years the Brehons gather to discuss and update the laws, and these are promulgated in the name of the Chief Brehon of the Five Kingdoms.'

Temnén suddenly relaxed and smiled.

'There is much resentment in this land, lady. I suppose I am a symptom of it. It is hard not to feel aggrieved when you see your territory being changed by defeat and conquest.'

Fidelma saw that Gormán was having difficulty restraining himself and she gave the young warrior a warning glance.

'We won't argue the rights and wrongs. In Cashel we feel it was wrong for Prince Eoganán to lead his people into rebellion against us and thus, being defeated, the Uí Fidgente reaped what they had sown. Unfortunately, as we have already discussed, in warfare the innocent are swept away with the guilty. That is the sad lesson of life that we must all live with.'

As Temnén was carving the cold ham, his hound, which had been lying so quiet they had almost forgotten it, suddenly gave a little whine and thumped its tail on the floor. It still lay stretched in the corner, but its eyes were alert.

The farmer chuckled. 'At least I have one faithful companion.'

He sliced some more meat from the bone and then picked it up, showed it to the dog, which sat up expectantly and uttered a soft growl.

'Here, Failinis!' He tossed the bone towards the hound who caught it with a mighty snap of its jaws and then turned away to its corner to gnaw on it.

'Failinis,' remarked Fidelma. 'That was the magical hound of the God Lugh of the Long Hand.'

Temnén chuckled again, though this time, it was a sound without humour. 'I do not consider myself a deity or even a great warrior, as Lugh was said to be. I named him as tribute to the fact that Failinis was a steadfast companion and guardian to the gods.'

'You need a decent hound on a good quality farm such as this,' Eadulf observed.

'Good quality? This is only classed as a third quality farm, according to the law. It is well watered, because of the river, but much of it is only arable in the groves and between the copses where I can sow a little wheat, oats and barley.'

'But you have animals?'

'A few milch cows.'

'So who milks them?' Eadulf pressed.

'I do,' replied the former warrior. 'It is astonishing what one can adapt to when the need arises. At least the pigs are no trouble.'

'Ah yes, you said you kept pigs,'

'I do, which reminds me – soon I must go into the woods to round up my animals. During the clement months I turn them loose into the forest to feed on mast and whatever else they can pick up. They give no trouble and can be left out day and night, except during the shortages of winter-time. Then I have to bring them into the enclosure I have behind my cabin.'

'So you own the woodland?'

'The woodland was the common land of my sept so everyone uses it, although we did have trouble with the neighbouring lord – that was the late unlamented Lorcán, no less. As I have said, he was an arrogant man who declared the woodland to be his and wanted unfair tribute for its use from all his neighbours. We refused and were appealing to the Brehon of Prince Eoganán when the war against Cashel started. Such things were forgotten when the fiery cross summoned all the chiefs and their clansmen to battle.'

'So the question of the land rights was postponed,' Fidelma summed up.

Once again, Temnén laughed without humour. It was a curious sound which he often used to express himself. 'It was postponed permanently after Lorcán's death. Our new Prince Donennach assigned the land to Lorcán's more worthy brother, who donated its use to the Abbey of Mungairit. So we pay a small tribute to the religious and all are satisfied.'

'So that was a good outcome?'

'For the likes of us it was,' agreed the farmer.

'It seems good that the brother of this Lorcán is a pious man,' murmured Gormán. 'Who is he? Surely not Torcán, who was also killed at Cnoc Áine?'

Temnén looked surprised. 'But you have been to Mungairit and must therefore have met him.'

'Who are you speaking of?'

'The stable-master at the abbey – Brother Lugna, that is the man. As I have said, he and Lorcán might have looked alike, but they were very dissimilar in character.'

'As I recall, Brother Lugna did not bear a resemblance to the meaning of his name,' mused Fidelma. 'The Little Brightness – yet he was a big, burly fellow.'

'As was his brother,' confirmed the farmer. 'But I see you have knowledge of the meaning of names, lady?'

'I like to know the meaning of people's names,' she agreed. 'Names should always mean something.'

'Then you will know the meaning of mine.'

'The Dark One,' she replied. 'Perhaps appropriate, for our meeting was during a dark storm.'

'Maybe more suited to the sadness that is in me now.' Temnén rose, went to the door and looked up at the sky. 'But it is appropriate that at this moment the storm has passed and the day has brightened.' He went across the room and extinguished the lamp.

It was true. The storm clouds had disappeared. The lightning and thunder had raced off to the distant eastern mountains.

Fidelma rose and stretched herself. 'And that is a signal for us to move.'

'You will not reach Dún Eochair Mháigh before dark but you should find shelter at the Ford of the Oaks,' Temnén advised. 'There is an inn there kept by Sitae. A good innkeeper much inclined to gossip.'

Gormán left to get their horses from the stables while Fidelma said quietly to their host: 'We hope that it will be a true saying that time helps to heal, Temnén. Above all, I hope you will come to accept that there is a future and that one must continue to live the present with the hope of making that future better. The past cannot be unmade but the future should be built more firmly from the lessons of the past.'

'I have said before, lady, that you are a wise woman,' Temnén said after a moment or two. He turned to Eadulf: 'You are truly a man to be envied, Eadulf of Seaxmund's Ham.'

They left Temnén's farm and turned south along the main track again. The storm had completely disappeared and hardy winter birds seemed to be raising their beaks in a chorus of thanksgiving for its passing.

'A sad man,' commented Gormán after a while, breaking the silence that had fallen between the three of them. He was riding just behind the couple.

'Life is sad,' returned Eadulf over his shoulder. 'But we can only mourn for a brief while and then must move on in life. Our friend seems to be making a virtue of his sadness.'

'It's a harsh judgement, Eadulf,' commented Fidelma. 'He has lost his wife and child.'

'I do not mean to belittle his loss. But I would hope that he moves on as you suggested to him.' Then Eadulf returned to the matter that had been worrying him. 'Brother Lugna was brother to Lorcán and Torcán, which makes him . . .'

'The son of the late and unlamented Prince Eoganán as well,' replied Fidelma. 'Yet it seems he is unlike his father or brothers. I remember Abbot Nannid telling us that he left his family when he was seventeen to serve in the abbey stables. It shows how, even in the same family, there will be differences in character.'

'But someone smothered old Brother Ledbán,' Eadulf pointed out. 'I was thinking . . .'

'You were speculating,' she reproved him.

At that moment, they came to a pillar stone and halted. It was a tall stone with a circular hole in it.

'We are approaching a township,' explained Gormán, who looked uncomfortable and kept peering round nervously.

'Indeed,' agreed Fidelma. 'This is the *gallan* that proclaims a territorial border.'

'A *gallan*?' asked Eadulf. 'I have heard these markers called by several names, but that is new to me.'

'It is said that they are so named because it was a colony of Gauls who came to this land in ancient times and were the first to erect such stones to delineate their territories. Come on, we should be able to get to the Ford of the Oaks before the daylight goes.'

She was about to move off when Gormán stayed her with a piercing whisper.

'Lady, do not look round. I think we are being observed. Be very still, Eadulf.' The sharp command was added as Eadulf began to turn.

Fidelma bent forward to pat her horse's neck and said, in an even tone, 'Have you spotted who it is, Gormán?'

'I've had a feeling for some time that we were being followed. I wasn't sure, otherwise I would have said something sooner. The feeling began soon after we left Temnén's farmstead when the forest began to thicken to our left. Several times I thought that I saw movement among the trees.'

'Brigands again? Well, they have already taken most of our valuables,' Fidelma said tiredly.

'If they were brigands, they could have attacked us at any time before now,' muttered Gormán. 'I wish I had been able to find a replacement sword.'

'We had best ignore them and ride on. They surely won't attack so close to a township.'

She led the way past the pillar stone and they moved slowly at a walking pace along the track. The treeline had come down to the road now, obscuring their view to the left, and as the road swung to follow the line of the river on their right, they were suddenly halted by three riders facing them in the middle of the track, forcing them to draw rein. One of them held a fluttering red silk banner with the design of a ravening wolf. It was the *meirge* or battle standard of the Uí Fidgente.

'Let your sword remain in its sheath, warrior!' the leading rider said to Gormán, who had been automatically groping for his non-existent weapon. 'Do not be foolish enough to throw your life away. There is an arrow aimed at your heart.'

A bowman had stepped out from the cover of the trees. The strange warrior had not been bluffing, for the man had a bow full strung, with an arrow pointing directly at Gormán. Six more mounted warriors now rode up behind them and sat at ease on their horses, their weapons carelessly displayed in their hands.

Gormán stifled an exclamation of anger and despair and raised his hands.

'I carry no weapons. My scabbard is empty.'

The leading warrior who had issued the order looked sceptical but one of his men soon acknowledged that Gormán spoke the truth.

'Welcome to the Land of the Uí Fidgente, Fidelma of Cashel,' the leader then said. 'We have been waiting patiently for you.'

CHAPTER TEN

Fidelma stared long and hard at the warrior.

'I know you,' she said, trying to dredge his name from her memory. Her eyes widened. 'You are Socht.'

There was a brief moment before the taciturn warrior grinned.

'I am flattered that you remember me, lady. Much time has passed since we were together at Ard Fhearta.'

Now Eadulf was beginning to recall the features of the Uí Fidgente warrior.

'Remember you?' went on Fidelma. 'It looks as though you have recovered from that crack on the skull delivered by the pommel of Slébéne's short sword.'

'Indeed, lady, the sword of the chief of the Corco Duibhne caused me many a headache for days afterwards. But thanks to you, he and his allies received their due.'

'So are we well met again, Socht, or is it ill met?' Fidelma asked, nodding towards his armed companions.

'All in good time, lady,' replied the warrior. 'I am ordered to take you to the fortress of Ath Dara, the Ford of the Oaks.'

Without another word he turned and, motioning them to follow, set off at a trot. The other warriors closed around them and forced them to follow at the same pace, and then that pace gradually increased to a canter. It was a short ride before they swung around a bend following the riverbank and came across several habitations and a narrow crossing which nestled among the tall oaks from which it obviously took its name.

The settlement spanned both sides of the River Mháigh, which twisted and turned like some giant serpent. The main settlement was on the far bank; doubtless because its higher elevation would provide the inhabitants with protection against flooding. Here the group noticed a large stockade – a fortress of timber with a square watchtower. A horn was being sounded from within: there were several short blasts.

Fidelma's escort did not hesitate on the riverbank but plunged forward, obviously aware of the existence of a ford. As Fidelma followed, she noticed that the ford had been reinforced, probably over many years, by deposits of stones and pebbles, creating an underwater pathway a few metres wide. The height of the water therefore barely reached above the knee of the forelegs or the hock of the hind legs of their horses.

Socht wheeled his mounted warriors towards the wooden fortress, whose gates stood open, although with sentinels on the walls above watching their approach. He halted the band in a small courtyard and swung down, shouting orders to his men. Then he turned to Fidelma and her companions.

'My men will take your horses to the stables, lady, so if you will follow me . . . ?'

Fidelma was about to retort that they had been left with no other choice, but thought better of it.

Socht moved swiftly off towards the main building. A guard opened the door and he led them inside. They entered what seemed to be a chieftain's feasting room, albeit an old-fashioned one and poorly furnished at that. A central hearth provided a fire whose smoke went upwards through a point in a conical thatched roof, which was supported by great timber supports and beams. A few shields adorned the walls as decorations, and at one side stood an ornately carved chair behind which hung a banner similar to the one Socht's men carried – red silk which bore the image of a ravening wolf.

Rising from the chair was a tall, well-muscled young man with a shock of black hair. His eyes were grey and sparkling, and a white scar across his left cheek would have given him a sinister impression had it not been offset by his wide smile as he moved towards Fidelma with his hands outstretched in greeting.

Fidelma responded with an answering smile.

'Conrí – King of Wolves!' she declared. 'Of course – with Socht here, I should have known that you would not be far away.'

'Fidelma – Eadulf! It is good to see you both,' declared the war chieftain of the Uí Fidgente with unfeigned warmth. 'We have not met since we were at the Abbey of Ard Fhearta.'

'Indeed,' Fidelma smiled. 'And chance continues on our travels for we were at Mungairit and encountered Brother Cú-Mara, the young steward of Ard Fhearta.'

Conrí was surprised. 'The young steward of Ard Fhearta was at Mungairit?'

'He was just visiting, but it was fortuitous that he was there.'

Conrí glanced at Gormán who was standing awkwardly in the background.

'This is Gormán of the Nasc Niadh,' introduced Fidelma, interpreting the question in his expression. 'Conrí was elected war chieftain of the Uí Fidgente after Donennach became Prince,' she explained.

'Welcome, Gormán. Yet you do not wear the insignia of the Nasc Niadh, and Socht whispered in my ear that you had no weapon when he encountered you. Well, that is strange for a warrior of the Golden Collar – but you are welcome. Welcome all! Seat yourselves before my hearth and let me offer you hospitality.'

Without waiting for an answer, Conrí clapped his hands and an attendant appeared and began to pour drinks as they made themselves comfortable. Socht took up a position at the side of his chieftain's chair of office.

Fidelma did not feel like recounting how they were robbed, but Conrí was already moving on to other things as he sat relaxing with his drink.

'When did we first meet?' he mused.

'Three years ago, as I recall, when we were dealing with those terrible murders at Rath Raithlen,' Fidelma reminded him.

For a moment a shadow crossed Conrí's face. 'Indeed. When my brother, Dea, and his men were slaughtered. Had you not shown that the Cinél na Áeda were innocent of their deaths then another war might have erupted between our people.' He sighed, then waved his hand around the hall. 'Now you are welcome as a guest to my home. As I told you three years ago, we are a small impoverished people who now labour under the yoke of defeat. My fortress does not resemble the grand palace of Cashel but, such as it is, you are welcome to its hospitality.'

'We are on our way to Dún Eochair Mháigh, but our journey was delayed by the storm. Now it grows dark, so we will accept your hospitality with gratitude.'

'You have but to ask, and if it is in our power, then you shall have it. We hope we may provide entertainment even for a noble warrior of the Nasc Niadh,' smiled Conrí, glancing towards Gormán.

'There is little of nobility in my blood,' grunted Gormán, who was not convinced that any noble of the Uí Fidgente was worthy of courtesy.

'Then, my friend, the fact that you are of the Nasc Niadh must be proof of your nobility in other ways,' Conrí said smoothly.

Gormán's hand went automatically to his neck where the golden collar of the élite warriors of Cashel should have been adorning him. He frowned: was there some hidden meaning to the smile that the action drew from Conrí?

'The Ford of Oaks is a beautiful spot, Conrí,' Fidelma said hurriedly, sensing the tension from Gormán. 'And your house is elegant. Do not denigrate it. Better to wake with the aroma of wood around you than cold and soulless stone. Don't you agree, Eadulf?'

Eadulf had been lost in his own thoughts and now started at the prompt that Fidelma had given him.

'Eh? Oh – oh, yes.' He managed to find the memory of the last remarks. 'I was brought up in a wood-built house in a similar situation to this. It too was a small settlement by the side of a river. My father was the *gerefa* – a *bó-aire*, you call it here and—'

'So you see,' Fidelma cut into Eadulf's sudden burst of nostalgia, 'it is not everyone who has to endure being raised in a stone palace. It is better to be among the perfumes of wood and the scents of the countryside.'

'I would agree with you, lady,' Conrí said pleasantly, 'but I think Eadulf has something on his mind that is preoccupying him.'

Fidelma turned to Eadulf with a question on her features.

'It was something Socht said when he met us on the road,' Eadulf mused.

Conrí's smile broadened. 'Which was?' he invited.

'He said that he had been waiting patiently for us. I was not sure that I had heard him correctly. Sometimes, my use of your language lacks subtlety. But now I reflect on it . . . yes, that *is* what he said. If that was so, how did he know that we would be on that road?'

Fidelma realised that Eadulf was right and that she, of all people, had overlooked the meaning of that innuendo.

Conrí glanced up at Socht and it seemed they were exchanging a silent joke. Then he turned back to them.

'Well, to be honest, we did not know where you would turn up. I had sent riders south to Dún Eochair Mháigh as the most likely place that you would head for. I had entirely forgotten that the Abbey of Mungairit might be another natural place for you to make your goal.'

Fidelma was looking bewildered. 'But how did you even know that I was in the territory of the Uí Fidgente?' she asked.

'You must forgive me, lady – and forgive me, friend Eadulf. I was enjoying the superiority of confusing you. Indeed, Fidelma, I was hoping that you would solve the mystery so that you might add another story to your fame as one from whom it is impossible to hide a secret.'

Fidelma was growing irritable but tried to disguise it. 'In this case, I have little enough information to present a solution to your conundrum, Conrí.'

'Then I will show you.' The warlord clapped his hands for his attendants again. Fidelma and her companions rose and followed him to a table at one side of the hall. The top was covered with a large linen sheet and it was clear there were objects underneath. The attendants hurried forward and, at a nod from Conrí, they grasped the cloth, removing it from the table and revealing the items that had been concealed from them.

Everything was there; everything that had been stolen from them when they had camped at the Hill of Ulla. Had it really been only the day before yesterday? There were the golden torcs that signified Gormán and Fidelma to be members of the Nasc Niadh. There was Fidelma's wand of office, Eadulf's ornate crucifix and the various pieces of jewellery. What Eadulf was particularly relieved about was the sight of the silver seal that Brother Conchobhar had given him. And there was Gormán's prize sword. All that had been taken from them now lay before them on the table.

Gormán recovered from his astonishment first and swung round to Conrí. 'Were they your men?' he demanded, his eyes narrowed in fury. 'Were those brigands your warriors sent to rob us?'

Socht had now taken a step forward, hand on his sword, ready to check Gormán's threatening stance.

'Have a care, warrior of Cashel,' he said softly. 'Were you not travelling in the company of the lady Fidelma, you might have to answer for unjust accusations.'

Conrí raised a hand. 'Peace. Peace. I did not mean to provoke anger by playing my game of mysteries. No, Gormán, those brigands were *not* my warriors in disguise.'

'Then you'd best explain,' Fidelma suggested.

'Perhaps it would be easier to show you.' Conrí gestured for them to follow him and took them to a door which led to the back of the fortress. Socht trailed in the rear keeping a careful watch on Gormán. They passed through the kitchen area and went across a back yard to the perimeter of the fortress where it seemed Conrí's warriors had their sleeping quarters.

'Prepare yourself, lady,' he instructed, 'for we of the Uí Fidgente are not as merciful as you of Cashel. We believe that in extreme cases, extreme penalties may be applied. Mercy was the old law of the Brehons and now we have been advised otherwise.'

'I do not understand, Conrí,' Fidelma said, puzzled by the elaborate prelude the war chieftain was going through.

He did not reply but moved on through a copse to a clearing. A few men were gathered there, but it was not these upon whom Fidelma and her companions fixed their immediate attention. There was a tall oak to one side of the clearing and from one of the branches a body was hanging. The twisted head in the rope had a shock of sandy hair and a beard. Fidelma did not even have to look for the livid white scar made by a sword from forehead across the eye, nose and cheek to recognise who it was.

'We came across him and his gang of cut-throats in the forest,' Conrí said sombrely. 'When we counted their spoils, we recognised your wand of office and the emblems of the Nasc Niadh. Before he died, we persuaded this fellow to tell us what had happened to those he took these things from. He described you so that we knew it was you, lady. He swore that he had let you go unharmed.'

'You are not the first travellers that this man and his companions have robbed,' added Socht. 'We have been seeking him for some time. His crimes are many.'

'So that is how we came to be searching for you,' Conrí ended.

'And so this man was hanged,' Eadulf stated the obvious. 'What of his men? He had four companions when he robbed us.'

It was Socht who answered. 'They were given the opportunity to surrender or to die fighting. They chose to die. Their bodies were buried where they fell. This one,' he jerked his thumb towards the dead man, 'seeing his men fall, pleaded for mercy, and threw down his sword. So we brought him here. For such a man, justice was swift. Perhaps it was too swift.'

'He should have been heard before a Brehon,' Fidelma said sternly.

'He was,' Conrí replied, to her surprise.

Fidelma's eyes narrowed. 'The spirit of our law is compensation for the victims and rehabilitation for the wrongdoer. He could have been made a bondservant and worked for the rest of his life to compensate for his crimes. What Brehon would sanction death as a punishment except in very exceptional circumstances?'

As if in answer, Conrí turned to the group of men and waved one of them forward, a man in religious robes with his head almost covered by a cowl. Beneath the shadow of his cowl, he was revealed as a youthful man but one who had obviously not shaved for days. He carried himself with an air of self-importance as he approached.

'This is Brother Adamrae who served me temporarily as my Brehon,' said Conrí before introducing Fidelma.

'I am told that you sanctioned the hanging of this man.' Fidelma's tone was curt and she did not spend time on niceties.

The young man's eyes glinted in the shadow of his cowl. 'I did,' he replied and there was truculence in his tone.

'Under what law?'

Brother Adamrae's jaw came up aggressively. 'Under the just laws of the Penitentials, the Canon of the Church. Does not Canon Four state that a thief found in possession of stolen goods may be put to death?'

For a moment or two Fidelma stared at the man in surprise.

'You have allowed the taking of this man's life under these Penitentials which are contrary to our laws. Tell me, young Brehon,' there was a hint of sarcasm in her voice, 'where did you study and qualify in law?'

'I studied at the Abbey of the Blessed Machaoi on the island of Oen Druim,' he replied after a slight hesitation.

'In the country of the Dál nÁraide of Ulaidh? I have heard of it,' Fidelma said. 'But I do not hear the accents of the Kingdom of Ulaidh in your voice. Your voice has the accent of these parts.'

The young man shrugged. 'That is because I was sent to be fostered by Uí Fiachrach Aidne before I return to my own clan.'

'The Uí Fiachrach Aidne? Their territory touches on the northern border of this kingdom. I would have placed your accent further to the south. Anyway, it is a long way even for fosterage links.'

'It was my family's choice,' asserted the man in a stubborn tone. It was hard for Fidelma to decide whether he was a youth or just youthful-looking.

'And what is your degree?'

It seemed for a moment that Brother Adamrae was going to refuse to answer. Then he said: 'I am of the level of *freisneidhed*.'

'You have studied law for three years only?' Fidelma's eyes widened.

'It is enough when there are laws yet to be written to bring our barbaric society into keeping with the laws of the Church,' retorted the man.

'Ah, so you make up the law as you proceed?' Fidelma's tone was sarcastic. She turned to Conrí, who now seemed uncertain. 'I would advise you to have a care of who you appoint as your advisers as to law. After three years of study, this youth has a lot to learn about the laws of the Fénechus.'

'What right have you to say so?' protested Brother Adamrae in anger.

Gormán, who had so far been silent, moved threateningly forward. 'You are speaking to Fidelma of Cashel, sister to King Colgú, *dálaigh* of the courts of the Five Kingdoms, qualified to the level of *anruth*. That is her right to say so.'

Brother Adamrae's reaction was marked. Almost as if he had received a blow, he took a step backwards. His features tightened.

'An Eóghanacht?' he breathed in surprise.

'You have a problem with that?' snapped Gormán.

'I had not realised the lady's legal rank,' muttered the man. The qualification of *anruth* was only one below the highest degree that the secular or ecclesiastical colleges could award.

'What brings someone from Ulaidh to the land of the Uí Fidgente?' asked Fidelma.

'I came to turn people from the ways of heresy and to teach the law of the True Faith.'

'Did you now?' mused Fidelma. 'Would it not be best to return to the Abbey of Oen Druim and learn something of the laws of your own people before coming and misleading others with your own?'

Brother Adamrae flushed. 'I protest,' he replied. 'The laws of the Faith take precedence over barbarian laws. We should adhere to the words of the truth Faith coming from Rome and—'

'I think even a student in their first year would know the introduction to the first of our law texts, Brother Adamrae,' Fidelma said.

'I don't understand,' he replied hesitantly.

'I quote that introduction – "What did not clash with the word of God in written Law and in the New Testament, and with the consciences of the believers, was confirmed in the laws of the Brehons by Patrick and by the ecclesiastics and the princes of Éireann, and this is the *Senchus Mór*". Do you not know that Patrick, and his blessed companions, the bishops Benignus and Cairnech, agreed to confirm those laws on behalf of the new Faith?'

Brother Adamrae looked confused.

'I suggest you retire and think about it, Adamrae,' Fidelma advised. 'Perhaps your thoughts might take your footsteps back to where you may continue your studies. Even though you are scarce qualified to pronounce any judgement, you are qualified enough, I see, for your cheeks to become blotched – which, we are told, is the blemish of one who gives false judgement.'

The young man's hand automatically went up to his red cheeks.

'Go, Brother Adamrae,' ordered Fidelma, 'and remember that even a judgement given in ignorance can still evoke penalties.'

The young man turned and strode angrily away.

Conrí shrugged and glanced at the hanging body. 'Even so, Fidelma, death is often better than habitual crime.'

'Not in our law,' she replied stubbornly. 'Our lawgivers believe if you kill the evil-doer, you are as bad as they are. These Penitentials being adopted by the religious are foreign ideas that are simply laws of vengeance. They resolve nothing. Those who adopt them are the enthusiasts for these new teachings from Rome. Well, they have not yet replaced our own legal system. You would have been wise to wait until you found a qualified Brehon before listening to that arrogant youth.'

'Perhaps,' the Uí Fidgente war chief said thoughtfully. 'I fear though that you have made an enemy in Brother Adamrae. Young, arrogant men take the questioning of their abilities as a personal insult.'

Fidelma smiled thinly. 'If I were worried about who I upset by the advocating of the law and my decisions pertaining to it, I would not have become a *dálaigh*. How did that young man come here – and how is it that you have no proper qualified Brehon?'

'Prince Donennach left for Tara last week to see the new High King, Cenn Fáelad. In his retinue he took the Brehon who serves us locally. Therefore, for this time, we had no one to give the sanction of the law.'

'So how did Brother Adamrae come here?'

'About a week ago, he appeared in our settlement to join Brother Cronan at the little chapel. It seemed Brother Cronan was in poor health, for he fell ill with a fever soon after Brother Adamrae arrived. The young man therefore started to conduct the services. He preached in favour of these new ideas coming from Rome. He said that councils of the church leaders had been deciding that the religious should cease to wear the tonsure of John and adopt instead the universal tonsure of Peter; that they should follow the new rules as laid down from Rome, which was the heart and centre of the Faith. He spoke of many things that were new to us, Fidelma.'

'And did he do so with the approval of Brother Cronan?' queried Eadulf.

Conrí frowned. 'Brother Cronan has been confined in his chamber at the chapel by his illness, which is said to be contagious. So it was opportune that Brother Adamrae arrived and preached for him.'

Fidelma sighed deeply. 'It is true that there have been many great councils in recent years in which the advocates of the new rules adopted in Rome have been victorious in debates with the churches in the Five Kingdoms, those in the island of Britain and those in Gaul. I attended the one at Streonshalh, which persuaded the King of Northumbria to follow Rome, so that all our religious had to leave the kingdom. And more recently, there was the great council at Autun in Neustria that demanded that all the abbeys and monasteries should adopt the new rules. Alas, the young man is right in that respect.'

'But religion is one thing; law is another,' Eadulf pointed out.

'True,' said Conrí. 'He spoke of the fact that he had studied law at the Abbey of Maolchai and I needed someone to judge our prisoner. I did not enquire just how much law he had studied. Perhaps I should. Now what am I to do? Chase him from this township?'

'I would refer the matter to your own Brehon when he returns. If Adamrae simply preaches whatever interpretation of the Faith he wants to, then he may stay. But if he speaks against our law and tries to govern lives by rules that are foreign to us, then he cannot be allowed that liberty. Two centuries ago, when the Faith was officially accepted among the Five Kingdoms, when our laws were inscribed in the great law books, they were examined and approved of by the leading clerics of the country. They remain our laws.'

'Very well, lady. We will keep a watch on the young man to see that he does not overstep his authority.'

Fidelma glanced up at the hanging body. 'I would cut the man down now and accord him burial. He was a stupid fellow, but now he and his followers have no chance to reflect on their stupidity and make recompense to the people they have injured.' Then she turned with a quick smile to Socht. 'However, our thanks are due to you for retrieving our belongings. I trust none of your men were hurt in the conflict with the brigands?'

'A few bruises and minor cuts, lady, that is all,' replied Socht more cheerfully.

They made their way back to the hall and were grateful for the *corma* that Conrí's attendants provided. Albeit used to encountering unnatural deaths, Fidelma still felt a sense of outrage when people were killed wrongly in the name of the law. The death penalty was no deterrent, merely vengeance. The ancients were right to emphasise that punishment must be coupled with repayment to the victim. Death was too easy. No one benefited from it, not the dead or the living.

Gormán went to the table, collected the items and handed them back to each of their owners. It gave them all a sense of security that their emblems of office were now returned.

'So, what are you doing in the land of the Uí Fidgente?' asked Conrí when they were settled.

'You have not heard the news from Cashel?' asked Fidelma.

'We heard news of an attack on your brother in which the Chief Brehon Áedo was killed. But we were told that King Colgú had survived. News travels fast these days.'

By the time Fidelma explained the details, Conrí had assumed a worried look.

'Brother Lennán was a name well known among the Uí Fidgente,' he said. 'He was respected as a physician.'

'He came from the outskirts of Dún Eochair Mháigh,' Socht said. 'I remember him as a boy, before we went our separate ways to study.'

Conrí nodded thoughtfully. 'The story was that he had been killed in the battle and, being a physician, that created a scandal here. He was also a religieux at Cnoc Áine and was there to tend the injured. If someone was using his name, that must mean the person knew the story. Perhaps it was a vengeance killing?'

'That was what we came to find out,' Fidelma confirmed. 'We had a word with his father, Ledbán, at Mungairit, but it did not help.'

'Ledbán?' Socht was frowning at the memory. 'Yes – that was his father's name. I remember him. He ran a stable for one of the lesser nobles and his wife died of the Yellow Plague. So Ledbán went to join his son at Mungairit? He must be very old now.'

'He is dead,' Eadulf said dryly. 'He died the night we arrived at the abbey.'

'Well, I suppose he must have been an old man,' Socht mused. 'But it was surely a sad coincidence that he died just when you turned up there.'

'If coincidence it was,' Fidelma said. 'Anyway, he was strong enough to speak with us when we arrived. It was during that night that he died.' She did not wish to say any more about the circumstances until she was on sure ground. 'But tell me, Socht, you say that you knew him and his son, Lennán?'

'When I was young, the family were well known along the river hereabouts.'

'When did Ledbán's wife die?'

'That was some eight years ago. It was when the Yellow Plague devastated the country.'

Conrí shivered. 'The Yellow Plague! We had several deaths from that pestilence here. Thankfully it was not as bad here as it was in many places, but no one was exempt once it struck. Not kings and bishops, warriors or cowherds.'

'Ledbán . . .' muttered Socht. 'It comes back to me now. They were a sad family. He hated his daughter's husband and that is why he decided to go and end his days in Mungairit with his son.'

'A daughter?' Fidelma was suddenly interested. 'Ledbán had a daughter? What was her name and what happened?'

Socht thought for a moment. 'I think she married a river fisherman who sometimes ran a ferry and—'

'It was a man who kept a boat at Dún Eochair Mháigh,' interrupted Conrí. 'Something bad happened. Didn't his wife run away and later he was found dead in the river?'

Socht was suddenly excited. 'I think the man's name was Escmug.'

'What happened to him? You say he was found dead in the river?' Fidelma tried to hide her interest at the news.

'Maybe he drowned. But this was about the time of the Battle at Cnoc Áine. No one at that time was worried about the stray dead body. There were too many bodies and all had unnatural endings.'

'This daughter of Ledbán, do you recall her name?' asked Eadulf.

'It was not Liamuin, was it?' Fidelma was watching their reaction to the name, but it did not seem to mean anything to either of them.

'Perhaps someone at Dún Eochair Mháigh would know it,' offered Conrí.

Fidelma suddenly glanced at the windows and realised it was rapidly growing dark.

'I want to see Brother Cronan before the hour grows too late,' she told them. 'There are a few questions to which I would like the answers.'

'But the contagious disease . . .' protested Conrí. 'No one has seen him since he fell ill. That is how young Adamrae came to take over his role here.'

Fidelma smiled. 'Tell me, where does Brother Cronan live?'

'He had a small cell which adjoins the chapel,' replied Conrí. 'It is part of the building – a little annexe and you enter from inside the chapel itself. But you must be wary, Fidelma. If it is a contagious disease, you may be at risk.'

'You say that Brother Adamrae has been nursing him during the week? And Brother Adamrae moves freely among you? Then if there was some contagion it would be too late to prevent its spread among you now. If the good Brother Adamrae has survived these many days, I doubt whether it is a disease that we need fear too much.'

Conrí suddenly realised the logic of her statement. 'I had not thought of that, lady,' he said contritely.

'No harm.' Fidelma was cheerful. 'Doubtless we shall talk more of it and of Brother Adamrae. Is the chapel far?'

'Just a few moments' walk across the square from the fortress gates. You can't miss it – but you'd best take a lantern as it is growing dark,'

Conrí advised. 'I was going to suggest that my attendants prepare the evening bath for you before the meal. We may be poor here but we can set a good table for honoured guests. And I will get chambers made ready for you; you must be our guests for the next few days.'

'That is excellent and we are honoured by your offer. I shan't be long so you may give your instructions as soon as you like.'

'We'll come with you,' Eadulf said as he and Gormán rose.

'It does not require all of us to visit a sick man,' Fidelma replied firmly. 'I won't be long. You and Gormán may take your baths to save time.'

Although it was still early evening, it was already a dark and cloudy night, for winter had distorted the hours of daylight. However, the settlement at the Ford of the Oaks was still active and there were lights from the bullrings around the square. Fidelma had taken the lantern, although she did not really need it now that she crossed the square towards the wooden chapel which stood apart from the other buildings and was surrounded by its own green space. A flickering light was provided by a lantern hanging at the side of the door of the chapel, and using this, she was able to follow the path from the gate to the entrance of the building.

She pushed through the gate, and the noise of the hinge was suddenly answered by the alarmed call of a nightjar and the hoot of disapproval from an owl. She moved cautiously up the muddy path towards the door. There was no sound inside the chapel and she hoped that she was not going to disturb Brother Cronan; however, there were questions that she felt had to be answered now.

She paused outside the chapel door before pushing it open. It was dark inside and she was glad that she had brought the lantern with her. She moved forward a few paces and then called softly: 'Brother Cronan?'

There was no answer, but spotting a side door, she felt that this must be the entrance to the living quarters.

At least Brother Adamrae was nowhere about. She did not want to encounter him before she spoke to Brother Cronan. Had he been in the chapel, he would have surely answered her call. Holding the lantern before her, she began to make her way towards the door.

It was no more than a slight intake of breath that alerted her: that and the instinctive feeling of someone behind her. She began to turn but not before a piece of wood had struck her arm, knocking the lantern from her hand and plunging the interior of the chapel into darkness. Had she not moved, the wood would have descended on the back of her head. As it was, her arm was stinging from the blow. She was aware of a grunt of frustration and the dark shadow of an upraised arm again, upon which she fell into a defensive crouch.

Ever since she was a young girl Fidelma had practised the art called *troid-sciathaigid* – battle through defence. When the missionaries of the Five Kingdoms had set out for strange lands to preach the new Faith and bring their learning and literacy to pagans, they could not carry weapons to protect themselves in case of attack from thieves and robbers. It was an ancient philosophy that went back to the time before time, when the ancient men and women of wisdom travelled among people of darkness. So to protect themselves they turned back to an ancient form of defence without weapons, a way of protection without returning aggression.

Now, as the figure advanced with weapon upraised, Fidelma slipped under the upraised arm and reached towards it, to use the momentum of the attacker to drag the figure forward and deflect the aim. At the last minute, the attacker seemed to guess her intention and sprang to one side. It was a clever move and for a second the thought passed through her mind that her opponent knew the art of combat as well as she did. She had leaped forward as the figure had moved sideways and it was her attacker who recovered first. As she tried to regain her balance, the figure turned, the weapon still upraised. In a split second she had a realisation of what was going to happen. The wood struck the side of her head. Then there was blackness.

CHAPTER ELEVEN

Fidelma came to her senses to find a dark figure bending over her. The calming voice of Eadulf bade her remain still.

'It's all right. Your attacker has fled. It was a lucky thing I thought better of you coming here alone.' Eadulf raised a lantern so that she could see.

'Who was it?' she asked, clearing her dry throat.

'Adamrae, who else?' Eadulf replied, helping her up with his free hand.

'The young religieux?' She was astonished.

'I saw him lurking outside under the light above the chapel door. I wondered why he was being so furtive so I doused my lantern and crept up the path as he entered the chapel. Alas, I was not quick enough. I entered just as he struck the blow that knocked you out. I launched myself at him but I swear, he moved with the strength and agility of a warrior. He pushed me aside as if I were a small child. Then he was out of the chapel with the speed of a hare.'

Fidelma was rubbing her bruised head ruefully. It was sticky and she knew her assailant had drawn blood.

'How do you know he has fled?'

'There was a horse waiting by the fence. I followed him outside just in time to see it speeding away into the night.' Eadulf peered at Fidelma's injury in the lamplight and said, 'We'd best get that bathed and tended.'

She was about to agree when she suddenly remembered what had brought her to the chapel.

'All in good time. Let us find Brother Cronan, if he is still here.'

She made her way, a little unsteadily, towards the door which separated the living quarters of Brother Cronan from the chapel. Eadulf followed, holding the lantern high. She twisted the iron handle and pushed. The door would not budge. She tried again.

'It's locked,' she said unnecessarily. 'You will need to fetch Gormán to help you. This is a heavy door.'

'And leave you here alone?' Eadulf said, aghast. 'After what has happened?'

'Either that or I must fetch him myself.'

Eadulf dithered for a moment or two before handing the lantern to her and turning and trotting off.

When he returned, he brought not only Gormán but Conrí and Socht with him. Conrí's face was a mask of dismay.

'Did I not tell you that young, arrogant men do not take kindly to having their abilities questioned? However, I had no idea that the young man would go so far as to attack you.'

'He did not attack me for any insult that he felt I had given him,' Fidelma corrected. 'There is something much deeper to this matter.' She indicated the door. 'It is locked and needs to be opened. If you would oblige me by forcing it . . . ?'

Gormán immediately put his shoulder to the door. Socht, after receiving a nod of approval from Conrí, joined him. A moment later the lock was wrenched from its holding as the door caved in. Fidelma followed the men into the room, holding the lantern high.

A figure lay on a bed covered in a blanket. It was very still.

Eadulf ran forward and pulled back the cover. An elderly man lay beneath it, tied hand and foot. A piece of cloth was fastened across his mouth.

'Brother Cronan!' exclaimed Conrí.

The man was alive but tied in such a way, with hands behind him, the rope connecting his hands and feet, that he was bent almost backwards. Eadulf untied the gag then drew his knife and quickly severed the bonds. The man was very pale. He looked weak and anaemic. There was a jug of water nearby and Eadulf poured some of the contents into a beaker. Conrí was trying to question the bewildered figure on the bed.

'Let him recover first,' Fidelma instructed, holding the man's head to allow him to sip the water. 'Everything in good time.'

The man, identified as Brother Cronan, began to sit up, coughing a little and rubbing at his wrists where angry weal-marks showed how tightly he had been bound. He looked from one to another of his rescuers in bewilderment.

Fidelma sat down on the edge of the bed.

'I am a *dálaigh*, Brother Cronan. My name is Fidelma of Cashel. We need to ask you questions. Are you up to answering?'

'How long have I been here?' he countered.

'We have not seen you for five days,' Conrí said. 'Brother Adamrae said you were taken sick and confined to your room.'

Brother Cronan's lips compressed for a moment. 'Brother Adamrae!' he echoed bitterly. Then: 'Five days? Yes, he came and fed me five times and I was allowed to perform . . . certain natural functions. Other than that he kept me tied up as you have seen. I am weak from hunger and need a bath. Forgive me, for I must insult your sense of smell, lady.'

Fidelma smiled encouragingly. 'Do not worry. These matters will be attended to shortly. But first you must tell us how you came to be in this predicament.'

'The young man, Adamrae . . . where is he?' He looked about nervously.

'He is fled,' Eadulf said.

'I will send some warriors in pursuit of him,' Conrí said quickly.

The religieux sighed and relaxed a little. 'It was roughly five days ago that he came here and told me that he had been sent by the Abbot of Mungairit to help me administer to the people of the Ford of Oaks.'

'Abbot Nannid?' pressed Fidelma.

Brother Cronan nodded. 'Yes. He said that he had come from the abbey. So I invited him in and he started asking questions about the lord Conrí and how many warriors he commanded here. I thought that strange. But then he said something that made me suspicious of him.'

'Which was?'

'He claimed to have studied at the Abbey of Machaoi. Yet he had no accent of the northern kingdoms in his voice.'

'I noticed that also,' Fidelma said. 'When I remarked on it, he told me that he was fostered among the people close to these borders.'

'Well, I once made a journey to I-Shona, where Colmcille built his abbey,' Brother Cronan said. 'On that journey I stayed in the Abbey of Machaoi before journeying across the narrow sea to I-Shona, so I knew something about it. It was clear that he did not even know that the abbey was on an island.'

'He certainly knew it was on an island when we spoke with him,' Fidelma pointed out.

'Because I was foolish enough to show my astonishment at his ignorance and told him. Stupidly, I revealed that I had become suspicious. I turned my back on him and the next thing I knew, I was trussed up as you discovered me, lying on the bed.'

'He came to see me soon after,' admitted Conrí, 'and said he had come to help you but found you ill and so you had to be confined to your chamber.'

'Did he give you any idea of who he was and why he was here?' Fidelma asked Brother Cronan.

'He left me more or less alone, except that at some time he would loosen the bonds to feed me. Usually, it was just a bowl of oats and water and he would allow me to use the bucket for decency's sake. But then he would stand in the room with a drawn sword so that I would not get any ideas. Most of the time I was bound and gagged to prevent my calling for help.'

'And no one thought to come and check on you?' Fidelma was frowning. 'Was there no physician or apothecary here? Surely someone would have come to discover what this illness was that confined you here?'

It was Conrí who replied, with a shamed face. 'I think Adamrae, whoever he was, has murdered our apothecary.'

'You have made no mention of this before!' Fidelma turned sharply.

'It is only now, listening to Brother Cronan, that this conclusion has come into my mind.'

'You had better explain,' Fidelma sighed.

Conrí looked even more contrite. 'When Adamrae introduced himself to me and pretended that he had found Brother Cronan ill, he told me that he had sent for our apothecary, Lachtine.'

'So what did this apothecary say?' asked Fidelma.

'I have not seen him since. That is why I think he is dead.'

'Did Adamrae comment on the disappearance of the apothecary?'

'On the next day, when I saw Adamrae, I asked him how Brother Cronan fared and what Lachtine had diagnosed. He said that Lachtine had prescribed some herbs and a potion, and had recommended that Brother Cronan should be kept isolated for seven days. In the meantime, he would go into the forests in search of some herbal remedies that would further alleviate the symptoms. That was why we have not been worried by Lachtine's absence. He often spends whole days at a time in the forests searching for plants and herbs with which to prepare his concoctions. But now, hearing what has happened, I do fear . . . truly I do now fear for the man's life.'

'Well, Lachtine never visited me, that is for sure,' muttered Brother Cronan.

'Why would Adamrae kill this apothecary?' asked Eadulf. 'And why keep Brother Cronan a prisoner?'

'If we had an answer to that, then we would know what his purpose was in coming here,' grunted Socht irritably.

'Well, we know it wasn't to preach the Faith,' Eadulf replied dryly.

'I am worried that he asked Brother Cronan here about the strength of my warriors,' Conrí said. 'Perhaps he is one of the brigands that have become active in recent times. The Ford of the Oaks is a strategic place right enough, but only for merchants. It is a good meeting place for them, being situated on the road from east to west, and a good navigable spot for small boats heading north along the River Mháigh to the great estuary of the Sionnan.'

'But if Adamrae is a brigand, why put himself forward as a judge to condemn that other thief to death?' Gormán said.

'I suppose he could have been part of another band of thieves and took the opportunity to get rid of a rival?' suggested Eadulf.

'Adamrae was interested in the local inn that serves merchants,' Socht said. 'He would go there several times a day.'

Conrí was not convinced. 'An attack on merchants here or an attack on my fortress would be futile unless he had a substantial gang. I have fifty men at my command here.'

'Whatever Adamrae wanted, or was going to do, he has either achieved it or would have achieved it soon,' Fidelma said thoughtfully.

'How do you come to that conclusion?' asked Eadulf.

'He told Conrí that Lachtine said no one should go near Brother Cronan for seven days. Why mention a specific time unless it had meaning? I would think it would have occurred to someone that Lachtine should have returned from wandering the forest in search of herbs by then. So a search would have been started about now.'

Conrí was still clearly embarrassed. 'That is true, lady. In fact, the matter did not even occur to me, but the time will soon be up. We are so used to Lachtine's wanderings in the forest but I suppose we would have started asking questions within the next few days.'

'I suggest that as soon as it is daylight, some search is made for this apothecary,' Fidelma said, 'although I suspect that you will be searching for a body rather than a living person.' She turned back to Brother Cronan, who seemed to be regaining his strength. 'You can recollect nothing else that Adamrae said that would give a clue as to why he came here?'

Brother Cronan shook his head. 'I was aware that during one or two nights, some people came to see him. I heard voices beyond the closed door of this chamber.'

'These people came to the chapel then?' asked Eadulf.

Fidelma turned to Conrí and Socht. 'Was anyone seen coming to the chapel at any time when Adamrae was here?'

'There were people who came for the services, of course,' pointed out Socht, 'but they were turned away by Adamrae, who used the excuse of Brother Cronan's illness. There are no reports of anyone visiting the chapel at night.'

Fidelma stood up. 'I think we should leave Brother Cronan to recover from his experience. Is there anyone we can send to tend to you after your rough handling?'

'You might send old Mother Muirenn to me,' the religieux said. 'She helps clean and wash this place from time to time.'

'I'll do so immediately, Brother,' Socht offered. 'I'll assure her that the tales of illness and contagion are false.'

They bade farewell to the exhausted but relieved religieux and walked back across the square in the semi-gloom of the lanterns. Attendants came forward to offer refreshment and remind them that it was time for the evening baths before the *praintech*, the evening meal.

They did not speak much until they were seated at the refectory table. It was Eadulf who then returned to the topic that had been occupying his thoughts.

'I find it curious that no one saw who went to the chapel to see this man Adamrae nor, indeed, does anyone in this settlement own to visiting him.'

'Rather Adamrae came to us, than we go to him,' Conrí pointed out. 'I think most people were afraid of picking up Brother Cronan's contagion, which we now know was non-existent.'

'And forgot that if there was a contagion, Adamrae would be carrying it to them,' muttered Fidelma.

'Tell me,' Eadulf asked reflectively, 'did Adamrae always wear that cowl of his drawn over his head?'

'Always. He said it was the custom of his Order to . . .' The war chieftain closed his eyes in a grimace. 'It could have been an aid to disguise.'

'Why would he be interested in how many warriors you have here?' Eadulf asked. 'Why kill the apothecary; why keep Brother Cronan a prisoner; why ask questions about the strength of your fortress and, indeed, why did he frequently visit the local tavern?'

Conrí was perplexed. 'I have not heard of any group of brigands strong enough to attack my fortress, and my warriors guard the merchants crossing through this territory.'

'I presume that the only other major fortress near here is Dún Eochair Mháigh?' Eadulf asked. 'Is there a large force guarding it?'

'Less than a score of men, I believe. There is little need of warriors to guard it when . . .' Conrí paused.

'. . . when Prince Donennach is in Tara with his personal entourage to have discussions with the High King,' Fidelma ended softly.

Eadulf considered the matter. 'When Prince Donennach succeeded after Eoganán was killed at Cnoc Áine, after Donennach made the initial peace treaty with Cashel, was everyone happy with that choice?' he asked.

Conrí gave a slight shrug. 'Of course not. Many thought the Uí Fidgente should have fought on to avenge the dishonour of their defeat.'

'But you were not one of them?'

Conrí flushed. 'I was not. After the defeat we had been occupied by the warriors of Cashel for months. We suffered much for the mistakes of Prince Eoganán. True, that created resentment among many. But others, like myself, believed it was wrong to try to take by force what was clearly a matter to be resolved among the Brehons of all the Five Kingdoms. The Brehons found the claim of Eoganán invalid. I stood by their decision.'

'Then let me put out this thought to you,' Fidelma said. 'We know that Prince Donennach has left the territory to visit Tara and pay his respects to the High King. Would he have taken most of his loyal advisers with him?'

'I remain to guard the peace of the territory,' Conrí replied defensively.

'What of his *tanaiste*, his heir apparent?'

'Ercc? He is a loyal man and accompanies Donennach to Tara.'

'Isn't it curious that both the Prince and his heir apparent have left the territory?' Fidelma observed pointedly.

'It was on the advice of Donennach's Brehon – Brehon Uallach.'

Fidelma was thoughtful. 'I can't recall him.'

'He has not been at Donennach's court for long. Uallach succeeded as the Prince's Brehon, when his former adviser, the one who helped Donennach negotiate the peace with Cashel, died in a hunting accident.'

'What reason did Uallach give for both Prince and heir apparent to leave their territory to go to the High King?'

'After the visit to the High King, the party were to call on your brother in Cashel to negotiate the new treaty. To do so, both Donennach and Ercc had to be present and in accord.'

'And Brehon Uallach also accompanies them?'

'Of course.'

'Yet it is a weak legal reason, for a Prince can agree a treaty without the presence of his heir apparent. Is Uallach trustworthy?'

'His advice was accepted as sound and lawful. Are you making some accusation against Uallach?'

'When did Donennach leave for Tara?'

'The party left about a week ago.'

Fidelma inclined her head pensively. 'So you are the only person who would protect the territory, should there be any manifestation of dissension?'

Conrí's eyes narrowed angrily. 'I hope you are not impugning my loyalty . . . ?'

'What I am saying is that this is an ideal time for anyone who wishes to overthrow Donennach, while he and his advisers are out of the kingdom! Perhaps this might be a reason for Adamrae's strange behaviour here.'

'A plot to overthrow Donennach? But why here? The conspirators would surely try to seize control of his fortress at Dún Eochair Mháigh,' Socht argued.

Conrí was thinking rapidly. 'If there is danger in this land, we had best be near the centre of it. We should ride to Dún Eochair Mháigh.'

Grey fingers of light were appearing over the eastern treetops when Eadulf and Fidelma made their way down to the main hall after a fitful night's sleep. Conrí and Socht were already at the table which had been laid for the first meal of the day. However, they saw that Conrí had been talking to two warriors who were just leaving the hall when they came in.

'It seems that an early morning search has found Lachtine, our apothecary,' Conrí greeted them sombrely. 'You were right, lady.'

'Dead, I presume?' she said quietly.

'Dead,' confirmed Conrí, gesturing for them to be seated.

'Where was he found?'

'Not far away. He was almost buried in a manure stack at the back of the chapel. It just so happened that one of the searchers we sent out this morning was passing into the forest that way and saw a hand sticking out of the stack. The apothecary had been stabbed twice in the chest.'

Fidelma grimaced sadly. 'I did not expect miracles,' she sighed. 'This Adamrae seems a ruthless man in pursuit of his purpose.'

'And you think his purpose is to overthrow Donennach?'

'It would be the logical conclusion – except for one point.'

They all turned and looked at her in surprise.

'But you said last night . . .' began Conrí.

'Oh, I made a speculation last night. I still think that speculation has to be followed. But if Adamrae's purpose was to claim to be Prince of the Uí Fidgente, then he would surely be known to people here. To you, for example. He would have to be kin to Prince Donennach and his family, even as Donennach was cousin to Eoganán. He would be recognised even with the disguise he assumed.'

Conrí saw the point immediately. Succession of a noble to office had to be approved by a gathering of the *derbhfine* of a family, usually no more than three generations of the family of the last approved chieftain, petty king, or even High King. Therefore, one claiming the office had not only to be of the bloodline but approved by the electoral college called the *derbhfine*. In ideal circumstances this ensured that the most worthy member of the family held the office and that no one usurped it; thus inheritance by the eldest son or daughter was almost excluded.

'You mean,' Conrí said after a while, 'we should consider which members of Donennach's family are conspiring against him?'

'It would be one way of approaching things,' agreed Fidelma.

'Well, then there are several people to consider. I know a farmer who is a cousin and even the master of the stables at Mungairit is a cousin to Prince Donennach,' observed Socht cynically.

Conrí suddenly chuckled. 'Not a likely choice of succession. Twenty years or more working in the stables of an abbey suddenly to be elevated to Prince of the Uí Fidgente is too far-fetched. I, too, must be a prime suspect. I am also a cousin, albeit distant. How else could I have become warlord of the Uí Fidgente?'

'I had forgotten the obvious, Conrí,' Fidelma sighed.

'That is unlike you, lady,' replied Conrí, amused. 'But I am afraid you would have too many suspects to contend with if you are looking just for relatives of Eoganán. Even old Abbot Nannid is uncle to Donennach. The descendants of the Uí Fidgente Princes are many, lady.'

'However, you have made me recall another obvious thing that you said yesterday.'

'Which was?'

'You pointed out that the Ford of Oaks is a crossing which many merchants often use.'

'That is so. Further along the track to the west is a large inn that caters for the merchants; they can rest there and keep their wagons and animals safe. You are returning to the idea that Adamrae was a brigand, planning a raid on the merchants who pass through here?'

'I had almost forgotten the visits he made to the inn.' Fidelma turned to Socht. 'You did say that Adamrae visited it several times?'

'I did. The inn is run by Sitae.'

'Then let us go and speak with the inn-keeper.'

'I'll take you there,' Conrí offered. 'It is just a short walk.'

The square was now bustling with people, some of whom saluted Conrí in elaborate fashion while others passed with a nod or courteous greeting.

Conrí was correct in that the inn of Sitae was just a short walk along the roadway to the edge of the settlement. It was a fairly large construction with a paddock in which several horses were enclosed – strong muscular beasts better suited to pulling wagons rather than carrying warriors or nobles. There was also an area in which a number of wagons were parked, many of them with a canvas cloth, called a *bréit*, covering them to protect whatever goods they held. Outside the building was a pole on which an unlit lantern hung. It was the duty of the inn-keeper to light this when darkness fell so that travellers could recognise the place as an inn.

Conrí led the way to the main doors, but before they reached them, the doors were flung open and a short, portly man with unkempt white hair and flushed features seemed to bounce out to greet them. He was light on his feet and his movements were almost comically dramatic. To imagine him in any other role than mine host would be hard.

'This is Sitae the inn-keeper,' Conrí announced as the man approached them.

'My lord, welcome; my lady, welcome, welcome.' He almost made obeisance to Fidelma, bobbing up and down as he spoke. Obviously the news of her arrival in the settlement had spread. 'But why are you on foot? The road is muddy after the rains yesterday and you will ruin your pretty shoes. Come in, come into the dry, I entreat you.'

Like a mother hen, the inn-keeper seemed to cluck as he marshalled them to enter his establishment and bade them be seated before a fire. Fidelma felt an overpowering impulse to tell him to stay still, for the man, in addition to moving his head up and down, had a disconcerting habit of stepping from side to side with tiny little movements as if performing some curious dance.

'I have heard about the finding of Lachtine our apothecary, and the flight of Brother Adamrae,' the inn-keeper began, glancing nervously towards Fidelma and her companions as they settled themselves.

'I am told that during the past few days, Brother Adamrae frequented this inn,' Fidelma said, once they had settled themselves. 'Why was that?'

The inn-keeper spread his hands apologetically. 'To explain, I must first tell a long and curious story.'

'Then the sooner you proceed, the sooner we will hear the story,' replied Conrí with an air of resignation.

'It was a peculiar story that Lachtine told me some time ago.'

'Go on,' Fidelma prompted impatiently.

'Well,' the inn-keeper grew confidential. 'It was a month or so ago when Lachtine came in, all breathless-like, and told me that he had seen something very singular in the forest. He was there gathering herbs, which he often did, when he witnessed a meeting in a glade. He saw two men – one was in religious robes. However, they both rode good horses, which is not usual among the religious. One was a thickset man, that was the religieux, and the other was a younger man. Lachtine said he thought the thickset man had a humped back, but it turned out he was carrying a sack on his back under his cloak. It was obviously heavy, as when he handed the sack to the younger man, he dropped it. It fell to the ground and the sack split open – whereupon the elder shouted at him to be careful; that it was a sacred object. Well, it did not look like any religious object known to Lachtine, although it was made of some sort of metal. He said it was more like an image of some animal, so far as he could see.'

'And what was Lachtine doing all the time this exchange was taking place?' asked Conrí. 'Why was he not spotted by these two men?'

'He had been crouching behind a bush gathering some herbs and remained so because of the curious way the men were behaving.'

'What was this animal that they dropped?'

'He could not see too well from where he was concealed. It might have been a dog. The elder man dismounted and examined it. Satisfied that it had sustained no damage, he handed it to the younger man. Then he said something to the effect that he had to go, but that he would leave it to the younger one to hand it to the merchant. No names were mentioned and the reference was just to "the merchant". The younger man said that the merchant was due to be at the very spot shortly so the elderly man mounted and rode off.

'Lachtine decided to remain hidden and time passed while the young man sat in the glade, apparently growing impatient. But, sure enough, eventually, a heavy wagon rolled along the forest track. The young man handed the bundle to the driver of the wagon and said, in curt fashion, "Remember, the best work must be done on it" and then the wagon rolled on. The younger man then rode off. Realising that he had spent too much time in the glade, Lachtine rose to come back to the Ford of the Oaks. He was trotting along the track towards the settlement when he encountered a group of local farmers and stayed to talk. It was just then that a horseman came trotting by. It was the young man he had seen in the glade. He did not pause but Lachtine felt that he had stared especially at him as he rode by.'

'This story is a curious one and makes no sense,' muttered Conrí. 'What is its relevance to Adamrae?'

'I will explain,' the inn-keeper said hastily. 'Lachtine recognised the man with the wagon as a merchant who frequently passes by here.'

'And you are going to tell us who that was?' Fidelma asked patiently.

'Of course. It was Ordan of Rathordan.'

There was a silence in which Fidelma could not help exchanging a quick glance with Eadulf.

'I presume that you know Ordan?' Sitae went on, noticing the look.

'Rathordan is next to Cashel,' Gormán answered for her. 'So yes, we know him.'

'And how does this answer my question of why did Brother Adamrae visit this inn so frequently?' asked Fidelma.

Sitae smiled as if he was about to produce some wonderful object to tempt them.

'Adamrae first came to my inn five days ago and asked after Ordan. He paid me to keep the matter between us but said that he had business with Ordan and must be told the moment he came here.'

'Why have you decided to tell us now?' asked Conrí. 'Adamrae has been here five days.'

'Because of the news of Lachtine's death.'

'Please explain.'

'Brother Adamrae was the young man whom Lachtine saw in the forest.'

'Did Lachtine tell you this?'

'It is my own conclusion. It was on that first day that Brother Adamrae arrived here and came into the inn to ask about Ordan. While he was here,

Lachtine came in. They did not speak, but I had the strange feeling the two men recognised one another.'

Eadulf saw a sudden look of excitement come into Fidelma's eyes.

'Can you be certain?' she demanded.

'As I say, they did not acknowledge one another. Lachtine hurried off while Brother Adamrae asked his question about Ordan. Then, as he was leaving, Adamrae asked me who Lachtine was. I told him. Then he left the inn.'

'You had not seen Brother Adamrae before that?'

'I had not. Anyway, I was suspicious of him as it is not often a religieux rides up on a horse more suited for a warrior. Later that day I heard he was supposed to have come from Mungairit to help Brother Cronan administer to our settlement.'

'Yet you did not alert anyone?'

'Who – and about what?' replied Sitae. 'I heard that Lachtine had gone off into the woods, which was a normal occurrence, and that the new religieux was helping Brother Cronan.'

'Let's return to Ordan of Rathordan,' Fidelma said. 'You say the merchant came here regularly?'

'He has passed through here several times during the past year. Sometimes he has arrived from the south and heads north, and sometimes he goes in the opposite direction. But he always stays at my inn.'

'It is interesting that he never travels from east to west or vice versa. That would be a more usual route for a merchant from Cashel.'

The inn-keeper gave a shrug.

'Did Brother Adamrae ever say why he was enquiring about Ordan?'

The inn-keeper shook his head. 'No.'

'Do you know who Ordan trades with?'

'I presume he trades with the Abbey at Mungairit, of course. Then, as he spent time in the country of the Luachra, he must have business with them. In truth, lady, Ordan is a man who speaks a lot but says little about his business.'

'Have you ever been curious about what he trades in?'

'I would not press someone who does not want to tell me,' the inn-keeper replied with some dignity.

'Not even one peek under the canvas awnings on his wagon?' It was Eadulf who intervened, having assessed the inn-keeper's curiosity correctly.

The man grimaced, then as Eadulf continued to stare at him, he admitted, 'Well, there was one time when I happened to be checking that the wagons were parked safely. There was a high wind and some of the coverings were coming loose, and not wishing my guests' goods to be ruined, I went to secure them. I could not help but see what was in the wagons.'

'And what was in his wagon?' asked Fidelma.

'Ingots. Metal ingots of the types smiths use in their forges. There was also scrap metal. Broken weapons, that sort of thing.'

'Broken weapons? An odd thing to trade in.'

'I could not tell exactly what they were. It was only a passing glance as I tied down the covering.'

Eadulf smiled cynically. 'A passing glance?'

'Truly, Brother. That was all I saw,' the inn-keeper replied defensively.

'Broken weapons? Bars of metal?' mused Fidelma thoughtfully. Then she rose to her feet, forcing the others to rise too. 'Very well, Sitae. We thank you for your information.'

They left the man at the door of his inn, still bobbing and clucking after them. Fidelma had become quiet. Eadulf knew enough of her moods not to press for information until she was ready. Nor did Conrí break the silence, for his mind was still considering the possibility of some impending conspiracy against Prince Donennach.

They were nearing the gates of the fortress when a mounted warrior rode across the square towards them.

'This is one of the men I sent after Adamrae last night,' Socht explained, turning to greet the man.

The warrior halted before them and swung down from his horse, raising his hand in acknowledgement of the warlord.

'What news?' demanded Conrí. 'Have you found him?'

'He has vanished, Lord,' the man said with a shake of his head. 'No trace of him to the north . . .'

'I was wondering if he might have been heading for Mungairit,' muttered Fidelma to Eadulf.

The warrior overheard her remark and said, 'If so, lady, then he has chosen a circuitous route to do so. One of my men found signs of him passing to the south.'

'To the south?' Conrí was puzzled.

'Yes. South on the road towards Dún Eochair Mháigh.'

chapter twelve

ೞ

For the principal fortress of the Princes of the Uí Fidgente, Fidelma saw that Dún Eochair Mháigh was surprisingly small. The arrogant Uí Fidgente rulers had called it *Brú Rí* – the King's abode – claiming it as the equal of Cashel. It was true that the stone fortress towered over the eastern bank of the river and the settlement that spread beneath its walls, but apart from its strategic position, there was nothing particularly awe-inspiring about the edifice. Apart from the grey stone dominance rearing above it, the settlement itself appeared as just a peaceful, small farming community. As they approached along the opposite bank of the Mháigh, the riders could see boats plying their trade along the waterway and hear the reassuring ring of a blacksmith's hammer combined with the noise of cattle being herded. People were moving here and there. But there seemed little movement on the walls of the fortress – whose gates, they could observe, stood wide open.

Socht had brought a company of twenty-five warriors as an escort. He rode at the head of ten of them. The war banner of red silk with the ravening wolf emblem was borne aloft by the standard-bearer at his side. Then came Conrí with Fidelma, Eadulf and Gormán. They were followed by the remaining warriors. It had been an easy ride from the Ford of Oaks. They had kept to a track on the western side of the river, as Conrí had said it would save them time rather than having to follow the wriggling path of the water on the eastern side. Beyond the Ford of Oaks the river seemed to increase the number of twists and turns in its path from where it rose in the distant southern mountains.

Conrí surveyed the settlement. 'It seems our fears might have been for nothing, lady,' he observed. 'The place appears tranquil enough. If there had been an attempt to attack it, we would surely have seen evidence.'

'Better to be wrong than to have one's fears set aside until too late,' Eadulf offered defensively.

Fidelma made no comment as they rode down the short hill towards the riverbank and found a wooden bridge, still under construction, across the river into the centre of the settlement. Although it was still being worked on, the bridge had been reinforced sufficiently to take the passage of horses.

Conrí turned to Socht. 'Take half of the men and wait on this side of the river. I'll go with the lady Fidelma to the fortress and see what can be discovered. If all is well, I'll signal you to join us.'

They walked their horses carefully across the construction, the hooves beating a hollow tattoo on the wooden planks while Socht dispersed his men as instructed. As they moved through the township, some folk recognised Conrí and hands were raised in greeting. Other folk regarded them with looks of curiosity while a few stopped and held whispered conversations as they watched them pass.

They moved directly to the pathway that led up to the gates of the fortress. Now they could observe sentinels. A thickset man was waiting for them in the middle of the open gateway. He stood legs apart and hands on hips, a broad smile on his face.

'Welcome, Lord Conrí!' His voice was almost a bellow. 'We saw your banner across the river. What brings you here?'

Conrí swung down and greeted the man as an old friend.

'Greetings, Cúana. We come here out of curiosity.' He waved a hand towards Fidelma and Eadulf. 'This is the lady Fidelma of Cashel and Brother Eadulf.'

The names registered with the man, who regarded them with a surprised expression before quickly acknowledging them.

'This,' went on Conrí, 'is Cúana, the steward to Prince Donennach. He commands the fortress while the Prince is absent.'

'That is, I have a guard of just a score of warriors,' Cúana added with a wry smile. 'Nothing so imposing as at Cashel, lady.'

Fidelma and Eadulf had dismounted. 'Is all quiet here, Cúana?' Fidelma asked.

The young steward frowned. 'Should it be otherwise, lady?' he countered.

'It is just that there have been some strange happenings, my friend,' Conrí explained. 'The lady Fidelma has come to investigate the attempted assassination of her brother, King Colgú – an attack which succeeded in killing the Chief Brehon of Muman.'

At once the steward showed concern. 'Is your brother out of harm's way then, lady?'

'So far as we know.'

'Then what brings you here?'

'A torturous path,' she replied. 'We will talk about it later. Right now, I would like to know if you have heard of any plot against Prince Donennach? Have there been any rumours that some rival to his rule may be plotting to seize this fortress?'

Cúana's eyes widened and he glanced at Conrí as if for confirmation that she was being serious. When he saw his friend's expression, he turned back to Fidelma. 'None that I have heard of, lady. All is quiet here, as I have said. If there is some plot to discredit the Uí Fidgente, then I have seen no sign of it.'

Conrí laid a hand on his arm. 'But what better time for a plot to be put in motion, my friend? What better time to overthrow the rule of Prince Donennach – when he is out of the territory? We must admit there are some among us who resent the peace that was made with Cashel. That is why I hurried here to make sure that all is well with you.'

'The country has never been quieter,' the steward assured him.

'In that case, my friend,' smiled Conrí, 'I would formally ask hospitality for myself and my guests as well as for my men.'

'It shall be granted. I had wondered why you left half of your men on the far bank of the river. Unless my eyes deceive me, Socht, the commander of your guard, is among them. Ah, but I have your strategy. You wanted to ensure all was well here first before you committed them to cross. Well, all *is* peaceful, my friend. You may signal them to that effect so that your warriors may join us. There is ale aplenty. Come, lady, the fortress is at your command.'

'I presume all Prince Donennach's ladies have departed with him?'

'They have, but we have female attendants if you wish to bathe after your ride. You may be assured that there are women enough to attend to all your wants.'

By this time, they were being led across the courtyard and stablemen were coming forward to take care of their horses. Conrí had ordered one of his men to go back to instruct Socht to bring the rest of his warriors across the river. It seemed that many of the warrior sentinels who paced the walls of the fortress were known to Conrí and his men, for cheerful greetings were being exchanged.

Cúana led the way into the great hall which seemed more impressive on the inside than the outside. Great tapestries hung on the walls, with shields bearing symbols of the owners who had once used them, displayed along with swords. At one end of the hall was the Prince's chair of office, ornately carved with the icons of the Uí Fidgente. Stretching before it was a long oak table with benches either side where the nobles would sit either in council or when they feasted with the Prince. It was, as Fidelma had noted, not as grand as Cashel, but as good as any territorial ruler could afford.

At the young steward's call, two attendants hurried in, and when refreshments for the guests were served, they went off to fulfil their tasks. Another attendant appeared and began to build a fire in the great hearth, and Cúana gestured for his guests to be seated before he gave orders for chambers to be prepared for Fidelma, Eadulf and Conrí. Gormán, Socht and the rest of the warriors were to be housed in the long wooden *laechtech* – the House of Heroes, as the warrior's' quarters were called.

Cúana seemed almost jovial as the attendants served the drinks. 'I will order bathing facilities to be prepared shortly,' he told them.

Once again Eadulf was reminded of the daily custom of the people to bathe in the evenings before a meal. Usually, fires were kindled and water heated and a large tub or *dabach* was filled. Often the water was scented with sweet-smelling herbs, and a soap or *sléic* was used. Now and then he had noticed that the tub was filled with water and then round stones were heated and dropped in to warm it. Fidelma had once told him an ancient story of a mythical king named Fergus mac Léti whose attendant did not properly heat the bath stones, or *cloch-fothraicthe* as they were called. He threw one of them at her and killed her. Eadulf was brought up in a culture where bathing was not such a priority and a dip in the river from time to time sufficed. The evening bath was the main wash of the day, while in the morning one usually washed the hands and face.

'So how have you traced the assassin to this place?' Cúana asked after they had settled with their drinks. 'And what are these rumours of an attempt to overthrow Prince Donennach?'

'I did not say I had traced the assassin here,' returned Fidelma evenly. 'As yet we do not know who he was or where he came from.'

'Then what . . . ?'

'I think that you had better let me ask the questions in my own way,' intervened Fidelma. 'It is my right as an advocate of the court.'

Cúana seemed a little put out but gestured for her to continue.

'I believe that there was once a ferryman here called Escmug. Did you know him or of him?'

'Escmug?' The steward seemed genuinely surprised for a moment. 'He is long dead. He was not only a ferryman but a fisherman who plied his boat along the river here. He would try his hand at anything that made him a living . . . or rather paid for his liquor.'

'He was a heavy drinker, then? Tell me something of him.'

'He was not a nice man, if the stories are to be believed. There was a rumour that he killed his wife. At least, she disappeared. He claimed that she had run away.'

'Do you recall the name of his wife?'

'I think it was Liamuin.'

'Do you remember any details of what happened?'

'Liamuin simply disappeared one evening,' the steward replied. 'Escmug said she had gone off in his boat. He searched for her but never found her. That was when the rumours started that he probably killed her.'

'Her body was never recovered?'

'No. Liamuin was never seen again.'

'And did Escmug and Liamuin have any children?'

'There was a girl, as I recall. Liamuin abandoned her, which supported the idea that her husband killed her, for it takes a strange woman to abandon her daughter. For a short time the girl lived with Escmug. He was a brute of a man and worked the girl from morning to sunset until one day, she suddenly took off. Some time later, Escmug's body was found upriver from here. Again, there were rumours and stories. No one ever saw the girl again.'

'Was it thought that the daughter had murdered her father?' asked Fidelma.

'Who would have blamed her, if she had? Whoever did it had made a mess of his head, or so the locals say. The daughter vanished as surely as the mother.'

'Does any of Escmug's family remain here?'

'None that I can recall. But I will ask around . . .' A bell interrupted him and he smiled at them. 'That signifies that the waters in the *dabach* have been heated for your baths. So we will continue this conversation at the evening meal.'

It was some while later that Fidelma and Eadulf sat in the guest chamber they had been allotted. They had both bathed and changed and were awaiting the bell that would summon them to the feasting hall for the evening meal.

Eadulf was reflective. 'So far as I can see, we have not learned much more than we knew before we started out. The girl, Aibell, seems to have told us the truth – except that she could have killed her father.'

'I don't believe she did. The father seems to have been killed just after he had taken the girl to sell her to Fidaig of the Luachra. Therefore, she was not free to do so.'

Eadulf acknowledged the point. 'Yet there is a curious pattern emerging. We have learned that Ledbán had two children. One was Brother Lennán and the other one was Liamuin. Someone calling themselves Lennán attempts to kill your brother, shouting, "Remember Liamuin!" – the name of the real Lennán's sister. Then Aibell, the daughter of Liamuin, finds herself in the hut used by the so-called Brother Lennán. Then the father of the real Brother Lennán and Liamuin is, so we think, smothered to stop him talking to us about his daughter. Then there is the matter of Ordan the merchant and his activities with the mysterious Adamrae. I have never encountered such confusion before.'

'It is a puzzle, right enough,' replied Fidelma calmly. 'There is a relationship between all these matters, of that I am sure. The question is finding the common thread.'

A distant bell sounded and Eadulf rose to his feet. 'Let's hope the quality of the food in this place is good.'

There was a tap on the door and it swung open to admit a female servant. She was young, not more than twenty years, with fair skin, dark hair and pretty features.

'I am to escort you to the feasting hall,' she announced.

Eadulf was about to remark that they could have found the way, unaided, but Fidelma interrupted.

'What is your name?'

'Ciarnat, lady.'

'How long have you served here, Ciarnat?'

'Since I reached the age of choice at fourteen years, but my mother was one of the *coic* of this household so I have known no other place but Dún Eochair Mháigh.'

A *coic* was one of the professional cooks who served in the households of the nobles.

'So you know this township well?'

'I do, lady. I was born and raised here.'

'Do you remember a girl called Aibell, the daughter of Escmug? You look about the same age.'

A troubled look crossed the girl's features. 'I knew her,' she said quietly. 'She was my best friend, once.'

'Once?'

'She and her father left here and never came back. Her father was found murdered. I fear she might have killed him.'

'What makes you think so?' asked Fidelma.

'Her father was a wicked man who used to beat her. He also beat her mother before she ran away. The local people say that he killed her mother.'

The bell rang again with more persistence and the girl raised her head with a fearful look.

'The evening meal, lady. I will get into trouble unless I take you there at once.'

'That's all right, Ciarnat,' Fidelma reassured her. 'We will come with you. But tell me, is there any of Aibell's family still living in these parts?'

The girl hesitated then said, 'Her uncle is Marban – he is a *saer-muilinn*.'

'A millwright?' asked Eadulf. 'Where would we find him?'

'He has a cornmill upriver,' she confirmed, lowering her voice and

giving an anxious glance over her shoulder as if looking for an eaves-
dropper. 'It is a place called An Cregáin. You turn west before the Mháigh
passes a tributary called the Lúbach. There is a fast-flowing smaller stream
that joins the river from the west. Go upstream along it. That stream is
still known as the Mháigh. You follow it through a forest and that is where
Marban lives. Now, please, we must go.'

'Just tell me what relation this millwright is to the family of Aibell? Is
he brother to her mother or to her father?'

'Brother to Escmug, but people say that he hated him. Marban rarely
came to Dún Eochair Mháigh.'

Then the girl turned and hurriedly led the way along the corridors
towards the feasting hall with Fidelma and Eadulf hastening in her wake.

Cúana and Conrí were waiting before a large fire in the central hearth.
They had been joined by Socht and Gormán. A table was already prepared.

Fidelma immediately apologised for keeping them waiting. 'I am afraid
I needed some adjustments to my hair and this young girl helped me.'

Cúana nodded, as if understanding, and gestured to the table.

'Pray, seat yourselves. I have asked Donennach's harpist to attend and
provide us with some distraction.'

Fidelma looked and saw an old man seated in a corner with his *clarsach*
in front of him; at a sign from the young steward, he started to pluck at
the instrument with agile fingers. It was the custom for musicians to play
while nobles ate, and Cúana obviously did not believe in stinting on the
rituals simply because his Prince was absent. As steward, he first ensured
that everyone was seated in the appropriate order of priority. In attendance
was a *deochbhaire* or cup-bearer to see that each guest's goblet was filled,
and a *dáilemain* who would carve and serve the meat dishes.

The meal was impressive. It was mainly composed of meat dishes:
spit-roasted venison joints, basted with honey and salt, sausages made of
pork and lamb, and a dish of hard-boiled eggs which, by custom, were
eaten cold. There was also fish, and Fidelma observed that these had been

cooked on an *indeoin* or griddle; nearby were complementary dishes of *craobhraic* or samphire, and a braised pottage of herbs. There were other vegetables such as onions and watercress, and kale spiced with wild garlic. Later, there would be platters of nuts and apples. The knife was used in the right hand and the left was used to pick up the food. When needed, an attendant came forward with a basin of water to wash the fingers and a *lámbrat*, or small linen cloth to dry them on. Throughout, the *deoch-bhaire* continued to keep all the goblets filled with ale. If Cúana was trying to impress them, he was succeeding.

Cúana took an opportunity presented by a pause in the harpist's repertoire to report to Fidelma. 'I have made enquiries about the matter you were interested in, and I am told no one exists these days who was connected with the family of Escmug or Liamuin.'

Eadulf's brow creased; he was just about to say something when Fidelma said quickly, 'That is a shame. It would seem that our enquiries here have come to nothing.'

Conrí nodded absently. 'So what do you intend to do now, lady?'

'I intend to take the road south to the territory of the Luachra,' Fidelma announced.

Cúana was astonished. 'The Luachra, lady? That is a dangerous country to travel.'

'Have no fear. I have met Fidaig before.'

'But why go there?' It seemed even Conrí was surprised.

'A few more enquiries, that is all.'

'You mean the Luachra might be involved in this affair at Cashel?' asked Cúana.

'That is what I intend to discover. In the meantime, I know I can leave this territory in the safe hands of Conrí and yourself, Cúana. But I would urge you both to be vigilant.'

Eadulf tried to hide his surprise. It was unlike Fidelma to give up so easily, especially now they had already learned that there was some relative of Aibell dwelling not far away. He realised that she was up to something.

'Of course,' Conrí replied at once. 'When will you leave Dún Eochair Mháigh?'

'I see little need to tarry here now. We'll be on our way tomorrow morning.'

'We can supply you with an escort to the borders of the Luachra territory,' offered Conrí, and Cúana immediately agreed.

Fidelma said politely, 'Thank you, but there is no need. We will not be long in their territory for we have already been away from Cashel too long. You forget that when I left, my brother was barely surviving his wound. I need to return as soon as possible.'

'Of course, lady,' Conrí replied. 'We would hope that, should the worst happen, it will be understood that whoever the assassin was, it was not a member of the Uí Fidgente loyal to Prince Donennach.'

'We know how the Uí Fidgente are regarded in some parts of this kingdom,' Cúana added. 'And perhaps this assassin tried to mislead you, making it seem that it was an Uí Fidgente plot while it was something that arose closer to home.'

'Closer to home?' Eadulf was puzzled.

'Why not?' Cúana replied with a thin smile. 'The Eóghanacht Áine dwell on our eastern borders. Isn't Colgú's heir apparent Finguine of that same clan?'

Fidelma remained surprisingly calm in the face of his outrageous suggestion. 'You have made an interesting point and I shall bear that in mind,' she replied coolly.

Gormán and Eadulf exchanged a look, for both of them knew that Finguine was greatly trusted at Cashel and had frequently shown himself to be a very worthy heir apparent to Colgú.

Fidelma suddenly smothered a yawn. 'Well, it has been a long day today and it may be an even longer one tomorrow. If we are to leave in the morning, then we should be a-bed now.'

She rose and they followed suit. Eadulf and Gormán declined an invitation to continue to sit longer before the fire and thus left the others in the feasting hall with jugs of *corma* and ale.

Outside, Fidelma grimaced in disapproval. 'We shall be well away from here before they are stirring,' she said. 'Perhaps that is good.' She turned to Gormán. 'Are you comfortable for the night?'

The young warrior grinned. 'I have had worse accommodation, lady. I have a good cot in a corner of the *laochtech.*'

'Then I want you to have our horses ready in the courtyard just before first light.'

'Very well, lady. Anything else?'

'For the time being, nothing. There is something that troubles me about Cúana. So have a care and sleep with one eye open.'

Gormán raised a hand to his forehead before turning towards the *laochtech* – the House of Heroes where the warriors slept.

As Fidelma and Eadulf made their way to the guest chamber, Fidelma saw that Eadulf was about to speak and quickly placed a finger on her lips, indicating that she felt it better to reach their chamber first.

Once inside, Eadulf said with a frown, 'I am missing something here.'

'I am afraid that we are both missing something – but I am not sure what,' Fidelma replied, sitting down on the bed, her brow furrowed in thought.

'The girl said that Escmug had a relative who ran a cornmill nearby. That would surely be known to Cúana, yet he denied knowledge of such a relative. A cornmill and its owner is not of insignificance in this sort of community.'

'Well observed, Eadulf. So what was Cúana's reason?'

'That he did not want us to know?'

'But why? That is the more important question.'

'And that is also the mystery.'

'There is a conspiracy here, but what is it? It is strange that Cúana attempted to place suspicion on Finguine. He may be my brother's heir apparent but he has demonstrated himself to be trustworthy many times. When Colgú was about to be betrayed by his then heir apparent, Donndubháin, it was Finguine who helped save the day and that was why he was elected *tánaiste* instead. Since then he has been loyal. Look how he dealt with the recent Osraige conspiracy.'

'However, you could ask how long Donndubháin was loyal to your brother as former heir apparent before he decided that he wanted to become King.' Eadulf felt he should play the devil's advocate.

'That is true,' agreed Fidelma quietly. 'Do not worry, Eadulf. I am not totally blind to treachery. But I cannot find any motive for our cousin Finguine to be involved in a conspiracy. The other credible motive would be jealousy, and jealousy is not in Finguine's nature. He is quite happy being my brother's administrator. He enjoys ensuring that the nobles pay their tribute, that the chieftains fulfil their obligations by taking care of the roads, the hostels and the hospitals. He is happy seeing that no one wants in any part of the kingdom. This, of course, may present a reason for enmity against him rather than from him.'

They were silent for a moment or two and then Eadulf said, 'Nevertheless, there is something going on that is dark and mysterious.'

'I agree and I am not abandoning the search for answers to the question. I merely think that it is time to part company with Conrí and Socht. That is why I am pretending to go directly to Fidaig's territory, before returning to Cashel.'

'Wouldn't that alarm Conrí and Cúana if they are involved in this?'

'It would alarm them more if we said that we had given up our search and were heading directly back to Cashel. Then they would know that we are suspicious. So I let them think we are heading to the mountains of the Luachra to search for more information.'

'So we are to see this millwright, Marban, on the way back?'

'That is the idea,' she smiled. 'We must ensure that we keep our wits about us at all times.'

There came a soft tap on the door. Eadulf and Fidelma exchanged a quick look of surprise before Eadulf moved to the door and unlatched it.

It was the girl Ciarnat. She looked nervous. She pushed quickly by Eadulf, who then peered out into the passageway. There was no one about and so he shut the door behind her.

Fidelma smiled encouragingly at the girl. 'You want to see me?' She patted the bed beside her. 'Come – sit down and tell me all about it.'

'I should not have told you about Marban,' the girl blurted out.

'Why not? Is he not the relative of Escmug? Did you not tell me the truth?'

The girl hesitated. 'I do not want to get into trouble, lady.'

'You will be in no trouble if you have told me the truth.'

Ciarnat bit her lower lip.

'One of the attendants told me of some of the conversation at the feasting table. The steward has denied knowing about Marban.'

'Why do you think he did that?' Eadulf asked quickly.

The girl looked uncomfortable. 'I don't know. Cúana knew Marban well enough. I think that I should not have mentioned Marban, for now it seems as if I was not telling the truth.'

'Or that the steward was not telling the truth?' Fidelma pointed out.

Ciarnat looked confused.

'Are you saying that Cúana knew that Marban was a relative of Escmug?' asked Fidelma gently.

'Why, everyone knows that.' She caught herself. 'I mean . . .'

'I know what you mean,' Fidelma said brightly. 'Don't worry. He shall not learn from me that you told us about Marban. However, if everyone knows this fact, we could have learned it from anyone. It is curious that Cúana does not wish us to know it.'

Ciarnat sat looking unhappy.

'Since you knew Aibell, tell us something about her,' invited Fidelma.

'There's little enough to tell. We were young girls growing up together. We explored and played together – but that was only when Aibell's father was away working. He had a boat and often went fishing, and sometimes that kept him away for a time. These were the happy times, for when he was at home he was usually drunk.'

'But during happy times, how was it?'

Ciarnat smiled. 'It was good. Aibell was a great friend.'

'What of Aibell's mother, Liamuin? What was she like?'

'She was young and attractive. But she was a sad person.'

'Was she now?' Fidelma was thoughtful. 'Was she younger than Escmug? I know it might be difficult to say, as a child is not a good judge of age.'

'Oh, but I do know. Escmug was evil and old. Liamuin was young, and many a man would have willingly exchanged places with him. I heard men speaking. I did not understand much then, but I remember what they said.'

'So she was attractive and what did Aibell think of her?'

'She loved her mother and it was not one-sided for Liamuin was Aibell's only protection against her father. Aibell would often appear with a bruise or two. After her mother disappeared, things were very bad for Aibell.'

'When was this?'

'About the time I came to the age of choice. That was . . .' she frowned '. . . four years ago, just after the great Battle at Cnoc Áine.'

'Did you think it odd that Liamuin disappeared and left Aibell?'

'I did. It was known that Liamuin loved poor Aibell and that she would never have left her behind at the mercy of Escmug. He drank more than ever and treated Aibell like . . . like . . .' She ended with a shiver. 'I cannot say the words.'

'But Aibell's mother did run away.'

'True. Everyone hoped that she had run away and found somewhere safe, but few places were safe at that time.'

'What do you mean by that?' Eadulf asked, curious.

'For six months after the defeat of our army at Cnoc Áine, we had warriors of the King of Cashel quartered throughout the clan lands, and many of our nobles who had sided with Eoganán decided to flee rather than live under their orders. They took to the fastnesses and fought in small bands. Eventually, they accepted defeat and Prince Donennach made a treaty with Cashel. Things became better after that.'

'But not at first?' asked Fidelma.

The girl was uncomfortable. 'Begging your pardon, lady, most of the Eóghanacht treated us fairly but there was one man, the commander, Uallach of Áine, who believed all Uí Fidgente should be treated no better than animals. He was eventually killed in an ambush. Then the treaty with Cashel was agreed.'

It was Eadulf who suddenly posed the question. 'Did the King of Cashel, did Colgú ever come to this place during that time?'

Ciarnat stared at him in bewilderment. 'Why would he do so?'

'I meant, after the Battle at Cnoc Áine, when Eoganán was defeated, I am told Eóghanacht warriors were quartered in all parts of the Uí Fidgente territory. Did Colgú come here?'

Ciarnat shook her head. 'I never heard that he was in this part of the country. He never came here to visit Prince Donennach. Donennach always had to go to him.'

There was a sound outside in the corridor. They stopped speaking and heard footsteps, the slap of leather shoes on wooden boards. The girl rose nervously. She waited until the steps faded.

'I must go. I have said more than I intended. I don't want to get into trouble.'

'Then say nothing further to anyone,' Fidelma advised with a reassuring smile, 'and you will not get into any trouble. We shall be gone in the morning.'

The girl paused at the door. 'If ever you find out what happened to Aibell and you can tell me, I would like to know. She was once my friend.' Then she disappeared, closing the door quietly behind her.

CHAPTER THIRTEEN

❧

Had Ciarnat not given them specific directions, Fidelma and her companions would never have found the mill of Marban. They had left the fortress as dawn was breaking over the distant eastern hills and begun to move south along the western bank of the river, whose path continued to frequently twist and change. It was Gormán who indicated where they should turn westward, following what appeared to be an insignificant watercourse that had entered the main flow of the waterway.

He was quietly confident, saying, 'We need to look for a rocky place – that is, if the name An Cregáin indicates the terrain.'

They could smell the cornmill before they came to it: it was the aroma of corn drying in the kilns in preparation for the grinding. Most mills would have large kilns or ovens which were called *sorn-na hátha*, heated by wood. These required skill to work. If the person looking after them was lax and the ovens overheated or caught fire, then the corn would be burned and ruined. In some rural parts Eadulf had seen a more primitive form of drying which was done by roasting the corn on the ear. The person in charge would set fire to the ear and then watch for the right moment when the outer husk or chaff was burned but before it had a chance to reach the grain. It was then that the burning chaff was struck off, using a stick.

The mill seemed to be well-hidden. They followed the smell of the drying corn along a small path through the trees, emerging from the treeline onto some high rocky ground, where they caught sight of the mill. It was a watermill, situated by a stream, a millpond before it and a spring behind it. To one side were storehouses and beyond them, at some distance, were two large stonebuilt kilns with smoke billowing and men checking the corn that was being fed into them or turning it to heat it evenly. There were several workers at the mill, which was clearly a large and important one.

Suddenly, one of the men spotted them; laying aside his fork, he came over to meet them. His eyes swept over them, taking in their clothes and lingering a moment on Gormán and his gold torc.

'Is this the mill of Marban?' Fidelma enquired.

'It is, indeed, lady,' replied the other with a courteous bow.

'Are you Marban?'

'I am not. Marban is in his millhouse. Shall I summon him?'

'No, we will go to him,' Fidelma answered as she dismounted. Gormán remained with the horses while Eadulf accompanied her to the mill. They had not reached the door when it opened. A giant of a man appeared. He was shirtless but with a leather apron covering his great chest and leaving his muscular tanned arms bare. He had a large head, covered with a mass of dark red hair, and a large bristling beard. His arrogant light blue eyes were half-covered by drooping lids. He gazed at them with a truculent expression.

'Are you Marban?' asked Fidelma.

The man did not reply immediately. If anything he seemed to intensify his scrutiny of her.

'I am Marban the miller,' he finally conceded. 'I do not know you, lady. You travel with a foreign religieux but I see you also travel with a warrior of the Golden Collar,' he indicated Gormán, still seated astride his horse behind them. 'Further, I see you wear the same golden collar round your neck. That means you are an Eóghanacht.'

'You have a sharp eye, Marban the miller.'

'A man with poor eyesight is no judge of cows on the distant hill.'

''Tis true for you. But we come in peace, my friend.'

'Then you may go in peace.'

Fidelma glanced around. The workmen had not stopped their tasks but she was aware that eyes were watching them, noting their every move.

'You are wary, my friend. What ails you?' she demanded softly.

Marban eased his weight from one foot to the other.

'You may recall that you are in Uí Fidgente country, lady. As yet I do not know who you are but the golden collar denotes where you come from.'

'Then know, Marban, I am Fidelma of Cashel, sister to Colgú.'

The big man's eyes narrowed further. He shifted his weight once again.

'There has been some talk of you in these parts,' he admitted. 'You are a Brehon. It was also said that you were married to a foreigner.' He glanced towards Eadulf.

'I hope you will also have heard that I am a *dálaigh*,' Fidelma said quietly. 'And you will know that you must answer when I put questions to you.'

Marban's mouth was barely discernible through his bristling beard but there was a movement of the facial muscles that might have indicated a smile.

'I have no fear of lawyers, lady. This is my own mill and I block no one's access to the water supply. Those farms about me have their fill. The mill has been assessed according to the eight parts as listed in the *Senchus Mór*, and anyone who is injured in the working of the mill is compensated according to the direction of the *Book of Aicill*. Sometimes accidents happen and the proper assignment of liability is provided for in accordance with the instruction of the local Brehon.'

Fidelma hid her amusement. 'You seem to know much about your rights and obligations under the law, Marban. Perhaps you are a lawyer, too?'

The big man shook his mane of hair. 'Not I.'

Eadulf was looking puzzled so Fidelma explained quickly: 'The law lists the eight components of the mill and the legal construction of them.' She turned back to the miller. 'Are you often in need of a Brehon?'

'No, not often, because Prince Donennach rules in justice.'

'Ah? So you approve of Prince Donennach?'

'He has done much to save our territory from devastation,' replied the miller gruffly.

'From devastation . . . from the warriors of Cashel?' Fidelma's voice was almost teasing.

'I have told you, lady, that you are in the territory of the Uí Fidgente.'

'I understand.'

'I don't think you truly do,' countered the miller. 'When our warriors suffered defeat on Cnoc Áine, our people were shattered. Your brother's warriors came among us to make sure that we continued to be weak enough not to challenge Cashel again. Many of those leaders who had supported Prince Eoganán and his vain attempt to gain the kingdom were dead or fled. For a while we were without order and law – unless it was the order of your brother's warriors and their law.'

'You cannot expect us to feel sympathy for the Uí Fidgente who unwisely followed Eoganán on his foolish venture to overthrow Colgú and who, being justly defeated, were also justly punished,' Eadulf intervened. 'I myself was taken off a ship on the high seas and sent as a slave to work in the copper mines which were being used by Torcán, the son of Eoganán, to trade for men and arms. Eoganán and his son were not so concerned about the treatment they gave to those they intended to conquer so I shall not feel much sympathy either.'

Marban stood regarding Eadulf as he spoke. Eventually he said, 'I can understand how you must feel. But an injustice faced by an injustice does not equate to justice.'

'A good philosophical argument, Miller.' Fidelma's tone was distant.

'But a discussion on the ethics of the conflict is not why we have come here.'

The burly miller sniffed. 'I was wondering if your visit had a purpose.'

'I am told that you are related to a ferryman, sometime fisherman, called Escmug.'

The miller's eyes widened for the first time and he seemed about to make an involuntary movement backwards but straightened himself.

'Escmug? He is dead.' The words came out emphatically.

'Then you will not object to telling us something about him?'

Suspicion was shaping Marban's features. 'Why?'

A fine, misty rain had started to spread, almost indiscernibly at first, like settling dew. Fidelma drew her cloak more tightly across her shoulders.

'Perhaps we could find a more comfortable place to talk, or is the custom of hospitality absent in this part of the world?'

Marban stared angrily at her for a moment and then pointed to some large sheds to which some of the workers were hurrying as the misty rain turned into heavier drops.

'Your . . . escort,' he indicated Gormán, 'can shelter your horses in the stable there. We can speak in the mill.'

Eadulf turned and hurried back to Gormán with the instruction before rejoining Fidelma and the miller in the interior of the mill. It was gloomy but warm and the atmosphere was heavy with the dust of ground corn. The miller indicated a bench for them to be seated on before he perched himself on the bottom of a stairway that led to an upper floor.

'Escmug is dead,' he repeated heavily. 'What would you want to know about him?'

'You were related to him, so I am told.'

'Since you know, why ask?'

'I ask in order to confirm it. We can either make this easy or spend the day, longer if you like, extracting replies.' Suddenly Fidelma's voice had grown brittle, threatening. 'You know the penalties for not answering the questions of a *dálaigh* or for not answering them truthfully? Now, is it so?'

The miller shifted his body uncomfortably. 'It is. He was my elder brother. I was not close to him, nor did I ever want to be. If you must know, I hated him. He only saw me when he needed help, and I grew tired of giving it to him.'

'Didn't he have a good business on the river?'

'When he was sober enough, which was hardly ever. He was a brute of a man. He beat his wife and his child and neglected them both. When they were alive, it was the only reason that I offered to help him – for their sakes.'

'You speak of his wife and child as dead.'

'They are all dead now. Escmug's body was found in the river.'

'And his wife?'

'Liamuin? She had run away from his ill-treatment and was reported dead. Why she ever consented to wed him, I don't know.'

'Tell me something about her.'

'Her father was Ledbán, who was the stableman to the lord Codlata at the Ford of Flagstones which is just north of here. When Ledbán's wife died of the Yellow Plague he entered the Abbey of Mungairit where his son was the physician.'

'So Brother Lennán was brother to Liamuin?'

It was now Marban's turn to look surprised. 'You know the story?'

'We were at Mungairit a few days ago. We saw Ledbán. He died while we were there.'

Marban let out a long sigh. 'He was old and made older by the fate of his family. His wife died of the Yellow Plague, his son was slain at Cnoc Áine while nursing the wounded, and his daughter . . . his daughter married a beast like Escmug. No wonder Ledbán sought tranquillity in Mungairit. If gossip is to be believed, I think his lord, Codlata, also sought refuge there.'

'Why would Codlata seek refuge in Mungairit?' asked Eadulf, intrigued.

'He was a nephew and steward to Prince Eoganán, and commanded a company of his warriors at Cnoc Áine,' replied the miller. 'Many of Eoganán's family sought ways of protecting themselves after the defeat.'

Eadulf cast a thoughtful glance at Fidelma but she was concentrating on other matters.

'Tell me more about Liamuin.'

'She was an attractive girl. I could not believe that she would be fascinated by such a beast as Escmug, even though he was my own brother.'

'The attraction between a man and woman is one of the great mysteries of the world,' Eadulf remarked.

The miller nodded. 'Is it not an old saying that the three most incomprehensible things in the world are the labour of bees, the ebb and flow of the tide and the mind of a woman – begging your pardon, lady.'

'So the wedding did not meet with the approval of Liamuin's family?'

'Everyone was unhappy. They all hated Escmug.'

'But Escmug was your own brother.'

'In every litter there is usually one who turns out bad.'

'And that was Escmug? But he and Liamuin had a child.'

'Aibell? A sad child, indeed. When Liamuin left Escmug, and not before time, the poor girl had to endure her father's wrath until finally, she too disappeared.'

'So what happened to Escmug?'

'His body was found lodged in a beaver dam on the river.'

'We have heard that he might have been murdered,' Eadulf said.

Marban gave another of his eloquent shrugs. 'Some thought that being the man he was, perhaps he was helped to depart to the Otherworld,' he said. 'If so, no one mourned his passing.'

'The story we heard was that some people thought he had killed his wife,' Eadulf put in.

The miller was silent.

'You said both his wife and child were dead,' Fidelma went on. 'Do you know that as a fact? Did Escmug find and kill them?'

'Escmug never did anything unless there was something to gain. Why kill his wife who had become a virtual slave in his household?'

'Even the lowliest slave can rebel,' Eadulf murmured.

'Liamuin left him,' said Marban, his voice hollow. 'I heard sometime later that she had died.'

'So she ran away, leaving her young daughter?'

'Liamuin could not stand her life any more. She would have taken the child with her, but the opportunity did not arise. She had to seize her own chance, and so she fled.'

Fidelma gazed thoughtfully at the miller and an idea came to her.

'Did she come here?' she asked.

For a moment the miller stared at her as if he would deny it – and then he shrugged. 'Where else would she go? Her brother had just been killed at Cnoc Áine and her father was serving in the Abbey of Mungairit. There was no one to protect her. Yes, she came here.'

'Were you in love with her?' This was Eadulf.

'Perhaps I was. But she was never in love with me.'

'When did she die? What happened? Did Escmug catch up with her?'

Even in the gloom, they saw a look of grief spread over the miller's face. 'As I say, she came here first. She could no longer bear life with Escmug but circumstances dictated that she had to leave young Aibell behind when she made her bid for freedom. When she arrived here, she and I both knew it would not be long before Escmug followed her. I suggested that she should seek refuge at a place in the hills further south. You see, I had a patron there who owned a fortified house just where the river rises. I felt she would be safe there as there was nothing to connect the place with Liamuin.'

'Obviously, since she is dead, it was *not* safe,' Eadulf commented.

'But not for the reasons you are supposing,' snapped Marban.

'Tell us then, who was your patron?'

'Menma. He was a *bó-aire* who sent his corn to me to be dried and ground. His rath lay on the side of the hills at what was called the Old Ridge, at the spot where one of the springs rises that come down to feed the river. That is An Mháigh. I was worried that Escmug was close behind her, so I took her to Menma myself and he promised me that he would protect her. When I returned here, I found Escmug. He was in a rage. He had a horse-whip in his hand and was threatening what he would do once he caught up with Liamuin. I denied all knowledge of anything to do with her, and eventually he returned to Dún Eochair Mháigh.'

'And then?'

'Some weeks passed.' The miller sighed and rubbed a hand over his face. 'Then I heard that Aibell had also disappeared. I hoped she had run away – but she never came here to me.'

'Was nothing done to rescue the child and reunite her with her mother?'

'I had discussed the matter with Liamuin once she was safe. Unfortunately, Escmug must have suspected such an idea, for he kept the child within sight almost the whole time.'

'But you said she was dead?'

'One day Escmug arrived here. He was smiling, calm and cold of temper. I feared the worst.'

'Which was?'

'I felt he had killed the girl. He then said that he knew I had helped to hide Liamuin. Someone had told him that she had been seen with me, and he said he was going to find her and make her pay. I had the choice to tell him where she was, or suffer the consequences. And then he boasted that he had taken his daughter Aibell and sold her in bondage to Fidaig. I protested that she was at the age of choice. He merely laughed. Said her bondage would be something for Liamuin to reflect on when he caught up with her.' Marban suddenly fell silent. 'I could not let him find her.'

Fidelma leaned slightly towards him.

'Before you consider what you have to tell me, Marban, I should explain that in law there is what we recognise as *colainnéraic* – the existence of circumstances in which the killing of another person is justified and entails no penalty. This is when the killing occurs as an act of self-defence.'

The miller stared at her, his face pale.

'You knew all along that I had killed Escmug?' he said heavily. 'Is that why you came here?'

'We knew nothing, until you began to tell us. Did you kill Escmug and then put the body in a beaver dam?'

The miller shuddered violently. 'I killed him right enough. And yes, it was in self-defence. When I refused to tell him where Liamuin was and said I would tell the local Brehon how he had placed his daughter in bondage, he went berserk. He grabbed an axe. There was a wooden stave nearby and I seized it. I caught him on the side of the head and he went down. It was a chance blow and he did not move afterwards. When I examined him, I found he was dead. I carried the body to the main river and heaved it in, thinking it would float downstream so that he would be found. But the current took him into the dam where his corpse lodged for a while. It was found sometime later.'

'And no one helped you? You did this alone?'

'It happened as I said. He was shouting and raving. His anger grew murderous as he realised that I had been helping Liamuin the whole time. No one else was involved.'

Fidelma nodded slowly. 'So his death was in self-defence,' she murmured.

'But what of Liamuin?' Eadulf wanted to know. 'You said that she was dead?'

'So I have been told.'

'You must know more. Explain.'

'All of this happened after the war against Cashel. With the defeat and death of our Prince, warriors of Cashel came to occupy certain places to ensure our people were pacified. It was not a good time for any of us.'

'Go on,' prompted Fidelma when he paused.

'Menma told me that a warrior came to his rath and demanded to stay.'

'Who was this warrior?'

'I do not know. Only that he was of Cashel and wore the same golden circlet around his neck as you wear.'

'Then he was a member of my brother's bodyguard?'

'Whoever he was, lady, my friend Menma was forced to give him hospitality. It seemed his task was to ensure there were no threatening disturbances in the foothills that border the territory of our lands with those of the Luachra.'

Even Eadulf had to chuckle at this. 'One warrior?'

'He was the commander of a troop that encamped in those hills between Sliabh Luachra and the Uí Fidgente territory. He would go and consult with them from time to time to ensure there were no rumblings of discontent while the peace negotiations were continuing.'

The miller stopped and wiped his brow with a piece of cloth before going on.

'As I said earlier, the mind of a woman is beyond understanding. Within a short space of time Liamuin and this Cashel warrior grew close; even though her own brother had been killed at Cnoc Áine, she and this warrior became lovers. Menma tried to warn her. He even sent for me to come and try to speak with her.'

'And did you?'

Marban sighed deeply. 'When I reached Menma's fortress, it was a burned-out shell. Menma, my good friend, was dead, along with his wife and sons and almost his entire household. Liamuin was also dead.'

'And this Cashel warrior?'

'I found out from neighbours that one day, after it was thought this warrior had gone into the hills, he and his men suddenly returned and without warning they attacked Menma's fortified house. I was told that Liamuin was struck down by one of his bowmen. The place was put to the torch. The folk from a neighbouring farmstead buried them.'

'And could anyone identify the warrior who had done this terrible deed?' Fidelma's voice had gone dry. When Marban silently shook his head, she went on: 'What of these neighbours? Did they not learn anything at all about him?'

'Only that he was from Cashel and wore the golden collar. It is some years now, but I think there was a survivor who reached the safety of the forest during the attack. I am not sure, but that is what I was told. A name might be known among those neighbouring farmsteads.'

Fidelma was surprised. 'Do you mean that Menma's farmstead was the only one torched? That the other farmsteads were left alone?'

'It seemed so. But such things were what we of the Uí Fidgente had to endure in those months after the defeat at Cnoc Áine,' the miller added bitterly.

There was a silence and then Fidelma said: 'I can assure you, Marban, that I will do all in my power to find out who that warrior and his men were. There is surely a way of tracking him down. When we do, he will find himself answerable to the law.'

The miller uttered a cynical laugh as he said, 'I am an Uí Fidgente, lady. The warrior was an Eóganacht, one of your kind. Do you seriously expect me to believe that the victor will punish his own?'

'That is the law, and if it is not applied then there is no justice.'

'I have seen enough Eóganacht justice,' the miller grunted.

'You *will* see it,' emphasised Fidelma. 'That is my promise.'

'And you will swear that on all that is sacred to you?'

'On all that is sacred to me, I swear it,' she replied solemnly.

There was a silence and then Eadulf said: 'And what of her daughter, Aibell? You have not said why you believe her to be dead.'

This time the man hesitated a moment. 'I went to Fidaig, as Escmug said he had sold her to him as a bondservant, but Fidaig denied all knowledge of the transaction. So I realised that either Fidaig was lying, or that Escmug must have killed the girl, as people suspected. My brother was a vile, vengeful man. Anyway, to all intents my niece was beyond rescue and therefore as good as dead.' The miller bowed his head, sighed, then rose suddenly, saying, 'I must attend to my workers. I presume you are anxious to continue your journey?'

'We are anxious,' replied Fidelma, 'but the giving and taking of hospitality is a sacred thing in itself. We will take food with you, Marban, before we continue our journey.'

After Marban had left, Eadulf commented, 'Vengeance seems the motive for the attack on your brother.'

'Vengeance? Indeed. The assassin chose to strike him down because he was the King whose warrior had done this. Yes, vengeance – but from whom? The would-be assassin was certainly not Liamuin's brother, or father or anyone else who was related to her . . . unless he was somehow connected with Aibell. But what did Aibell know of her mother's death and who killed her? Also, the assassin shouted, "Remember Liamuin" as if that name would mean something to Colgú. Yet Colgú swore – even as he might have been dying from his wound – that the name meant absolutely nothing to him. No, Eadulf, there is still a mystery here.'

'You think the miller knows more than he is saying?'

'No, I don't think so. He did not have to give us such details – even down to admitting that he killed his own brother. I think he has been completely honest and told us all he could.'

'Then what do we do now?'

'There is only one path for us, and that is to see if we can find the survivors of Menma's house. Above all, we must try to identify the warrior who killed Liamuin.'

Just then, the door of the millhouse swung open and Gormán came in. 'The horses are safe, lady,' he said, 'So I thought I would come and see what is happening. The miller and his men are securing the kilns as the rain seems to have ended their day's work.'

Fidelma turned to him with a frown.

'Did you fight at Cnoc Áine, Gormán?'

'Alas, lady, I did not. I was still trying to convince my master that I had the skill to be a warrior. I was studying at the school of the Múscraige Breogain then.'

'I don't suppose you know which of the warriors of the Golden Collar went into the land of the Uí Fidgente at that time?'

'Capa was the commander at that period. It was not until after that time that I was allowed to serve in the bodyguard at Cashel. Indeed, it was when Capa was replaced by Caol that I was admitted into the Golden Collar. As you know, Capa had tried to convince the King that I was responsible for the abduction of your child . . .'

'I remember well enough, Gormán,' Fidelma replied tightly. 'I presume Caol was at Cnoc Áine?'

'A lot of the Nasc Niadh were, lady. It was a great battle. Enda, Aidan, Dego, all of them were there.'

'Did they ever speak of the months afterwards, when my brother sent them and some of their companies to ensure that peace prevailed in the territory of the Uí Fidgente?'

Gormán thought for a moment and then said: 'I don't recollect anything specific. I think everyone wanted to boast about their deeds in the main battle rather than focus on the more mundane action of making sure the peace was kept after the Uí Fidgente were defeated.'

'But most of the warriors of the Golden Collar, who were the élite commanders, had territories to oversee.'

'So I understood. But that did not last for long, only until the new Prince of the Uí Fidgente struck his accord with your brother. Prince Donennach accepted that if there was any infringement to the peace, he was answerable to Cashel and therefore it was in his interest to ensure there was no such unrest.'

'Would it be hard to discover which of the warriors of the Golden Collar were sent to this area?'

'I am not sure, lady. But we are near Dún Eochair Mháigh, which is the chief fortress of the Uí Fidgente. Would it not be logical that Colgú himself would have come here to oversee the peace?'

There was a brief silence and a troubled look crossed Fidelma's features.

'We are told he did not. The King would not spend months in some remote spot in the foothills south of here,' Eadulf said quickly, knowing what was passing through her mind. 'Those foothills lead into the mountains of the Luachra. We are looking for a warrior of the Golden Collar who was based there.'

Suddenly, voices were raised outside – then the door burst open. Gormán swung round, hand on the hilt of his sword, and Fidelma and Eadulf rose to their feet.

Marban stood on the threshold, his face grim.

'We have word that some of Fidaig's warriors are coming this way. I suggest that you go up to the top of the mill building and make yourselves inconspicuous.'

'Fidaig? Of the Luachra?' breathed Fidelma. 'But this is not his territory.'

'There is no time to debate borders, lady. His warriors are not given to intellectual discussion. They come by right of their swords.'

'Why would you think that we should hide?' asked Gormán.

'Because you are who you are,' the miller replied simply. 'Fidaig's men are hard to control once they sense sport, and their idea of sport is not one that you would appreciate. Hide.'

'But why are you doing this?' Fidelma asked. 'You are an Uí Fidgente.'

'I am willing to see if you are right about Eóghanacht justice. Above all, I want justice for Liamuin.'

'I have sworn justice will be done,' Fidelma assured him.

'Then go above the stairs and wait until they have gone.'

With that he left them, shutting the door behind him. They did not delay but climbed the stairs through the millhouse until they reached the small top-floor area. There were two windows, one overlooking the stream and sluice gates from the spring which, when the gates were opened, started the water-wheel moving by the passage of the water into the millpond. The other overlooked the grounds outside with the kiln and stables.

Eadulf glanced quickly round. 'Well, if we are about to be betrayed, they have to come up those stairs. Only one man at a time. We can easily defend this place.'

Gormán grinned. 'True, friend Eadulf. Except that I do not think they would bother if they were intent on catching us. They would merely wait at the bottom of the mill until we came down.'

'Starve us out?'

'Probably set light to the mill and we would have the choice of perishing in the flames or perishing by their swords.'

'You are a cheerful soul, young Gormán,' Eadulf replied without enthusiasm.

Fidelma told them to be quiet and moved carefully to the window overlooking the working area before the mill.

'Keep down,' she hissed. 'A dozen horsemen are arriving. Marban is going forward to greet them.'

They could hear brief snatches of conversation. The leader of the horsemen asked a series of sharp questions to which the burly miller seemed to reply in obsequious manner, bowing and pointing to the north-west. To their relief the exchange did not last long. The horses cantered off. Moments later, they heard the miller climbing the stairs until finally his head appeared in the aperture in the floor.

'You can come down,' he said. 'They've all gone.'

Fidelma had a strange expression on her face. 'I recognised the young warrior leading them by his tone of voice. Who was he, Marban?'

'That was one of the sons of Fidaig. His name is Gláed.'

'Gláed?' Fidelma drew in a breath. 'I would have said his name was Adamrae.'

CHAPTER FOURTEEN

❧

They had left Marban's mill and followed the narrow course of the Mháigh as it snaked its way towards the point where it rose in the south-western hills. On Fidelma's instruction, Gormán had removed his golden collar emblem of the Nasc Niadh. She too had removed her own collar, and they had placed them in their saddle-bags. Obviously, as they proceeded into the territory of the most truculent of the Uí Fidgente septs and their neighbours, the Luachra, it was wise to be cautious. Most of the area was thick with forest, although now and then they came across large plains of intersecting waterways; small streams and water-filled gullies that rose from springs in the distant bank of hills. At times it was almost hard to follow the main course of the Mháigh, as it was so interspersed with other watercourses. But it was from all of these waters eventually merging together that the great River Mháigh was created.

The long line of low hills to the south of them began to grow higher as they approached them. Gormán pointed out a number of rath-like buildings, fortified enclosures that could be seen along the hilltops.

'One of those must be the one we are looking for,' he said.

Fidelma glanced at the hills in front of them. 'We should be looking for a burned-out ruin.'

They began to guide their horses up the side of the hills. Across the gentle slopes were bands of hill sheep, black and brown with wiry wool and crooked horns. Fidelma felt it was surely time that they were brought into more protected pasture for the winter months. The animals gazed indifferently at the three riders as they moved slowly along the path. Now and then they passed patches of ferns of various varieties and gorse that would, in the early spring months, burst forth in a glorious fiery yellow.

Fidelma decided to stop at the first hill farm they came to and make enquiries. It could just about be called a rath because it was surrounded by an earthen bank and wooden fencing. A middle-aged woman was seated outside the main building plucking a chicken. She had not observed their approach and was disconcerted for a moment, rising to her feet and discarding the half-plucked bird on the wooden bench beside her. She watched them halt at the gate; her dark eyes scanned their clothes before their features to decide what sort of people they were.

She answered Fidelma's greeting with a lack of enthusiasm.

'What do you seek here?' she demanded gruffly.

'We are looking for what used to be the rath of Menma,' called Fidelma without dismounting, unperturbed by the woman's hostility.

'The rath of Menma, is it?' Her eyes narrowed. 'He is long dead and his rath is no more than a pile of firewood.'

'So I have been told. And in which direction do we go from here?'

The woman gestured along the path to the west. 'Keep on this track and you will come to it. But there is nothing there now. As I said, Menma is dead. They were all killed years ago.'

'Were there no survivors?' asked Fidelma.

Again she was met with a suspicious frown. 'Why do you ask?'

'If there were survivors of that tragic event, I would like to speak with them. I am a *dálaigh*.'

The woman blinked. 'A lawyer? We do not have many lawyers coming along this track.' She suddenly gave a grunt; it took them a while to realise it was a sardonic laugh. 'In fact, you are the first strangers I have seen since the harvest.'

'Have you lived here long?'

'I was born on that far hill. My husband, Cadan, runs this farm. He's away with the sheep right now.'

'So you lived here at the time when Menma's place was burned down?'

'Why the questions, lady?'

'I want to know what happened.'

'That I can't tell you in detail. One day we saw smoke rising above Menma's homestead. I called my man. He and my son ran to help – but by the time they reached it, all that was left were slain bodies and smoking ruins.'

'You knew Menma, of course?'

'Of course.'

'And what of his household?'

'He had a large household. There was Menma, his wife and two sons who worked the farm. He had cornfields on the plain below. He also had two servants . . . oh, and there was a woman. She was a guest. I think that she might have been a relative. I forget her name now.'

'Was anyone else at the farmstead that day?'

She shook her head. 'Not on that day.'

Fidelma caught the inflection. 'So, on other days there were people staying or visiting.'

'There was one warrior. I was told that he was one of the Eóghanacht troops sent to keep us in order. It was in those days following the great defeat and there were several Eóghanacht soldiers encamped around here. He was their commander. I only saw him from a distance, riding across the hills with his men. Thankfully, he had no cause to come to our farmstead.'

'You do not know who he was – his name, or what he looked like?'

'Why all these questions?' the woman muttered impatiently. 'Who are you, lady?'

'I told you, I am a *dálaigh* and I want to know what happened at Menma's rath.'

The woman sniffed. 'A bit late for that isn't it, when all these years have passed.'

'And you say no one survived?'

A cunning look spread across her features. 'Did I say that?'

'Then someone did survive?' Fidelma pressed.

'Old Suanach survived. She had worked for the family ever since she was a young girl.'

'Suanach? Where would we find her?'

'You just carry on beyond the ruined rath. The track leads into a forest. She took refuge there afterwards and still lives there. My man and my son found her more dead than alive and brought her here at first. We nursed her as best we could, with the help of the local apothecary, until she eventually said she would go to live across the hill. Old Menma had a cabin in the forest where he once employed a woodsman, for the forest was partially his.'

'Thank you. That is very helpful. Did she ever tell you what happened?'

'That the Eóghanacht horsemen attacked the rath for no reason. Cadan, my husband, was able to confirm that.'

'Why do you say that?'

'My man is a good woodsman. He saw the signs of several horses. Most people had been killed by sword blows. The woman who was staying with them had been shot with arrows and so had one of the servants. Old Suanach would have been dead too from a hefty blow to the back of her skull from a sword but, thanks be, it merely knocked her unconscious but left such a bloody mess that they thought she was dead.'

'You've been very helpful,' Fidelma repeated. 'What is your name?'

'Flannait is my name.'

'Then my thanks, Flannait.' Fidelma turned and led the way along to the track across the hillside.

It was not long before they came across a large site of overgrown scrubland. Half-hidden amidst it were the remains of stone and burned wooden constructions; the stones were scarred and blackened by fire. Already nature was beginning to claim the site for grass, shrubs and trees were spreading across it. A quick glance assured them that it had once been a substantial rath, a large house with many outbuildings. They paused only momentarily before moving on along the track towards the forest beyond. It was a large area of evergreen, holly, mixing with blackthorns. The many-branched trees rose to contest the hardy grey alders with their pointed leaves and smooth grey bark. Even rowans spread towards the ridge of the hill. Moss, fern and lichen all clustered among them giving the impression of a dark, impenetrable forest.

Yet the forest was alive. A snipe suddenly flitted from a tree, arrowing down to the mud banks of the water-courses below. This set off some alarmed chattering from a couple of red grouse who had sought sanctuary here from the open moorland behind. However, their flight had been noted and followed by a small dark object rising rapidly skywards, with fast shallow wingbeats. The tiny merlin was an unforgiving bird of prey.

Led by Fidelma, the three travellers walked their horses along the path and entered the darker space of the woodland. It was not long before they saw the shadowy shape of a hut; it was well-hidden in the gloom and could easily have been missed, had they not been specifically looking for it. Even so, Fidelma and Eadulf had to leave their mounts, under the care of Gormán, on the main path and push through the ferns and bracken that grew almost to their own height, presumably in their search for the sun, as if reaching up towards the top of the forest canopy.

To their surprise, they found themselves in a cultivated space in front of the wooden cabin, a place where a few hardy root vegetables had been planted.

Fidelma paused and called: 'Suanach! Don't be alarmed. We wish to talk with you.'

There was a movement inside the hut and then the door creaked open.

A woman stood there with wild grey hair and a pale skin, creased with wrinkles. Her eyes were bright but the flesh seemed aged by weather as much as time. She was wrapped in a thick woollen shawl which covered an equally thick dress of wool.

'What do you want?' she demanded.

Fidelma reflected that suspicion seemed a natural reaction in this territory.

'Flannait the farmer's wife told us where we would find you,' she began.

'For what purpose?' came the uncompromising response.

'I am a *dálaigh*,' Fidelma went on, unperturbed. 'I understand you are a survivor of the attack on Menma's rath some years ago.'

If anything, the woman's eyes narrowed with increased suspicion. She looked from Fidelma to Eadulf – a disapproving expression on her face as she regarded him. Then she turned back.

'It was a long time ago.'

'No more than four years, so I am told.'

'A long time,' Suanach repeated as if she had not heard her.

'Can we speak inside your cabin?'

The woman sniffed and actually stepped out onto the porch, closing the door behind her.

'No, we cannot. There is scant room for myself and none for strangers. If you must talk, there is a seat on that log. I shall sit on the porch.'

Fidelma glanced at Eadulf with a smile of resignation and went to sit on the log that the woman had indicated. Eadulf preferred to stand.

'I merely want you to tell me the details of the attack on Menma's rath,' Fidelma said quietly.

'Details?' The woman gave a hoarse laugh. Suddenly she turned her head away and raised her long hair from the back of her neck, revealing a livid white scar. 'Is that detail enough? Menma and all his family were all killed. I was the only survivor. A curse on the strangers from Cashel!'

Fidelma shot a warning look at Eadulf before continuing. 'Tell me what happened. Who was at the rath that day?'

Suanach shrugged indifferently. 'What good does it do to speak of them now? They are all dead.'

'It may help to bring the guilty to punishment,' Fidelma replied.

'After all these years? I doubt it. And who will punish the Eóghanacht? Still, I shall not go to my grave without passing on the truth.' She paused and seemed to gather herself before continuing. 'It was a normal day. The sun was up and the warrior had gone . . .'

'The warrior?'

'It was after our defeat by the Eóghanacht. Part of our punishment was that we had bands of warriors from Cashel set to watch over us until we agreed the terms of the peace. One warrior who commanded them demanded the hospitality of the rath.'

Fidelma leaned forward eagerly. 'Do you know his name?'

Suanach frowned. 'It is so long ago, I forget. All I remember was that he wore a golden collar, a gold torque around his neck, and boasted that he was of the warrior élite of Cashel come to maintain order over us. He was tall and slender.'

'Perhaps his name will come back to you as we speak,' Fidelma replied, disappointed. 'Let us continue. How long was he here?'

'A long while, I think. Months, but not years. Long enough for him to pretend to be in love.'

Fidelma ran her tongue over lips that had gone dry with excitement.

'With whom was he supposed to be in love?'

'A woman from Dún Eochair Mháigh who was under Menma's protection. She had come to be with us some months before. She was an attractive woman, with dark hair the colour of black night. When the sun shone on it, it danced with a blue light.'

'What was her name? Do you remember that?'

'Oh yes, her name I *do* remember. It was Liamuin. I think she had been newly widowed, but she had come here under Menma's protection. Menma was a *bó-aire*, a cow lord, and influential in these parts.'

'And this warrior from Cashel, you say that he fell in love with her?'

'Pretended to be in love with her,' she corrected. 'Liamuin certainly fell in love with his deceitful looks and lying tongue.'

'Very well. What then?'

'On the day it happened, Menma and his sons were shearing some sheep. Menma's wife was preparing the meal with Comnait, a young girl serving the household. Liamuin was outside with the *muide* churning the butter.'

Seeing that Eadulf looked puzzled, Fidelma quickly explained: 'A *muide* is a small hand-churn.' The popular word that Eadulf knew was a *cuinneóg* but this seemed to be a local term known to Fidelma.

Suanach had not noticed the interruption for she was continuing. 'I had gone down to the boundary wall to look after the pigs and was—'

'And did you say that the warrior with the golden collar was not here?' interrupted Fidelma.

'He was not. He was in the habit of leaving every few days. He would vanish on his horse and then return. I suppose he went to meet with his men who were encamped elsewhere in the territory.'

'So, what happened?'

'Everything was peaceful that morning and then . . . Then he appeared with a dozen of his men. They jumped their horses across the border fence and made straight for Menma and his sons. They struck them down with their swords. Burning torches were flung into the house. I saw Liamuin, her black hair flashing in the flames. She grabbed a sickle and rushed to defend Menma's wife and little Comnait. She actually wounded the leader of the attack – yes, her former lover with the golden collar.'

'You say that she wounded him?'

'Yes. I saw him drop his sword as blood gushed from his hand. Then two of his men released their arrows and shot her down.'

'And what of Menma's wife and Comnait?' asked Eadulf.

'Both cut down. God forgive me, I turned and fled. I heard one of the warriors riding after me. I was trying to run into the forest to hide, but before I got there I felt a blow on the back of my head and everything went dark. I don't really remember any more. I am told that I was over a week in fever until I came to my senses in the cabin of Flannait and her man. Cadan and his son had found me and taken me there. May they be blessed. They managed to get the local apothecary to come and tend me. It was from Lachtine that I learned that everyone had been killed and the rath burned to a cinder.'

'Lachtine!' exclaimed Eadulf, glancing excitedly at Fidelma.

'He was the apothecary here. He waived his fees for he had also been in love with Liamuin. Of course, he was not alone in that. She was that sort of woman – men fell easily in love with her. God's curse that she fell in love with the Eóghanacht warrior!'

'You said Lachtine *was* the apothecary here?' Fidelma picked up on the tense.

'He left some time later. I do not know where he went.'

'And you say that the attackers were led by this warrior wearing a golden collar, the one whose name you cannot remember?'

'That is correct.'

'And you recognised him – face to face?'

'Not exactly – I was some distance away.'

'How did you recognise him then?'

'He wore a golden collar.'

Fidelma breathed out softly. 'So you recognised him simply because he wore a golden collar at his neck. Was there anything else?'

'I know he had a stag rampant on his shield. It was picked out with jewels.'

Fidelma started, a hand came up to her throat. 'A stag rampant with jewels?' she repeated faintly. 'Do you know what that symbolises?'

'No. I know nothing of shield emblems, nor do I wish to. I only know that he wore the hated symbol of the golden collar.'

Fidelma paused for a moment to collect herself before asking: 'Did Liamuin, so far as you saw, make any form of recognition as she swung at him with the sickle?'

Suanach frowned and shook her head. 'I was too far away to see what was on her face.'

'Why would this attack have taken place? Do you know of any reason why this warrior, having lived with Menma for so long, would suddenly turn and order his men to attack and destroy the rath and its people?' demanded Eadulf.

'It is not for me to give reasons. I only know what happened that day and will forever bear the scar.'

'So, as far as you are concerned, there was no reason?'

'He was an Eóghanacht warrior. Did he need a reason? They spread death and destruction wherever they go.'

Fidelma compressed her lips for a moment. Eadulf had noticed that she had been tense since the woman had mentioned the shield. Now she seemed to allow herself to relax a little.

'Did anyone come to investigate this matter?' she asked.

'None to my knowledge. Oh, I did hear that someone had been asking questions about the attack some time afterwards. But no one knew who it was. I was still confined at Flannait's cabin and in no fit state to answer questions. I am told that after that, there was no sign of the warrior who led the attack or anyone else. Of course, by then a peace was agreed between our people and the Eóghanacht. Much good did it do us.'

To their surprise the old woman suddenly spat at her feet.

'I say this to the Eóghanacht of Cashel – may they melt off the face of this land like snow melts off a hedge when the sun appears. May guinea fowl cry at each new birth from the loins of their women. May the old ones die roaring. May they have only ashes in their hearth through the coldest winter. And may they sustain no comfort in this world nor the other one.'

Fidelma shivered suddenly at the chill intensity of her voice. Eadulf looked angry.

'Christ forgive you, woman. It is against the Faith to make such a curse. It is bad and penance should be made,' he admonished.

'Bad was its inspiration,' muttered the old woman, 'and the bad seed only produces a bad harvest. I have already served my penance and now it is the turn of others to serve their due.'

Fidelma gave a warning glance at Eadulf when he would pursue the moral rebuke. She rose to her feet and reluctantly Eadulf followed.

'I thank you for telling your story, Suanach. It was bad, what happened to you – but you cannot curse a whole people for what one person has done. It is wrong to live with such bitterness in old age.'

'It is that bitterness which sustains me in what is left of my life, *dálaigh*,' she replied emphatically.

Fidelma led the way back through the fern-covered path to the main track.

'Where now, lady?' asked Gormán as they rejoined him.

'I think we will return to Flannait's farm. There are some further questions I would like to ask.'

'The old woman was still very angry,' remarked Eadulf, after they had quickly told Gormán what had happened.

'I cannot believe someone of the Nasc Niadh could do such a thing,' the young warrior said. 'It goes against all our training, all our code of chivalry.'

'Yet it must be true,' replied Fidelma. 'Warriors have sometimes been known to betray their code as well as loyalty to those they claim to hold dear and to serve until death.'

'It is hard to accept that a warrior of the Golden Collar could have done this thing, but if the evidence shows it then we must accept it,' Eadulf said sadly. 'We must then find out who is the man responsible and secure his punishment.'

'If only Suanach had not forgotten his name,' replied Fidelma. 'She is certain she saw him lead the attack, but only because he wore a golden collar.'

'And carried a shield,' added Eadulf. 'Remember? The shield bore the symbol of a bejewelled stag rampant on it.'

Gormán's reaction was a sharp tug on his reins so that his horse came to an abrupt halt. He turned a pale face to them.

'You did not mention this before,' he grated.

Eadulf looked at him in bewilderment. 'Is there something I should know?' he asked uneasily, recalling Fidelma's reaction when Suanach had mentioned it.

'There is only one person who is allowed to carry on his shield a bejewelled stag rampant.' Fidelma's voice was almost inaudible.

'The stag rampant is the symbol of the Eóghanacht. That shield is only carried by the King of Muman,' Gormán added grimly.

They rode on in silence for a while. It was Eadulf who finally broke it.

'If the old woman was the sole survivor of the attack, then she must have told someone who also knew who carried such a shield.'

'Suanach did not know the meaning of the shield,' Fidelma objected.

'But the person she told might have done. That person thought it was your brother, and if we find the person she told, we know the assassin. Don't we need to go back and ask who she has told?'

'You believe that the assassin came to Cashel to claim blood vengeance?' Fidelma was reflective. 'I am not sure. The fact that he cried "Remember Liamuin!" and not "Menma" would indicate that he sought vengeance for her and no other. It is logical, but then why wait all these years?'

'Time? Opportunity? And isn't there a saying that vengeance is a dish best served cold?' offered Gormán.

'This is true,' Fidelma conceded. 'But there are many things that concern me about this explanation. Suanach did not know who this warrior was. She merely described his gold torque and then the emblem on the shield of the attacker. I have never known my brother to lie. He claimed that the name Liamuin meant nothing to him. If he had stayed at Menma's rath for the time it was said, he must have been known. His warriors had just defeated the Uí Fidgente. What was he doing here? How could he have stayed here long enough to have an affair with Liamuin? And then what purpose would have been served by this massacre?'

'All good questions,' Eadulf replied thoughtfully.

'Better if we had answers,' muttered Gormán.

'And that is why we are going back to Flannait's farmstead,' Fidelma said.

'And there is another question to be answered,' added Eadulf. 'Lachtine was the name of the local apothecary who attended Suanach, and he too was in love with Liamuin. He bore the same name as the apothecary at the Ford of Oaks. Is this a coincidence, or was he the same man and is there a connection?'

'I have not forgotten,' Fidelma replied. Then she indicated the farm buildings that spread before them on the lower slope of the hill. 'Let us hope we shall now learn more from Flannait.'

As they approached Flannait's farmstead, a swarthy man, of medium stature, was emerging from the cabin. Ice-blue eyes stared out from a face that wore an expression of curiosity mixed with anxiety. He called something over his shoulder and was joined in a moment by the woman Flannait, who said something hurriedly to him before coming forward to greet them. This time Fidelma slid from her horse.

'Well, *dálaigh*, did you find Suanach?'

'We did,' Fidelma replied. The others dismounted and Eadulf joined her while Gormán secured the horses to a nearby wooden fence. The swarthy man had taken his place beside Flannait.

'This is my man,' muttered the woman by way of introduction.

'My name is Cadan, lady,' he introduced himself. 'How may we serve you?'

Fidelma smiled reassuringly. 'Just a few questions more. I understand that after the attack took place on Menma's rath, you and your son were the first to arrive there and that you managed to rescue Suanach?'

The farmer shifted his weight from one foot to the other and bobbed his head in acknowledgement. His hands were clenching and unclenching at his sides in his nervousness.

'That is right, lady. We brought her back here.'

'I understand. Can you tell me any reason why Menma's rath should have been burned?'

The man raised his shoulder expressively. 'It was an Eóghanacht attack,' he said, as if that should explain everything.

'So I am told. But why was only Menma attacked? It makes no sense.'

'Menma was a *bó-aire*. He had the biggest and richest farmstead,' Flannait said almost defensively. 'I suppose they attacked it for those reasons – or because of Menma's rank.'

'Did they sack it or carry off anything?' demanded Fidelma.

'Nothing was taken as far as we could see,' replied the farmer.

'Then there was no question of it being done for profit or gain,' Eadulf decided. 'It was a case of simple destruction. People killed, the place torched.'

'Who knows the reason? It was done by the man who stayed there. The Eóghanacht warrior.'

'I need to know more about this man,' Fidelma said. 'Can you tell me anything at all about him?'

'It was long ago.'

Fidelma looked round. 'You said your son was with you. Perhaps he might remember something?'

Cadan and Flannait looked uncomfortable.

'Maolán? He is no longer with us, lady,' Cadan said.

'What do you mean?'

'Soon after the attack he left us to join the religious. He was very . . .' the man chose his words carefully, 'very sweet on the woman who was staying with Menma.'

'Liamuin?'

'That was her name. He took her death very badly.'

'But she was in love with the warrior who stayed with them?'

'So she was. But Maolán had his hopes. So did others, like our local apothecary, Lachtine. He also left us not long after. Liamuin was an attractive woman and she had plenty of admirers. We tried to persuade our son not to leave us. We have no other children. Who will look after us when the winter of our days comes upon us, which must surely be soon?'

'Did he know that it was the warrior she apparently had affection for, the one who carried out the attack?' asked Eadulf.

'He did. For he left after Suanach had recovered and told her story.'

'Where did he go?'

'Alas, we don't know. Maolán was talented and set out to make his way in the world. He had an eye, that boy.'

'An eye?' asked Eadulf curiously, not understanding the expression.

'He was a good copyist. He went off to do that as a means of earning his living.'

'So is there nothing you can tell me that would help identify this warrior?' Fidelma asked in frustration, returning to the main question. She was looking intently at Cadan as she spoke and he tugged at his lower lip with one hand under her scrutiny.

'What sort of things?' he countered. 'I only saw him once or twice from a distance. All I know is that he wore the Eóganacht golden collar.'

'Was he old or young? Fair or dark? That sort of thing,' intervened Eadulf.

'He was not a boy, he was a young man. That is all I recall.'

'Surely you could tell whether he was fair or dark.'

'Fair.'

'Not red-haired,' Fidelma suddenly said. 'Say red hair like mine?'

The farmer looked at her red tresses and then shook his head. There seemed an easing of tension in Fidelma's body.

'Presumably this warrior with fair hair carried a shield? A warrior has on his shield his *suaicheantas*, his emblem, by which his friends and his enemies alike would know him,' Eadulf said.

Cadan's brows drew together in concentration as he tried to remember. 'His shield was plain. There was no motif upon it except . . .' He paused. 'No, the shield was coloured red with a single, narrow blue strip across it.'

Fidelma glanced at Gormán, who shook his head.

She knew that the warriors of the Golden Collar who formed the *Lucht-tíghe*, the house company, were the chosen élite among the bodyguards of the King. But each had his own individual emblem or insignia. These men were classed as the *ridire* or champions. Beyond them the King could call on larger forces in times of danger, but he usually kept one *Catha* or battalion, of 3,000 warriors, permanently on call throughout the kingdom. These were divided into various units: each unit was marked by a shield emblem.

'Is there no way of identifying which unit held such an emblem?' asked Fidelma, knowing vaguely that the position of the stripe on the shield had some significance. 'After all, the man wore a golden collar as well.'

Gormán took out his sword and traced the outline of a shield on the wet soil.

'Now, you say the narrow blue strip was placed this way?' He drew the line.

Cadan the farmer looked at it quizzically and shook his head.

'No, the other way – horizontally, as if dividing it in half.'

'I think it was one of the units that fought at Cnoc Áine and belonged to the *amuis* command.' The *amuis* were companies raised in times of conflict, often hired from territories outside the immediate clanland of the King.

Fidelma sighed and shook her head.

'Well, it might help us a little.' She turned back to the puzzled farmer and his wife. 'As far as you were aware, was there anyone else in the vicinity of Menma's rath when it was attacked?'

'As soon as I saw smoke rising, my son and I went running across the hill,' the man replied. 'It took us a while to get there as we have no horses. When we reached the rath, there was no one else there.'

'What of other neighbouring farmsteads? As I approached these hills I thought I saw several rath-like buildings spaced along them.'

'We were the nearest. After those times, some of the farms fell into disuse.'

'Did Menma answer Prince Eoganán's call to arms?' Eadulf suddenly asked.

'He did not agree with the cause,' replied the farmer with a shrug.

'So what you are saying is that no one saw the rath on fire except yourself?'

'So far as I know.'

'Who is the lord of this territory?' asked Gormán. 'Rather, who was lord in Menma's time?'

Cadan looked quizzically at him. 'You mean who was Menma's lord?'

'Was there anyone who could tell us something about him? I mean, someone more local than the Prince at Dún Eochair-Mháigh.'

'These are the borderlands, the edge of the lands controlled by the Múscraige Luachra. Beyond the hills behind us are the mountains of the Luachra. Although we are of the Uí Fidgente here, Fidaig of the Luachra claims tribute from us.'

'That is correct, lady,' the farmer's wife nodded. 'Once a year, after harvest, Fidaig sends his warriors to collect tribute from us. We are Uí Fidgente but some of those who dwell here among us are Luachra.'

'I thought his territory was further south in the mountains?' Fidelma said.

'It is not far enough away,' Flannait remarked bitterly.

'So, is he not a good lord?'

Flannait seemed to be suppressing a sour remark but Cadan said quickly: 'I have known worse.'

'How did he stand in the rebellion?' asked Gormán.

'Rebellion?' queried the farmer uncertainly.

'The war against Cashel,' Fidelma said, with a frown at Gormán for giving away their allegiances.

'Oh, Fidaig likes to see which way the wind is blowing before he commits himself.'

'He did not support the Uí Fidgente at Cnoc Áine?'

'He did not, even though he owed allegiance to Prince Eoganán. His excuse was that his warriors were needed to guard the southern borders against the Eóganacht Locha Lein and the Eóganacht Glendamnach. But it was at Cnoc Áine that the Eóganacht attacked.'

'So Fidaig remained neutral in the war?'

'Neutral while the wind blew against him,' muttered Flannait. 'He abandoned the Uí Fidgente.'

'How did Menma stand in this conflict?'

'Menma was first and foremost a farmer and had little time for the politics of ambitious princes. He and his sons believed their first duty was to the land. Those days were bad when death and disaster ravaged this land.'

'But peace is restored and the kingdom is one,' pointed out Eadulf.

'Blood never wiped out blood,' the farmer commented dourly. 'The Uí Fidgente will never be at peace with Cashel.'

'One more question,' said Fidelma, ignoring the comment. 'You had an apothecary here who helped nurse Suanach back to health. His name was Lachtine.'

The farmer nodded.

'I am told that he too was in love with Liamuin.'

The farmer grimaced. 'That he was. Just like my son, Maolán. Soon after the attack, he left here. I heard he became the apothecary in a town further downriver – ah, yes, a place called the Ford of the Oaks.'

They had taken their leave of Cadan and Flannait and ridden back down the hill towards the plains.

'Where to now, lady?' enquired Gormán.

'There is nothing left but to return to Cashel. We need to speak to Ordan again, but above all, we must find out something about the warriors who served in the *amuis* company at that time.'

'There are many questions to be answered,' Eadulf said, 'but are you sure that all the answers lie back in Cashel?'

They had barely reached the bottom of the hill and started along the track in the direction of the eastern hills when a whistling sound caught their ears, followed by a sudden thud. An arrow transfixed itself to a tree at the side of the track. Gormán was attempting to pull free his sword as the silence was abruptly pierced by shouting and the thunder of hooves.

A band of half-a-dozen horsemen came racing towards them brandishing weapons. It was obvious they were outnumbered, and any attempt to fight would end one way only. Fidelma had already seen the flash of weapons, and one of the riders had halted a little way and was stringing an arrow to his bow. The riders looked a motley bunch, but clearly had some professional training. They had an assortment of weapons, and each man was capable of using them.

For a moment, Fidelma's blood ran cold. She thought the leader was Adamrae. Then a closer examination revealed that although he bore certain facial similarities, he was not Adamrae. Now he nudged his horse forward and scrutinised them carefully.

'A warrior, a lady and a monk.' He paused and grinned wickedly. 'Well met. Undoubtedly you are Fidelma of Cashel?'

Fidelma looked at him with disfavour. 'Well met? That arrow could have killed or wounded one of us,' she said coldly.

'That would have been the intention, unless you halted and surrendered.'

'Why?'

'We have heard of you. Visitors from Cashel, I believe, and intent on asking questions.' The young leader was still smiling.

'It is my right to do so as a *dálaigh*.'

'My father might question that right,' he replied. 'You will come with us now. It is only a short ride from here, lady. But first your escort must hand over his weapons.'

Gormán glanced round at the well-armed men surrounding him and gave a philosophical shrug. Then he took out his sword and handed it to the man nearest him.

'To whom have we surrendered – and why?' Fidelma demanded.

'The why, I shall leave for my lord to explain. The who? You have surrendered to Artgal, son of Fidaig of the Luachra. It is Fidaig who asks for your company. So it is to him that I shall now escort you.'

CHAPTER FIFTEEN

୧୬

Their escort set off at a brisk trot along the wide track towards the south-western mountains. But dusk was descending before they reached the ford of a broad river, beyond which dark shadows of the mountains began to rise sharply.

'That's the territory of the Luachra,' Fidelma muttered for Eadulf's benefit.

'So this is Sliabh Luachra?'

'The whole mountain range is known by that name,' she confirmed. 'Once it was a vast, uninhabited marsh area guarded by the surrounding mountains and so inhospitable that little could be farmed there. Sliabh Luachra is not a single mountain but several, with seven glens between them. The place is filled with peat bogs – and woe betide if you fall into one of them, for you will never get out.'

The leader of their escort, without checking the forward momentum of his horse, turned in his saddle and pointed to where a group of lights flickered in the darkness on the far bank of the river.

'This is the ford of the Ealla. My father, Fidaig, is encamped on the far side.'

A moment later they were splashing through a shallow ford and entering an encampment, where fires were burning and lanterns were lit. It was not a large encampment but enough, so Fidelma estimated, to contain one hundred warriors. Nor was it a permanent encampment. Fidelma knew that even when warriors halted for one night, certain officers were in charge as to the placing of tents, bathing, cooking and rest places. Everything was planned in detail to fortify it and set up sentinels.

A concentration of several lanterns showed where the *pupall* or the pavilion of the chieftain was. A short distance from this, their escort halted them and Artgal indicated that they should dismount. Then Fidelma and Eadulf were separated from Gormán, who was led away, while they were instructed to follow the young man to the main tent, where he ushered them inside.

Fidaig, lord of the Luachra, protector of the Mountain of Rushes and chieftain of the Seven Glens of Sliabh Luachra, was not as Eadulf had envisaged he would be. In fact, Eadulf realised that the man had been a guest at their wedding in Cashel and that they had briefly met before. He was not a tall, imposing figure, but elderly, with a shock of white hair and an intelligent but heavily lined face of the sort that comes with age and experience. He looked more like a learned elder of his clan than a chieftain used to handling weapons in defence of his people. His eyes were dark, almost pupil-less, his mouth thin. He gave the impression of frailty, but there was something in his features that made up in shrewd-ness and ingenuity what he lacked in physical strength. That he had survived so long as leader of the Luachra was evidence enough of his astute qualities.

Fidaig was standing ready to greet them when they entered. There was the trace of a smile on his features as he looked from one to another.

'Welcome to my humble camp. I would have made you more comfortable at my fortress up in the mountains, but you find me travelling and, alas, the accommodation I have to offer is but a poor warrior's makeshift tent.'

'Then perhaps my companions and I should have been allowed a choice in the matter?' Fidelma's voice was icy.

Fidaig raised his eyebrows in mock surprise. 'You were given no choice? Ah, I must reprimand my son, Artgal. His task was merely to invite you to be my guests. I had heard that you and your companions were travelling in my territory, and I was sure that you would come to pay your respects to me in accordance with custom. Concerned that you might not know where I was encamped, not being at my fortress, I sent my son and his men to find you and assist you to meet me here.'

His tone betrayed none of the sarcasm that his words implied. His son, Artgal, took a stand behind his father's chair, apparently unconcerned at the rebuke. Fidaig clapped his hands for his attendants and ordered chairs to be brought forward for them all to be seated.

'Let us take some drink and talk of what brings you here.' Fidaig sank into a high-backed chair and smiled at each of them in turn as they reluctantly took the seats offered to them. 'I have ordered sleeping accommodation to be set up for you and there will be feasting later tonight. Alas, the washing facilities are not all they should be, but as you will have noticed, this is a marching camp and so we camp by the river.'

A young male attendant appeared and poured beakers of *corma* for them before he withdrew to the side of the tent ready for the next summons.

Fidelma regarded Fidaig unsmilingly. 'A marching camp?' she repeated. 'And where do you march *to*, Fidaig of the Luachra?'

Fidaig chuckled. 'It seems that each year, a number of those who owe me tribute as their lord get forgetful as to the time that the tribute falls due. Therefore, I have to disrupt my cosy existence at my winter fortress to ride forth and remind them. Forgetfulness is especially prevalent on the borders of my territory. In fact, in the very area that my men found you.'

'How did you know that we were there?' asked Eadulf, unable to restrain himself.

'It was not hard, my Saxon friend. Not hard at all. A chieftain without knowledge of what is happening in his own territory is a poor fellow indeed.'

Fidelma pursed her lips thoughtfully for a moment. 'So, you knew that we had gone to the rath of Menma?'

This drew a soft breath from Fidaig. 'Menma? He is long dead.'

'Indeed, he is. His family are dead with him. I presume that you knew him?'

Fidaig inclined his head slightly. 'Yes. At least he was never late with his tribute. The area of which he was *bó-aire* has become less forthcoming in that regard of late. I must encourage his replacement with someone who will help the farmers remember the time when their tribute is due.'

'You are familiar with what happened to him? With Menma, I mean.'

Fidaig's eyes widened slightly. 'Is that why you are in my territory? You want to find out who destroyed his rath?'

'That is why we were there,' she replied.

Fidaig looked at her slyly. 'I would have thought the answer was more easily obtainable at Cashel.'

'Meaning?'

'The story, as I recall, went that it was a warrior of your brother's own bodyguard that did the deed.'

'And you are satisfied with that explanation?'

'I am not particularly concerned. It was a long time ago. That war is over and there has been peace ever since.'

'For some among the Uí Fidgente, the old wounds do not heal.'

The chieftain sniffed. 'We are of the Luachra. The Uí Fidgente have their own problems.'

'And the Luachra do not?' snapped Eadulf.

'That remark is somewhat oblique. I have no understanding of it.'

'Before we explain, let me return to Menma. Did you know him?' asked Fidelma.

'I met him only on the occasions when he brought me the tribute of his people. We met annually here by the River Ealla.'

'He was of the Uí Fidgente.'

'Borders are not stone walls that cannot be passed through. The Luachra are to be found among the Uí Fidgente and Uí Fidgente are found among the Luachra. That is not to be wondered at. The line of those hills mark the northern reaches of my territory.'

'During the war between the Uí Fidgente and Cashel, where did Menma's loyalties lie?'

Fidaig sat back and thought for a moment. 'A good question. I did, in fact, once ask him.'

'And what was his reply?'

'He told me that Muman was a kingdom, and that the King of Muman ruled it. While others ruled territories and chieftains ruled clans, yet it was the King of Muman who ruled the entire kingdom. Therefore, unless the King was unjust, to raise one's sword against him was treason.'

'So he was loyal to Cashel and there would be no reason why a Cashel warrior should attack his rath,' Fidelma pointed out.

Fidaig leaned back and shook his head. 'Are you trying to tell me that Cashel was not responsible for the destruction of Menma's rath? Well, it's little enough to do with me. I did not support the Uí Fidgente nor did I side with the Eóghanacht. Sliabh Luachra is my domain. I do not care much about outside squabbles so long as I am left alone.'

'I have heard that not all Luachra agreed: some supported Eoganán of the Uí Fidgente in his war against my brother.'

Fidaig grimaced dismissively. 'I am the only lord of Luachra and it is my voice that matters. Eoganán was a young fool. Anyway, Eoganán or Colgú – I would wind up having to pay tribute to one or the other so why should I bother which one?'

'I presume that you have heard of the attempt on my brother's life?' she asked abruptly, her eyes on him.

To her surprise, he smiled. 'Nothing travels faster than bad news, lady. But in this case, I hear that the news is good.'

Fidelma looked uncertain. 'I don't understand?'

'A rider on his way to my good neighbour and enemy, Congal, lord of the Eóganacht of Locha Léin, was persuaded to break his journey with us. He left Cashel two days ago with news that your brother, the King, is no longer awaiting Donn to transport him to the Otherworld. He is well on his way to recovering.'

Eadulf recalled that Donn was the dark Lord of Death, who collected souls and took them to the House of Donn, said to be an island to the south-west. There the souls were judged before they were allowed to proceed to the Otherworld.

Fidelma sat back, trying to control the surge of emotion that went through her. She suddenly felt weak.

'Is it true?' she whispered.

'Oh, true enough, lady,' Fidaig assured her. 'Your brother has survived his wound and is recovering.'

'Thanks be to God,' Eadulf muttered automatically.

Fidaig glanced at him and chuckled. 'Thanks be to the unskilled hand of the man who struck the blow, my friend.'

'And what of the messenger from Cashel?' Eadulf asked.

'Have no fear. Having told us his news, we allowed him to ride on and inform Congal, who I think was already calling himself King of Iarmuman, west Muman. He's a man to watch, is Congal, for didn't his grandfather once claim the kingship at Cashel? As I recall, he lasted no more than a few months, having killed your father's own father. You talk of the Uí Fidgente plots, lady, but I would seek out the whisperers among your own family.'

Fidelma was uncomfortable because Fidaig had pricked the weakest spot of her family. She was suddenly thinking about what Cúana had implied about rivalry in her family. It was true the Eóganacht of Cashel were the senior line descended from Eóghan Mór but, at times, other branches of the family, from Locha Léin to Raithlin, from Áine to Chliach and Glendamnach, had made successful claims for the kingship. Wasn't her brother's own heir apparent, Finguine, of the Eóghanacht Áine branch? She shook her head to drive the thoughts away and saw Fidaig smiling at her as if he knew what was passing through her mind.

'The Kings of Cashel can only succeed through law, Fidaig,' she snapped, bringing herself back to the present. 'No one who has tried to seize power has prospered. Not even Aed Brennán of Locha Léin, the King that you referred to just now. As you say, he lasted barely a few months before the rightful choice of the *derbfine* overthrew him.'

Fidaig was not put out. Instead he asked, 'What has Menma's death to do with the attack on your brother?'

'Perhaps nothing; perhaps much,' replied Fidelma promptly.

'Then I have no understanding of this.'

Fidelma decided to change the direction of her questions. 'I am told that some years ago you made a transaction with a man called Escmug.'

A frown crossed Fidaig's features. 'I can't recall the name.'

'Perhaps the name Aibell will prompt your memory.'

Artgal, who had remained standing behind his father's chair, bent forward.

'Aibell, Father. She is the *éludach*.'

Eadulf took a moment to identify the word, which meant a servant who had absconded. He was feeling uneasy that Fidelma had suddenly raised the subject.

The lord of the Luachra had cast a glance of disapproval at his son for admitting that Aibell was known to him. Then he shrugged. 'The girl absconded from my fortress over a week ago. As an *éludach*, she can be offered no legal protection, not even by someone of high rank such as yourself. Where is she?'

'She is safe enough, Fidaig. And will remain so.'

'She was legally exchanged under the law of the *Gúbretha Caratniad*,' protested Fidaig.

'Her father sold her to you illegally,' corrected Fidelma. 'The *Gúbretha* mentions that some parents have been known to sell their children into bondage, mostly to foreigners, and actually condemns the practice. It is as evil for those who buy as it is evil for those who sell. In this case, it is criminal, for the girl was of the age of choice. She was fourteen years old when she was sold to you, and therefore a free woman, not bound to her father nor bound to you. You kept her in bondage for four years without legal cause.'

'And you can prove it?' There was a slight sneer in Fidaig's voice.

'Do you doubt it?' replied Fidelma coolly.

Fidaig stared at her for a moment and then forced a smile. 'We should not be quarrelling over a bondservant.'

'I am not quarrelling,' corrected Fidelma. 'Certainly I am not quarrelling over a bondservant but a freeborn girl whom you kept in your household against her will. There are legal consequences.'

'By the old gods!' Fidaig exploded in temper. 'I doubt whether the Morrígú possessed such an uncompromising attitude as you, Fidelma of Cashel.'

'How much did you give Escmug for the girl?' Fidelma demanded, ignoring his anger.

Fidaig struggled visibly with his temper, but then he seemed to relax. 'It is some time ago. I believe I gave him four *screpalls*, the honour price of the girl after he tried to claim a higher price.'

'Ah!' Fidelma could not help an ejaculation of triumph. 'You have just proved that you knew she had reached her legal maturity. You have already quoted the *Gúbretha Caratniad* at me, so you must know the law. Had she been a minor, you would have had to offer far more than that, for as you know, until the age of fourteen years her honour price would be half that of her father. Escmug must have told you her proper age and held out for her full honour price.'

Fidaig had lost his smile. 'You are a clever woman, Fidelma of Cashel. You are also a woman of courage to come into my camp and accuse me . . .'

'I am an advocate of the law, Fidaig. That is all. And you invited me into your camp and offered my companions and myself hospitality. You know the consequence if, having done so, something untoward happens to us. You would find the Eóghanacht might exact compensation that you would not be happy to pay.'

Fidaig stared at her with open mouth. Eadulf held his breath, certain that Fidelma had gone too far in confronting the lord of Luachra. Moments of silence passed and then Fidaig exhaled slowly. There was a reluctant admiration in his voice as he told her, 'Your wit is as sharp as your tongue, lady.'

Fidelma seemed unperturbed. 'You have held a girl in bondage from the age of maturity until she was eighteen years. I would judge that compensation to be four *screpalls* per year. Sixteen *screpalls* . . . Ten *screpalls* to the *séd*.'

'Ridiculous!'

'Your own honour worth is seven *cumal*, twenty-one milch cows. Since you have now been dishonoured by knowingly and flagrantly breaking the law, then your fine will be those seven cumals that I have indicated. We will round up the fine, compensation to the value of twenty-three milch cows.'

Fidaig sat staring at her in disbelief. Behind him Artgal was fingering his sword nervously, awaiting his father's next order.

'Tell me, Fidelma of Cashel,' Fidaig's voice was cold. 'Tell me, do you not fear that you are in the territory of the Luachra and that Cashel is far away?'

'Cashel is indeed a few days' ride from here,' Fidelma replied. 'But we are not speaking of Cashel. We are speaking of the Law of the Fenéchus whose writ runs everywhere in the Five Kingdoms and is respected from the High King down to the lowest *daer-fuidir*, or unfree servant. While I am an advocate of that law and offer just judgements, then what have I to fear – any more than you would fear the pronouncement of the *glam dicín*, the solemn curse which is the appropriate action that a Brehon or other member of the law courts would bring against the person who disobeys the law? Once pronounced, then it would be the duty of all, even the High King himself, to punish the wrongdoer.'

There was a strange silence as two wills clashed on some invisible plane. Speculative dark eyes challenged fiery green ones and, in the end, Fidaig blinked. He blinked for a second and then his face dissolved into a mask of mirth and he was guffawing with laughter. He banged his fist on the arm of his chair as he laughed and then motioned the attendant to refill the glasses.

'By the gods of our ancestors, Fidelma of Cashel, I admire your courage, indeed I do. Very well, twenty-three milch cows it is and we will speak no more of this matter.'

To Eadulf's horror, she was shaking her head. 'But speak some more, we will,' she said. 'I will give you a chance to earn back your fine, so that all you will have to pay me is two extra *séds*.'

Fidaig looked surprised. 'What game is this, lady? What is it that you now seek?'

'It is no game. I am utterly serious. Cooperation and information is what I seek.'

Fidaig shrugged. 'Ask away and, if it is in my knowledge to give you the information, you shall have it.'

'Do you know a merchant from Cashel named Ordan?'

'I have heard of him,' Fidaig nodded. 'He is often known to be in my territory, though he never trades with me.'

'What does he trade in?'

'So far as I know, anything he can get his hands on. Why are you interested in this merchant?'

'Your son seems to have a special interest in him.'

'My son? Which of my sons?'

'Gláed.'

A sad expression crossed Fidaig's features. 'Gláed the Howler, Lord of

Barr an Bheithe, the Head of the Birch Forest. Alas, he is my youngest son. His mother died, giving him life. For a while it seemed he would not survive, but he fought – yelling in his crib and hence he earned his name. Anyway, survive he did.'

'There is a sadness in your voice, Fidaig,' observed Fidelma.

'Sadness because he has not been a dutiful son, like Artgal here, who is my heir apparent. Gláed goes his own way and pays me scant courtesy. When he was young he went to train as a Brehon but left barely reaching the level of *freisneidhed*. After that he was impossible to advise. Even during the Uí Fidgente war with Cashel, when I tried to keep my people out of it, he took some warriors and went to answer Eoganán's call. The Uí Fidgente promised to make him lord of some territories they expected to conquer. He fought at Cnoc Áine and managed to survive.

'Artgal has a wiser head and that is why he is my heir apparent. Gláed treads his own path. I found he has even become fanatical about these new rules of the Faith coming from Rome because he finds in them an excuse to mete out physical punishments on his people which I find it hard to contradict. He espouses something called the Penitentials and does not even celebrate the Pasch at the same time that we do. I have long since given up trying to influence him.'

'What was the place you mentioned, the one that he is lord of?'

'Barr an Bheithe, the Head of the Birch Forest? It is further west in the hills, where the An Abhainn Mór – the Great Black Water – rises. And you say he has dealings with this Cashel merchant, Ordan? Why is that of concern to you?'

'It intrigues me, that is all. I presume there are mines around Barr an Bheithe?'

'None that I know of.' Fidaig looked puzzled. 'Why do you say that?'

'Ordan trades in metals and stones. It seems that he and your son Gláed meet secretly, with Gláed disguised in religious robes and calling himself Brother Adamrae.'

Fidaig was staring at her in astonishment. 'I have told you that he has become something of a religious fanatic. However, I know nothing of this trade. What is the purpose – do you know?'

'I was hoping to find out.'

'Then perhaps it is time that I paid my son a visit.'

'Would Gláed continue his allegiance with any dissident Uí Fidgente after all these passing years?'

'I know he has been restless and often rides forth with his small band of cronies. The times I have seen him since Cnoc Áine I can count on the fingers of one hand.'

'So you would have no idea why Gláed would disguise himself as a religious and be seen at the Ford of the Oaks on the River Mháigh and have to kill to keep his identity a secret?'

There was no disguising the painful look of surprise on the face of the Lord of Luachra.

'You had best tell me the entire story, lady,' he said quietly.

Fidelma told him as simply as possible what had happened at the Ford of the Oaks, mentioning how she had later identified Adamrae as Gláed at Marban's mill.

Fidaig was left silent; his bewilderment obvious. 'I have no understanding of these matters,' he confessed. 'But I swear that I shall have answers. Tomorrow I shall take my men across the hills to Barr an Bheithe and seek those answers from my son.'

Fidelma hesitated for a moment and then said: 'Perhaps we should come with you.'

Fidaig seemed to shake himself, as a dog might shake off water after an immersing. 'Very well. Then tonight, you shall both be my guests at the feasting and entertainment. Tomorrow we will set off to Barr an Bheithe and ask for an account from Gláed. He will be called to account for the death of the apothecary and for his attack on you.'

* * *

Later, having ensured that Gormán was informed of the situation and was comfortable, Fidelma and Eadulf were escorted to a small tent and provided with water to wash themselves and prepare for the evening feasting.

Eadulf was direct. 'Do you trust him?'

'Fidaig is a wolf but in wolf's clothing. He does not hide his nature and so we can trust one thing – that he can be treacherous,' Fidelma replied.

Eadulf commented, 'That is a curious way of expressing trust.'

'He tries to make his son Gláed appear like a disobedient child,' Fidelma replied, 'but I think he suspects there is something deeper behind this.'

'Don't you feel we shall be in danger by going to Barr an Bheithe and confronting Gláed or Adamrae, whatever he is called?'

'One cannot eat an egg without taking off the shell,' she replied enigmatically. 'So we are at the mercy of fate.'

Eadulf stared at her for a moment. 'I thought you believed in the teachings of Pelagius, that we are the masters of our own destiny, and that you did not believe in fate.'

'Now is not the best time for a discourse on theology, Eadulf,' she admonished. 'However, when you cast a stone into a pond, the ripples are inevitable. It is important how you deal with the ripples.'

'Which means putting ourselves in harm's way?'

'We were in harm's way the moment that we entered the country of the Uí Fidgente.'

'Our main task was to find out who the assassin really was and why he attempted to kill your brother.'

'I have not forgotten that,' Fidelma said irritably.

'Then surely we should be about that task, not chasing after this Adamrae or Gláed!'

'Eadulf.' Her voice was patient, 'I am sure that I don't have to point out the connections. There is a link between all these matters.'

'Do you never allow for mere coincidence?' he countered. 'This matter of Gláed and what he did at the Ford of the Oaks may have nothing to do with what happened at the rath of Menma or, indeed, at Cashel. We are merely wasting our time on it. Let Fidaig discipline his own son, if discipline is needed.'

Fidelma sat back on the rushes and soft branches that had been provided for a bed.

'Tell me how you interpret the events of the attack on my brother.'

'Easy enough. There was a warrior who seems to have been a member of your brother's bodyguard. After the defeat of the Uí Fidgente at Cnoc Áine, he was sent into this country, as were many others, to keep the peace until the Uí Fidgente concluded the treaty with your brother. He stayed at the rath of Menma. For some reason he turned on his host and slaughtered him and his family. That included this woman, Liamuin.

'Suanach had seen this warrior with a shield which bore your brother's emblem on it. She did not know what it was but she described it well enough for it to be recognised. She certainly told someone else who recognised it. That someone knew or was very close to Liamuin. We are told that Liamuin was someone with whom men easily fell in love. That person came to Cashel and tried to kill your brother in revenge . . . seeking an atonement of blood.'

'And what of the questions that arise?' Fidelma asked with an indulgent smile.

'Such as?'

'Why would this lovesick fury wait four years to seek vengeance? Why take the name of Liamuin's own brother, an apothecary killed on the slopes of the Hill of Áine? Why did he come to Cashel on the very night that Liamuin's own daughter came there? Why did they go to the very same woodman's hut, but at differing times? And what was Ordan's role in all of this, having come from this very area . . . And from there we get into his connections with Gláed, who called himself Adamrae.' She threw up her hands in a dramatic gesture. 'Oh Eadulf, Eadulf! Don't you see that this is not like following a single strand of string until we reach the end? It is like . . . like . . .'

She seemed on the point of exasperation and then Eadulf shrugged.

'I know there are complications,' he said. 'It is just that I feel we are adding unnecessary ones.'

'A search for the truth is like following a river. It does not always run straight,' Fidelma replied. 'It twists, turns and has many little tributaries. Show me a line that you think is truly straight and I shall show you the kinks in it.'

'Even if we confront this Gláed, do you think that the truth will be revealed?' asked Eadulf. 'Remember, he tried to kill you once.'

'Trying to kill someone in the dark and in secret is not the same as doing so in the open in front of his father.'

'His father . . . whom we do not trust?'

'My mind is made up,' she declared firmly.

Eadulf had seen Fidelma in such obstinate moods before and he knew that no powers of persuasion could convince her that she was wrong.

At that moment the sounds of music came to their ears.

'It seems Fidaig's feasting has started,' Fidelma said. 'We had best go to join it.'

They left the tent and made their way to a square which had been laid out before the *pupall* of the chieftain. Branches, rushes and ferns, and bundles of sedge grass had been laid out in order to lessen the amount of mud that would be churned up on the ground where the feasting was to be. In the centre, a great fire had been lit and round this were makeshift tables and log benches that had been erected for those who would sit down to the feast.

To one side were a group of musicians with their instruments – those playing the pipes, trumpet players with wide-mouthed horns, and even chain men, who produced music from chains and bells by shaking them in rhythms, along with bone men who beat out their music.

'Fidaig provides well for his warriors when they travel,' Eadulf observed, glancing around.

Once again Fidelma was reminded that this was only a 'marching camp' but containing a hundred warriors and their supporting attendants, travelling from place to place to collect tribute for the Lord of the Luachra. It was an entirely male gathering that could, if need be, have been turned into an aggressive war party. But the men were well prepared with entertainment and food. And it was only by the fires and lanterns that now lit up the encampment that she saw the heavy wagons drawn up around it. These were the wagons in which the tribute was gathered and, at the same time, they served as a form of protective barrier after the camp was set up.

In the flickering light they met Gormán, who was standing surveying the construction of the camp.

'The person who planned this encampment has a good eye,' he greeted Fidelma. 'All arranged in an orderly fashion . . . but I am concerned, lady.'

'Concerned?'

'Look at the area before the chieftain's tent. It is an oblong space, bounded by poles – and on each pole is a lantern, giving light onto the area. I saw the like of this when I was training as a warrior at the school of the Glendamnach – and I am wondering what sort of entertainment is planned.'

Fidelma was considering the matter when Fidaig emerged from his tent and greeted them.

'Come, lady, you and your companions must sit by me,' he instructed, before turning back to those gathering round. A silence fell on the camp, even before he held up his hand.

'Tonight, my friends, is a night to feast – for this is the last day of gathering in the tribute. We should all be able to drink our fill and look forward to returning to our beds and our women.'

'Whose women?' called out a bawdy voice, which sparked laughter among the warriors.

'A good question,' responded Fidaig. There was an expectant silence. Fidaig waved a hand towards Fidelma. 'Tonight we are honoured with the presence of the lady Fidelma, sister to King Colgú in Cashel, her husband Eadulf and one of her brother's bodyguards, a warrior of the Golden Collar.'

A ripple of interest went through the assembly. Eadulf and Gormán exchanged an anxious look.

'The lady Fidelma is a *dálaigh*, an advocate of our ancient law,' Fidaig went on. 'It is apposite that she should be with us tonight, for this evening we have to resort to an ancient ordeal to determine a dispute. It is the *fír cómlainn* – the truth of combat.'

Eadulf noticed that Fidelma had gone very pale. By his side Gormán leaned towards him. He was also looking nervous, his hand resting tensely on the hilt of his sword. 'That means a single combat to the death,' he whispered. 'I thought it was illegal.'

Fidaig overheard and turned to Fidelma. 'Is single combat illegal, lady?'

Fidelma stirred uneasily. 'It is not illegal. No Brehon council had felt it necessary to proscribe it as it is so ancient that it is almost irrelevant. The idea of quarrels being agreed by the sword is thought to be uncivilised when our law provides for arbitration.'

'Then you are in an uncivilised land, lady,' grinned Fidaig. 'I thought the law provided for the settlement of dispute by single combat.'

'So it does,' admitted Fidelma. 'However, there are stringent rules laid down for deciding whether the cause itself is legal. Who has issued the challenge?'

Fidaig raised his hand and beckoned. A tall warrior stepped forward. He was fully armed and clad with fighting helmet and shield. To the other side emerged Artgal, Fidaig's own son, who was also fully armed.

'Loeg issued the challenge and Artgal has accepted it.'

'And what is the dispute?'

Fidaig chuckled almost lewdly. 'Over a woman, what else? The wife of Loeg is now the mistress of Artgal.'

Fidelma pursed her lips in disapproval. 'Surely the law is sufficient to deal with this matter? We have enough grounds for separation and divorce in our laws.'

'It may be so, lady, but the Luachra prefer the challenge to combat when there is a dispute over their women.'

Fidelma regarded the would-be combatants with disapproval. 'It is said that there are three kinds of men who fail to understand women: young men, old men and middle-aged men.'

Fidaig laughed. 'That may be so as well – but the challenge remains. Will you be the judge of it?'

Fidelma realised that the wily lord of the Luachra had placed her in this position in order to test her determination and courage. He was trying to force her into an arbitrary decision. Here, in this time and this place, it was impossible to make a judgement without precedent. She had to follow the only path left open.

'The challenge has been issued, you say? And has been accepted?'

'It has.'

'Have both men offered to submit to law before proclaiming the combat?'

'Both men have agreed that they felt no recourse to deciding the matter than by combat until death.'

Fidelma was silent for a moment or two, trying to think of a means to stop the fight. But the existing legal criteria had been fulfilled. Both men, it seemed, were determined to pursue the matter.

'Very well. Let them step forward.' When the combatants did so, Fidelma addressed each of them in turn. 'There is no other way you will resolve this?'

The warrior Loeg said, 'There is no way but death!' and Artgal was smiling as he agreed. 'Loeg challenged me this morning and I accepted. Now it shall be resolved.'

Fidelma was about to confirm the proceedings when she paused. 'When did you say that the challenge was issued?'

'This morning. We agreed,' replied Artgal in a confident tone.

'They have witnesses,' Fidaig said quickly, seeing a smile on her lips. 'I recalled the law and there stand the witnesses on each side. Each combatant has sworn to abide by the result of the fight.'

'But the fight will *not* take place, for it is illegal,' Fidelma stated firmly.

Fidaig gazed at her in astonishment. 'What squeamish judgement is this, lady?' he sneered. 'I have ensured that everything is done within the law, as you have heard.'

'All except one thing, Fidaig. You should know that according to the *Senchus Mór*, five full days must elapse between the challenge and the duel.'

Fidaig clenched a fist in annoyance. 'Where does it say this?' he demanded. 'This is not right.'

'There is a story of two famous champions – Conall Cernach and Laegaire,' explained Fidelma. 'They quarrelled and challenged each other to a single combat in legal form. The Chief Brehon Sencha decreed that five days should elapse for them to cool their tempers before they fought. Thus all other combats since then can only be held five days after the formal challenge is made.'

Fidaig struggled to find an answer and could not. Fidelma ignored him and dismissed the combatants and their companions. 'At least it gives them five more days to think it over,' she explained quietly to Eadulf.

Even as they were finally relaxing and someone had signalled for the music to restart, there came the sound of a warning horn piercing the darkness close by with three short blasts. Gormán looked round, wondering what new threat was emerging.

'Don't be alarmed,' Fidaig called immediately. 'It is a signal from one of our sentinels.' Then he frowned. 'Curious. We expect no other guests.'

He was looking towards the edge of the camp where the bulky shape of a wagon had emerged, having just crossed the river. It was being escorted by a couple of warriors.

'I thought all my wagons had been safely gathered in for the night.' Fidaig was surprised by the new arrival. 'I do not know this one.'

The wagon had halted on the rim of the encampment with the other wagons. The stocky driver had climbed down. One of Fidaig's warriors was escorting him towards the *pupall*. They noticed that he was not so much guiding him as propelling him forward with the point of a sword.

The driver of the wagon was a balding man of stout proportions. He came wheezing before them, his head lowered, his pudgy hands rubbing together.

Fidelma glanced at Eadulf in surprise before turning back to the newcomer.

'Well, Ordan, I did not expect to meet you again so soon and in this place.'

CHAPTER SIXTEEN

⟋⟍

The merchant recovered quickly from his obvious shock and forced a sickly smile to spread over his fleshy features.

'Lady Fidelma,' he bowed his head briefly. 'I, also, hardly expected to find you here and in such distinguished company.' He looked at Eadulf and made his curious bow again. His small glittering eyes missed nothing, observing Gormán behind them. Then he turned to Fidaig and made an artificial obeisance.

Fidaig simply ignored him but raised a questioning eyebrow to the warrior who had escorted Ordan into the camp.

'Lord,' began the warrior, 'we were returning from the north, and just by the place known as the Hill of Green we saw a campfire. There we found this merchant.'

'I had camped there for the night, lord,' Ordan explained hastily. 'Had I realised your encampment was nearby, I would have hastened to join you. Better to spend the night in numbers than in isolation. I have heard that the wolves and bears are many in these fastnesses.'

The warrior gave the merchant a pitying glance and went on, 'Your campfires, lord, were clearly visible from where we found this man.'

'Yet I had failed to see them until your warriors kindly pointed them out to me and invited me to join you,' the merchant said suavely.

Fidaig stared at the fat man in distaste. 'So you are Ordan of Rathordan? I hear you have often been in my territory but have never once come to my fortress to pay your respects to me.'

'When we questioned him, he told us that he was heading for the Ford of Oaks in the land of the Uí Fidgente,' interrupted the escorting warrior.

'Your route is curious for one heading to the Ford of the Oaks,' pointed out Fidaig.

The merchant spread his hands nervously. 'I missed the road. I mean . . . the road I usually take was muddy and impassable.'

'Yet you have put an entire day or more on your journey to see Gláed, haven't you?' Fidelma said softly.

'It was better to arrive safely than . . .' Ordan suddenly stopped, realising that he had unwittingly admitted he was going to meet Gláed. His jaw went slack and he was at a loss to continue.

'Perhaps, lord,' said the warrior, 'you might like to see what is in the wagon of this merchant?'

'That will not be necessary,' protested Ordan. 'I am trading a few weapons, that's all.'

Fidaig's expression did not favour the merchant. 'I have heard of you, Ordan. Reports have reached me that you have often been in my territory but that you favour my son to trade with. I am curious.'

'I trade with many people,' Ordan muttered sullenly.

'We shall see what goods you bring to my son.' Fidaig turned to one of his warriors. 'Keep our guest company while we look at his wagon.' Then he gestured for Fidelma and Eadulf to accompany him.

Led by the warrior who had escorted Ordan into the camp, they walked across to the place where the wagon had been left under guard. Lanterns were called for and Fidaig climbed up and drew aside the covering. His gasp was audible. Without a word, he turned and signalled for Fidelma to join him. Eadulf assisted her in climbing onto the heavily laden wagon before he followed her. Gormán, not to be left behind, also climbed up.

The wagon was packed with an array of swords, spears and shields as well as bows and quivers of arrows. There was no room in the wagon for anything else.

Gormán whistled softly.

'It looks as though your Cashel merchant was ready to start a war,' Fidaig said, turning a suspicious glance on Fidelma.

'Don't get the idea that this merchant came here with Cashel's blessing,' Fidelma said. 'I am as anxious to find out what use your son would put these weapons to as you doubtless are.'

'My son shall have much to explain,' replied Fidaig. 'But weapons of this quantity and quality are not part of a simple trade.'

Gormán had picked up one of the swords and examined it. 'You have observed well, Fidaig,' he said. 'These swords are new and the work of the famous smiths of Magh Méine. I know their work well.'

The smiths of Magh Méine, the 'Plain of Minerals', were also known to Fidelma, for Fhear Máighe was the centre and it was at the library there that Fidelma had managed to piece together the secret that had led to the murder of Donnchad of Lios Mór.

Gormán was continuing to examine the other weapons and shields.

'Indeed, these are all new-made, lady,' he said to Fidelma. Then he came across something wrapped in sacking. Gormán bent forward and picked it up. It was a battle standard. The shaft was new polished wood. He tore the sacking from it. On the top of the shaft, exquisitely worked in gold metal and inlaid with semi-precious stones, was the image of a ravening wolf. They immediately recognised the Uí Fidgente symbol.

Fidaig appeared to recognise something else. He drew a long breath and said slowly, 'By the powers of the Mórrígan!'

Fidelma turned a cold eye towards him. 'Is there a reason to invoke the ancient Goddess of War?'

Fidaig blinked, staring at the standard that Gormán held. The lanterns of the onlookers flickered on the golden image and the red stones set as the wolf's eyes. Fidaig's warriors had fallen silent, almost in awe.

'The reason is that this is the symbol of the ancient Goddess of War,' Fidaig said slowly. 'It is the sacred totem of the Uí Fidgente. It disappeared after the great defeat of Cnoc Áine.'

'A sacred totem?' demanded Fidelma.

'It is the *Cathach* of Fiachu Fidgenid,' Fidaig uttered reverently.

Eadulf knew that most clans, when they went to battle, usually carried into the conflict a sacred object which they believed gave them strength and protection. The object was known as a *cathach* or battler. More recently, as the New Faith spread, some clans carried a copy of one or other of the Scriptures while others carried a reliquary of the great teachers of the Faith. But this was an ancient symbol from the time before the New Faith.

As if reading his thoughts, Fidaig said: 'This is supposed to be the very standard that the Goddess of Darkness and Sorcery, the Mongfhind, gave to Fiachu Fidgenid, the progenitor of the Uí Fidgente, at the time before time.' His tone was a mixture of wonder and dread.

'Are you saying that it is the battle standard of the Uí Fidgente, last seen during the conflict at Cnoc Áine?' asked Fidelma.

'It disappeared from the battlefield. It was thought to have been looted and taken to Cashel, but your brother denied all knowledge of taking it as part of the spoils of battle.'

'Had it been taken to Cashel, then it would have been destroyed,' Fidelma assured him. 'Its symbol would have aroused too many passions among the Uí Fidgente. The question is – how has it fallen into the hands of Ordan?'

'A question we should now attempt to answer,' Eadulf said, turning and jumping down from the wagon before he held out his arm to assist Fidelma down.

Her feet had barely touched the ground when there were shouts coming from the direction of Fidaig's tent, followed by the sound of a horse galloping off.

'If the guard has let that merchant escape . . .' began Fidaig, stifling an oath.

They were running for the tent across the campsite. The warriors milled around in confusion as Fidaig began yelling orders for the wagon to be protected, for others to chase after the fugitive.

They halted at the entrance of the *pupall*. There, lying on the ground, was the rotund form of Ordan. Eadulf went immediately to kneel by him. Ordan was clutching his side where blood was seeping over his clothing. His face was deathly white. One look into his eyes and Eadulf knew that Ordan had resigned himself to death. A tongue licked over the pale lips.

'Wealth . . . more wealth than I ever dreamed of. He promised me . . . he promised . . .'

Fidelma knelt by his other side, glancing at Eadulf who shook his head.

'Who promised you this, Ordan?' she asked softly.

'He would be King . . . he promised.'

'Gláed? Did he promise you wealth? What was he to be King of?'

The dying merchant stared at Fidelma as if not recognising her.

'Not Gláed. Must get it . . . get to Mungairit. He promised . . . he . . .'

With a sigh, Ordan suddenly went limp. Fidelma did not have to ask Eadulf whether he was dead or not.

Slowly, she and Eadulf stood up. Fidaig had just been speaking to his son Artgal. He came towards them with an angry expression.

'It seems that one of my warriors drew his knife and killed Ordan. Then he leaped on a horse and rode away. It was Loeg, one of the men you prevented from engaging in the single combat earlier.'

Fidelma glanced into the darkness beyond the campfires. 'Was Loeg one of Gláed's men?' she asked.

'He came from Barr an Bheithe,' acknowledged Fidaig bitterly.

'I suppose there will be no chance of overtaking him in this darkness?'

'Half a dozen of my men are now chasing him,' Fidaig replied. 'I doubt that they will be able to catch him. Come daylight, they might be able to track him, but I suspect that he will have gone to ground before then.'

'Was the attack unprovoked?' Eadulf asked, although he already knew the answer. 'Did Ordan make an attempt to escape?'

'It was when you discovered the *Cathach* and the news spread that Loeg struck,' Artgal said, having followed his father to their group.

'You think that he did it to prevent Ordan revealing where he obtained it?' queried Fidaig, troubled. 'If my son was buying arms then he was surely plotting against me – plotting my overthrow.'

'That might well be,' replied Fidelma. 'Except that I think it was a bigger conspiracy – and one to which the *Cathach* of the Uí Fidgente is the key. You heard what Ordan said. The answer is at Mungairit.'

The lord of the Luachra shook his head stubbornly. 'My concern is to stop Gláed's folly. If he wants to take over the chieftainship of the Luachra, then he must confront me first. I am taking my men to Barr an Bheithe tomorrow. Gláed has much to learn if he thinks he can outsmart me, lady.'

'Then I suggest that we split up and go our separate ways. I think it is important that we get to Mungairit in view of the discovery of the *Cathach* and Ordan's dying words, so Eadulf, Gormán and I will continue north to Mungairit at sun-up.'

'It could be a trap.'

Fidelma disagreed. 'I think the totem of the Uí Fidgente is essential to this conspiracy – whatever it is. If Loeg reports that you have it, Fidaig, then they will not come after me. So I suggest that you take good care to hide Ordan's wagon. I also suggest that you hand over this totem to me for temporary safekeeping. I think it will help to solve the many mysteries which now lie hidden. I promise that I will keep it safe. Will you trust me with that?'

Fidaig rubbed his chin thoughtfully and then he finally gave a quick nod of confirmation.

'The Uí Fidgente mean little to me. I am content as lord of the Luachra.

You may take their totem back to them or destroy it as you will. But remember, it is a powerful symbol. Even some of my own warriors have followed it and been seduced by its power. You saw how they reacted just now when it was discovered. So have a care, lady. Guard it safely.'

Fidelma turned to Gormán but before she spoke he said solemnly: 'My honour and sword hand will defend it, lady, or I will be dead when it is taken from me.'

'Rather you remain alive than dead, my friend,' she replied dryly.

'To ensure that you reach Mungairit, I can give you two of my men to accompany you,' offered Fidaig.

To Eadulf's surprise, Fidelma accepted the offer.

Later that night, in the darkness of their tent, Eadulf rolled over and peered towards the figure of Fidelma. The sounds of her breathing made him realise that she was awake.

'I still don't trust Fidaig,' he whispered without preamble.

'Trust does not come into it,' she whispered back. 'I think Fidaig is genuinely concerned about Gláed, although I don't believe it is Gláed's intention to overthrow his father. I return to my earlier thought about the overthrow of Prince Donennach. Why else would Gláed, in his guise of Brother Adamrae, be trading for new weapons with Ordan? I know that Ordan was a merchant without morals and that he had traded with the smiths of Magh Méine for years. Perhaps it is as simple as that. It is not every merchant who has such connections or who is willing to trade in weapons and is not too scrupulous with whom he trades. But the *Cathach* is something else.'

Eadulf stared into the darkness. 'I would have thought your law system would control such things as the way merchants trade.' He did not mean to sound rude.

'A merchant is the one occupation that is not included in the lists of the professions,' replied Fidelma. 'It is not even mentioned in the law texts such as the *Uraicecht Becc* or the *Bretha Nemed toisech*.'

'And why is that?'

'Because such a merchant of death is so abhorrent to us that we cannot conceive that he exists.'

'And yet exist he does.'

'Exist he does,' she confirmed hollowly. 'Or did so until Loeg ended his existence.'

'Yet if there is a conspiracy to overthrow Prince Donennach, what would Gláed of the Luachra hope to achieve by it? He is not even an Uí Fidgente, let alone having a claim to the succession.'

'I am beginning to see some light in all this darkness, Eadulf. But we have some way to go first.'

Eadulf peered at her. 'You see some light?' he demanded. 'I see nothing but complications.'

'I think that by nightfall tomorrow you will have a better understanding.'

'Why tomorrow?' he asked, bewildered.

'Because tomorrow we shall be on our journey back to Dún Eochair Mháigh and our first stop will be at the watermill of Marban.'

'I still don't understand.'

There was a long sigh from the darkness. 'Go to sleep, Eadulf. Tomorrow will be a long day.'

They set off after the first meal of the day. A weak sun was trying to shine, with banks of white clouds being blown rapidly across the sky by the wind from the west. Fidaig's camp was in the process of breaking up. The heavy wagons were already moving off towards the spot where Fidaig's fortress lay, while the warriors were saddling up ready to ride with Fidaig for Barr an Bheithe. The two who had been designated to accompany Fidelma and her companions were sturdy, capable men, professional warriors who knew their art. When Fidelma had asked them about their qualifications, they answered that they were of the *fubae* – warriors whose task was usually to hunt down brigands, especially horse and cattle thieves, and to keep the wolf population under control.

They made their farewells to Fidaig and, with Gormán leading, they rode back across the River Ealla, retracing their way along the track they had been forced to take on the previous day. Gormán carried the totem slung across his back, with the sacking securely tied over the gold ravening wolf so that no one would recognise it. Behind him rode Fidelma and Eadulf, and behind them came the two watchful warriors.

Most of the journey was in silence for it was a cold day, and now and again the wind brought a fine spray of rain. Fidelma and Eadulf were thankful for their *lummon* – thick woollen cloaks edged in beaver fur. The wool was from the black-fleeced sheep that were prevalent in the country; it was of a thick texture and could protect against the most persistent rain, having an oily quality that allowed water to drain off it without penetrating.

It was not long before they were passing north of the hills on which the rath of Menma could just be glimpsed. Then they were heading back over the marshy plains to pick up the small stream that would eventually emerge as the great River Mháigh. The trees began to grow thickly, so that woods became forests before thinning out again.

Just after midday, the smells and then the sounds of Marban's watermill assailed their senses. A short time later, the fields, kilns and the mill itself came into their vision.

One of the workmen at the kilns saw them and, with a shout, went running to the mill, doubtless to inform Marban. Sure enough, the burly miller came out of the mill, greeting them with a raised hand.

'Welcome back, my friends. I did not expect you to return.'

Fidelma swung down from her horse. 'In truth, Marban, we did not expect to do so . . . at least not in this direction. My intention was to return directly to Cashel after we had visited Menma's rath, or what remained of it.'

A sad look momentarily crossed the miller's features. 'And did you see it?'

'We did and more.'

'More?'

'We were invited to encamp with Fidaig himself. Our new companions are two of his warriors.'

'Fidaig was there?' The miller looked concerned.

'Not there exactly,' smiled Fidelma. 'However, from our journey there are a few more questions we have to ask you before we move on.'

The miller hesitated a moment. Then he said: 'Stable your horses and let your companions rest as they will.' He turned and ordered one of his workmen to look after Gormán and the other warriors. Gormán seemed unwilling, but Fidelma glanced at him and nodded slightly.

'Now,' said Marban, 'come into the mill where we may be warm and I may provide you with hospitality and information.'

Inside, the mill was indeed as warm as they had previously experienced. They took off their cloaks and spread them on the wooden benches to sit more comfortably while Marban poured the inevitable beakers of *corma*.

'Did you find out what you wanted?' he asked Fidelma as he handed the drinks to them.

'I found out what I was able,' she countered. 'Now I think you could add to that knowledge.'

Marban frowned. 'I will answer if I can.'

'I would like you to tell me the real reason why Liamuin ran away from her husband, Escmug.'

Marban looked astonished at the abruptness of the question. 'He was a bully and an evil man,' he said defensively.

'Then why did she not leave him before?'

'Her daughter was the reason. I told you.'

'Yet what happened this time that she fled and abandoned her daughter? She had put up with Escmug's beatings for fourteen years. Why choose this moment to run away?'

Marban could not meet her eye.

'Come!' snapped Fidelma, suddenly becoming angry. 'Are there no

Brehons here? Women are equal to men in their right to divorce or to separation. Women who have been ill-used or beaten can be divorced with full compensation – especially if blemishes have been raised on the skin by such ill-treatment. Why did Liamuin not have recourse to the law? Instead she flees – and the law states that a woman who flees from her marital contact without sufficient cause is classed in the same manner as a fugitive thief.'

The miller raised his hands, spread slightly outwards. 'Liamuin is dead, lady. Surely the dead should be allowed to rest in peace?'

'Not if their resurrection goes to explaining their death and exonerating their reputation. And not if their resurrection will save lives.'

'I cannot help, lady,' the miller replied stubbornly.

Fidelma turned to Eadulf. 'Would you ask Gormán to bring the . . . the object in here.'

Eadulf rose and went off to fulfil his task. He knew that Fidelma had an idea but he was not sure what it was. He was back with Gormán within moments.

'Gormán, unwrap the sacking and show the miller what you have there.'

As Gormán obeyed, Fidelma watched the miller's face turn pale. A number of expressions chased across his features. He reached forward and ran his trembling hands over the golden wolf.

'It is the same, yet it has been expertly repaired,' he breathed at last.

'Repaired?' Fidelma asked sharply.

'When I last saw it, one of its legs and its tail had been broken off. I think, perhaps, by sword blows. This has been repaired and by a smith with much experience and talent in the art of working with this metal.'

'So you are sure this is the *Cathach* of Fiachu Fidgenid and the one which Liamuin brought here when she fled from Escmug?'

'I am sure—' began the miller before he halted and stared at her in astonishment. 'How did you know?'

'Is it the same?' repeated Fidelma.

The miller sighed and pointed to the object. 'There is a special incision on the metal in Ogham, the ancient script, just under the belly of the animal.'

Fidelma reached forward and felt for the incised letters. 'Buaidh!' she read aloud. 'Victory!' She sat back and looked at Marban, her silence inviting him to speak.

'Very well,' he said finally. 'I will tell you the story as Liamuin told me and will subtract nothing.' He paused to refill the beakers of *corma*, taking a large swallow of his own before beginning to speak.

'When Liamuin came to me for help, not knowing where to turn, it was not that she was merely fleeing from her husband and abandoning her child, Aibell. You were right. You have already learned that her father was old Ledbán and that her brother was Lennán, who had trained as a physician and entered the Abbey of Mungairit.'

Fidelma waited without commenting.

'Lennán had decided to join Prince Eoganán's warriors when they marched against your brother's army. Not that he supported the Prince but he was sworn to follow his calling as a physician. So he went to care for the sick and wounded.'

'We have heard as much,' Eadulf muttered. 'He was killed on the slopes of Cnoc Áine by Eóghanacht warriors.'

The miller glanced at him. 'That is not exactly so,' he said quietly.

It was Fidelma's turn to be surprised. 'What are you saying? That he was not killed by Eóghanacht warriors or that he was not killed on the slopes of Cnoc Áine?'

'He was mortally wounded but did not die there.'

'You'd best continue the story then.'

'It happened on the very day of the battle. As Liamuin told me, it was, thankfully, one of those evenings when Escmug was away drinking. And yet the battle was raging on a hill less than twenty kilometres away. Liamuin was mending her husband's nets when a wounded rider arrived at her cabin. It was her own brother Lennán. He was dying. He had strength enough to tell her of the defeat of the Uí Fidgente army at the hands of Colgú. He had, indeed, been nursing the wounded on the field of slaughter.

'One of those mortally wounded was the standard-bearer of Prince Eoganán. He was lying with the *Cathach* of Fiachu Fidgenid almost hidden beneath him. As Lennán turned him over to assess his wounds, he saw the golden wolf and its broken haft. He was about to treat the standard-bearer when he felt a sharp pain in his side. He turned to see a warrior bending over him, sword still in his hand. The warrior's face was a mask of maniacal desire as he stared at the *Cathach*. He was screaming, "It's mine! It's mine! I will have the power." He made another lunge towards the *Cathach*. Realising that this warrior had stabbed him with his sword, Lennán grabbed the remaining haft of the *Cathach* and swung it at him, catching him on the forehead. The warrior fell down and lay still.

'Lennán knew what the *Cathach* symbolised. He knew that if the warrior seized the *Cathach* it would mean more bloodshed and destruction for the Uí Fidgente as well as the Eóghanacht. And this fear caused him to flee to his sister. The fear of that warrior on the battlefield who had struck the fatal blow at him . . .'

'Some Eóghanacht warrior, no doubt?' Gormán's voice was almost a sneer.

To their surprise, Marban shook his head.

'Not so. The warrior was Lorcán, son of Eoganán. Everyone knew and feared Lorcán's ruthlessness. The man was killed not long afterwards and few among the Uí Fidgente mourned his passing. But at the time, he was a man to fear. Lennán realised that he was badly wounded, but he derived an extraordinary strength of purpose from the knowledge of what might happen if Lorcán got possession of the sacred totem. He managed to stagger from the battlefield with it, mount a horse and, wounded as he was, he rode that agonising distance to his sister Liamuin. He entrusted the emblem to her, telling her to take it and hide it somewhere safe.'

'And then he died?'

'While knowing full well that death was at hand, he remounted his horse and rode back towards the battlefield. It seemed that he did not make it, but he was close enough for the others to think he had been killed on the field of battle or died trying to leave it. At any rate, his visit to his sister was not known.'

'Except to you. This is the story that Liamuin told you?'

'He had impressed his fear into the poor girl. She took the metal wolf of the *Cathach*, placed it in a sack, and realising she could not wait for her daughter to return from the fields, she left Dún Eochair Mháigh and so headed upriver to me.'

'So you weren't simply concerned with Escmug chasing after her?'

The miller shook his head. 'Not just Escmug, although I knew he would guess where she had fled. As I told you, Menma, the *bó-aire*, was one of the most moral people I knew. That is why I sent her to his rath. I suggested that we take the *Cathach* and have him hide it.'

'And what of her daughter, Aibell?'

'The plan was for her to be told where her mother was later. Escmug believed that Liamuin had simply run away from him and for no other reason than she was tired of him. In revenge, he decided to do something that would wound Liamuin. That was when he sold Aibell to Fidaig as a bondservant. As I have already told you, I had no regrets in killing that animal.'

'So Liamuin hid with Menma and nothing was done about her daughter?'

'What could we do? The child had become a slave – to Fidaig of all people. As I told you before, she was as good as dead.'

'Yet she did not die. I have spoken with Fidaig and he accepts that he has done wrong in law by taking the girl from Escmug knowing she was at the age of choice.'

The miller's expression was one of incredulity.

'Lady, you have seen that we are not far from the great fastness of the

Luachra, where Fidaig and his sons rule. His power extends even over the hills where my friend Menma used to dwell. I swear that I gave up all hope of Aibell being rescued when I heard that Escmug had given her to the Luachra.'

'Let us speak of Gláed first,' Fidelma said. 'I am told he played a role at Cnoc Áine – even against the wishes of his father. His ambition lay with the Uí Fidgente.'

Marban's mouth tightened. 'That is true, lady. Fidaig was not really interested in Eoganán's claims to the kingship of Cashel nor, indeed, in the Uí Fidgente at all. He was concerned in building up his own fiefdom within the fastness of the Sliabh Luachra. There is a natural fortress with its great mountain barriers.'

Eadulf rubbed his chin thoughtfully. 'How well known is Gláed among the Uí Fidgente? Surely he would be recognised by all the Uí Fidgente nobles? Conrí, for example.'

Fidelma saw what Eadulf was driving at but Marban was shaking his head.

'Outside of these borderlands, I doubt many know him at all. Although he is ambitious, don't forget he was from Sliabh Luachra and joined Eoganán with only a small band of followers – against his father's wishes. After Eoganán's defeat, he was not considered of any importance to the Uí Fidgente. The war was four years ago.'

'Would Gláed know the worth of the *Cathach*?'

'It would not mean much to him personally, but he might know that any dissident prince of the Uí Fidgente would do anything to have it returned to Dún Eochair Mháigh. In the hands of our nobles it is a powerful symbol; a symbol of our past and a promise of our future – a symbol that we are not a defeated people.'

Gormán stirred uneasily but Fidelma shot him a warning glance.

'As you say, the war is long over, Marban. Hopefully, the Uí Fidgente no longer have any ambition to fight to assert their superiority,' she said firmly. 'Too many have died for that ambition. Too many mothers have lost sons.'

Eadulf added softly: '*Bella detesta matribus* – wars, the horror of mothers.'

'I believe in peace as well as the next man,' Marban stated. 'I pray Prince Donennach will last long enough to ensure that this peace, a peace we have known for the last four years, continues. But it is a fact that the only outcome of war is hatred and more war. And I fear it will be so. War will come again out of resentment. Don't forget, lady, in a conquered land, the defeat of its army leaves three armies in its place. An army of wounded and cripples; an army of mourners and haters; and an army of thieves and opportunists. Out of those three comes the growing resentment to seek atonement from the conquerors. An atonement in blood.'

Fidelma said sadly, 'You sound like a philosopher, Marban. All I know is, Cashel had to defend itself once attacked. But I agree that victory in war does not determine who is right, only who was the strongest. The victory is not a solution and that is why my brother engaged in finding a solution with Prince Donennach. At least, he seemed to understand the path to peace between Cashel and Dún Eochair Maigh.'

'Well, let us hope he has time to establish that peace. There is much resentment here.'

'And there are people who will attempt to overthrow him and end the peace?' queried Eadulf.

'Isn't that the nature of things?' The miller looked sad. 'Anyway, now you have heard the full story of Liamuin. She was a lovely girl, albeit a foolish one. Many loved her, but she chose the wrong man and suffered for it. Beaten, forced to abandon her own daughter, fleeing to a place where she was killed along with the family of my dear friend who gave her shelter. That is the tragedy of her life.'

Fidelma sighed. 'I am not sure it is the full story of Liamuin as yet. At least, Marban, I can confirm some good news to alleviate the tragedy.

Aibell is, at this moment, safe in Cashel, having escaped from Sliabh Luachra. Furthermore, when I challenged Fidaig he was forced to admit that he acted illegally, as I have already said, and he has agreed to pay a fine and compensation for doing so.'

The miller stared at her in disbelief. 'Liamuin's daughter is alive and well?'

'Your niece is safe, Marban.'

Tears sprang into the eyes of the big man. Then he tried to pull himself together. 'Liamuin would be overjoyed. The old saying is truly spoken – that dark stormclouds are sent to prove there is such a thing as sunshine. The impossible *can* happen.'

'I am sure she will want to meet with you and hear the real story of why her mother had to abandon her,' Fidelma said kindly. 'Even more, my friend, I believe that soon we will find out exactly what happened at the rath of Menma – and who is responsible for it.'

As the words left her lips, one of Marban's men came banging at the mill door and burst in before he could respond. 'Horses are approaching,' gasped the man. 'It is Gláed and his men.'

CHAPTER SEVENTEEN

❧

Marban turned pale with apprehension. It was Gormán who sprang into action and snapped at the miller: 'Are our horses under cover? Will they be spotted? Quick, man!'

The miller seemed in a panic. 'No, they are standing outside in clear sight. They will be seen before we can run them to the stables.'

Eadulf was glancing up the stairway to the room where they had successfully hidden before, but Fidelma, reading his intention, said: 'It won't work twice, Eadulf.'

They could hear the approach of a band of horses and any initiative seemed to drain from them as they realised how close the riders were. Gormán put his hand on his sword in a futile gesture – but Fidelma reached over to stop him.

'Resistance will only bring about your death more quickly. Our only defence is in my rank and office – not that Gláed seems to be concerned about that. As we cannot hide, let us go and confront him.'

Eadulf would have preferred to have made a run for it rather than be faced with the wayward son of Fidaig, but Fidelma was already moving towards the door with Marban behind her, wringing his hands.

As they exited from the mill a band of thirty horsemen swept up to the mill buildings. Among the first of the horsemen was the man they had spotted previously from the mill room and whom Fidelma had identified as Gláed or rather Brother Adamrae.

Then they halted in surprise, for next to Gláed rode the familiar figure of the warlord of the Uí Fidgente, Conrí, with Socht on the other side of him.

The men reined in their horses before Fidelma and her companions, with Conrí clearly astonished at seeing them.

'Lady!' greeted the Uí Fidgente warlord. 'What are *you* doing here?'

Fidelma recovered her poise. 'I would ask you the same question, Conrí . . . and riding in such company.'

She turned towards Gláed and only then noticed his sullen features and the fact that his hands grasped the reins at an odd angle, the wrists having been tied tightly together with rawhide. She turned back to Conrí with a puzzled look.

Conrí was dismounting with a grin.

'You were right in your suspicion, lady. There *is* a plot to overthrow Prince Donennach. But I thought you would have left the hospitality of Marban long ago. The girl at the fortress, Ciarnat, told me where you had gone. If Marban will extend his hospitality so that my men and I can water our horses in the stream here and rest before we take our prisoners back to Dún Eochair Mháigh, I will tell you what we have been about.'

Marban hobbled forward quickly, almost sobbing in relief.

'By all means, Lord Conrí.' He looked nervously at Gláed, who sat impassively on his horse, looking neither to right nor left, his mouth set in a firm line.

'Have no fear, miller,' Socht assured him. 'He won't hurt you. This man is our prisoner. Have you somewhere safe where I might put him? Preferably a well-used pigsty?'

'Still amazed?' smiled the warlord as they settled themselves back in the warmth of the mill. 'You may not have recognised him, but that is actually our missing Brother Adamrae, and Adamrae is—'

'Gláed, son of Fidaig of Sliabh Luachra,' finished Fidelma. 'We spent last night with Fidaig.'

Conrí looked disappointed for a moment. Then he continued his explanation. 'We took Gláed as a prisoner. He had a few men with him who put up a fight, neglecting to notice I had a couple of good bowmen with me. Gláed finally preferred discretion to valour. Now he will answer for Lachtine's death and for what he did to Brother Cronan.'

'He will have to answer for much more than that,' Fidelma replied grimly. 'How did you find him? And what happened to confirm my idea of a plot to overthrow Donennach?'

The warlord ran his hand through his hair. 'It was pure luck,' he confessed. 'After you left us at Dún Eochair Mháigh, a messenger came to the fortress. We had decided to stay on for a day or two as Cúana used to be an old friend of mine.'

Eadulf picked up the past tense and looked hard at the man.

Conrí interpreted the question. 'I am afraid he came off the worst in an attack on me.'

'What happened?'

'It was as simple as being in the right place at the right time. Night had fallen and I could not sleep. I was still wondering what the purpose of Adamrae, or Gláed as I now know him, was in the Ford of Oaks. I heard a messenger arrive at the fortress and curiosity brought me from my chamber. The messenger was speaking with Cúana in the antechamber. I was about to enter when I heard him say that the moment to strike was at hand. That made me pause.

'The messenger then said that Gláed and his men were waiting at a certain place – a small ford north-west of here. The merchant had been told to take his wagon there, and then Gláed would escort him to Mungairit. The merchant would bring "the object" with him. I never learned what that referred to. Cúana was instructed to take those loyal to him and join Gláed in Mungairit, where he would be given further instructions. All I could gather from this was that there was some kind of plot afoot.

'The messenger left and I was going to withdraw quietly but unfortunately, I slipped on the stone floor and Cúana found me. He knew that I must have overheard what had been said, even though I could make no sense of it except that it promised intrigue and danger for our people.

'Cúana drew his sword and said, "I am afraid you must die for what you have heard". I tried to protest but the sword was descending . . .' Conrí flinched at the memory, 'and then Socht's dagger caught him in the throat. Had that not happened, I would not have been here to tell the story. It was fortunate that Socht, being a light sleeper, had followed me.'

'There is much to learn here,' Eadulf said with satisfaction. 'Ordan was bringing a wagonload of weapons obviously to Gláed – swords, spears and shields from the best smithies of Magh Méine. He also had this . . .' He pointed to the standard that Gormán had placed in a corner.

Conrí observed it for the first time in the dark corner of the mill. His mouth opened in silent astonishment as he recognised it.

'So you bested Gláed at the ford?' Fidelma said hurriedly before Conrí could speak. 'What has he said since then?'

Conrí turned reluctantly away from the standard. 'Said?' he repeated. 'He has said nothing.'

'Nothing at all?' pressed Fidelma.

'Well, merely that all would be revealed if he was taken to Mungairit. I think it sounds like a threat.'

'Then we should avoid Mungairit,' Eadulf shrugged.

'I think not. It is at Mungairit that this mystery will conclude,' Fidelma contradicted firmly. 'Let us go and have a word with Gláed.'

'But, lady, you know what that emblem means,' protested Conrí.

'I know full well. You must keep it a secret until we have resolved the mystery of how it was meant to be used and by whom.'

Socht had tied the son of Fidaig to a metal horse ring in one of the barns. Gláed watched their coming with a faint smile of derision on his features.

'Well, Gláed son of Fidaig,' Fidelma greeted him coldly, 'you already know who I am.'

He did not respond.

'You will wish to know that Ordan's supply of weapons for your followers has now fallen into safe hands.'

There was only a tiny narrowing of the eyes to indicate that he understood.

'That also means that the *Cathach* of Fiachu is no longer available to arouse the Uí Fidgente to rise against Cashel again.'

Gláed continued to remain silent.

'*Cum tacent clamant,*' snapped Eadulf in frustration, using the words of Cicero. When they remain silent, they cry out.

At this Gláed turned and actually spoke: 'There is an old saying of my people that a silent mouth sounds most melodious. I will say nothing to you, nor will I tell you anything.'

'A pity. I would have liked to know what a petty chieftain of the Luachra would be wanting with the sacred battle emblem of the Uí Fidgente,' Conrí intervened.

'You will learn nothing from me,' the young man sneered.

Fidelma saw the determined look in the prisoner's eye and gave a silent sigh. She was a good judge of character and knew resolution when confronted with it. 'It will not add to our knowledge to question him further,' she said quietly.

Eadulf and Conrí followed her back to the mill.

'I don't understand,' Conrí said in frustration. 'The plot has been revealed – so why does he remain silent?'

'Because all is *not* revealed. He remains silent because he is only one of the conspirators. He is protecting the others. There is someone at the heart of this who is more powerful than Gláed.'

'More powerful? You can't mean Cúana? He is dead now. Anyway, he was only the steward of Prince Donennach's house.'

'How many trustworthy men do you have, Conrí?' she asked abruptly.

'As you see, lady, about twenty-five warriors. The number that accompanied us from the Ford of the Oaks.'

'Who did you leave to secure Dún Eochair Mháigh?'

'I found a few good men there who were unaware of what Cúana had been planning. I also sent a messenger to my own fortress to raise a dozen more men to join us.'

'It would be better if we had a hundred warriors or more,' muttered Fidelma. 'Still, with luck, it might not come to a confrontation.'

Conrí was still puzzled. 'Confrontation? A battle?'

'What would be the effect of raising the *Cathach* Fiachu among your people and calling on them to rise up against Cashel again?'

'No effect at all – unless it was raised by a prince of the blood,' Conrí told her. 'Certainly no effect if it had been raised by Gláed, as he is not even of the Uí Fidgente.'

'Gláed will not raise it. The person who will do so is to be found in Mungairit,' she replied confidently.

Three blasts on a hunting horn cut into the air. A moment later, Socht burst in.

'More horsemen are coming! I've told our men to stand to their arms.'

Fidelma sprang up. 'The fact they have given us warning of their approach may mean there is no hostile intention,' she pointed out as the warlord clasped his sword. 'Let your men stand ready, but don't provoke anything until we know who they are and what their intentions are.'

It was not long before they knew the answers as they gathered in a nervous group outside the mill building.

Fidaig, lord of Luachra, came trotting into the mill complex with a score of his warriors. He halted a little distance away from them and slid from his saddle, handing the reins of his horse to Artgal, who rode beside him. He then walked towards them, his face serious. His keen eyes swept the company before they alighted on Fidelma.

'I did not expect to see you again so soon, lady,' he said.

'Nor I you, Fidaig,' she replied. 'What does this mean? I thought you were chasing the man who killed Ordan the merchant to Barr an Bheithe?'

'That was my intention, lady,' he said heavily.

'And now?'

'My son, Gláed, was not at Barr an Bheithe. I was told that he was attacked and taken prisoner by Conrí of the Uí Fidgente. I am come to find and to claim my son.'

'If I remember correctly, Fidaig, the purpose of you going to his fortress at Barr an Bheithe was to ask an account of him and to punish him if there was wrongdoing,' Fidelma stated evenly. 'There *has* been wrongdoing and the Uí Fidgente have a prior claim on your son.'

'It is a father's right to punish a son.'

'What your son has done is no longer a matter of discipline from a father or, indeed, the chieftain of his clan,' Fidelma said.

'What then?' demanded Fidaig. 'Is he to be tried by strangers? The Uí Fidgente?'

'He is involved in a plot against the rightful Uí Fidgente Prince and probably against the King of Cashel,' Fidelma said. 'Therefore, if it comes to trial, he will be tried by a Brehon of Muman.'

Fidaig snorted. 'I say that my son is of the Luachra and he will answer to the Luachra. I allow no one to interfere in my family or the people of Sliabh Luachra.' The lord of the Luachra glanced towards his warrior escort.

Fidelma caught the implied threat and her eyes narrowed dangerously.

'What you allow is of no consequence to me, Fidaig. I am a *dálaigh*, qualified to the level of *anruth*. Even the High King has accepted my legal advice. Further, I speak with the authority of my brother, Colgú, rightful King of Muman. Now, do you deny the law I represent and your King? Deny me by force and there is nothing I can do. But should you do so, you will know that the consequences will be severe, for it will not be just a defiance of those authorities that I have spoken of but of the Chief Brehon of the Five Kingdoms and therefore the High King himself. Are you ready to accept those consequences?'

Fidaig stood defiant for a while. Then he seemed to acquiesce with a gesture of his shoulder.

'You make your point with your usual eloquence, lady,' he said softly. 'Where will you take my son?'

'We leave here for the Abbey of Mungairit. It is your right to accompany us, to see that your son is properly treated.'

Fidaig was still looking at Fidelma. 'I would like to have a word with my son before he is taken to Mungairit.'

Fidelma inclined her head towards the barn. 'He is being held there.'

Fidaig hesitated. 'I would like a word alone with him. Perhaps I have been a bad parent and could have prevented this. But I would like one chance to speak to the boy before it is too late.'

'Boy?' It was Eadulf who cut in. 'The boy is now a man, Fidaig. It is too late to treat him as a boy still. The damage is done.'

Fidaig swung round to him, anger on his face. 'Damage?'

'*Ego enim sum Dominus Deus tuus Deus aemulator reddens iniquitatem patrum super filios in tertiam et quartam generationem,*' intoned Eadulf unctuously.

'I have no understanding of what you say, Saxon!' snapped the lord of the Luachra.

'It is from Deuteronomy, one of the Holy Scriptures. For I, the Lord your God, am a jealous God, visiting the iniquity of the fathers on the children, and in the third or the fourth generation . . . And by the way, I am an Angle, not a Saxon.'

Fidelma shook her head warningly at Eadulf, before addressing Fidaig. 'You may have your word with your son but then we must start for Mungairit.'

Fidaig gave a deep sigh, then took back his reins from the man who was holding his horse before leading the animal across to the barn.

Fidelma had turned back to Eadulf with a look of reproof. 'You are free with your quotation from Holy Scripture.'

'I thought the passage from the translation of the Blessed Jerome was appropriate,' Eadulf replied with a smile of satisfaction. 'I don't trust Fidaig.'

'Then quote for quote – *non portabit filius iniquitatem patris . . . et pater non portabit iniquitatem filii*. That's from Ezekiel.'

Eadulf's mouth turned down, for it was a contrary statement. The son shall not bear the punishment of the father's iniquity, nor will the father bear the punishment for the son's iniquity.

Conrí scratched his head. 'Whatever this saying means, I think friend Eadulf here is right to suspect Fidaig. Perhaps I should send someone to keep an eye . . .'

'I promised Fidaig a word alone with his son,' snapped Fidelma.

There was a sudden yell from Socht. They swung round. The figure of Gláed had emerged from the barn and leaped onto his father's horse. Within moments, he had jumped a fence and sped away towards the surrounding forest.

Socht was bawling for his men to give chase, but the Luachra warriors had formed a barrier with their horses.

'Damn Fidaig!' cursed Conrí. 'He's released his son. I knew he couldn't be trusted.'

Fidelma looked shocked at the defiance of her legal authority by the lord of the Luachra. It was obvious that he had cut his son's bonds and allowed him to escape. Eadulf and Conrí were running towards the barn. As Fidaig had not emerged, two of the mounted Luachra sent their horses over to the barn at a trot. Eadulf thought their purpose was to help Fidaig to escape, recognising one of the riders as his son, Artgal. Eadulf increased his speed and reached the barn just moments before them. They all came to a stunned halt at the entrance.

Fidaig was lying on the ground, covered in blood. Next to him was the iron ring to which Gláed had been secured by ropes. The pieces of rope lay cut and discarded nearby.

Eadulf fell to his knees by the side of the stricken man as Fidelma caught up and pushed her way between Artgal and his companion, who had jumped from their horses to crowd inside. Conrí had joined them. They were staring in disbelief. Fidaig's eyes were barely open, his face twisted in pain. He groaned and then caught sight of his son across Eadulf's shoulder.

'Artgal, get him . . . Gláed . . . he has killed me . . .'

Artgal's companion did not hesitate but turned and ran out of the barn, yelling the news to his followers.

'Gláed has murdered his father! After him!'

The Luachra warriors wheeled their horses round and within moments were indistinguishable from Socht and his men as they formed a body racing after the fugitive.

Fidelma and Eadulf were now joined by Artgal at the side of the fallen Fidaig. The lord of Sliabh Luachra was coughing blood.

'You were wiser . . . than I,' he gasped, peering towards Fidelma as if he found difficulty in focusing.

'Don't speak,' advised Eadulf. 'Save your strength.'

The man's mouth twisted in a parody of a grin.

'It will not . . . not need much strength to die, Saxon,' he grunted. 'Must tell you – I thought I knew best how to treat my son. I cut him loose. Told him . . . there'd be no fair trial from Uí Fidgente. Told him I . . . would hear him at Sliabh Luachra. Tried by his own . . . people.'

Eadulf raised the man's shoulders to make him more comfortable. 'It is hard to believe ill of your own,' he said softly.

'Didn't think he . . . think he would kill his own . . . father.' Another spasm of coughing seized the dying man before his fading gaze sought out his son Artgal. 'You are now . . . now lord of the Luachra. Rule more wisely than I . . .'

A spasm suddenly wracked Fidaig's body and then he was still. Eadulf laid him down gently and rose to his feet.

Fidelma was still in a state of shock. Eadulf had never seen her so distressed before. She was obviously blaming herself for the tragedy. Eadulf turned to the pale-faced Artgal. The young man was still staring at the body of Fidaig as if he did not believe what he had witnessed.

'Artgal!' he said sharply.

The young man reluctantly drew his gaze from the dead body to Eadulf.

'I am sorry for your loss, Artgal. You have heard your father's dying words. Alas, he has brought this upon himself by releasing your brother.'

Artgal's eyes suddenly flickered with a curious fire. 'My brother will answer for this. He will answer for the death of our father.'

Fidelma moved suddenly, as if coming out of a stupor. 'So he shall,' she said. 'But Gláed must answer for other matters as well. He must be recaptured and brought back here alive.'

Artgal's face was grim. 'That he shall be, if it can be accomplished. But he must be taken back to Sliabh Luachra where his own people shall sit in judgement on him.'

'I am more than willing to let that happen, Artgal – but *after* he has provided witness to his part in this Uí Fidgente conspiracy.'

They faced each other stubbornly. Then the young man's face seemed to crumple in lines of grief. This time it was Fidelma who reached out to comfort him.

'You are now the lord of the Luachra, Artgal,' she said softly. 'Responsibility often comes upon us before we are prepared to receive it. If we can recapture Gláed, I suggest that you and some of your men shall accompany us to Mungairit. It is my intention to gather the witnesses there and resolve this conspiracy. After that, you may take him back to Sliabh Luachra and you and your people may judge him as you see fit. You have my word.'

The young lord of Luachra glanced down at his father's body. He was quiet for a few moments. Then he gave a deep sigh.

'It shall be so, lady. You also have the word of the lord of Luachra. And with your permission, I shall send some men to take my father's body back to Sliabh Luachra.'

She bowed her head slightly in acknowledgement and he left the barn. Conrí had gone to consult with some of his remaining warriors. Not everyone had chased after the fleeing Gláed. Fidelma stood for a long while, shoulders hunched, staring down at the body of Fidaig. Eadulf saw the guilt on her features.

'It is not your fault,' he said finally.

'We have an old saying, Eadulf. "A sharp hound knows its own faults". Alas, I knew my fault and I ignored it. It is my error that is responsible for Fidaig's death.'

'My people also had a saying before the arrival of the New Faith,' Eadulf replied. '"Only the gods are without fault".'

Fidelma said nothing but she seemed to rally a little before striding back to Marban's mill. Eadulf followed a moment later. Gormán was waiting for them.

'So, Fidaig paid for his folly?' he said without sympathy and did not seem to notice Eadulf's warning look.

Ignoring him, Fidelma asked Marban if there was any of his *corma* left.

'Do you think Gláed will be caught, lady?' asked the miller, pouring the drinks as they seated themselves once again in his mill.

She did not reply, but made a gesture as if to say, 'Who knows?'

Conrí entered abruptly, saying, 'There is nothing we can do for the moment, lady.'

Fidelma took a sip of the *corma* and then looked up at the warlord.

'We can't delay long. We need to press on to the Abbey of Mungairit. I was hoping to gather all the necessary witnesses. That also means you, Marban,' she addressed the miller.

Conrí looked astonished. 'Is it necessary?'

'I deem it so,' she said distantly. 'A Brehon, presenting evidence, must have the backing of witnesses. This territory is in danger and that danger has spread to Cashel. The mystery now has to be resolved. We must ride on to Mungairit before this conspiracy brings down Prince Donennach as well as Cashel.'

'I will defend Prince Donennach so long as I live, lady,' declared Conrí.

'Then live a long time, Conrí,' she replied dryly. 'What men do you have left here?'

'About ten. Socht ordered them to remain in case of . . .' He hesitated and ended with a shrug before adding, 'The rest are chasing after Gláed with warriors of the Luachra.'

'Artgal has ordered some of his men to carry his father's body back to Sliabh Luachra. There will be no trouble from the Luachra. Choose five of your men, Conrí – the most trusted men you have. They are to ride towards Tara and intercept Prince Donennach and his party who should be returning from their meeting with the High King along the Slíge Dalla, the main road from Tara to Cashel. It is vital that they intercept them *before* they enter the territory of my brother's kingdom, for that is where I believe there will be an ambush. Once Prince Donennach crosses the border into Muman, I am certain the assassins will strike. Make sure they take Brehon Uallach prisoner. He has a hand in this conspiracy, I am sure.'

Conrí looked astounded. 'I don't understand, lady.'

'This is part of a carefully laid plan to assassinate Prince Donennach and those loyal to him. It is intended to appear that my brother or the Eóghanacht are responsible. Anyway, Donennach is not supposed to return alive to the land of the Uí Fidgente. It will be claimed that he was killed by the Eóghanacht in retaliation for the assassination or attempted assassination of my brother. Cashel will be blamed, and in the turmoil a Prince of the Uí Fidgente blood is to come forward to raise the *Cathach* Fiachu, the sacred standard of the Uí Fidgente. The *Cathach*, therefore, must remain hidden until we uncover the identity of the leader of this plot.'

Conrí stared at her in horror. 'But which Uí Fidgente Prince? As warlord, I am now the most senior among the Princes. Am I to be accused?'

'The answer will be revealed when we get to Mungairit.'

'Why Mungairit?'

'Because I now know who attempted to assassinate my brother and why. I also know who it was who persuaded him to carry out that attack. At Mungairit, we will find the person who has unleashed this conspiracy of death.'

A sudden shouting and clamour could be heard outside. They jostled each other to get through the door of the mill and see the return of the horsemen. One man was on foot. His hands were tied before him and a rope formed a halter around his neck. One end of the rope was held in the hands of a grinning warrior of Luachra. The prisoner had clearly been pulled along behind the horse for some distance, running to keep up. His neck was raw and bloody where the rope cut into it. It was Gláed.

The rider halted before Artgal and dismounted.

'We caught him when his horse stumbled, lord,' the man said. 'We were sorely tempted to hoist him from one of the trees and hang him there and then – but we thought you might like to choose the place of hanging.'

Artgal, the new lord of the Luachra, stared with anger at his breathless and bloodied younger brother.

'Our father is dead by your hand,' he hissed.

Gláed stared back with hatred. 'He would have taken me back to Barr an Bheithe and hanged me there. He did me no service.'

'He tried to deliver you from the Uí Fidgente,' snapped Artgal.

'He never did anything for me unless he expected me to pay for it. You were always his favourite, Artgal. That's why he chose you as his heir apparent. Well, you are in the ascendant now. Hang me – go on! I will curse you from the next world. You can watch for me at the Feast of Samhain when this world and the Otherworld meet and the dead return to wreak their vengeance!'

A silence had fallen over the warriors of the Luachra. They shifted nervously. Artgal's face was a mask of fury. He took a step forward as if he would strike down his brother there and then.

'Artgal!' Fidelma moved forward. 'Remember your promise. Have Gláed cleaned up and secured on a horse. You and two of your warriors may accompany us to Mungairit. Afterwards, you may take him back to Sliabh Luachra.'

Gláed's anger was turned on her.

'I will say nothing! Don't think I have any gratitude to you for stopping my brother from killing me.'

'I do not expect any,' she replied, turning away from him in disgust. Then she looked up at the sky. 'The sooner we set out for Mungairit, the sooner we shall arrive.'

CHAPTER EIGHTEEN

∽⊘∾

For Eadulf, the ride back to Mungairit seemed to take a curiously short span of time compared with the outward trip. Artgal and two warriors of the Luachra took charge of Gláed. Accompanied by Marban, they had halted at Dún Eochair Mháigh to rest their horses. When they moved on, Conrí ensured that the principal fortress of the Uí Fidgente was secure in the hands of some of his trusted warriors. They spent the night at the Ford of the Oaks where Conrí increased his escort of warriors, once again ensuring that the fortress was left well-defended.

Early that morning, they moved northwards along the banks of the turbulent River Mháigh. They had one more stop to make before the final part of their journey back to the abbey. Fidelma insisted that they halt at Temnén's farmstead and request the former warrior-turned-farmer to accompany them as a further witness. Temnén reluctantly did so, on the condition that he could bring his hound, Failinis, and that he would not be long away from his farmstead.

'If I cannot demonstrate my case within an hour of reaching Mungairit, then I will have failed anyway,' Fidelma assured him.

They arrived at the gates of the abbey as darkness was falling. Lanterns and brand torches were already in evidence, lighting the courtyards and buildings. Unlike their previous visit, the arrival of some sixty horsemen caused excitement among the brethren, many of whom came crowding into the courtyard in a state of curiosity. The steward, Brother Cuineáin, came hurrying out with an expression of anger on his features as the company came to a halt.

'What is the meaning of this?' he demanded, gazing at them all in horror. 'This is a House of God and you have no right to bring warriors into its sanctuary.'

'I am Conrí, warlord of the Uí Fidgente,' called Conrí, still seated on his horse. 'I act in the name of Prince Donennach.'

Fidelma and Eadulf swung down from their horses and went up to the steward. His eyes looked almost malignant in the flickering light.

'Ah,' was all he said; the syllable expressed in a long and slow breath.

'You will observe, Brother Cuineáin, that this time I am wearing the badge of the Golden Collar?' Fidelma addressed him quietly.

The steward sniffed in disapproval. 'I have noticed.'

'You will also know what this is?' She continued presenting the official hazel wand of office, the emblem of her authority from the King of Muman.

'I know it.'

'Then you know what it symbolises and the recognition that must now be accorded me and my party?'

'It is so acknowledged,' the man admitted reluctantly. 'You are both representative of the law of the Five Kingdoms and of the personal authority of the King of Muman.'

'That is good. Then you shall conduct me, and those I choose, to the chamber of Abbot Nannid immediately.'

'But . . .' the steward began to protest, throwing out an arm to encompass her warrior companions, 'are they necessary?'

'They are here because there is treason in these walls. Now, this is not a request,' Fidelma expressed herself firmly. 'Take me to Abbot Nannid. It is an order and you will carry it out *now*.'

The steward's shoulders sagged a little in defeat.

'Very well. But the abbot will complain to the High King and Chief Brehon of the Five Kingdoms.'

'That is your right,' replied Fidelma. She turned to her companions. 'Conrí – your men are to secure the gates of the abbey in case of any attack on us. I do not think there will be, since I believe that the conspirators' warriors have been sent to ambush Prince Donennach. However, we must be cautious.'

Conrí issued the orders while Fidelma gathered her party, which consisted of Marban, Temnén and the still silent Gláed, escorted by Artgal and Socht, with Eadulf, Gormán and Conrí. Ensuring that Conrí's men had secured their positions, Fidelma instructed Brother Cuineáin to lead the way to the abbot's chamber. As they did so, the steward noticed that Temnén was being followed by his hound, Failinis. He immediately began to protest again.

'You can't bring that creature into the House of the Lord. It is an affront and a sacrilege!'

Fidelma was in no mood to allow any further protests. 'Do you then deny Holy Scripture, Brother Cuineáin?' she snapped. '*Nimirum interroga iumenta et docebunt te*. Ask the animals and they will teach you . . . in God's hand is the life of every creature and the breath of all mankind.'

Eadulf smiled. 'The words of Job,' he said, and added, 'the creature has as much right to be here as you do.'

Brother Cuineáin gave an angry exclamation as they marched through the stone corridors towards the chamber of the abbot.

Abbot Nannid rose from his chair, his outrage obvious, as they crowded into his chamber. Before he could speak, however, Fidelma pre-empted him by holding up her wand of office.

'Look closely on this, Abbot Nannid. I am here first to speak with the voice of the law and then with the voice of the King of Muman.'

'You do not speak with the authority of the Church,' snapped Abbot Nannid. 'You have no authority within these abbey walls. You have admitted that you are no longer a member of the religious. You come here by the power of the sword – so I refuse to acknowledge your right to be here!'

'You will find that I also act by the authority of Ségdae, Abbot of Imleach, *comarb* of the Blessed Ailbe and Chief Bishop of this kingdom.' Eadulf's voice rang out as he moved forward and, to Fidelma's surprise, produced a small round, silver object from his leather bag. He laid it on the table before the abbot. 'I carry the seal of Abbot Ségdae of Imleach, Chief Bishop of Muman. So the authority of the Church *is* upheld. Do you recognise it?'

Brother Cuineáin made one last effort to challenge them. 'You did not present these authorities before,' he began. 'Why—'

It was Conrí who answered this time. 'You were told that brigands had robbed the lady Fidelma and her companions. Thankfully, my men encountered the thieves and thus we were able to return these symbols of authority.'

The abbot was still staring at the silver seal. Then he looked from Eadulf to Fidelma, and then at those who had crowded into his chamber, sweeping them with a puzzled gaze. He did not even question the presence of Temnén's large hound, who now sat patiently by the foot of his master.

'What do you want here?' he asked Fidelma.

'To prevent a plot that would provoke civil war among the Uí Fidgente,' she replied evenly. 'To stop a war that will cause bloodshed throughout all Muman. To resolve the unlawful bloodshed that has already marred this kingdom, and to identify the culprits.'

The abbot raised his arms a little way then let them fall in a hopeless gesture. 'I know nothing of such things,' he said. 'When you were here last, you claimed it was Brother Lennán who tried to assassinate your brother, the King. But Brother Lennán had been dead these many years. Have you now managed to resurrect him? Do your powers extend that far?' Somehow the abbot found the courage to be sarcastic.

'You hold a key to the door of a certain room,' Fidelma said, ignoring the abbot's gibes. 'You will unlock it for me.'

Abbot Nannid shook his head. 'I do not know what you are talking about.'

Fidelma turned to Brother Cuineáin. 'If the abbot has no knowledge of the room of which I speak, I am sure that *you* do. It is the room in which the items are stored that are kept in remembrance of Cnoc Áine.'

The steward started nervously and glanced at the grim-faced abbot.

'You have acknowledged my authority,' Fidelma said forcefully. 'You do not need the abbot's permission to respond to my request.'

Abbot Nannid leaned back in his chair with a sigh. 'That room?' There was a thin smile on his lips. 'Come, come, lady. There is nothing in that room that needs such suspicion as I see on your face. Brother Cuineáin may unlock it if he will, but I can tell you already what is in there. Some years ago, I authorised Brother Cuineáin to gather some of the sad debris that was left on the battlefield of Cnoc Áine. We have placed it there as a reminder of the evils of war. Isn't that correct, Brother Cuineáin? It is a shrine.'

'A shrine it is,' Brother Cuineáin agreed quickly.

'I have a mind to see this shrine,' replied Fidelma. 'And we will see it now.'

With another quick glance towards the abbot, Brother Cuineáin pointed to a small door to one side of the abbot's chamber.

'It is through there,' he mumbled.

'Take us inside,' Fidelma instructed. She paused only to turn to the two Luachra warriors guarding Gláed, saying, 'Keep him safe here. The others will come with us and that means you as well, Abbot Nannid.'

'It is unnecessary. I know what it is in the room.'

'But I do not want you to accuse anyone here of placing something in it that was not there before,' she warned him.

They moved in a body, led by Brother Cuineáin, through the door – which opened onto a long corridor. Along one side, high windows would have emitted daylight, had it not been well past nightfall. The sounds of horses showed they were either near a courtyard or the stables. Brother Cuineáin asked Marban to light some lanterns to help and then, with Marban and Temnén holding them aloft to light the way, he preceded them along the corridor until he paused before a stout oaken door.

From his leather belt, he took a bunch of keys, selected one with his left hand and thrust it into the lock. It turned easily and he pushed the door open. Marban had set down one of the lamps on a nearby wooden shelf so that the steward could see to open the door.

'Brother Cuineáin, the lantern please,' said Fidelma as she moved into the room.

The steward, still holding the keys in his left hand, bent to pick up the lamp in his right but that hand shook so much that Eadulf took the lantern from him.

'It is a palsy,' the steward hastily explained. Eadulf glanced at the steward's wrist without comment.

With Eadulf now holding the lantern above shoulder height, they moved forward into a small storeroom. Conrí and Gormán came behind while the abbot and the others followed.

'This is a shrine of the weapons used at Cnoc Áine,' explained the abbot. 'What else other than the debris of war should be gathered to show its futility?'

'Except,' Conrí pointed out, 'these weapons seem highly polished and well-maintained for a battle fought over four years ago.'

It was true that the pile of swords and other equipment seemed almost new, but Fidelma appeared uninterested by them. She had taken note of several gold torcs placed on a tabletop, but was intent on looking for something special. Then she spotted a pile of shields in a corner and, beckoning Eadulf to bring the light closer, she began to look through them. It was only a short while before she gave a small grunt of satisfaction and picked one out.

'Very well. I have seen enough,' she announced.

They returned silently to the abbot's chamber. Fidelma placed the shield on the table. It was a red shield on which was an emblem of a stag rampant, picked out with semi-precious stones.

'I shall be glad to return my brother's shield to him,' she said coldly.

'I did not know your brother had lost his shield on the field of battle,' Abbot Nannid said. 'I am glad that we have become the means of saving it so that it can be safely returned to him.'

'Indeed. I am sure he will be grateful for its return and for the restoration of his good name,' she replied solemnly.

'His good name?' queried Brother Cuineáin, running his tongue around his dried lips.

'Oh yes,' Fidelma said. 'There is a story, which I am now able to tell you. All the pieces now fit together.'

'Is it connected to this plot to overthrow Prince Donennach?' queried Conrí eagerly.

The abbot exchanged a nervous glance with his steward. Fidelma pretended not to notice. 'It is,' she confirmed. 'The plot has been a long time in the hatching. Perhaps it was first conceived on the bloodied slopes of Cnoc Áine, when Eoganán was killed and many of his nobles fled.'

Abbot Nannid was shaking his head in disbelief. 'Are you claiming that there is a plot in my abbey to use those weapons from Cnoc Áine to overthrow Prince Donennach? Why, there are scarce enough weapons to arm a company of warriors!'

'The arms were not significant,' replied Fidelma. 'However, all will be explained in good time. I shall tell you a story – and here stand witnesses to various parts of it, if I go wrong.' She indicated the assembly. 'Of course, Gláed of the Luachra has preferred to remain silent. I doubt, therefore, he will bother to correct anything I say.'

'Except to say it is all lies!' spat the young man, finally speaking.

'Even to your attack on me and the slaughter of Lachtine the apothecary?' she replied. 'Well, no matter. We shall proceed. Oh . . .' She turned. 'Socht, would you bring the stable-master here? I am sure he will not be far away, fretting about how to deal with an extra sixty horses gathered into his abbey.'

Socht was not gone long before he returned with Brother Lugna.

'Ah, Brother Lugna. I am sorry to bring you here but I need you to witness some things I have to say.'

The man looked around, seemingly puzzled by the company, and gave a quick shrug.

'You did not want me to make arrangements for the horses, lady?'

'Not for the moment. I just wanted you to confirm a few things about your old friend, Brother Ledbán, and his son.'

'Brother Ledbán and Brother Lennán were good men and I will defy anyone who says otherwise,' asserted the stable-master with spirit.

'That is fair enough.' Fidelma paused, collecting herself. 'I am afraid that I have to start with the Battle of Cnoc Áine. When Eoganán and his standard-bearer were cut down during the battle, Brother Lennán was tending the wounded and dying. In accordance with the rules of war, as the Blessed Colmcille postulated before the Brehons at Druim Ceatt, he was not to be harmed by either side, being a non-combatant. He found the body of Eoganán's standard-bearer. Next to him lay the *Cathach* of Fiachu, the battle emblem of the Uí Fidgente, which was considered sacred by your people. Its haft had been splintered and, being of gold, the more delicate parts of the metalwork had been broken off. Brother Lennán stooped to pick it up.

'As he did so, he was attacked and mortally wounded by a warrior who desired the emblem above his honour. Lennán turned and saw the threatening face above him. Even as he did so, the man thrust his sword into him. Lennán recognised him as Lorcán son of Eoganán . . .'

Brother Lugna winced. 'My poor misguided brother,' he muttered sadly. 'God be merciful to his soul.'

'Realising what would happen if the sacred battle emblem fell into the wrong hands, Lennán found a horse, and taking it, rode from the field. He was dying. It was a painful ride but he knew that his sister, Liamuin, dwelled only a short distance from the battlefield. She was married to a fisherman on the nearby River Mháigh. Lennán handed the standard to his sister with the instruction to hide it. He then tried to return to the battlefield in order not to give his sister away. His body was found near the battlefield where loss of blood from his wound had overcome him.

'I will not go into the personal details but suffice to say, Liamuin had an unhappy relationship with her husband Escmug, a brutal, dominant man. Fortuitously, he was away when Lennán had brought her the *Cathach*. She knew if her husband returned, she would not be able to carry out the dying wish of her brother. Her daughter was also away from the house, working in the fields. Liamuin had no time to waste. She decided to flee to a relative, Marban the millwright, whom you see before you. She told him the whole story. Marban sent her for safety to his friend Menma. It was at Menma's rath that she buried the *Cathach*. Is this not so, Marban?'

The miller shuffled awkwardly. 'It is even as I told it to you, lady.'

'It was then that Liamuin's evil husband played a cruel hand. He went searching for her. He threatened Marban. In his rage he even illegally sold his own daughter, Aibell, as a bondservant to Fidaig of the Luachra, to spite his runaway wife.'

Gláed showed some surprise for the first time.

'You did not know that Aibell, who served your father, was the daughter of Liamuin?' asked Fidelma. 'Ah well, the fate of Aibell does not concern us for the moment; I will deal with it elsewhere. Marban, tell us something about Liamuin's character.'

'She was a dutiful wife, even though Escmug beat and ill-used her,' Marban told them. 'It was only when her brother gave her a sacred charge to take the *Cathach* and hide it that she found the courage to finally break away from Escmug. She had remained with him simply to protect her daughter.'

'A dutiful wife,' mused Fidelma. 'Was she also a dutiful daughter?'

'She was,' affirmed Marban.

'Her father was Brother Ledbán, who had come to this very abbey to work as a groom in the stables after his wife died from the Yellow Plague,' Fidelma went on. 'Isn't that so, Brother Lugna?'

The man started when his name was called but he nodded quickly in agreement. 'It is so. I became the stable-master here long ago, as anyone will tell you. When Brother Ledbán came to join his son Lennán at the abbey, I realised he had served in the stables of our nobility. It was natural that I gave him work in our stables. It was only recently that age and illness caught up with him.'

'So, surely you would know if Liamuin communicated with her father while he was here?'

The stable-master frowned. 'After he came here? Of course, all this was a long time ago. I am not sure.'

'Well, if old Ledbán told anyone here about his daughter, surely it would have been you?'

'Not necessarily so,' replied Brother Lugna. 'Ledbán was friendly with many people. There was a young scribe here that he often talked with. I also remember that he was once visited by a very disagreeable man, who shouted at him – I had to intervene. As I remember, he kept shouting the name Liamuin. Maybe that was this Escmug that you have mentioned?'

Fidelma sighed. 'Then this is where I must speculate, which is something I do not like to do. Liamuin managed to contact her father and tell him not only where she was, but that she had possession of the *Cathach* given her by her brother. Liamuin was a dutiful daughter. In the joy of hearing from his daughter, old Ledbán revealed that information to someone he trusted.'

There was a silence and then Marban said: 'Are you saying that Liamuin was killed – indeed, that Menma's rath was attacked and burned – because of the *Cathach*?'

'That is precisely what I am saying,' Fidelma replied.

'But we know that a warrior of the Golden Collar led the raid that destroyed Menma's rath,' Marban declared. 'It was the same warrior who had been staying at the rath and with whom Liamuin was supposed to have fallen in love. Are you trying to exonerate whoever that Cashel warrior was?'

'I do not intend to exonerate anyone,' Fidelma returned in an even tone.

'I intend to uncover the truth. The truth certainly is that, in the aftermath of Cnoc Áine, my brother sent his commanders and warriors into this territory and stationed them in certain areas to maintain the peace while Prince Donennach negotiated the treaty. Such a warrior was, indeed, sent to the rath of Menma. Apparently he fell in love with Liamuin and she with him. I should add that Liamuin's husband had already been killed by Marban, who justly claims self-defence. Is that not so, Marban?'

'I have no shame in admitting it,' Marban said sombrely. 'He was my own brother but he was evil and a brute. I should have dealt with him many years ago, and much anguish could have been avoided.'

'I have already said that there is no legal consequence from what you told me,' replied Fidelma gravely. 'Liamuin was, apparently, a woman of beauty and charm. Several men fell in love with her when she was at Menma's rath, but she responded only to the warrior from Cashel.'

'And *he* was the person who killed her!' Marban said heatedly.

'Not so. The person who wanted to recover the *Cathach* killed her. A raid was led by someone wearing a gold torc and carrying my brother's shield – the very shield which is on the table before you. It was a shield abandoned at Cnoc Áine. That same person took some men to Menma's home and killed all the inhabitants, including Liamuin, in order to recover the *Cathach*. The ruse worked, for the one survivor – an old woman named Suanach – described the leader as wearing a golden collar, and she also described the shield. She did not, however, know the significance of its device. The story was then handed down among locals that it was the warrior from Cashel and his men who were responsible. The blame was laid squarely on them.'

'You claim that this shield, your brother's shield, was the one used in that attack? But this shield has been kept in the abbey all these years. You are making wild speculations.' Brother Cuineáin's tone was angry. 'You are trying to shift the blame onto the abbey.' He went suddenly pale. 'In fact, you are accusing the abbot or myself – as we have the keys to the shrine!

You are trying to say that whoever led the raid on this Menma's rath came from the abbey and used items from our special collection to mislead people. You are trying—'

Fidelma decided to bring a halt to his rising hysteria. 'I am not *trying* to say this, Brother Cuineáin,' she said sharply. 'I am *saying* it.'

Conrí was frowning, attempting to follow her arguments. 'I do not see how this fits in with your claim of a plot to kill your brother or overthrow Prince Donennach and all else that follows?'

'Be patient, my friend,' Fidelma chided gently. 'I will explain. This story of the raid on Menma's rath was swiftly spread, much to the real culprit's satisfaction. The blame was put on the nameless Cashel warrior and his men – the horror being that he had this relationship with Liamuin and claimed her love, only to ruthlessly cut her down. But two other men happened to be hopelessly in love with Liamuin.

'One of them was the apothecary who had nursed Suanach, the survivor of the attack on Menma's rath. His name was Lachtine, as Gláed will know because he killed him a few days ago. We will come to that in a moment.' Gláed made no response and Fidelma continued: 'The other lover of Liamuin was a young man, the son of a neighbouring farmer and his wife, who heard the story of her death from the lips of the sole survivor and witness. He was told that the man who led that raid wore the golden collar of the bodyguards of the King of Cashel. Further, he was also told of the particular device on the shield of the warrior who led the attack. He did not know what it meant – but brooding with his grief and anger, the Fates had it that he came to this abbey to work among the copyists. Here he fell into the hands of the conspirators. He was told what the shield device meant – and so was groomed to become the assassin of my brother.'

Chapter Nineteen

The silence that followed was one in which only the quickened breathing of those gathered could be heard.

'I am speaking about Maolán,' Fidelma finally announced.

Abbot Nannid let out a startled exclamation. 'Maolán the copyist! He was a farmer's son – a talented copyist, but hardly a conspirator!'

'I said he was the tool of conspirators, not one of them,' Fidelma replied.

'He came to study and work in our abbey library . . .' The abbot's voice trailed off as he began to assess the consequences of the accusation.

'He was not one of the brethren,' said Brother Cuineáin hurriedly. 'He took no vows; he remained a layman.' The steward was clearly trying to point out that the abbey would not be legally responsible for someone who was not one of the brethren.

Fidelma ignored him and continued, 'Curiously, he came here to recover from his grief. Maolán was the archetypal rejected lover: he had convinced himself that, had Liamuin lived, he would have eventually won her favour.'

'Maolán was the young scribe I mentioned,' Brother Lugna said excitedly. 'He and Brother Ledbán often spoke together.'

'But Maolán could not have betrayed the fact that Liamuin was hiding at Menma's rath to anyone in this abbey,' pointed out Eadulf quickly. 'He only arrived at the abbey after the attack in which Liamuin was killed. Someone else betrayed where Liamuin was hiding long before Maolán came here.'

Fidelma glanced at Eadulf with appreciation before she continued. 'Once Maolán's story became known, it was realised that he was in the right emotional state to be manipulated. With his hatred festering of the warrior whom he thought had killed Liamuin, he was told about the shield and that it belonged to none other than King Colgú of Cashel. Maolán needed little persuasion to go to Cashel and attempt to kill Colgú, even if it cost him his own life. He was well schooled with information, doubtless gained by the treacherous merchant Ordan. Ordan passed on the information of the location of a hut in the woods where he could change his clothes and leave his equipment and horse ready if he was able to escape from Cashel. He was even told that the woman on whose land he could leave his horse, possessed a dog.'

Gormán's eyes widened. 'Of course, my mother's dog was sedated.'

'It could have been worse. The dog could have been poisoned, but Maolán was a farmer's son. He cared about animals. That is why he did not turn his horse loose in the forest, as doubtless he had been advised. But he decided to leave it in Della's paddock, safe from any ravening wolves.' Fidelma glanced at Conrí. 'If you'll forgive the choice of words.'

'Except that he had no chance of escaping alive from Cashel after the manner of attack that you described to me earlier,' Conrí replied.

'That poor frenzied creature had no wish to live. Once he had killed the person whom he thought had destroyed the woman he loved, he was prepared to give his own life. It was a suicidal attack.'

'Maolán . . .' Abbot Nannid was muttering. 'He had been with us for several years, working as a copyist. He never joined the religious. But I was told that he left the abbey over a week ago to go east . . .'

'Maolán was told lies that made him into a tool of conspiracy. He was sent to assassinate my brother.'

'You spoke of Lachtine,' interrupted Conrí. 'We know that Gláed, in his disguise as Adamrae, killed him – but why?'

'You remember what Sitae, the inn-keeper, told us?'

'Remind me.'

'Sitae told us what Lachtine had witnessed in the forest. He saw Gláed, or Adamrae if you like, receiving the broken *Cathach* from a man in religious robes and then passing it to the merchant Ordan. Ordan had contacts with the smiths of Magh Méine, renowned for their brilliant metalwork. Ordan was the go-between to get the damaged *Cathach* repaired. Gláed – Adamrae – must have spotted Lachtine and realised that he had witnessed that exchange some weeks before. Gláed had arranged to meet Ordan at the Ford of Oaks. He was some days early, and while in Sitae's inn he encountered Lachtine. It was obvious that they both recognised one another. That was when Gláed decided to kill him. He did so, but he still had to wait for Ordan. Hence the complicated method of disguising himself, so that he could wait at the Ford of the Oaks for Ordan to show up. But the one thing he did not allow for was the arrival of my companions and I.'

'So once uncovered, he had to flee?' asked Conrí.

'Exactly so. And instead of waiting for Ordan to bring the repaired *Cathach* to the Ford of the Oaks, he had to make other arrangements. Ordan was bringing the *Cathach* by a circuitous route when he was waylaid by Fidaig, whose guests we were at the time. When we went to question Ordan, one of Gláed's men, Loeg, killed him to stop him telling us what he knew. Loeg escaped to warn Gláed but Gláed had already been captured by Conrí.'

'It's complicated but it begins to fit,' Conrí said thoughtfully. 'The *Cathach* is a powerful symbol that would cause the Uí Fidgente to rise up to support the person who held it. And you say the man who handed the broken *Cathach* to Gláed to be repaired was a religieux?'

'So you *are* accusing my abbey?' cried Abbot Nannid, scandalised. 'The abbey is plotting some uprising against Prince Donennach? Nonsense!'

'Is it such nonsense?' Fidelma said coolly. 'The attempt to assassinate my brother, the confusion that would be created, the fact that Prince Donennach was away visiting the High King in Tara and being advised to take most of his loyal advisers with him, with the exception of Conrí, his warlord . . . presented the ideal opportunity.'

Some suspicious looks were cast towards Conrí by those surrounding him. Brother Cuineáin was quick to seize on the idea.

'So why was Conrí left behind, to ensure all was peaceful during the Prince's absence?' he demanded. 'It was a perfect position to be in if he was one of the conspirators. He is a Prince of the Uí Fidgente.'

Conrí flushed angrily. 'Are you accusing . . . ?'

Fidelma held up her hand to still the inevitable outburst. 'Things were coming together for the person who had probably begun plotting this when he left the bloody field of Cnoc Áine.'

'I did not fight at Cnoc Áine, as you know,' snapped Conrí.

Brother Cuineáin glowered at Fidelma. 'This sounds like fairytales spun for the entertainment of children. You will have to do better than simply speculate that someone in this abbey is orchestrating this so-called conspiracy.'

'Only someone of the ruling family of the Uí Fidgente could make such a claim to re-animate our people to rise up once more,' Brother Cuineáin said nastily.

'Suanach has already told us who that person is.' Fidelma spoke casually but the effect was gratifying. Astonished faces were turned towards her. She paused a moment and then resumed. 'Let me show you the way forward. Remember that Suanach was the sole survivor of the attack on Menma's rath.'

'But you say that this survivor saw only what she was meant to see and spread the word that this unknown Cashel warrior led the attack,' pointed out Marban. 'She did not even identify him correctly, for she described the shield whose emblem was that of your brother.'

'All true,' Fidelma admitted. 'Except that you have forgotten the most important part. She added something else.'

They waited patiently while Fidelma relished the dramatic pause she had often practised in pleading cases for a Brehon. However, Eadulf spoiled it.

'She was able to describe how Liamuin was killed,' he intervened excitedly. 'Liamuin apparently picked up an axe to defend herself as the warrior rode towards her. As he lunged at her, she swung the axe and knocked the sword from his hand. She wounded him so that the blood flowed from his wrist. Liamuin was then shot by the warrior's companions – killed by two arrows.'

Fidelma glanced in approval at Eadulf. 'Such a wound would have left a scar on the man's sword wrist,' she added. 'Even weakened it.'

Gormán turned quickly to Brother Cuineáin, whose face now had a pallid tinge. He began to back away from the young warrior.

'You have all seen how he is constantly massaging his right wrist with his other hand,' Gormán said in ringing tones. 'When we were here days ago, he dropped a beaker because he was unable to hold it. It was the same when he nearly dropped the lantern a moment ago.'

Fidelma smiled grimly. 'I suspect that Brother Cuineáin did enter this abbey after the defeat at Cnoc Áine not to escape attention but because he was steward to Prince Eoganán. I think he is actually Codlata from the Ford of Flagstones.'

'I did not know Codlata,' Conrí said, staring in curiosity at the man. 'His relationship was distant to that of my family.' He moved towards the steward, hand on the hilt of his dagger. It was Eadulf who intervened.

'It is not a wound that causes Brother Cuineáin's hand to shake. It is what you call *crithlam* – a palsy. It is just as he said – he suffers from some strange ague that causes the hand to be weak and to shake uncontrollably.'

The warlord stepped back, blinking. He turned to Fidelma for guidance, then glanced towards Abbot Nannid.

'If he is Codlata, then Abbot Nannid must have known him.'

'One's relations are not proof of guilt,' blustered the abbot. 'I gave sanctuary to Codlata and will maintain it. He was only administrator to Prince Eoganán.'

'You are at liberty to do so,' confirmed Fidelma. 'That is, unless Codlata or Brother Cuineáin, as he is now called, is proved guilty of some crime.'

She had been looking at Abbot Nannid as she spoke. As if in answer, the abbot drew back the sleeves of his robe, showing that he had no blemishes on his wrists. He stared back at her in silent challenge.

'I was not about to accuse you, Abbot Nannid,' she told him, 'although, of course, you are Prince Donennach's uncle and also of the bloodline. It seems this abbey has become home to several Uí Fidgente nobles. No, it is the man Suanach described that I want.' Then, turning quickly: 'And you have a scar on your right wrist, don't you, Brother Lugna?'

The stable-master started in bewilderment. 'Yes, I do. Everyone knows it. You saw it when you were here before. A horse bit me years ago. It was an accident, I told you.'

'Brother Lugna has served this abbey for many years as my stable-master,' Abbot Nannid said irritably. 'He entered the abbey when he was seventeen years old, many years before Prince Eoganán started his war against Cashel. Brother Lugna was renowned for his piety and devotion to the abbey as well as his love of horses. He never wanted anything to do with his father's claims nor did he have sympathy with his brothers Torcán and Lorcán. Why would he suddenly want to lead such a conspiracy, and claim power after all these years?'

Fidelma was aware of the looks of doubt on the faces of her companions.

'People do change with experience,' she conceded. 'When Brother Cú-Mara was here a few days ago, he mentioned that he had noticed a change in Brother Lugna's attitudes after Cnoc Áine.'

'Brother Lugna is a man of great piety,' insisted the abbot.

'Indeed he *was*,' Fidelma assured him. 'His brother Lorcán was not. Perhaps it is time for you to speak as yourself, Lorcán!' She added the last sentence sharply, wheeling round on the man.

In the silence that followed, Temnén was shaking his head. 'No, no, no, lady. Lorcán was killed. Everyone knows that. It was Uisnech who killed him.'

'I am afraid not. Lorcán killed his twin brother, Lugna, so that he could take his place as stable-master in this abbey. You, Temnén, were not alone in remarking how alike the brothers were physically but how unalike in temperament. Brother Cú-Mara, who had known Lugna for some years before Cnoc Áine, noticed a subtle change in the stable-master's temperament. But everyone was willing to agree that attitudes had changed after that great defeat.'

'But I have known Brother Lugna for . . . This is impossible!' stammered Abbot Nannid. 'I also knew Lorcán. He was not only a son of Prince Eoganán but one of his chief commanders. Speak up, Lugna.'

'What better way of hiding, after the defeat, than in full view of everyone, passing as his own twin brother? People see what they expect to see,' Fidelma said. 'Lorcán's twin brother was renowned for his lack of interest in Uí Fidgente pretensions, and for his piety and goodwill, having served a long time in the abbey. What a perfect disguise!'

'But to kill his own brother and switch identities . . .' Conrí was shaking his head in disbelief.

'There is an easy way to get confirmation,' Eadulf murmured. 'Any competent apothecary or physician can tell the difference between the scar left by an axe and the bite of a horse.'

Brother Lugna, who had remained silent the whole time, went to move forward, as if to extend his arm for inspection, but then he suddenly turned and made a grab for Gormán's sword, his placid features twisted in anger. Gormán was quicker and his dagger was at the stable-master's throat. Brother Lugna wisely halted his action and stood glowering at them.

Eadulf glanced briefly at the man's wrist. 'No horse made that scar,' he confirmed.

Fidelma pointed to the forehead of the erstwhile Lugna. Anger had caused the blood to flush his features. In so doing, a faint white scar was shown in relief.

'A further proof? That is doubtless where poor Brother Lennán struck his killer when he tried to seize the *Cathach* on Cnoc Áine.'

'I can hardly believe it,' the abbot almost wailed.

'This fits with Lorcán's character.' Temnén was reflective. 'I knew him, as I told you. He was ambitious and cruel. I did say that physically, Lorcán and Lugna could pass as one another except for their differences in personality.'

'I am afraid that it was Lugna who was slain,' repeated Fidelma. 'And it was not by Uisnech, although he received the blame – presumably from tales circulated by Lorcán. He, as you say, had no morality. After the defeat and death of his father, he fled to this abbey. He did not think twice about killing his own twin brother and taking his place. Brother Lugna would not be suspected. Who would question him? Then he was free to plot for the future. As the surviving son of Prince Eoganán he determined he would find a way to claim the princedom and continue the war against Cashel. It was as simple as that.'

'Yet not so simple to me,' Conrí said. 'Explain the details of this.'

'It was Lorcán, in his guise of stable-master, who learned from poor Brother Ledbán, working as a groom under him, where his daughter Liamuin was hiding. He also learned that she had the *Cathach* which her brother had given her for safekeeping. Having heard that a warrior of the Golden Collar was living at Menma's rath, he conceived the idea of retrieving the *Cathach* in the guise of Eóghanacht warriors, even taking the shield that he knew had been retrieved from the battlefield and kept in the shrine here, along with one of the Cashel torcs. It was not hard for him to gain access to the shrine room.

'But when he recovered the *Cathach* from Menma's rath he found it had been damaged during the battle. It needed repair – and who were the greatest smiths in the kingdom? The almost legendary smiths of Magh Méine, the Plain of Minerals on the Great River.'

'And so they restored the *Cathach*?' queried Temnén.

'The task was given to Gláed, one of his loyal followers. Gláed knew Ordan of Rathordan and made the deal with him to take the *Cathach* to the smiths of Magh Méine. When it had been repaired, Ordan was to bring it back to him at the Ford of the Oaks. Gláed also gave Ordan money to purchase some new weapons – swords, spears and shields, for the quality of items produced by those smiths is known throughout the Five Kingdoms. And this Ordan did . . . he fulfilled his task – except that he fell into our hands. Then Gláed was caught by Conrí.'

Brother Cuineáin was aghast. 'I served with this man for four years and was fooled. He was my cousin, and I was fooled. Why did he hide here for four years in disguise before acting?'

'He had to await the right opportunity. That was when Prince Donennach felt secure enough to make a visit to Tara to see the High King. It was then Lorcán decided to use another weapon. As I have told you, that weapon was poor demented Maolán, whose secret he had learned. He told Maolán that it was my brother Colgú, the King of Cashel, who had led the raid on Menma's rath. Maolán was advised to dress as a religious and say he had a message from this abbey in order to gain entrance to Cashel. Perhaps it was his own idea to give his name as that of Liamuin's brother, Brother Lennán. That I do not know.'

Conrí was undecided. 'I am not sure what to do with him.'

Lugna scowled. 'You would know what to do if you were a true Uí Fidgente! Call yourself a warlord? If you hold the sacred banner of our people in respect, you would turn on our oppressors! You, too, Temnén – you fought against the Eóghanacht. Are you still possessed of any Uí Fidgente manhood and pride? Will you let an Eóghanacht trample on your people?'

Gormán and Eadulf edged protectively close to Fidelma. But Conrí's sword arm did not waver.

'It is out of respect for the sacred banner that I do what I do now,' he returned coldly. 'Many Uí Fidgente would be alive today, had they not listened to the siren call of your father. And now you, too, would have them follow you into the field of blood again. Follow *you*? In your ambition you even slaughtered your own brother, who was a good, moral man. The blood of many is on your hands.' He turned to Fidelma. 'What do you suggest, lady? Is he to be escorted to Cashel for trial?'

Fidelma was shaking her head.

'I believe Lorcán and his confederates should be tried by his own people. It is to them that he owes an atonement of blood. The decision of what to do with Lorcán will be made by the Uí Fidgente, so that it will create no fresh cause for the Uí Fidgente to nurture any more grievances against Cashel.'

Temnén grinned. 'Did I not say that you were a wise woman, Fidelma of Cashel? That is a sound judgement.'

'A judgement that shall be carried out,' Conrí said firmly.

'My suggestion is that Lorcán be taken to Dún Eochair Mháigh. He can be imprisoned there until the return of Prince Donennach.'

Lorcán chuckled sourly. 'If he ever returns.'

Fidelma cast a look of satisfaction at Conrí. 'Well, then, I will let you await in your prison cell to hear whether Prince Donennach survives the ambush you have set for him and returns with Brehon Uallach as a prisoner.'

She saw the dismay spread over Lorcán's face as he was led away. He had obviously been banking on the fact that she had not worked out a major part of his plan to kill Prince Donennach on Cashel territory.

'You are forgetting Gláed, lady,' muttered Conrí.

Artgal took a pace forward. 'You promised that I could take my brother back to Sliabh Luachra to be tried for the murder of our father, lady,' he reminded her.

'And so it shall be done,' she said without hesitation. 'I think Gláed will receive the justice he deserves from his own people.'

A grim smile was on Artgal's lips. 'You may be assured of that, lady.'

'What about the abbey?' Abbot Nannid sounded uncharacteristically humble.

'What about the abbey?' Fidelma enquired innocently.

'If this conspiracy was nurtured in this abbey, are we not culpable for fines under the law?'

'Not in my judgement,' she assured him. 'However, I will, as I have said, take my brother's shield back to him as well as the golden collars of those of my brother's warriors who died in battle. They belong to their widows and children. I would advise you that a shrine to a battle is one thing, but a shrine which has the potential for perpetuating hatred is another. Any representations you may want to make are best submitted to the Brehon of the Uí Fidgente – that is, once a new Brehon is appointed.'

'So what can we do now?'

'Now?' Fidelma glanced out into the darkness that had enveloped the abbey. 'Now I think we shall avail ourselves of your hospitality. Hot baths and an evening meal. Then a good night's rest, before my companions and I start back for Cashel in the morning.'

ChAPTER TWENTY

It was late the next morning when Fidelma, Eadulf and Gormán began to cross the marshland to the south-east of Mungairit and turn along the road that would lead them back to Ara's Well on their way home to Cashel. For the first time in a while, Eadulf felt he could talk freely.

'I shall be glad to get back to Cashel and our son,' he said to Fidelma, looking at the distant hills. 'I cannot say I have much desire to return into the country of the Uí Fidgente.'

'It is all the Kingdom of Muman, Eadulf,' she reproved.

'It may well be, but this is not a territory in which I am at ease. Anyway, I feel strangely dissatisfied. It seems to me that there are still questions that remain unanswered.'

'Such as?' she asked innocently.

It was Gormán who answered. 'We have not identified the warrior of the Golden Collar who stayed at Menma's rath. Why did he leave it and never return after Lugna, or rather Lorcán, destroyed it? If he was in love with Liamuin, why did he not want revenge or even to punish the attackers?'

'Now that is a good question, Gormán. Yet in the overall scheme of things, his identity does not matter. However, I think I will find an answer to that, once we return to Cashel.'

The young warrior rode on in thoughtful silence for a while before suddenly addressing no one in particular. 'Knowing what I now know, I realise that I was too hasty in condemning that young girl, Aibell. She was very attractive and to have been a bondservant to that man Fidaig, unjustly enslaved and . . . Well, one can forgive her temper and . . .'

Fidelma and Eadulf glanced at each other and Eadulf thought his wife had a smile on her lips.

It was a bright winter's day as Fidelma and her companions rode into the outskirts of the township sheltering beneath the great stone palace of Cashel. Although the sky was blue, a frost still showed in places where the advancing day had not chased away the shadows. Few people were stirring, apart from those whose work necessitated them to be outside on such a cold morning. They smiled and called a friendly greeting as the three rode by. There was an air of happy prosperity about the town, which was reassuring for Fidelma, for had Cashel been in mourning for her brother, it would have shown. Some part of her had remained sceptical when Fidaig told her a messenger had passed with news of her brother's recovery.

They were nearing Della's cabin and paddock and Fidelma saw Gormán look across.

'Perhaps you would like to inform your mother that you are safely returned?' she suggested with a smile.

The young warrior raised his hand in acknowledgement and nudged his horse towards the cabin. The other two continued on through the almost deserted town square. They turned up the slope towards the gates of the palace. Enda was on guard and his features broke into a ready smile of welcome as he saw them.

'It is good to see you home, lady – you, too, friend Eadulf,' he called. 'The news of your brother is good, lady. He is completely out of danger. He is still weak, but improving every day.'

'That is good news, Enda.' Fidelma was enormously relieved to have the news confirmed. 'And Brother Conchobhar – is he still in attendance on my brother?'

'That he is, lady. He was with the King day and night for several days until all danger passed. Praise be, the King is well enough.'

They had walked their horses into the courtyard and dismounted while attendants rushed forward to lead the horses off to the stables.

'Where is Gormán?' Enda asked. 'Did you succeed in discovering who the assassin was and why he carried out this attack?'

'We left young Gormán at his mother's cabin,' Eadulf assured him. 'And yes, we have resolved the matter.'

'You found out who the assassin was?' Enda said eagerly.

'We did, but that must wait,' Fidelma interrupted before Eadulf could reply. 'We must first report the matter to the council.'

Enda looked disappointed but then said: 'Should I tell my lord Finguine to summon the council?'

'Not yet, Enda. First, Fidelma must see her brother,' Eadulf replied, and added softly, 'And then we must see our son.'

Fidelma caught the intonation. 'No,' she said determinedly. 'We will see our son first – and then I shall see my brother.'

Eadulf turned so that she did not see his smile.

As soon as they entered their chamber, little Alchú gave a scream of delight and came running towards them, abandoning some toy he had been playing with. Muirgen the nurse looked on approvingly as they embraced the boy.

'Has all been well, Muirgen?' Fidelma asked, detaching herself from the child.

'Everything has been very well, lady,' she replied.

There was no need to ask as to the health of their son, for the little boy's robustness demonstrated it. Alchú was even now excitedly tugging at the sleeve of Eadulf.

'*Athair, athair*, I can play *fidchell*.'

'Really?' Eadulf regarded him with wide-eyed solemnity. 'But that is a very difficult game.'

Fidchell was one of the popular board games among the intellectual class of the Five Kingdoms.

'It is so! It is so! But I can play it. Isn't it so, *muimme*?'

Muirgen smiled at her small charge. 'It is so, my pet. You can play *fidchell*. Goodness, he is a bright boy. I never learned the game,' confessed the countrywoman.

'If you have become so good, I dare not play the game with you,' Eadulf told the boy, keeping back his amusement by assuming a serious tone. 'Who taught you this wonderful skill?'

'Why, King Am-Nar, *athair*. King Am-Nar came and played with me,' the child said.

'King Am-Nar' was the term by which the boy called his Uncle Colgú, as he could not pronounce the word *amnair*, the word for a maternal uncle, when he was younger. The name had stuck.

Fidelma turned to Muirgen in surprise to ask a question, but the nurse preempted it.

'The King is recovering well, lady, and has visited here several times to play with the boy.'

A short time later, Fidelma and Eadulf made their way to the King's chambers. Caol, the commander of his bodyguard, was on duty outside the doors. He smiled a nervous greeting.

'Is all well?' he greeted them.

'Surely that is what we should be asking you?' Eadulf answered in amusement, clapping him on the back.

'Oh.' The commander of the King's bodyguard looked flustered for a moment. 'Everything is well here – very well. The King is almost recovered. It is good to see you both returned unharmed from the country of the Uí Fidgente.'

'Is my brother within?' asked Fidelma.

'Brother Conchobhar is with him. He comes to check on the King twice a day.'

'Excellent.' She knocked, and then without waiting for an answer, she opened the door. Followed by Eadulf, she stepped into the familiar chamber beyond.

Fidelma's brother was seated before a blazing log fire. He was clad in loose-fitting clothes and she could see that he still wore bandages under his shirt. He glanced up and his features broadened into a grin. Fidelma went over and leaned down to embrace him.

'Brother Conchobhar told me that he had heard that you had just returned,' smiled Colgú, extending his hand to Eadulf. 'Are you both well?'

'Better for seeing that you are improved, brother,' replied Fidelma, before turning to beam at the old apothecary who had risen from the other chair at her entrance.

'I was just about to take my leave, lady,' the old man said. 'Your brother is fitter than I am. But try to make him relax more. He has been the worst of patients.'

Colgú grinned at the apothecary. 'And you have been the most dictatorial of physicians,' was his riposte. When the old man left, he waved Fidelma and Eadulf to seats. 'Now you must tell me everything.'

'Everything?' protested Fidelma. 'Not now. I do not want to have to repeat my story to the council meeting.'

Colgú looked disappointed for a moment. 'Well, Finguine is here, and so is Aillín.' He hesitated and then said: 'Following Áedo's death, the Council of Brehons decided to confirm Aillín in his place as Chief Brehon of the Kingdom.'

He knew Fidelma had earlier aspired to the office. However, she responded with a shrug of dismissal. 'Brehon Aillín has many years of experience. Anyway, perhaps it will not exhaust you if you could call the council this evening – I could make my report then.'

'That is a good idea. Why not immediately?'

'Because there are a few things I must do first. For example, I need to see the girl that I had confined on suspicion. She should be released with something to compensate her. I did her an injustice.'

'You mean the girl, Aibell?' replied Colgú with a smile. 'Don't worry. I have spoken with her and allowed her to stay with Della in the township. Della has promised to look after her.'

Fidelma's eyes widened, annoyance spreading on her face. 'You saw her? But I gave Dar Luga strict instructions that—'

Colgú held up his hand. 'I am not that incapable, sister. I had her brought here and questioned her and she told me her sad story. You are not the only judge of character in this family. I thought it more appropriate that she stay with someone who would show her some sympathy and friendship. She is an attractive girl, the sort that people easily fall in love with.'

Fidelma winced at the familiarity of the phrase. 'So was her mother,' she muttered. 'So Aibell is being looked after by Della?'

'I have someone check surreptitiously each day. But, so far, she has proved that I made the right decision. I am told that they get on like a mother and daughter.'

Fidelma and her brother stared at each other, jaws thrust out pugnaciously, each determined to be right. At that moment Eadulf saw the similarity of temperament between the two red-haired siblings. There was tension for a moment and then they both relaxed with smiles.

'I would have done the same,' Fidelma admitted. 'In fact, I can think of no better place for Aibell to be at the moment than with Della, especially now that Della's son Gormán has returned home.'

Her brother looked uncertain. 'What has Gormán to do with it?'

'Oh, I think we might safely leave the future in Gormán's hands,' Fidelma said enigmatically. Then she added: 'I am glad to see you so well again, brother.'

'No more than I am happy to be well and look forward to your explanation behind this assassin's attempt on me. I am still sure that the name Liamuin does not mean anything to me,' he added. 'Aibell told me about her mother and I have certainly never heard of her, nor any other woman called Liamuin.'

'I know it. However, there are a couple of things I would like to know from you, before you call the council.'

'Which are?'

'I just wanted to clarify something that happened during the Battle at Cnoc Áine. I understand that you were wounded there. I heard it was a grievous wound.'

'Stories spread after battles. Not everything you hear is strictly accurate. It was not serious at all,' Colgú said. 'Stupidly, it was in the first charge: a blow from a spear hit against my head and knocked me unconscious. As I was being hurriedly carried to my tent, to a physician, I came to and demanded to return to my men. You see, in such moments come victory or defeat: if the men are dispirited by seeing their leader injured, then a battle can be lost. Why, the blow did not even break the skin but caused a bruise, that's all. Why the concern now?'

'I presume that it was in this incident that you lost your shield?'

'That's a curious question,' replied Colgú.

'I just need to have it confirmed.'

'As a matter of fact, I don't remember. I suppose that when I was unconscious and the attendants picked me from the battlefield, they left my shield lying where I had fallen. Anyway, due to the privileges of a King – I had three shields in my tent ready for use.'

'I have brought the one you lost back to you,' Fidelma said. 'Back from the Abbey of Mungairit.'

Colgú stared at her in surprise. 'I don't understand.'

'I will tell you everything later, during the council. But now a third question. When the battle was won, when Prince Eoganán fell, and his nobles were dead or had fled, you appointed your commanders, members of the Golden Collar, to take charge of various Uí Fidgente territories. It was my understanding that this was only a temporary measure to ensure the country stayed at peace until Prince Donennach had negotiated a peace with you. Is that so?'

'That is exactly so. It worked well except . . .' He hesitated. 'Except that I made the mistake of appointing Uisnech, of the Eóghanacht Áine, in overall command. It was a bad choice. He bore a deep hatred against the Uí Fidgente that I had not counted on. I later heard reports of many evil things he did. When these stories came to me, I was on the point of recalling him, but then I heard that the Uí Fidgente had taken matters into their own hands. They ambushed and killed him.' Colgú shrugged eloquently. 'I cannot blame them. Thankfully, about that time, the *derbh-fine*, the electoral college of the Uí Fidgente, had met and Prince Donennach was made Prince. He had been the son of Óengus, whom Eoganán had displaced years before, so the choice was a just one.'

Fidelma had waited patiently while her brother explained. 'Can you recall what territories your commanders were given?'

Colgú frowned for a moment and then said: 'I don't think so.'

'South of their territory, along the border with the Luachra . . . who was sent in charge there?'

'I can't recall. Capa was the commander at that time and made those dispositions. Then came the peace treaty and so there was no reason for our warriors to be in Uí Fidgente territory at all. They were all withdrawn. Why do you want to know?'

Fidelma smiled in satisfaction and shook her head. 'It does not matter. It is of no significance now.'

'And are you going to tell me everything?' Colgú demanded.

'As I said, brother, all in good time. Call the council to meet this evening.'

'It shall be before the evening meal. I shall be impatient to hear what you have to say,' sighed Colgú as she and Eadulf rose and left.

Outside, Fidelma turned to Eadulf. 'There is one more thing I need to do. Will you go back to little Alchú and I'll be along shortly?'

Eadulf wondered what she had in mind. He knew there was something she was not sharing with him. However, he was sure she would reveal it in her own good time.

After he had left her, she turned to Dego, another of the King's bodyguard, who had replaced Caol on guard duty, and asked where she might find the commander.

'He has retired to his chamber, lady,' Dego replied. 'It was my turn to guard the King's chambers.'

Caol was alone in his chamber when Fidelma entered. He rose to his feet and stood nervously while she closed the door behind her. For a moment they stood facing one another without speaking.

'Well, Caol?' she said.

Caol shifted his weight.

'Well, lady?' he repeated.

She motioned for him to be seated and lowered herself into a chair opposite.

'You probably know why I have come to see you and to speak with you alone?'

'I have some idea, lady.'

'You fought alongside my brother at Cnoc Áine?'

'True enough.'

'When my brother dispersed warriors throughout the country of the Uí Fidgente, with companies to support them, I think you were sent to the southern borders, along the hills that separate it from the territory of Luachra.'

'I was.'

'You went to stay at the rath of Menma.'

He made no reply but did not deny it.

'So you were the warrior of the Golden Collar that the locals came to believe led the attack on the rath.'

'They would have believed anything of a warrior of the Nasc Niadh. I did not lead any such attack.'

'I know. But you were the warrior who fell in love with Liamuin.'

'And she with me,' Caol replied defensively.

'You knew about her background?'

'She told me that she had been married and had a husband who had mistreated her. She also had a daughter.'

'When I brought Aibell into the palace, I think you recognised her. I saw the astonishment on your face.'

'I thought . . . I thought I was dreaming. She seemed so like her mother. While you were away, I have spoken with the girl. I did not tell her about my relationship with her mother. I allowed her to tell me her story.' Caol shook his head sadly. 'If only her mother had known. Menma's rath was only a short distance from Sliabh Luachra. Perhaps I could have taken some men there and . . .'

'And perhaps not,' replied Fidelma. 'Even a relative of Liamuin, the one who sent her to Menma's rath for safety, felt he could do nothing to rescue the girl. Why didn't you tell her that you were the lover of her mother?'

Caol sighed. 'I do not have that sort of courage, lady.'

'You may well have to find it. But there are questions first. How and when did you come to know of the death of Menma and his family; the death of Liamuin?'

'There was trouble in the east and I had to take my men to the settlement at Finnan's church. Some Uí Fidgente rebels had fortified the hill fort that is nearby. We were kept at that place for three months. I was told the news of what had happened at Menma's rath by a wandering monk. I learned that Liamuin had been slain, along with the others – and during these last four years I have tried to forget.'

'What was the story that you heard?'

'That the attack was led by a warrior wearing a golden collar.' He raised his hand to touch the emblem at his neck. 'I heard also that he carried a shield with the stag rampant encased in jewels – the personal emblem of Colgú.'

'Local people did not know that.'

'Any member of the Eóghanacht could decipher its meaning. The wandering monk told me.'

'Would he not have passed that on?'

'He did not have the opportunity. Moments after he told me, the Uí Fidgente rebels made an attack and the man was killed.'

'So only you knew about the shield. Did you think Colgú was responsible?'

'I was with him on Cnoc Áine when he was wounded and lost his shield. Anyone could have picked it up. Indeed, several warriors of the Golden Collar were killed that day and much looting went on. It would have been easy for someone to go off with a golden collar and the shield.'

'There is something that I don't understand, Caol. I could guess, but perhaps you will tell me.'

'What is that, lady?'

'When the man calling himself Brother Lennán came into the feasting hall and thrust his sword at Colgú, he shouted, "Remember Liamuin!" You must have recognised him.'

'No, lady, I did not. He did seem familiar – I tried to think where I had seen him before, but I could not recall him. Four years is a long time.'

'But he recognised you.'

Caol gestured helplessly. 'It was not reciprocal.'

'Let us think back to the moment. He wounded my brother and then poor Brehon Áedo intervened and he was killed. The killer tried to with-draw his weapon for another blow. Then you moved to prevent that second blow. As you did so, he looked up and hesitated a moment. In that hesitation, he recognised you. Obviously he knew that you were the warrior of the Golden Collar who had been Liamuin's lover and not my brother. Did you kill him because of that?'

Caol's expression was serious. 'I did not, lady. All I knew was that he had attacked Colgú shouting, "Remember Liamuin!" I recognised her name but I did not recognise the assassin.'

'In fact, he was named Maolán. He was the son of Cadan and his wife Flannait.'

The warrior breathed in sharply. 'So that was who he was! Maolán. I remember him now. He was the son of a neighbouring farmer and his wife. Where had he been these last years, nursing this hatred?'

'He had gone to Mungairit to work as a copyist. He was found by the conspirators, who took advantage of his brooding resentment and anger. He was told that the leader of the attack carried the King's shield and was therefore the King himself.'

'So that is why he struck at the King! He really believed it was Colgú who attacked Menma's rath?'

'He did. That brings me back to my next question. If you did not recognise him, why did you kill him when you could have easily disarmed him?'

Caol bit his lip and was silent.

'You knew that it was not Colgú who carried out that attack so you were surely not trying to conceal it,' said Fidelma.

'But that is *precisely* why I killed him, lady,' asserted Caol.

Fidelma regarded him in astonishment. 'I do not understand.'

'I killed him because I knew the King had not done this deed. But, had the assassin been captured alive, he would have had the opportunity to justify his act to the Brehons. Even a false accusation against Colgú would have created untold alarm and unease in the kingdom.'

'I still don't understand,' she repeated.

'You know that Prince Donennach of the Uí Fidgente has been to Tara and is even now on his way here to Cashel to conclude new agreements with Colgú about the relationship of his territory within the kingdom.'

Fidelma suddenly saw the connection. 'Of course, that was the missing piece of the puzzle! Maolán was their cat's paw of Lorcán's conspiracy. Even if the assassination had not been successful, Maolán's accusations against Colgú would have caused such rumours that it would have spelled disaster for the negotiations. Either Prince Donennach would have had to break off the peace, or his own nobles, led by the conspirators, would have ousted him, preparing the way for a new Prince who would have had no compunction in renewing the war against Cashel.'

There was a long silence while Fidelma thought through the situation.

'You have left me a difficult choice, Caol. What you did was wrong. It was against the law. You killed a man when you could have taken him alive. And yet the reason you did so was a laudable one.'

Caol raised his hands in a gesture of resignation.

'I know that in law I did wrong in killing the assassin when I could have taken him alive. I am willing to pay the *éraic* payment to his parents. Yet I would argue that it was an act done in defence . . .'

'Self-defence?' Fidelma sounded sceptical.

Caol shook his head. 'No, lady. In defence of your brother's reputation so that Prince Donennach would arrive here, conclude his treaty and remain in peace with us. Therefore, it was an act in defence of the King – of the peace and prosperity of the kingdom.'

Fidelma actually smiled. 'You have argued your case well, Caol. I have to say that was the conclusion I was coming to. Maolán did not need to die, but had he not done so, countless others might have died. Perhaps only you and I should know the reality of this matter.'

She stood up and went to the door, where she paused. 'I believe that you are still in love with Liamuin, Caol.'

Caol smiled tightly, trying to conceal his emotion but there was some redness around his eyes. 'I still dream of her, lady. She comes to me in my dreams at night, and that goes some way to compensate me for the hopeless longing of the day. That is why I have not taken a wife.'

'I can't advise you on that, Caol. You must follow your own path. However, I don't think Liamuin would want you to be in mourning for the rest of your life.'

'Perhaps not. Thank you, lady, for your wisdom and understanding. But tell me – why did Maolán agree to the role of assassin? Just because he believed that Colgú had led the raid on Menma's rath? As I said, his parents had an adjacent farmstead and they were friends with Menma.'

'He did not shout "Remember Menma!" He shouted "Remember Liamuin!",' Fidelma reminded him.

Caol frowned . . . then his face lightened as the realisation struck him. 'Ah! So he was in love with Liamuin?'

'Yes, but in his case, it was unrequited love. This kind of love often stirs deeper passions than love exchanged,' confirmed Fidelma.

Caol's features were sad. 'Liamuin was easy to fall in love with. In a way, it was not Maolán's fault but those who manipulated his emotions.'

'And used them,' agreed Fidelma. 'When I explain these events to the council, I will simply say that your action was motivated by defence of the King's life. As for the rest, that will remain between you and me.'

'I feel responsible about Maolán; more so now that I know who he was and why he did what he did. Even though you have absolved me in law, I still feel guilty. If there is some way I could make atonement, I would do so. Maolán was misled by his emotions and now his parents have to pay for that with a lonely old age for, as I recall, he was their only son.'

'Then it must be your decision of how to make that atonement, Caol,' Fidelma replied firmly. She went to the door, opened it and paused for a moment 'We are all prisoners of the consequences of our actions,' she said softly. 'I am sure you will make the right decision.'